Quickening

Volume Two

AMY LANE

DSP PUBLICATIONS

Published by

DSP Publications

5032 Capital Circle SW, Suite 2, PMB# 279, Tallahassee, FL 32305-7886 USA
www.dsppublications.com

Quickening, Vol. 2
© 2017 Amy Lane.

Cover Art
© 2017 Anne Cain.
annecain.art@gmail.com
Cover content is for illustrative purposes only and any person depicted on the cover is a model.

ISBN: 978-1-63533-440-1
Digital ISBN: 978-1-63533-441-8
Library of Congress Control Number: 2016918940
Published June 2017
v. 1.0

Printed in the United States of America

This paper meets the requirements of
ANSI/NISO Z39.48-1992 (Permanence of Paper).

These books are for everyone who picked up a self-pubbed book written by nobody special and loved it, and has stuck with me ever since.

These books are for everyone who followed me from urban fantasy to gay romance—and then read everything in that new genre and loved it.

These books are for everyone who followed me from gay romance back to my roots—and told me that they loved the Little Goddess series too.

And these books are especially for everyone who wondered, asked me, begged for the answer to the singular question of "Goddammit, is she going to be pregnant for frickin' *ever*?"

No. She is not. And this is how that happens.

I hope you love this book as much as I've loved having readers as wonderful as you.

Character Lexicon

Cory. Corinne Carol-Anne Kirkpatrick op Crocken Green started this little adventure as a gas station clerk, and then she met Adrian, a vampire who loved her, and Green, who loved them both. She is now married to Green, Bracken, and Nicky, carries three of Adrian's marks and so leads his kiss of vampires, and is still trying to get that degree.

Green. Vernal Green, Lord of Leaves and Shadows. The leader of most of the supernatural peoples in Northern California, Green is not a warrior. Instead he leads and heals with sex and love, and people would die to protect him.

Bracken. The youngest full-blooded sidhe on the hill, Bracken was Adrian's lover and fell in love with Cory at first sight. He stepped away from her then, because Adrian loved her and they didn't share well, but upon Adrian's death, he became her full-time lover.

Adrian. Adrian started life as the sexually abused cabin boy whom Green rescued on his way to America. Adrian became a vampire so he wouldn't age and leave Green alone, and even after he fell in love with Cory, he couldn't survive without his ties to Green.

Arturo. Arturo came from the jungles of South America to the new world in the fifties, trying to find an easier life. He found Green's hill instead, and instead of conquering, fell exquisitely in love (in a very heterosexual way) with a leader who would lead with compassion instead of violence.

Grace. A devoted family woman, Grace was dying of untreated breast cancer in Redding when Adrian heard her yearning to see her family grow, with or without her. He granted her wish and made her a vampire, and Grace has come to love her Green's hill family even more intensely than she loved the mortal family she left.

Mitch. Mitch was Renny's first lover. Renny loved him since they were kids—when Mitchell was accidentally transformed into a were-kitty, Renny actually seduced him so he'd bite her and turn her too. Mitch was skittish and independent and refused to accept Green's generosity and live in the hill, but Renny's heart was so twined with his that she almost lost all of her humanity when he was one of Sezan's first victims.

Max. Max is the police officer who tried to 'save' Cory from Green's hill when she first met him. In the end, Green's hill saved him, and he ended up beguiled by a girl who was more cat than human.

Renny. Renny became a werecat to follow her first husband, Mitch, into the life. When Mitch was killed, Renny's cat personality became dominant and nearly feral. She's become more human since she and Max have become a couple and gotten married… but not by much.

Marcus. Marcus was a history teacher with a passion for snow skiing. He's got curly brown hair, big brown eyes, and a teacher's affection for Cory, who wants to document the world they've found themselves in now that he has fangs and a taste for blood.

Phillip. Phillip was a stockbroker with a passion for snow skiing. After Marcus found him buried in an avalanche and brought him over as a vampire, the two spent twenty years struggling with their sexuality and their boundless love for each other. What they finally decided upon was a relationship based on the sentiment "I apparently can't live without you, asshole," and that seems to be working for them.

Sezan. Part sea-nymph, part human, Sezan is what happens when someone is warped from conception on. He came to NorCal to torment and kill Adrian—but he had help.

Crispin. Crispin was the kiss leader of the Folsom vampires until Sezan arrived and brainwashed/drugged/threatened him to force Crispin into Sezan's own vendetta.

Crocken and Blissa. Bracken's parents, Crocken and Blissa, are a study in opposites. Blissa is a flittery sex kitten of a four-foot pixie, and Crocken looks like an undusted pile of rocks. Together (and with a little bit of Green's magic to make everything fit the way it should) they managed to produce Bracken, whom they love to distraction.

Leah. Leah's little brother died and Leah descended into a spiral of sex, drugs, and self-destruction. Adrian saved her from all of that, but Leah's emotional makeup does not include any sort of monogamous relationship. Still, she misses the stability of having a small nuclear family and has spent years trying to find a balance in the hill.

CHARACTERS INTRODUCED in *Wounded*:

Nicky. Nicky is an Avian—a shapeshifter who turns into a bird. He met Cory while she was attending CSU San Francisco immediately after Adrian's death, when he was working for Goshawk, the bad guy. Nicky accidentally bonded to Green and Cory in the course of saving Bracken's life, but because he was trying to atone for his assault on Cory at the time, Green and Cory took them into their family—and their bed.

Mario. Mario was an Avian who worked for Goshawk, the bad guy in *Wounded* who convinced Nicky to mind-rape Cory on their first date. Mario's wife, Beth, was killed in an assault on Green's hill, and Green gave Mario back his will to live. Mario is midheight, stocky, and very proud of his Mexican heritage.

LaMark. LaMark is another sweet-tempered Avian who had the misfortune to meet up with Goshawk while struggling with his identity. Unfortunately, LaMark's identity is not a comfortable one—a gay, black Avian is sort of doomed wherever he goes, isn't he? In spite of that, LaMark is a nice guy with a sense of humor and a blinding smile.

Andres. Andres is the leader of the San Francisco vampires. In *Wounded*, he allied his vampires with Cory's—and passed up on an opportunity to take both Cory and Bracken into his bed.

Orson. Orson is the leader of the San Francisco werewolves. He's not a particularly physical fighter, but he is an aggressive advocate for his people.

Mist. Green's old lover, Mist betrayed Green to Titania and Oberon. When Green escaped their faerie hill, Mist watched jealously as Green fought for a place of his own. Mist was responsible for sending Sezan Adrian's way—he couldn't stand that Green was happy, especially with someone Mist considered inferior.

Morana. Mist's lover at the time of *Wounded*. She's mostly just a smug, superior, elitist bitch who thought Green was a good lay. For that alone we despise her.

Goshawk. Goshawk was the leader of the Avians in San Francisco. He was working on world domination when he convinced Nicky to mind-rape Cory in order to get her most powerful memories to drive his power. Nicky was guilt-ridden and turned against his former leader in order to help the girl he hurt.

Timmy and Danny. Timmy and Danny were two of the Avians who were set against Green's hill. They were captured instead and given sanctuary. Like LaMark, Mario, and Nicky, they chose to stay at the hill instead of rejoining Goshawk's forces.

Titania and Oberon. The traditional leaders of the sidhe in England, Titania and Oberon ruled over a court full of sexual excesses and cruelty. They held Green prisoner in their famed faerie hill because nobody could provide sexual satisfaction like Green. Green hoarded his power, though, and eventually snuck himself and his lime trees out of their garden and across the sea.

Characters introduced in *Bound*:

Chloe. Grace's bitter, unpleasant daughter. Chloe had to have her memories of her vampire mother and of Green's hill wiped in *Bound* because she was not the kind of mortal Green allowed at the hill (i.e., she was a *real* bitch).

Gavin and Graeme. Chloe's sons, they *adored* Green's hill and completely accepted all of the strangeness within. Once a year they come back to the hill—Green has arranged a sham "camp" to cover for their chance to visit with their grandmother and all the other people they have come to love.

Sweet. Sweet is one of the more promiscuous sidhe at the hill—but also one of the most pleasant. She's also one of the three sidhe who are known for being healers.

Ellen Beth. Ellen Beth was brought to the hill when her lover was infected with some poisonous blood. Her lover died horribly, and Ellen Beth was turned over to Sweet for emotional healing. Sweet decided to keep her, and Ellen Beth has been happy to be kept.

Erik. Erik is a werecoyote with a sad past and a long-ago history with Green, Bracken, and Adrian. He is content to live in Austin and run his own company, until he meets up with Green and Green introduces him to Nicky. Both of them realize that they have something in common—too low-key for the intense emotions of the hill, they both make better secondary characters... except to each other, where they are the heroes of their own story.

Kyle. The lone survivor of the Folsom vampires, Kyle's beloved, a girl named Davy, was killed because she and Cory vaguely resembled each other—and because they were friends. Cory took Kyle into her kiss and forced him to want to live.

Hallow. Hallow is a sidhe and a professor at Sacramento State University, where Cory and the other students attend school. He is also—by Green's request—a counselor for the students themselves. Although Green usually counsels his own people, he felt that he was way too close to the situation as Cory's lover *and* her leader to be objective or effective, and thus his trust in Hallow.

CHARACTERS INTRODUCED in *Jack & Teague (& Katy)*:

Jack. Jack is actually a nice, quiet young man. When his sister—who became a werewolf by choice—is killed, Jack asks Green for some answers to her world and the people who would kill her. Paired with Teague to be human liaisons to Green's hill and to go out and deal with violent and legal matters outside the hill, Jack fell utterly and irrevocably in love with his damaged, noble partner. When the two of them become werewolves (Jack by accident and Teague by choice), Jack's transition to the hill is marred by his realization that Teague really is the great man Jack has always believed—and that means that his loyalties cannot ever be exclusively Jack's.

Teague. Teague was brutally abused as a child and inculcated in the same ideas of hate and prejudice that killed Jack's sister. One night while hunting a werewolf, he is injured while saving the life of a young man who looks very human—and Adrian pays him back by bringing him to Green. From that moment on, he is Green's devoted subject. When Jack is injured and Cory comforts him while waiting for the injury to heal, Teague's loyalty is transferred to the lady of the house, even while he pursues a relationship with Katy and Jack, whom he loves beyond reason.

Katy. Katy has loved Teague Sullivan since she was barely old enough to talk. When she found that fate had brought him to Green's hill too, she pursued him—and Jack—with a single-minded quest for happiness. Now that they're a family, she wants to be a part of Teague's adventures whenever she can be.

Lambent. Lambent joined the hill just before Jack and Teague were bitten. He had always been semi-independent of Titania and Oberon, but until he ended up on Green's Hill, he had no idea how much he'd valued his autonomy—or how much he hated the antique laws that governed sidhe behavior in the old country.

Ellis. We officially meet Ellis—a young vampire with little self-control—in *Bound*. He shows up again in *Being*.

CHARACTERS INTRODUCED in *Rampant*:

Tanya. A not-yet-mated sylph.

Sam. Offspring of "the other" and a human.

Walter. A sweet, young, newly made vampire.

Rafael. The leader of the Redding vampires.

Annette. Nicky's unpleasant ex-girlfriend.

Gretchen. A child vampire who is eventually allowed to meet the dawn, because child vampires are such terrifying creatures in so much pain.

John and Terry. Nicky's parents.

CREATURES:

Sidhe. High elves—lots of powers, humanoid attributes and physical beauty.

Fey. All the underclasses of elves existing at Green's Hill—pixies, nixies, sprites, gnomes, sylphs, red-caps, trolls, fairies, etc. etc. etc.

Weres. Shapechangers, they age at about 1/3 – 1/4 the speed of a human, have super strength, super speed, and whatever characteristics their creature possesses. Were-creatures reproduce by biting humans. They probably can carry young of their own species, but interspecies mating is so prevalent at Green's hill that no one knows for sure.

Vampires. The blood-sucking undead—but in a nice way.

Sylphs. Sexless fey, they choose their gender when they choose their mates.

Avians. The only shapechanger that's born and not made by another shapechanger. The Avians are bonded for life with the person/people involved in their first sexual experience. If this mate doesn't produce offspring within ten years, the Avian is doomed.

CHARACTERS ADDED from other works:

Whim and Charlie. Originally introduced in *Litha's Constant Whim,* which can be found in *The Green's Hill Novellas.* Whim and Charlie first met on the shortest night of the year, when a miserable adolescent Charlie was planning to kill himself. Whim's company was too captivating for that idea to stand, but Charlie was too young for Whim to want to bind to a life on Green's hill. What followed was thirteen-year courtship of meeting on one summer's night a year. By the time Charlie ended up on the hill, he and Whim were so stupid in love, even the gods couldn't separate them. But why would the gods want to do that?

Shepherd and Jefischa. Shep and Jefi were the two angels in *Guarding the Vampire's Ghost*—their job was to make sure Adrian didn't do anything he wasn't supposed to while in the anteroom to heaven. Trouble was, heaven doesn't *do* vampires, and nothing about Adrian was like Shep and Jefi were expecting. Including the way they were coming to feel about each other.

CHARACTERS WE meet in *Quickening*:

Iris Masterson. Bad guy's assistant—although that's not what she wanted to do with her life.

Conno. Werewolf made specifically to be a soldier in the bad guy's army—but he got away and got imprisoned.

Dylan. Half elf psychic busted for a poker game—then imprisoned to keep him out of the bad guys' radar.

Cami. Half elf psychic friend to Dylan, who begs Green's help to get Dylan out of jail.

Cerise. Another reluctant werewolf

Dr. Nieman. World's worst obstetrician

GREEN
Victories and Small Mercies

GREEN HOVERED in the air and watched as the latest batch of werewolves went sailing to the lake. Bracken and Cory had not, as Cory had suggested, combined forces and set their penises on fire while making them bleed out the asshole. (She'd been particularly cranky, and he couldn't blame her, but still… bloodthirsty, his beloved, oh yes she was.)

But he knew the time was nearing when they would have to take definitive action. They could not continue to live under siege when they were so close to having the means to defeat this enemy—one way or another.

Nicky touched down on one of the oak trees and changed form, sitting on the branch with his bare feet dangling beneath him. "Have you noticed," he asked musingly, "that they don't visit when the vampires are here?"

Green looked up and smiled at him, at his playfulness and helpfulness and his desire to be whatever they needed of him.

"I have," he said. "I think they're afraid."

"Well, they should be. As far as they know, *all* of our vampires belch power and cook RVs." Nicky executed a cherry drop, landing at Green's feet, and Green was so charmed he wrapped his arms around Nicky's shoulders and placed a series of tickle kisses on his neck. Nicky laughed and turned into his embrace, standing on his toes so they could kiss in earnest, and Green closed his eyes to savor. Oh yes—Nicky was a blessing. He loved them all, and all he wanted from *any* of them was to be loved in return. He didn't have the depth or complexity of Cory or Bracken—but Green had the feeling he'd made his peace with that. He was content to be simple, to give them affection, to take it as it was offered, and to savor joy from every small moment.

Green would celebrate a lover like that to the moon and back. Nicky Kestrel was not the love of a life that spanned two millennia, but he was absolutely a lover for *now*. And now Green needed what Cory had needed—to just for a moment forget the depth of his fear for the people he loved.

Nicky opened his mouth under Green's kiss, and Green fell into it happily. Who could have known two years ago that the timid, slightly phobic young man who had been tragically forced into Green's bed would turn into this sensual, happy lover. Green pushed the kiss, backing Nicky into the tree behind him, then ran his hands from Nicky's neck down the outside of his arms and circled his slim hips with long-fingered hands.

Nicky bucked against him, aroused almost instantly, and Green chuckled against his neck.

"Goddess, that's good. What was that for?" Nicky gasped.

"Suddenly very much in love with you, lad. Is that a problem?"

Nicky smiled sunnily. "I am *so* horny. Can we do something about that? You and me? Hell, throw in Bracken and Cory, and my day is complete. Can we? Huh?"

Green nodded and continued to nibble on that flushed, pale neck.

The sense of air being disturbed around them called him away from Nicky's frustrated moans, and he grinned at Cory, Bracken, Arturo, and Lambent as they all touched down around him. Shepherd and Jefischa hovered above them, great wings providing a constant breeze on this crisp autumn day.

"We're doing this now?" Arturo asked, sounding disgusted. "Because mine doesn't wake up for another two hours, and that's no fair."

Green pulled away from the taste of Nicky's skin and grinned suggestively at Cory and Brack, who were standing hand in hand.

"But that's the point, isn't it?" he asked, because this thought felt profound. "The vampires *aren't* up. Why is that? Why stage an attack in broad daylight? Why would she do that?"

"'Cause elves don't like vampires, and we kicked her ass at night?" Cory said, sounding bemused.

"Oh no they don't, and oh yes we did!" Green said, nodding. Cory's realization—her acceptance about her pregnancy and her limitations— as painful as it had been for *her*, had suddenly freed Green in ways he hadn't known he'd been bound. "And why have an attack right now, in the middle of the afternoon?"

They all stilled, the great gusts caused by the angels' wings making the late October day suddenly that much chillier.

"There are cars off the road for miles," Cory said soberly. "I saw them. This wasn't planned—it was like they all suddenly got called. And the werewolves we just pitched in the lake now were the stragglers. We got the first wave when the alarm sounded, but these guys came from farther away. Like suddenly an emergency, right?"

Everybody at the top of the Goddess grove nodded, and Teague, who had just come trotting up after roaming the perimeter, changed forms so he could speak.

"She lost Iris," Teague said succinctly. "She felt it. Wanted to attack immediately, see if she could stop it, or distract us, or—"

"It's a thrown shoe!" Cory said excitedly, breaking away from Bracken to bounce in the center of their attention.

"A what?" Green looked at her with some relief. She'd been fierce in battle, as she always was, but she'd also been through a bit of a trial today. Watching her, excited as she became when putting together a puzzle, soothed something in him. She would be fine, he thought. She would breathe fire and brandish wisdom the way they depended on her to do.

"It's a family legend, right? My dad was supposed to work late, and my mom was home alone. But my dad got off early, and my mom had gone to sleep all freaked out because she didn't like being alone in the country. When Dad showed up, she didn't recognize him at first, so she sat up in bed and started screaming—and he threw a shoe at her head."

"He did *what*?" Bracken asked. They all stared at her, fascinated. This could be the one story from home she'd ever told that didn't appall them.

"She *scared* him," Cory said, nodding. "Don't you see? He said she sat up and started screaming, and it scared the crap out of him. It was all he had, so he threw it to shut her up!"

"But a shoe isn't going to do anything!" Bracken argued. Green *didn't* argue. He saw where she was going with this.

"That's the point!" Cory swept around in the circle, arms wide. "Don't you get it? Even Mom said it. She thought there was a stranger in her house, and she was going to get raped and murdered and left for dead, but she saw the shoe and thought, 'If this is all he's got, I can take him!'"

Bracken did a double take, and so did Green. He felt Nicky jerk under his arm, and he wondered if it was the same for all of them. It was the first time in three years he could actually see a resemblance between their beloved and the woman who'd given her birth.

Green started nodding and stepped away from the tree, Nicky in tow.

"Your father was startled and frightened," Green said, grinning. His blood was up, thrumming through his body—and he felt like celebrating with his wife and husbands, because this here, this was *huge*.

"And he threw the only weapon he had," Cory said, grinning. Green caught her hand and whirled her against his body, holding Nicky on one side undulating against his hip and kissing Cory on the other side sweetly, yearningly.

"She's afraid of us," Green said, feeling hopeful for the first time in months.

"She just threw a shoe," Cory agreed, smiling sunnily at him. Bracken stood behind her, arm wrapped around her waist and chin rubbing softly on her hair. The moment caught, lengthened, stretched warmly over their bodies and spun into sex, and a breathless silence filled the grove.

Cory licked her lower lip and gazed at him from under her lashes, an unexpectedly coy move from a woman who would swear she didn't know coyness or seduction in any form.

Green lowered his head and nuzzled her, waiting for her caught breath, her tiny sound of acquiescence.

He heard it, and the want that had begun with him and Nicky suddenly rolled out from their four touching bodies in thick waves.

"And now we're all gonna fuck?" Lambent grumbled. "Where's the fun in that?"

"*They're* going to fuck," Arturo said dryly. "The rest of us are going to *fuck off*."

Green heard him in the back of his mind, Arturo's voice growing more and more distant as he led everybody down the staircase. A burst of wind blew by them, but just as he looked up to ask Shep and Jefi for some privacy, perhaps, the fallen angels touched down on their platform in the top of the tallest oak. The gnomes were busy building a house underneath it, but for now the platform had a bed and covers and the sunshine, and the two seemed particularly happy.

And Green could forget about them.

Cory tilted her head back, and he took advantage by nibbling his way down her throat to the neck of her hooded sweatshirt.

"We could always go inside," she suggested. Another gust, chill like the encroaching evening, blew around their ankles, and for a moment, a shining moment, all Green could see was her, with Bracken behind her and Nicky's hand stroking through her hair.

Adrenaline, yes, because the fight had been fierce, but also the sense of a burden being lifted. She wasn't in denial, wasn't in pain. They'd made love the night before just from sheer relief, but this was different.

The wind, the light, the warmth of her skin beneath his lips—this was joy.

"Snow is coming soon," Green breathed in her ear. "But now there is sun and glorious wind and sweetness."

He slid his hands up under her sweatshirt, and her heat burned through his palms. She gasped and leaned back against Bracken, who held her with ease.

Oh, yes—her nipples springing against the cupped center of his palms, the sensuous weight of her filling breasts. She was strong and fertile and fierce—a warrior goddess—and it was their duty to pleasure her.

He fell to his knees, tall enough against her to bury his face in her belly, kissing the softness, the roundness, the curves. Bracken stripped off her sweatshirt and bra, then draped his body against her back, keeping her warm.

"Skin," she demanded. "I can't be the only one naked."

Well, it was only fair—she was the only one without the heightened metabolism or the resistance to the elements. There was a scramble as Bracken stripped off his own sweats and Nicky danced out of his sweater and jeans. Green was only wearing jeans, and his cock strained against the fly torturously.

He let it.

He was busy kissing along the skin of her lower stomach, peeling her jeans and cotton panties down her thighs, and smoothing his thumbs along the inside of her knees.

She gasped when Bracken lifted her gently so Green could strip her out of her pants and shoes. Then he spread her thighs and teased his tongue along her tenderest button of flesh.

She cried out unashamedly and spread her knees wider, cautioning, "My knees are gonna go!" before Bracken squatted down and hefted a thigh in each hand.

Ah, a banquet for Green if ever there was one. Her body had changed, her sex growing darker and bolder with her pregnancy, her tang sharper on his tongue.

He savored each taste, each unabashed wiggle as he plunged into her, gorging himself on her, the day, the freedom, and the joy.

She cried out, a short, hard sob, and he felt the first contraction start deep in her womb. It wasn't a full orgasm, no—but it would make her tender inside, accepting, able to take pleasure from him with one thrust.

He looked up, saw Nicky's head bent over her chest as he suckled on her breasts. Nicky must have been exquisitely gentle, because her hands were convulsing in his hair, clenching, unclenching, but there was no pain in her movements at all.

Green pulled away. Bracken let her feet touch down, then held her, whimpering with need, while Green shucked off his own jeans and let his member free.

Cory turned to kiss Bracken, and he returned the kiss with interest, his big hands roaming her tiny body, warming, marking, arousing. Then he turned her and gave her a little push, one Green recognized from previous lovemaking.

Bracken was giving her permission to put Green first, letting her know he wouldn't be hurt, because she was always so exquisitely careful not to hurt her big gruff lover even when she wanted Green and no one else.

Green was grateful—but not grateful enough to give her up. He swept her into his arms, hefting her thighs around his waist and seeking out her heat even as he backed up, searching instinctively for the cushioned bench that was the grove's sole decoration.

"Nicky," he sighed as she sank down upon him, "bring Bracken to the bench, and then—"

Nicky had forgotten.

The rule was that Bracken could touch Green and Nicky as much as he liked as long as Cory was touching him—but Nicky, in his arousal and carelessness, and his desire for Bracken, had simply sunk to his knees and taken Brack in his mouth.

And all that happened was that Bracken tilted his head back and groaned, holding Nicky's head tenderly and using him with gratitude and gentle lust.

Meanwhile Cory used her stomach and thigh muscles to lift herself and fall back down, and again, and again. Green wanted her so badly that watching Nicky and Bracken, no matter how beautiful, could no longer be on his agenda.

He found the bench with his thighs and sat down on it, Cory still riding him with her head thrown back, hair an autumn array around her head. Her fingers were clenched on his shoulders hard enough to leave marks on his pale skin, but still he wanted her harder, faster. "Oh Goddess, beloved," he gasped. "Use me *more!*"

"So good," she gritted. "Oh damn, Green, so close. So… ah!" She moved a hand from his shoulder to the apex of her thighs, reaching for her nerve bundle and touching herself more roughly than Green dared, needing the force of fingers.

Her back arched and her muscles clamped down on him hard, her channel spasming around him, milking him until….

"Ahh!" The groan was long and drawn out like his orgasm, thrusting up into her heart and losing himself there—awash in pleasure, body tingling, mind set free and as joyful as the day.

He barely caught her magic as it poured from her open mouth and up into the trees.

He was used to this by now—forming a shield over her, a dome of power over every place he held power, as the magic escaped her body and remade the earth he'd enchanted with his bare hands.

Her climax went on and on and on, washing through the grove and through Nicky and Bracken, both caught in the middle of their own climaxes. Nicky was still crouching on his knees before Bracken, who stood godlike, accepting his attentions, and apparently Nicky's excitement at having Bracken in his mouth was enough to bring him off—with Cory's help, of course.

Green let the last shivers tremble through him, the last trickle of light easing through her lips and eyes like smoke, before he took stock.

Above them he heard what sounded like *very* postcoital noises coming from the angels. Then Jefischa said, "Shepherd, look—do you see that?"

"Huh?" Shepherd mumbled, and Green smiled. Oh, Shepherd. So vigilant, unless distracted by the vibrant young angel—who would have followed him to hell, but was just as glad they'd ended up in Green's garden.

"The shield, down where it touches the earth, she added something. Do you see it?"

Jefischa sounded eager, and Green was curious himself.

He gazed into Cory's hooded eyes.

"Feeling good about yourself?" he asked. She smiled, catlike, and nodded.

"Can we ask what you did?" he prodded.

"Her blood," Cory mumbled. "We know how it smells. I made the defenses do something special when it smells her blood."

He was going to ask her what the difference was when he was interrupted by a groan and a sound of mild exertion. Bracken bent and scooped Nicky up in his arms, much as Green had with Cory, and wandered over to sprawl on the bench next to them. Green and Cory watched them, because watching Bracken naked, being tender, being sexual, was a treat even if they hadn't been the ones servicing or being serviced by him this time.

When he was situated, Nicky lying on him unashamedly, he reached a big hand out to Cory's naked thigh. She covered it with her own, smiling sweetly.

Green palmed her head so she was resting it against his chest, not because she was helpless and *needed* protection, but because it pleased him to have her there, and she was kind about indulging him.

"So what did you do?" Bracken asked, eyes twinkling.

"It puts them to sleep," she said, her shoulders coming up to her ears in delight with her own cleverness. "Anything that's attacking with *her* blood in it falls asleep. And then we can set down a steak and…."

"Oh, yes," Nicky said. He went to sit up, but Bracken's big-palmed hand stopped him. "But… wait… won't we have to do the whole… screaming thing after the addiction is stopped?"

"No," Green said decisively. "What Iris did today, with the words, that was because she was a leader. Our elf queen has been pretty casual about throwing bodies into the fight, and you don't do that kind of binding with someone you expect to lose." He shook his head. "No," he repeated. "What happened to Iris happened because she was valued—as she should have been. From what you've said, poor Judge Griffith was kind but probably not as strong in spirit, so she killed him and let him out of her service. But Iris—you don't just let an Iris Masterson go without a fight."

"It would be like letting Lambent or Max go," Bracken said unexpectedly. "Or Mario or LaMark. Iris probably wasn't her lieutenant or her second, but she *was* a valued member of the team. That was a real loss—our elf queen pulled out all the stops."

"Except if it was a choice between letting them go or killing them," Cory said darkly, "we'd let them go."

"An important distinction," Green acknowledged, clutching her tighter. "And one to remember." She purred and cuddled closer, and he felt the urge to sleep descend on them all. "Later. For now I think a nap is in order, then a strategy meeting tonight. All aboard, run naked to the bedroom."

"I like those sweats!" Cory protested needlessly.

"Then we'll make sure they're cleaned and ready when you wake up," Green assured. Of course he would—the sprites would see to it whether he asked or not, but he always asked.

"Thank you." Her head was heavy on his chest, and her eyes closed as she fell asleep on him.

Bracken straightened up abruptly and dumped Nicky on his ass.

Nicky grinned up from the ground, naked and happy. "I don't get carried down to the bedroom?"

"Are you pregnant?" Bracken asked, eyebrow arched.

"Nope!"

"Ready for round two?"

Nicky considered it. "Considering I pretty much came from my toes while *giving* a blow job, I'm gonna say 'peace out' for now."

Bracken shrugged. "Then you have my permission to walk."

Nicky picked himself up and dusted off his behind with his hands, then reached for Brack's discarded T-shirt, which he pulled over his head.

Together they descended the stairs into the bedroom, where, yes, they all settled down for a nap with Nicky and Cory rolled in the middle, Bracken and Green on the outside.

But Bracken and Green were elves, and now that there was no longer a psychic parasite screaming agony into the vampire vault, they had caught up on their sleep. Both of them lay still for a few moments, until Nicky curled up against Green's chest and Cory curled into Bracken's and both of them fell fast asleep.

Green caught Bracken's eye.

"You didn't need to touch her," he said, referring to Bracken and Nicky's coupling in the grove.

"Thank Goddess," Brack grunted. "He caught me unprepared."

"It was bound to happen," Green said pragmatically. "So much contact, so often. The Goddess believes in shades of gray, I think—especially for bindings like this one."

Bracken nodded and very deliberately reached over to stroke Nicky's rust-and-black hair from his forehead.

"It took a while," he admitted, a corner of his mouth pulled back. "But yes, I think Nicky and I are included in the marriage bond now too."

"Good," Green said softly. Very deliberately he covered Bracken's hand with his own.

Bracken closed his eyes, and his smile softened. "And you and I could be too?" There was a bit of longing in his voice. Back when Adrian had been alive, Bracken had been one of his favorite playmates.

"There's no reason why not," Green said. "We stopped when the two of you got together, because…."

Bracken grimaced. "Because she is all-consuming," he said, the truth from both their hearts.

"Yes." It couldn't be denied. "But that's not what she needs right now. This was nice"—Green grinned, because that was not nearly the word—"but it's not going to happen as much, not for a little while. And if we can fill ourselves in that way, we can be there for her in the others."

Bracken looked at him deliberately and licked his full and pouty lower lip. "Goddess should strike you down with cramps for that evasion," he said, his hooded eyes twinkling. "It always was amazing."

Green laughed, his heart full of something besides fear for the first time in quite a while.

"That it was, brother. Since the heart of our hearts approves, I think we should see if it holds up."

Bracken turned his hand palm up, and Green laced their fingers together. The hum of Cory's power breathed through them all, but it was a sleepy, sated sort of hum, and what it really did was prove to the both of them that no, two weeks of being depleted and depressed by a tortured soul could not be negated by one very passionate afternoon.

They would need another nap.

Their fingers parted in sleep. But as a family, they breathed as one.

CORY
*Mothers and mother*fucker!

"RENNY AND Nicky," I said, making sure this was the final head count.

"And me," Bracken said darkly.

"And me!" Katy interjected hurriedly, rushing in from the outside stairway. "You weren't going to invite me?" She sounded so hurt that for a moment I panicked. I'd worked so hard to woo Katy as one of my few—three!—female friends that summer, and I was terrified I'd fucked it up.

"She was going to forget me!" Renny snarled in disgust. "I can't believe you weren't going to take me shopping."

I stared at her helplessly. "I can't believe all of you *want* to come shopping—with my *mother*, no less." I grimaced at Bracken. He *hated* my mother. "Are you sure?"

He nodded adamantly. "She's not going to get you alone," he promised, his expression still thunderous.

"Well, obviously not!" I laughed. "Look, Bracken, I've got Nicky and Renny and Katy—"

"And me." His eyes narrowed, and for the first time in quite a while, I shivered.

The shiver snapped me out of it. Oh, yeah. I wasn't just going shopping with my mom. I was going shopping with my mom when I was pregnant and there was a *war* on.

"Fine," I conceded with little grace. "Just remember—she's the grandmother of our children, and you can't kill her and hide the blood spatter like you can with anybody else, okay?"

He managed to look affronted. "I don't just hide the blood spatter. I hide the entire body!"

I blinked and looked at Nicky in exasperation.

Nicky shrugged. "He does!"

"You're just saying that because you want him to get inside your pants."

Nicky nodded with some enthusiasm. "Well, *duh*. But also because he's a damned effective killing machine. Give the guy props where they're due."

I shook my head, refusing to *not* be irritated. We could be home. We could be home, doing homework and eating whatever luxury protein-and-vegetable masterpiece Grace had cooked to entice me to eat today while making plans for how to make sure there was enough blood-drugged hamburger along the perimeter of the hill to last the bad guys until Thanksgiving.

We could be home having *amazing* sex.

In fact, we could be home doing any number of things that didn't involve my family talking to my blood relations—but now?

We were going shopping.

With my mother.

There was not enough divine mercy in the universe.

MY MOM looked nonplussed as we all piled out of the SUV in the parking garage at the Galleria.

"Cory, you brought… brought…." She was wearing a flowered peasant tunic over tight jeans, and she shifted from one comfortably soled brown leather shoe to the other and checked her graying brown hair with nervous gestures of thin fingers.

Oh, she was not happy with this arrangement. That was clear.

"Two of my husbands and my friends? Yeah. They wanted to come."

"Well, okay," she said, sounding… well, funny. Odd. "We, I mean, I didn't want to go here. I, uh, looked up a place nearby, in Lincoln, if that's okay. It's a strip mall by a Target, so even if they don't have clothes in the boutique, we can go to Target afterward."

"Well, uh, sure, Mom." There was a Target right down the road, right? And a Baby Gap in the Galleria and a pregnancy boutique in there too. "Uh, why don't we just go here for the day? I mean, we're here. If you wanted to meet us somewhere else, we could have met somewhere else."

"Well, that's okay," my mom said, giving a patently fake smile to the rest of the group. "Your friends can just stay here and shop. We'll go look there and come back. It'll give us time to talk."

My mother was lying about something. I mean, I *thought* my mother was lying about something. The truth was, she'd never lied about *anything*, to my knowledge, which would mean that if she tried it, she'd be really bad at it.

And brother, did this seem like somebody being bad at lying.

"I'm coming in the car with you," Bracken said unequivocally.

"Me too," said Renny.

"I'll drive and follow," Nicky said, sounding serious. "Renny, you and Katy talk on the cell phone in case we get lost."

Katy nodded soothingly, and I felt marginally better about getting into my mom's little Sportage. In the *back* of the little Sportage, because Bracken's legs were just too damned long.

"Well, heavens, Cory," Mom said, sounding weak. "It's not as if you need a bodyguard or anything."

Bracken and I exchanged looks, even though he was busy stretching out his legs as much as he could in the front.

"She doesn't go off the hill without accompaniment," he intoned.

Mom's eyes darted from Bracken to me until she had to concentrate on backing the Sportage out and getting out of the garage.

But it wasn't like conversation just picked up after that. After a couple of sallies about the weather and school, Mom pretty much clammed up and kept her conversation to darting nervous glances my way, then asking if I was sure I was going to go back to school after I had the babies.

"Yeah, Mom—lots of women have their babies and then go back to take their finals. That's what I'll have to do." I finished saying that—as painful as it was—then looked in dismay at the strip mall Mom had brought us to.

"Mom! This isn't Target!"

Mom cast an apologetic look back at me and an apprehensive one at Bracken.

"Well, I'm sorry," she nonapologized. "It's just that you didn't seem to be taking this baby thing seriously. In our family we need to make sure the babies are okay, do you understand?"

I looked in dismay at the little collective of ob-gyn doctors occupying a four-office suite.

"No," I said stonily. "No, I do not understand. Renny, how far away are Katy and Nicky?"

Renny texted violently next to me—hopefully something like *Abort! Abort! Abort! Mother is* not *friendly!* Her phone beeped, and she spat softly.

"They had to get gas," she said unhappily. My mom looked hopeful.

"That's great, because the appointment is in about two minutes, and it shouldn't take long at all."

"No," I said, crossing my arms. "No. Nicky and Katy will be here in a minute, and we'll take off. I'm not going in."

And then, oh horror—had we not suffered enough?

My mother began to cry.

I didn't notice it at first, because she didn't sob, and her face didn't crumple. No, that would be too dramatic for Ellen Kirkpatrick. She just… shed tears and wiped them off stoically with the back of her hand.

"Cory, please. I… I know you think you've got it all nailed down. You've always been so… so self-contained, you know? All I ever wanted to be was a mother, and you popped out, and it was like you didn't need any mothering. What was I supposed to do with a kid who could brush her own hair at four? How was I supposed to protect you when you could talk to strangers and… and *order them around* by the time you were six? Your third-grade teacher—"

"Ms. Belcher?"

"Yeah. She *quit* because you kept correcting her, and you were *right*!"

I grimaced. "I didn't mean to make her quit!" I had unclear memories of a harried-looking woman with a really vast bosom and fuzzy blonde hair who kept losing kids as they dodged out the door. Well, hell, congratulations to me for winning the pain-in-the-ass award.

"Well she wasn't that bright anyway," Mom said, looking a little pathetic. "But that's not the point."

"I'm dying for the point," I said, scowling and remembering that I had been *ambushed* into submitting my body for care that was potentially detrimental to the unborn *nonhuman* children in my uterus.

"The point is, our family doesn't have a great history with pregnancy," Mom said, uncertainty wobbling her lip and crumpling her chin. "You were not… not my first pregnancy, Cory. I mean, we closed up shop after we had you, because… we just couldn't keep trying. But my mom, her mom—a bunch of only children, and the babies…." She bit her lip. "Sometimes the birth defects are just too severe. I had to abort two pregnancies because the fetuses… that much damage…."

My stomach roiled. Partly because I was beginning to suspect something, and partly because… oh hell….

"Mom—you couldn't have told me this before?" I shoved my hands through my hair, and my rubber band went splanging out the back and rebounded. I'm pretty sure it hit Bracken in the ear. "I mean… *Jesus*. This might have been something to know before… I don't know, marriage? Sex? Conception? All of the above!"

Mom looked away and bit her lip, a gesture so vulnerable that my heart broke a little. "When do you tell your daughter a thing like that?" she asked, voice breaking. "I just… you didn't go to the doctor, and you keep telling me that Green will take care of you—"

"He will," I said gently. "Mom—"

"He's not a doctor!" she snapped. "He's not a god! He can't do everything—"

Oh, but he could. Green, Bracken, and I had *flown* the day before. It took a tremendous amount of power, yes, but we *could fly*—could hover and swoop, could scoop up werewolves and defend the crap out of ourselves. I'd seen him heal heinous wounds—some of them mine— with a touch. When his palm slid over my abdomen, I could *feel* him communing with our children.

Green could do everything, but my mom—my mom couldn't know that.

"Mom, we're going to talk about how Green can know—"

"*Just get in the goddamned clinic!*" Mom screeched. I jerked and kicked the back of Bracken's seat in surprise.

He turned in his seat and waved a finger very slowly in my mother's face. "Don't. Scream. At her."

While Mom gasped for a minute, Bracken took his chance to calm me down.

"Go in, let the doctor listen to the heartbeats. They do that. I want to hear."

I grimaced. "Bracken. Ultrasounds. I mean… *pictures*."

"Let them make of the pictures what they will. Nothing will happen without your permission. Renny and I will go in with you—"

The SUV entered the parking lot full bore, then screeched into the spot next to the Sportage. Nicky and Katy hopped out, glaring at my mom.

She glared defiantly back.

"We're going in," I said. My hostility didn't ease up. "Brack, you ready with the mind-wipe if we need it?"

He grunted. "How many years of med school do you want to delete?"

Oh, hell. "I'll do it," I decided. "These are not the space-alien babies you're looking for." I shot my mom a dirty look. "Mom, you're lucky Brack's in a good mood." We got out of the car, and she came around to take my elbow and escort me inside. I shook her off, still pissed and hurt beyond measure. "Don't. Just… just don't. You couldn't have told me this shit when I wasn't backed into a corner? Just no."

Her hand dropped to her side, and she opened the glass door nervously—and then held it while the whole stinking lot of us trooped in.

We must have looked like a royal entourage, except I'm pretty sure that not even the Princess of Wales walked into *her* doctor's office with an extra husband and two ladies-in-waiting.

I didn't care. I was fuming and hurt and angry with myself all in one go. *My fault,* I kept thinking. I'd tried to cut my parents out of the big parts of my life, but if they loved me—and I'd never doubted it—they wouldn't be content with that. *I* wouldn't have been content with that. I would have fought and kicked and begged and cried to be let into more of my kids' lives than that.

But maybe first I would have simply asked them what was wrong and reassured them there was nothing they could tell me that would change how much I loved them.

Goddess knows it would be a change and a half from what my parents did to me.

Witness me and my four attendants crowding the anteroom and then filing down the mazed hallways into the exam room.

The nurse who led the way reminded me a lot of my mom, in fact. Lean, weathered, tough from gardening probably, or running, or horseback riding. Pretty in a tanned, strong way, and into her fifties. She and my mom talked like old cronies, and my mom asked her how she'd been since leaving the hospital.

"Oh, better, Ellen. You know how it is—nobody drops a 350-pound patient on you when you're doing ob-gyn clinics. After my back surgery, this was the best way to go."

Mom agreed, but she'd told my dad sometimes that she liked the hospital. Said a clinic would bore her to tears. I kept that in mind as I watched her deal with Nurse Rogers.

So we had all crammed into the tiny exam room—Nicky in the far corner with Renny perched on his lap and Katy and Bracken and me sitting on the bed—when the nurse actually looked around at all of us, and her eyes widened.

"You know, I didn't really think you meant *all* of you were coming in here," she said, her voice taking on that adult timbre that suggested we weren't going to get what we wanted.

"Well, lucky for us, that's what we meant," I said perkily. Her eyes narrowed in recognition.

"Cory? Oh, dear Lord. Ellen, I just didn't put it together. I didn't realize she was old enough. Cory, how're you doing? You probably don't remember me—I used to come out to your parents' house all the time. You couldn't have been more than two or three, but God, you were smart as a whip."

I summoned up a social smile. "I'm sorry," I said, shaking my head. "That was quite a while."

"Oh, I know it." She waved her hand and looked at the chart propped on her other arm. Apparently knowing me meant she would conveniently forget about my entourage. Awesome—sincerely, awesome. "So, this is your first pregnancy and your first visit to the doctor," she said, hmming. "And is the father...." She trailed off and looked at Bracken and me. I was sitting *on* the exam table, toes dangling in front of me, with Bracken half sitting, half leaning next to me, his long legs and frame making standing the more comfortable option. As always, he had his arm securely wrapped around my waist, and he eyed her with unfriendly acknowledgment as she took in the two of us. "...here?" she finished, both eyes opened exceptionally wide.

"Mm-hmm," I said, smiling neutrally. But I couldn't make myself be a bitch to her. She seemed like a genuinely nice woman, and she was apparently doing a favor for my mother and didn't know about the duplicity that had brought us there. "Uhm, Janine, this is my husband, Bracken."

Bracken inclined his head with the naturally regal posture he got from being an only child with rock-awesome parents and the youngest sidhe on the hill.

"And you haven't seen a—"

"She's under the care of a doula," Bracken said. I wrapped my head around the word. Yeah, I knew what a doula was, because I'd been a good little Easy-Bake oven and did the required reading, but to call Green a doula was... well, brilliant, actually. Hands-down brilliant. Because he *was* a trained healer, and his job, in this instance, was to make sure the babies and I were well. Wasn't that the definition of a doula?

"Cory!" Mom protested, and I looked her dead in the eyes.

"Green's a trained healer, Mom. He understands the workings of the babies and my body, and I trust him with my life—and the babies' lives as well."

"So, Mr. Green?" Nurse Rogers asked, and I gave her a medium grunt. Could be "Mr.," could be "Dr.," could be "don't fuckin' bother me." I'd learned that grunt from Bracken and was getting particularly good at the nuances. She nodded as though I'd said yes and asked, "Can he come with you for your next visit?"

I looked at her, smiling slightly. "There's not going to be a next visit," I said, keeping my voice even. "This isn't your usual situation."

"You're telling me," Mom said under her breath, but I silenced her with a glare. Goddess, even Nicky and Renny were staying silent. This seemingly innocuous situation could turn so bad if we gave too much away.

"But honey," Nurse Rogers said gently, "you *have* to have prenatal care."

"I do." I smiled a little. "I have Green."

She met my mother's eyes, and the two of them sent me pitying looks that almost—but not quite—sent me into a homicidal rage. Damn my mother. *Damn* her. It was my fault for trying to block her out, but dammit, this was why. Always interfering in the wrong kind of way. But I couldn't shake the way her lower lip had trembled, or her hurt at the independent kind of child I'd been.

Oh, hell. I hadn't meant to be a changeling, a foundling, nursed on rainwater and fairies' milk—but that was who I'd been even before I'd met Adrian and come into my power. Never the child she'd wanted, but the only child she'd had.

I refused to give blood. Supposedly all of Bracken's blood from my field transfusion had been absorbed and changed in my bloodstream, but I didn't know for sure—and the babies would definitely be sending weird shit into the mix, so I wasn't going to chance it.

I got on the scale and was tsked at until I told her I was carrying twins.

"And how do you know that?"

"Green told me." I'd given him the magic name of "doula," so she didn't ask how he'd know—she probably assumed a Doppler, and I wasn't going to disabuse her. She had me lie back and pull up my shirt, then placed the Doppler wand against my stomach.

Two distinct rhythms filled the room, fast as raindrops on tin.

For a moment, all was wonder.

"Listen," I whispered—unnecessarily, of course, because all of us were listening. "Bracken, that's—"

"The trippy one," he said, eyes closed. "The one that goes ba-pop ba-pop ba-ba ba-*pop*—that is our daughter."

Oh.

"Yeah?" I asked, enchanted.

"The solid one, do you hear it?"

"Boom-boompa-boom-boompa-boom," I said, because I *could* hear them. Two distinct beats, one fey and dancing, the other as deep and solid as warriors beating spears on stone.

"That is our son," he said, then lowered his face to nuzzle against me. I nuzzled him back, my chest swelling, swelling, and suddenly, without warning, filled with a thing that was not fear.

"They will be so beautiful," I said with deep conviction. Look at him. Look at Green. My beautiful men, my beautiful sidhe. Oh Goddess, my lovely, amazing lovers—what choice did these children have but to be beautiful like the sun on snow, like the moonlight on water, our children.

"How far along did you say you were?"

The nurse's voice cut into our communion, and for a moment I was irritated. Then I remembered that we had to be careful, and I had to think—middle of August, middle of September, end of October… "Three and a half months," I said. "Four on the fifteenth."

"You know the conception date for sure?"

I nodded. "Yup. The night the sure-fire birth control failed."

She frowned. "So fifteen, sixteen weeks along. Those heartbeats were damned strong for fifteen weeks. Here—you lie back, and I'll get the ultrasound."

"No!" I struggled to sit up, but Bracken, surprisingly, touched my arm.

"She will not know what she sees," he said lowly. "But we will." His smile, on that rugged, grim, warrior's face—oh, Goddess, it would melt an ice meteor in deep space.

Helpless before Bracken, before Green. I marveled at the miracle that I'd fought enough to conceive. I was helpless against their smiles.

Nicky broke my besotted silence. "This isn't gonna be the… you know, wazoo ultrasound, is it?"

Bracken looked over his shoulder. "The what?"

"You know, they've got the big mighty 'wand' that they push up her wazoo and it takes a picture?"

I gaped at him, and Bracken's eyes grew even rounder. "I don't even want to—"

"Hey!" Nicky protested. "You're not the only one who's been reading instruction manuals. The way our luck works, you and Green are gonna be off saving the world, and *I'm* gonna be the fuckin' doula."

Renny snarked, "You mean you're gonna be keeping Cory from wrecking the planet, and I'm gonna catch."

"You both suck," I said with deep feeling, and Katy patted my arm.

"No worries. I've been reading the same books. Those two can have the Sylvester and Tweety show, and me and Jacky can do all the delivering."

Oh, bless her. She meant well. "Katy, I love you, but how many people are going to see my wazoo by the time all this is done?"

Suddenly Nicky and Renny broke up. "Sylvester and Tweety! Oh my God, Katy, that was epic!"

I let a grin sneak through. "Yeah—I gotta admit, that was pretty good, hon."

She patted my arm again and leaned her head against my shoulder, loyal and trusting and good-humored as always. "I've been listening to Teague and Jacky. Teague's got so many teasing names, I can't think of any more for Jack, but those two? They're fair game."

I laughed, loving them all so very much in that moment. "But seriously. How many people are going to have to see my wazoo?"

Bracken made an unhappy sound. "From what I understand, the entire fucking world, beloved. Would you like me to trim it up and add ribbons?"

I stared at him in horror. "You wouldn't."

His grin was pure joy. "You heard them, right?"

Because that's what all the laughter and jokes were about.

"Yeah," I whispered, and Katy moved when Bracken leaned forward to claim my space.

"I will add sequins and beads and braids and—"

"My bush is not that big," I said, still a little horrified.

"Then I will have to decorate the room."

The room. I gasped softly because the room had sat, unused and un-looked-in. I'd been so afraid to admit they were coming, I'd missed out on some of the excitement of what to do when they got here.

"We all need to decorate the room," I said thoughtfully. He cupped my jaw and kissed me, and we were suddenly the only two people on earth.

The moment was interrupted by a knock at the door followed by a shortish, fiftyish man with thinning gray hair and a drinker's complexion.

He smiled winningly at me, then looked confused by the number of people in the room. Of course he was.

"It's my entourage," I said gamely. "All pregnant women have them, right?"

He didn't even crack a smile! I automatically didn't trust him—a real healer would have laughed at my joke.

"I understand there's some problems with the heartbeat?" he said, sounding sober.

"They sound a little farther along than they should be," Nurse Rogers said. "I was hoping you could supervise the preliminary ultrasound."

The doctor—Nieman, by his name tag—turned to look at her. They had one of those raised-eyebrow conversations that people who have worked together for a while have.

They thought there was something wrong with the babies. I smacked down the impulse to panic just because they were wearing scrubs and smocks. Dammit, I had *not* spent my first nineteen years distrusting authority, and my last couple of years *becoming* authority, just to let two humans frighten me now.

"They're fine," I said, keeping eye contact with Bracken. "Nothing to worry about here."

"Now, young lady, that's very fine for you to think, but let's take a look, shall we?"

Oh, awesome. "Mom, how do you know this guy?"

"We worked together for quite some time when he was at Mercy San Juan," Mom said. "He's very good."

That was code for "he could abuse the nurses and nurse's aides like a boss." I remembered her discussions with Dad. Wonderful. For the first time since we'd herded into this increasingly stuffy room, I made eye contact with my mom.

"He's a tool," I mouthed. She had the grace to look embarrassed, which meant she knew that. Ugh. I should have pitied her, actually—she'd been condescended to by doctors for her entire career. Of course I'd heard her talk about the male nurses and aides, and apparently the *entire* fucking world had it out for *them*, so I'm pretty sure she gave as good as she got, but still.

Must be a shitty way to spend your working hours.

Dr. Tool wasn't looking at me, though. No. He was clicking on the ultrasound machine with great authority and managing to ignore the other seven people in the eight-by-ten-foot room. "So, Ms. Kirkpatrick—"

"Green!" I snapped. "Mom, I've been married for more than a year!"

"Sorry, honey," she said automatically. "I forgot."

"Well, I remember *everything*," I told her darkly. Oh, yeah. This was not going to be just brushed off.

"Yeah," she sighed. "I know."

"So your doula is a relative?" Nurse Rogers said, putting things together slowly.

"Of sorts. Are you going to have to put the ultrasound wand up my wazoo?" I asked, because I was not interested in playing the Green name game anymore.

"Uh, no," Dr. Tool said, looking at me for the first time as though I was a person. An irritating person, but a person nonetheless. He forced some joviality into his bedside manner and elaborated. "No, we don't need the internal ultrasound for a preliminary checkup. When you come back around week twenty, we'll do the full workup, but this is just a checkup. Now, I need you to pull your shirt up again and your… uh…"

"Husband," Bracken supplied, his entire body turning to granite. He didn't like this guy either, and I didn't even need to read his mind to figure that out.

"…husband can step out of the way—"

"His name is Bracken," I said flatly. Yes, I was baiting him.

"Uh, Bracken. Hi, so nice to meet you. I'm Dr. Nieman." He smiled and held up his hands, which were already gloved. Bracken looked at him as though he wouldn't have touched those gloved hands with two inches of hazmat lead between them.

"Bracken Green," he said tersely. "Touch her carefully."

Nieman smiled nervously. "Of course. I'll just, here." He squirted half a gallon of K-Y onto the wand and glopped it onto my stomach.

"And that was hella fucking cold," I hissed. Wow. At least Nurse Rogers had made sure the lube that came with the Doppler was warmed before she slid it around like a squid on an ice rink. "And fucking ouch!" God, he was pushing hard.

"Sorry about that," he lied. "Okay, so here's where we're looking... at."

He trailed off, because he couldn't see.

I mean he could see, but he couldn't *see*.

Bracken and I could see. Tiny, separate, and crouched as babies were in all the pictures, they presented the perfect outlines of two elvish babies.

Their ears were pointed, even in the womb. Their torsos were too long, and they had vestigial tails that I knew might or might not disappear with birth. They had hands too big and too long to be human, and while we were watching, one of the little outlines in the alpine snow of the ultrasound picture turned and looked at the source of his or her discomfort.

The dips and shadows that probably signified eyes and ears and nose exploded across the black screen, the form of the little squidder morphing—becoming even more impossible, deformed even—and terrifyingly so.

But it didn't matter.

We'd caught him or her—for some reason I assumed this one was a he—before the little nipper knew we were watching. We had some solid footage of a perfect little elf baby in his natural habitat.

Me.

Both of the figures on the screen started to freak out, blurring in impossible ways now that they knew they were on camera, and Bracken and I chuckled.

"Nope," I said, my voice catching. "That's the last we'll get out of them today."

"It's not something we do consciously," Bracken said thoughtfully. "But by the time we're born—"

"Shh...," I said, holding his hand. "No logistics of magic, Bracken. Not today."

I'd seen my children today.

But that didn't mean this yo-yo could keep shoving at my uterus with the ultrasound wand like a chimp with a stick looking for ants either.

"You're done," I said, not caring if it was rude. "The show's over, they're not going to perform for the camera anymore."

"But—did you see the abnormalities? Young lady, I don't think you know the ramifications of those unusual shapes, or the hearts—I think those hearts had six chambers!" I probably would have sympathized with him, but he kept *shoving* at me with the damned wand the whole time. I grabbed his wrist and threw a little power into my grasp, hauling his hand and that thing slowly but surely away from my stomach.

"Please stop touching me," I said evenly. I let go of his wrist, and he put the sensor wand back in its little slot on the ultrasound tray.

"Look, Ms. Green, I'm not sure if you realize—"

"I was never here," I said, keeping eye contact with him. "We didn't show." I stopped for a moment and looked at Bracken, who turned to Nurse Rogers and started murmuring to her as well. I know I said I'd do it, but this sitch had gotten epic quick. The minute I saw her eyes glaze over, I turned back to my problem.

"Do you hear me?"

Dr. Nieman looked up, and our eyes met. "Yes, but I don't understand—"

"You will forget we were here," I repeated patiently. "You will forget my name. You will forget what you just saw on the ultrasound. You will forget the names and faces of everyone in this room. Do you understand?"

"I understand what you're saying," he said, looking at me and shaking his head. "I just don't understand why you're saying it."

Oh, for fuck's sake.

I stared him in the eyes and thought *sleep* until his eyelids fluttered and he yawned, slouching down on his little stool. "Wow, just got really tired… but we've got to talk about… the abnormalities…."

I knew how to put power in my voice. It was one of my first tricks, but not one of my favorites. I used all of my will for this, because I sensed it was extremely important.

"My babies," I whispered fiercely, "are perfect. Do you understand?"

"Perfect," he said through a yawn. "But the hearts…."

"Perfect!"

"Talk… need to…."

"*Perfect!*" I shouted, and he collapsed with his head on the exam table. He stayed there while I got up, moving awkwardly around him and freely using Bracken's hands as levers. Nicky and Renny had already gotten up and guided Nurse Rogers to their seat, and my mom was standing in the middle looking confused and terrified.

Well, I wasn't happy either.

I grabbed a wad of tissues, wiped the gel off my stomach, and chucked it in the trash can before stepping around the sleeping doctor. He was still struggling, mumbling "defects" and "viable," and I felt queasy and angry at once.

He was sort of fixated on it.

Sometimes, Green had told me, certain humans were resistant to magic. I was one, because I *had* power—but sometimes there were smart people with no imagination, and *those* people couldn't be manipulated. Dr. Nieman might be one of them, and he'd stumbled onto something so very important and deadly secret.

"Nicky?" I asked as we all slid out of the exam room. "Think you can erase our files from the computer?"

"Yeah," Nicky said thoughtfully. "Yeah. Can you guys get rid of the receptionist? Whammy her or something?"

"God, I hate to whammy people." It was the truth. I'd always called it "mind-fucking," and it didn't sit well with me. "I hate to think of how many brain cells I just transmogrified."

"I'll do it," Bracken said with relish. "I have had enough of this place anyway."

Ah, bless Bracken. He never saw a mountain that couldn't be carved with a straight line and a ruler.

"Groovy," I agreed, taking a right down the taupe corridor and then a left. There were nurses at a station, but they barely looked up as we passed. I'd noticed six names on the little placard outside—that must have meant six doctors and probably ten exam rooms and a couple of offices. Good. If nobody was watching us pass, then people must come and go all the time, and Dr. Nieman and Nurse Rogers might not be discovered for a little while.

Jesus, what a clusterfuck.

"Cory?" Mom had been in a state of shock as Bracken and I had reacted to the ultrasound and then mind-fucked our health-care practitioners. She was coming out of it now. "Cory, what in the hell did you—"

"Later, Mom," I said absently. "Smile and wave, folks, smile and wave."

"Ellen!" We had finally emerged at the reception area, and the woman at the desk turned toward my mom with a welcoming smile on her face. "How did it go with your daughter—"

"She never showed," Bracken and I said in unison. The woman nodded briefly and then continued.

"Oh, well, that's too bad. I hope you can talk some sense into her soon—prenatal care is really important!"

"Yeah, it is," my mom said numbly, and we charged ahead.

Outside, the wind had picked up, and I grabbed the hoodie I'd taken off in the stifling doctor's office and slid it back on while Bracken held my purse. When my head emerged, I stood for a second, staring at the merciless sun and gulping chill autumn air.

"That's gonna bite us in the ass," I predicted.

"Yeah," Bracken confessed, grabbing my hand. "I'm sorry."

I turned to him, aware that he was apologizing for wanting to see our children, for wanting to hear their heartbeats. But I couldn't blame him for that. "It was awesome," I said, smiling softly into his pond-shadow eyes. "I wouldn't trade it for anything."

"Corinne Carol-Anne K—"

Renny and Katy had been standing by silently, but now Renny clapped a hand over my mother's mouth.

"Don't," she said soberly. "You can't say it. It's important."

I stood, quivering, outraged—because *dammit*, that was a weapon, and it was unfair that my mother, the person who knew the least about my life, had what amounted to a nuclear weapon she could aim at my head, and she thought it was a wooden gun.

"Mom, you don't get to say it," I ground out. I realized a vein in my eye was throbbing, and if I hadn't just had my blood pressure taken and my heartbeat monitored, I'd wonder about my health. "What did you think you were doing, ambushing me that way?" Rhetorical question. Stupid. "Scratch that. I don't want to know your motivation. In fact, I need *you* to know a few things about *me*."

"You don't like authority," she snapped. "I get it! What I don't get is—"

At that moment, Nicky came out and nodded. "We're good to go."

"Jeez, are you sure you don't have magic or something?" I asked, seriously impressed. I thought people only worked that fast in movies.

"No, I just used your magic. The receptionist was still reeling from the mind-fuck—I had her delete your visit entirely."

"Nicky, you're brilliant," I said, grabbing his hand and kissing his cheek. He held me there for a moment and bumped his forehead against mine.

"Did you see?" he asked quietly. "Did you see our children?"

My eyes burned. Oh, yes—they were his too. "They're beautiful," I replied, kissing him softly. "Our babies are perfect."

"They were *not*!" Mom interrupted, almost in tears. "Cory, I saw those images—I *know* what you have to do! Don't you know that's why I did this? You weren't my first pregnancy or even my third, you were my *seventh*. Seven babies, three ultrasounds like that one, three spontaneous miscarriages. With those features, I'm surprised they made it this long! Don't you understand? Cory—" She was crying so hard that when she approached me I couldn't stay mad or shy away. "—baby—sweetheart. Your children—they're not going to make it."

I took her hands. "Mom," I said, swallowing against the nausea. I didn't want to imagine her pain. It made her too sympathetic, and right now my rage was keeping me upright. "Mom, I need you to look at Bracken. Right now. Close your eyes and think about how he looks, and then open them and look at him again."

I heard Bracken's annoyed sigh and watched as my mom closed her eyes dutifully, then opened them, looking at my husband with fresh, tear-washed eyes.

"Holy fucking Jesus," she blasphemed. Then she passed out. Literally. Her eyes rolled back in her head, and she would have fallen, but Brack was a full-blooded sidhe and was behind her catching her in his arms as she fell.

He'd replaced his glamour already, for safety probably, but I bet also because he felt naked around my mother.

Well, join the club. "Put her in the SUV," I whispered. "Katy, can you drive her car? We're going back to the hill."

"Yeah, mommy." Katy kissed me on the cheek, and I leaned into it, comfortable as I hadn't been with my mother.

"Okay," I said, letting out a shaky breath. "Renny, do you want to go with her? I think Nicky, Bracken, and I need to be in the SUV when she wakes up."

"Yeah, mommy," Renny said with a crooked grin. She hugged me hard. "That was awesome, seeing your babies. But…." She sobered. "That's rough with your mom. I'm sort of glad my parents don't ever want to talk to me again."

I kissed her cheek. "Maybe they do—"

She shuddered. "No, no. Don't jinx it—it's fine as it is!"

Well, they'd been mad when she'd rejected school to move in with Mitch, and *furious* when she'd gone back to school and married Max. Sometimes, if you couldn't win for losing, it was best just to leave the game.

But I didn't think that was the case here—that was what made it worse. Mom and Dad—I couldn't believe he wasn't complicit with this—actually loved me. In fact, I'd almost sort of thought they *knew* about Green and Bracken. The guys had kept their glamour minimal since their first meeting, and I'd thought… well, how could they *not* know? How could they *not* guess? But then, guessing, or having a funny feeling, or talking about your sons-in-law on the way home from dinner with a "Do you think they're cousins or inbred or something?" might be one thing—but realizing your daughter had married two aliens out of three husbands was apparently sort of a shock.

Renny hugged me again and hopped in the car with Katy. Before she shut the door, she looked out and said, "We're going shopping on our way home, by the way! I mean, *real* shopping. For you. And the babies. So you know."

Then Katy drove off, and I felt a sudden pang. "Should we worry about them?"

"I'll text Teague and Jack and have them meet at the Galleria," Nicky said. "But we'd better get in the car—they'll start to snap out of the whammies in a minute."

Bracken shook my mother's limp body meaningfully. "Aherm?"

Fuck. "Okay, fine. Put her in the middle seat, and you and Nicky get the front. It won't do our cause any good if you make her faint again."

Nicky sniggered. "But it would be hella fuckin' funny."

I couldn't help it. I smirked. "Well, yeah. Seriously. Goes without saying."

'Cause, you know, making your mother pass out from shock? Every naughty kid's dream, right?

Bracken laughed evilly. "Perhaps we can make it happen again," he said, depositing Mom in the middle seat and belting her fragile human body in.

I hopped up next to her and did my own belt. Just as I was about to close the door, we all smelled it.

Oh, hell. Playtime was over.

Nicky gunned the engine but pulled out of the parking lot moving at an average speed. Nothing to see here, folks—an elf, a shape-shifting bird, and a pregnant sorceress got into an SUV and that's all—no punchline, no fear.

But as he pulled away, I saw them—a big, beat-up Ford F-350, originally blue but now covered in primer spots, pulling up in front of the survivalist shop at the corner of the strip mall. They were shaking their heads as though they smelled something off, but none of them looked up at us as we drove away.

"Fuck," Nicky breathed, driving like butter. "That's... you just don't think you can meet them in front of your local...."

"Guns and ammo specialty store?" I asked dryly. "Yeah. Yeah, we should. But we were a little preoccupied."

Next to me my mom gave a little moan and eyelid flutter, and I wrapped my arm around her shoulders.

Preoccupied. Yeah. Wasn't going away.

BRACKEN
Breaches and Breeches

SHE WAS looking at me. I could see my mother-in-law—horrible phrase—looking at my profile as we drove. She might not have had any of Cory's power, but I could feel her gaze sinking into me like teeny-tiny lead weights burrowing under my skin.

"*What?*" I snapped just as Nicky took the exit to Foresthill. I usually loved this stretch of road, *loved* the vast bridge spanning the canyon. And especially around this time of year, when snow could be around any corner, I loved the brilliant scarlet leaves of the trees on the hillsides. In the mornings as we drove to school, I celebrated seeing the hills come into being, emerging from the shadows to entertain features—crooked trees, rock formations, granite hearts beating in time with the mountains that were their masters.

But right now I'd trade this stunning glimpse of autumn to be asleep in the back of the car with Cory in my arms.

"I just…." Ellen waved her hands in front of her—a gesture that, had she known it, was very much like her daughter. "You… I mean, I kept thinking you looked different from other men," she said, her throat working. "But… what are you?"

"I am sidhe," I said proudly, not willing to let her depersonize me with the word. "Green and I are high elves. We're the most powerful of our people."

"By power you mean…." Ellen looked up at her daughter—

And then jerked away to the other side of the car.

"What did you *do* to those people?" she asked in horror. "They were my *friends*!"

Cory sighed and leaned against the door, putting herself as far from her mother as possible. "They're fine," she said. "They just don't remember that we were there. Although Nieman—Jesus, what a tool. Bracken, we may have to send someone to finish off the job. He was not going under easy."

I grunted. I'd seen that. I had also not cared for the way he shoved the ultrasound wand on her body. I knew a certain amount of pressure was necessary, but he'd been completely without finesse. She didn't complain about physical discomforts much as a rule. It had better be somebody else who went back to finish the job. I would kill him, and that was—possibly—unnecessary.

"Yeah," she said, as though I'd spoken actual words. "We can send someone less homicidal. I hear you."

"What do you mean, homicidal?" Ellen asked suspiciously.

"Figure of speech, Ms. Kirkpatrick," Nicky said smoothly. I shot him a glance, and he glared at me narrowly. Fine.

"Look," Cory said, sounding like the young leader I had followed since Adrian had brought her to Green's hill, "Mom. Bracken and Green aren't human. *Nobody* at Green's hill is human—"

"Nicky—"

"Nope," Nicky said cheerfully. "If that had been my baby, you probably would have seen feathers and a beak."

"That's a lie." I laughed, because Avians didn't come into their shape-shifting abilities until after they could walk.

"Happy exaggeration," Nicky replied. "For effect."

"Nobody," Cory repeated calmly, ignoring us. "Including me."

I lost track of the conversation at that point. I heard a lot of Cory's mother insisting it wasn't true and Cory trying—and failing—to finish a sentence. There was a lot of faulty reasoning on Ellen Kirkpatrick's part, and there was a lot of devolvement of my beloved to the frustrated, angry, inarticulate child she must have been before Adrian had met her.

I shouldn't have been surprised about that. Not really. When my mother or father spoke to me, I became the happy, obedient child I'd always been. My nearly eighty years on the planet were forgotten, and I was again the boy who fetched things, ran errands for Green, or needed to be reminded to do his chores before he fucked. But my parents had been indulgent, happy every moment I drew breath—excited even with my missteps, to have a chance to love me in any way possible.

Cory's mother, though—she had apparently been twisted by sorrow. She'd wanted a child so badly, she'd become too attached to the idea of Cory as that perfect image in black and white on the doctor's monitor. She'd spent a lifetime trying to cut off Cory's wings because she believed wings were an anomaly, a birth defect, by nature dangerous to her child's welfare.

Cory had learned that she needed to shriek in order to fly.

My beloved was certainly shrieking now.

"Mom, just because you can't see it and hear it doesn't mean it doesn't exist—"

"You're just playing with words, Cory. I think I should have skipped the ob-gyn and taken you straight to the shrink! Or certainly tried to talk you out of joining a cult or—"

"*This is not a cult!*" Cory screamed. Then she did something truly terrifying.

We were going around an outside curve at the time, and the road ahead of us was clear. I could feel the wraparound ball of magic envelop the car, fueled by her power and fury, and then....

I could feel us fly.

The car lifted—not in a slow or stately way, but going the same speed in the air as it had been going on land. It vaulted the space between one curve and the next, flying free, the whole of the canyon underneath us while Cory's mother let out one ear-bursting screech.

When the car touched down, Nicky, bless him, hit the gas smoothly, barely swerving as the tires gripped the road again. Cory wasn't taking any chances, though. I could still see the shield sparking sunshine in a long autumn glare into our eyes until Nicky said, "Kill it, Cory, I can't see."

Ellen's screaming stopped when the glow did.

The unmistakable smell of urine filled the car, and I was not entirely sure it wasn't mine.

"Beloved?" I said, keeping my eyes straight ahead.

"Yeah?" She sounded frightened and small, terrified of her own uncertain temper and what she had tried so hard not to do with it.

"Maybe we can finish the conversation back at the hill." We only had fifteen more minutes to go, but I had no idea what she could do with that time.

"Yeah," she agreed. "Uh, sorry about that." Tears threatened her voice, and I couldn't be mad at her. She had everything so locked down, so often. Balancing the three of us, balancing the hill. Apparently being a mother and being a daughter were the two things she didn't have in balance. Given that my mother still wept copiously over me whenever I helped her move something in Grace's kitchen, I thought perhaps it was something that *had* no balance. There were no scales that could measure what was going on in the backseat, so Cory had, in one great tantrum, wiped the scales clean.

I twisted around in the seat and offered my hand, which she took, squeezing hard.

"So sorry," she whispered.

I wanted to hold her, let her cry, let her be remorseful, but we were in a fucking car.

"No sorry," I told her, all of my temper faded. "No sorry. We're okay, you're okay, the babies are okay. No sorry."

She smiled weakly and nodded, and by necessity I turned back around.

"Cory—"

"Not now, Mom."

"Yeah. Yeah, okay."

In my head, I heard Green. *"What. Did. She. Do?"*

"She showed her mother she could fly."

WE WERE a subdued lot getting out of the SUV in the garage under the house, and as I brought up the rear, I saw that Ellen Kirkpatrick's jeans were wet. When we got to the top floor, Cory turned to her mother and said quietly, "My room is the first door on the left, the one that sort of sticks out into the hall a little. Put your clothes in the hamper and grab something of mine from the drawer."

I gave a little mental nudge to the sprites and bumped Cory's arm.

"Actually, there will be clean clothes your size on the bed," she said without missing a beat.

Cory's mother nodded and ventured down the hallway on uncertain legs. As soon as we heard the door close, Cory turned to Nicky and me with a wobbly chin.

"I am *so* sorry—"

"Shh…." Nicky, for once, was the first one there. He always had this way of standing with her, eye to eye. I was the one who was her equal, but he was the one who lived the most in the mortal world. We'd had to deal with *his* parents this past summer, and it hadn't been pretty. You'd think people who grew up to become big shape-shifting birds wouldn't be so judgmental about other nonhumans, but that had not been the case.

"But… it was so stupid, and I let my temper get the best of me, and I *made the SUV jump the canyon, and…*"

"Shh… shh…," he calmed her, and maybe because he *was* the most human of her men, he was the one who needed the biggest apology but who understood the most. "I get it, okay?" He leaned back and cupped her face with his hands, wiping the tears with his thumbs. "Remember my parents? Brought my homicidal ex-girlfriend to visit so I could get a divorce? Have effectively cut me off? You had to deal with that. And you haven't blamed me for it. Not once."

She sniffled and gave a wobbly smile. "Nothing to blame you for," she hiccupped. "You didn't almost…."

She was about ready to lose it, fall completely apart, and Nicky had grown wise about her this summer. With a little nod of his chin, he invited Green to take over, and Green did, holding her as she sobbed hysterically into his chest—

And then fell asleep.

Suddenly, like a child.

I looked accusingly at Green, and he shook his head as I reached to pick her up. "Not me, mate," he said. "Not me at all. Given what I picked up in her head as she was fighting with her mother, it was a big fucking day, that's all."

I grunted and shifted her weight, feeling guilt for this all over again. "My fault. I should have just walked away." But I'd wanted to *see* them. I could feel them, but in the vague, generalized way of rerouted blood and dividing cells. Green could *feel* them—their particulars, even their moods—but I didn't get those details. As much as I'd loathed this day, with the invasiveness and the hard human clinical curiosity, I couldn't deny the deep satisfaction of those snowy images on the black screen.

Green bit his lip, looking shy and not at all like our fearless leader. "When you get back, you'll have to tell me," he said, looking instead like a child asking about a glimpse of the Easter Bunny.

I kissed Cory's head gently and smiled at him, soft as a child myself. "It was wonderful," I breathed. So much worry, so many enemies, so many ways for our people to be exposed, to die….

And all the hope I had in the world was heavy and sweet in my arms.

I turned and took her down the hall, knocking softly and opening the door when I didn't hear Ellen protest. The shower was running, so I settled Cory down, stripping off her shoes and socks and jeans. When I was getting her sweatshirt, she woke up a little and frowned at me.

"Don't I have heavy-duty emotional shit to—"

"To let us handle," I said, smiling a little. "Not that you won't have to do your share of it, but not today."

She nodded. "Yeah, okay. I'll take the coward's way out."

I smoothed back her hair. Since she'd pushed it out of her ponytail, it had flown rampant around her face, and I enjoyed seeing the curls and spikes of it.

"Maybe not the coward's way out," I said, stroking her cheek. "Maybe, the *prudent path* is more like it."

She grinned, still sleepy but slightly more at peace. "Okay. We'll go with that."

"Good. Now pretend you're asleep when your mom gets out of the shower. Will solve *so* many problems."

She nodded and turned her head to kiss my palm. "I want to wake up with all of you," she said plaintively, making a demand on our time as she seldom did. "I want to celebrate, even though it's a small thing."

The shower shut off, and I leaned forward for one more kiss. "It's a tremendous thing. It's the world."

She slid down the bed and curled up, not having to feign falling asleep too much, and I stood and made my way toward the door. Just as I put my hand on the knob, her mother emerged, dressed in a rather sleek tracksuit that made her look decidedly more metropolitan and less country nurse's aide. She'd dressed hurriedly, and damp tendrils of hair still clung to her neck. Her tennis shoes and a clean pair of socks were dangling from one hand, and she looked surprised to see me.

"Oh, it's you. I thought it was—"

I held my finger to my lips and looked meaningfully at the bed. Cory wasn't pretending to sleep—her breathing held an even rhythm I knew well.

I opened the door, and Ellen followed me down the hall.

Green was waiting at the end of it, wearing jeans and a T-shirt, his golden hair braided loosely behind him. Between the bare feet and the friendly look on his face, he didn't appear anything like the leader of thousands of people—but I'd followed him my entire life, now more than ever.

"Ellen," he said slowly, "I do recall, shortly before our wedding ceremony, you were witness to some things on this hill that we had rather you not be privy to. Do you recall that?"

Ellen blinked, and so did I. Yes—I *had* forgotten that.

"Yes," she said softly. "I do seem to recall some strangeness here."

"I remember that at the time, I gave you an option—to walk away in full knowledge that this place was not your usual human residence, or to have your memories erased. You chose to keep your memories, and I recall being very impressed by that. Would you care to tell me what happened?"

Ellen swallowed. "It just… it didn't seem real," she whispered. "The things I'd seen here—they didn't seem real, compared to… to grandchildren. To what it would cost Cory if she was going to lose the babies."

Green nodded. "I can understand that," he said. "The babies seem to make it all so much bigger. So much more real. But now you understand, don't you? The ramifications of what you saw that day to the children your daughter is carrying. You understand?"

There were four of us in the living room, all other souls besides Arturo having fled as we'd walked in.

"I… those children I miscarried—those were… were *elvish* children?" Her voice cracked. "How can that *be*?"

Green smiled at her, as gentle with her as he'd been with Cami and Connor during a recent fight, as gentle as he'd been with Jack and Teague or Phillip and Marcus when their tumultuous love affairs threatened to rip apart the hill.

"You and your husband," he answered. "You must have carried this blood in your veins your entire lives and never known. And then your DNA met and was determined to make a child of those parts."

"But…." She was trying not to sob. "But the babies I… I aborted, because the doctor said they wouldn't thrive… but… I killed—"

"No, no no no…." Green held out his arms, and she rushed in, as much a child as her daughter.

"Ellen Kirkpatrick," he said softly, "you need to listen to me, yes?"

She nodded mutely.

"When an egg is fertilized in a woman's body, that is not the beginning of pregnancy for us. For elves, there is a moment—a few days, actually—when we can decide. Usually, Bracken and I simply tell that child not to be. And this time…." Green grimaced at me. "We did not, and so the children implanted, became, are growing and thriving. But if Cory wanted, she had days to tell them now was not the time. She could have asked me to tell them that, and I would have. It would have pained me, but I would have done it, knowing they would return at a better moment."

"She didn't?" Ellen asked, sounding lost and a little hopeful.

"No," I said. I'd almost been waiting for it—which is why, as irritating as it had been, her denial that it was even happening hadn't infuriated me. Much. "No, it didn't even occur to her. She's terrified, but she doesn't back down from a challenge."

"So really," Green picked up, "those children you lost, the children you banished from your body, they were waiting for the better time. And when they returned, they returned as your daughter. You are probably thinking that's simple poetry, but I assure you it's not. For years we have wondered where *does* that stunning amount of power come from. You saw it, did you not?"

"Holy Jesus," Ellen said, with feeling.

Green nodded. "Indeed. And that—that was child's play compared to what we've seen her do. She's angry at herself because she did it out of temper, but even then she did it with control."

"Damned good thing, or we'd be dead!" Ellen snapped, pulling out of his comfort.

"No," he said soberly. "Do not under any circumstances underestimate your daughter. Even today, angry and hurt and feeling trapped, she didn't attempt anything beyond her ability. You were not so much lucky she didn't kill you, as you were lucky that she's the girl you raised. The girl you raised, that *we* love, wouldn't have risked doing that even in a fit of pique. And that's the point. A human sorceress does not just *happen* out of nowhere. I assumed there were some hidden bloodlines that created her, but normally being even a half elf doesn't guarantee anything *near* the power your daughter possesses."

"That's true," I said, our interactions with the half elves who'd been *dying* to hear they were not alone haunting me as we spoke. "Half elves have small things—psychic abilities, some small parlor tricks—but nothing near what she has."

"So what you are saying...."

She was right to sound uncertain. This was a tremendous thing we were putting together after all these years.

"The reason she has all this power is that she had to wait many times to return. Every time you miscarried or aborted, the core of her—the elvish magic of her—bided its time and grew. When she was finally born, she was blessed with a prodigious gift from all who had gone before."

Ellen nodded. Her mouth worked, and suddenly I understood her dilemma. She had held on to that pain for over twenty, perhaps thirty years. Time and time again, hoping for a child, being told that the ones in her womb could not thrive. And when she finally had a child, it was not the one she had been hoping for. What she was hearing now could heal so much—Cory *was* the child she'd been hoping for. She was *all* the children Ellen had been hoping for. Her very existence was forgiveness and reward, all rolled into one.

But it's hard to let go of pain.

"She…." Ellen swallowed. "She was such a pretty baby, you understand?"

And then she wept, folded in Green's arms, until she too fell asleep.

Nicky drove Ellen home before flying back. She didn't say much after she awoke and before she left, but she thanked us graciously for letting her nap on the couch and for being "So very understanding."

We cautioned her to please not say anything else about her daughter or her pregnancy, and especially to not call her by name in front of her friends. It was a hard thing to explain, but she was humble and seemingly willing to let herself be schooled in things that—finally—she could admit she didn't understand.

As Nicky drove her away, Green and I were left in a strangely silent hill.

"Do you think she understands now?" I asked tentatively.

"I thought she understood *last* time," Green said, irritated. Then he let some of that fall away. "Probably. Yes. But…." He looked at me honestly. "Women—human women—are complex. She is going to want a say in the raising of the children, and that will be complex. She's going to forget, time and time again, that Cory isn't human, and the children aren't human. She's going to *want* to forget."

"Even after—!" I flailed my arms, so certain this had been the final conflict that the prospect of going through it again left *me* a little nauseous.

Green put a hand on my shoulder—and then, oh Glorious Goddess, pulled *me* into his body for some much needed comfort.

"Bracken, my love, you and I and Nicky, we took Cory with all of the flaws. It doesn't change a thing that not all of those flaws are her own."

I thought of Cory's look as she'd fallen asleep, the vague sadness, the certainty that she hadn't done enough.

We loved her for so many things, and so many of those things she'd gotten from her mother, whether we cared to admit it or not.

I snuggled into Green's arms, remembering that we were going to try to regain that closeness, tumble in each other's beds, each other's bodies, once again.

"The children," I said, relaxing into him fully. "You had to see them. They were… simply *being* at the outset. And once they realized there was a third party involved, the little shits completely distorted the picture."

Green pulled back and grinned. "Did they? I had no idea that was a conscious thing! I thought it was something that hit when glamour hit." In adolescence—that was our common wisdom.

"Maybe as fetuses or embryos it comes to repel invasion. Perhaps it evolved," I reasoned, suddenly liking the science very much. "I wish we could have taken the pictures, but we had to delete them instead."

Green sighed and kissed my temple. I made no effort to move from his arms.

CORY
Fall-ing

FALL ALWAYS passed so fast.

Maybe it was because you were always looking at that dazzling sky, wondering when it was going to change, turn gray, dump snow on your head when you least expected it.

Maybe it was that the days were so short. Everything was nighttime, and after an hour or so every night socializing with the vampires, it was time to go to bed.

Maybe it was school, which pumped away with well-worn gears, oiled and smooth and massive, the assignments and lectures all bent on churning out a suitably indoctrinated little clone of Western civilization's best and brightest. *Okay, so maybe still a little bitter about school. Shall have to work on that.* Maybe it was the wind, which blew long and short, sweet and bitter, and made every walk on the campus into either a slog or a game of tag. We were so preoccupied by the wind that the classroom was a brief respite, shelter from the ocean storm.

I'm not sure what it was, really, but we always seemed to go from the end of September to Christmas at a dead sprint, and this year was no exception. In fact, this year was worse, because every day became a desperate race to see how much I could accomplish before my body absolutely demanded rest, food, and a bathroom break—and no, not necessarily in that order.

During the first week of November, we spent some time strewing the invisible border that surrounded Green's property with blood-seasoned steak. The next time the alarm went off, we all propelled ourselves above the hill to see twenty sleeping werewolves on the border.

For a moment we entertained the notion of inviting them all into the hill and making nice, but Bracken, ever practical, put the kibosh on that.

"Hi, hello, you've been trying to kill us for months, but now that you're no longer addicted to sex, I think we should be friends?"

Arturo, Green, and I all glared at him. Arturo turned his back and dropped out of the sky in disgust, and Bracken rolled his eyes and folded his arms, the wind whipping around his shorn black hair like it was getting vengeance.

"You all know I'm right," he said, then extended his arms over his head so he could touch down. Show-off. He'd gotten a lot better at flying in these past months.

Green and I were left, feet dangling over thirty yards above the ground as we watched the poor bewildered werewolves turn into poor bewildered naked people and approach each other warily.

"He's right, you know," Green said, but he didn't sound happy about it.

"Yeah. Prick."

Green laughed and extended his hand. Together we descended slowly, oh so slowly, until our feet touched, and then he draped himself over my back to still my shivering. I'd gotten *really* good at flying this autumn, but it still took a great deal of power, and when I was putting all that power into flying, regulating my body heat went right out the window. I often spent a good half hour trying to get rid of the shivering after we'd warded off the bad guys, and it only got worse as winter got closer.

Iris agreed with Brack when we asked her opinion—looking surprised when we did so. Of course, Iris was constantly surprised to just be alive and well these days.

She'd agreed to stay on at the hill as a sort of willing prisoner. She didn't have much memory of her thralldom to Nimuetia, so she was little to no help, but we all knew that it would be a death sentence to send her off the hill. She'd been too close to the head of the snake—now that she was no longer envenomed, she'd probably be killed. We gave her a room and a bodyguard—an unattached female elf who was fiercely loyal to Green but *very* compatible with a dominator like Iris—and hoped they'd be happy during her stay. I'd seen her and Sky running the cross-country track together, and though Teague and I kept our distance, we'd gotten uncertain hand raises of acknowledgment when we'd seen her.

So we didn't ask the poor, lost, forcefully recruited werewolves in, but we did put Teague and Mario and the vampires on special alert for the new shape-shifters. Apparently they organized some sort of "bar watch"—and in an odd way, that reminded me of Adrian's subtle, unstructured recruitment of the lost youth of our world.

We were recruiting lost werewolves—it was a noble calling.

But ultimately not one I was allowed to take part in, which was probably a good idea. Adrian had been the one who'd seen the good in everyone. I was not nearly the bitch I'd been before Adrian met me, but my world was… more centered now. The children were the core. I surrounded them, and the men surrounded me. Our friends surrounded us, and the hill surrounded them, and I loved everybody, but….

But at the moment, it all came down to the tiny creatures in my womb. They were the center.

I didn't have the energy to debate it, not now.

THANKSGIVING WAS… fast. I wish I could be ashamed at how much I slept, but it *so* wasn't happening. I indulged myself with running every morning with Teague, because I missed that, and with helping Grace in the kitchen even though she complained that I shouldn't put myself out.

I love the kitchen during Thanksgiving. It's warm and homey and social, and Katy and Renny were totally with me on that this year. Last year Katy had been consumed with Teague and Jack, so we hadn't spoken much, but this year she was throwing herself into the preparations with all her heart. Apparently holidays hadn't been a thing when she or Teague had been kids. Jack had the sense-memory guidebook—he remembered stuffing and gravy and turkey and cookies and mashed potatoes and….

For that matter, so did Renny and I. So did Grace and many other members of the hill. But for the people like Katy and Teague, or like Adrian had been, making Thanksgiving amazing and Christmas spectacular became a mission, something important, something sacred.

I was proud to be a part of that this year.

On Friday night, after the food coma had worn off and after my zillion-and-sixtieth nap of the week, I awoke between Bracken and Nicky in the early evening—happy, comfortable, and….

Oh holy Goddess, was I primed.

I yawned and stretched and turned toward Bracken, conscious of Nicky's hands roaming my back in a desultory, skin-feeding way. Bracken was sitting up in bed doing our homework. I actually *did* my homework, but he had a thing about rewriting it in some sort of neutral handwriting. On the one hand, I felt bad about that, but on the other, it seemed to keep him out of trouble while I was sleeping.

He turned to look at me, smiling slightly as he set the notebook on the end table.

"Awake?"

"Isn't that a rhetorical question when my eyes are open?" I asked, sliding my hand up under his T-shirt. Oh... yes. The skin of his stomach was almost entirely smooth. Nicky had a happy trail, and I enjoyed that—a *lot*—but Bracken's body, mostly hairless, pleased me no end. He was the reason I moisturized my hands in the morning—so I could feel every inch of his skin.

Bracken gave a little purr and arched his back, bucking under my touch.

"Yes," he said, "it's a rhetorical question. Are you happy now?"

I thought about it. Were we still at war? Well, yes. A whole new wave of sleepy werewolves had awakened naked at our borders that morning, wandering away to try to find their cars and figure out what had happened to their lives.

My parents hadn't come to Thanksgiving. It was a blow, but not unexpected. Sometimes my mom was asked to a friend's house, and that was where they'd gone this year. She'd thanked me when I called to ask her, but she didn't mentioned shopping again. She *had* mentioned that Dr. Nieman had called her to ask why I hadn't shown, and then called again to ask whose ultrasound records were in the monitor. Nicky had been furious—he hadn't been aware that the machine backed up twice to the office computer—so we'd sent Sweet, one of Green's lieutenants who might leave less of an impression than one of the male elves, to go wipe his mind again.

But Mom hadn't said anything else about seeing me, or about my children, or about my husbands.

Maybe Christmas.

And my stomach, which had been gently swelling, suddenly popped out. I wasn't grossly tremendously huge yet—but I was obviously showing at twenty-one weeks.

I had not, as of yet, felt anything resembling a kick, but Green assured me they were in there and moving. He seemed to think I was confusing their movements with gas. I told him if that was the case, they were training for the Olympics in backstroke.

He'd nodded sagely and said that yes, I was feeling kicks—but as of yet I hadn't identified them as kicks, so I thought that didn't count.

But my stomach was tight and my body was fit, and my men seemed to enjoy touching me as much as ever. And the tenderness in my breasts had eased off and so had the nausea, just a tad.

And I'd eaten well, surrounded by people I loved, and finally, after five days of vacation, I felt like I had enough sleep.

Was I happy?

"I'm so very happy," I told Bracken. I'd had enough of thinking. My hand drifted up to his nipples—he had tiny, pointy nipples that perked up with my touch. He grunted, stretching in a leisurely way, and I pushed up on my elbow. "But you know what would make me even happier?" I teased.

Nicky rolled over and started to kiss the nape of my neck. I dropped my head and let him, hissing with how good it felt.

Nicky was someone I should be worried for, I thought vaguely, appreciating his touch. I'd asked him if he was going to invite his boyfriend, Eric, to Thanksgiving, and his response had been oblique and a little troubling. I had the feeling they'd broken up, even though they'd seemed so very tight in the summer, but I hadn't pushed.

Right now, it didn't matter. Nicky's focus was on me, and for once, I wasn't embarrassed to be the focus and the center. Both of them had their hands on me, and that was all I craved.

Bracken's hands cupped the rise of my stomach, and his eyebrows arched.

"Did you feel—"

"No," I complained. "No, I felt nothing. Now stop trying to make me feel bad about it and kiss me!"

His chuckle rumbled low in his throat, and he slid down on the bed to wrap me up completely in his bulk. He left just enough room for Nicky to keep kissing as he lifted my shirt and stripped off my sleep pants, leaving a warm trail of smooth kisses against my skin.

I moaned, my thighs growing wet almost immediately, and when Bracken cupped my breasts and massaged gently, I brazenly propped my knee up, exposing me to the both of them, hungry for whatever touches they wanted to give.

Nicky took the touching-the-naughty-parts job today, and Bracken took touching everywhere else.

It was hard to think with Bracken's lips nibbling my neck and Nicky's evil fingers gliding around my most sensitive flesh, but then, thinking wasn't what I'd wanted in the first place. What I'd wanted was sort of the *opposite* of thinking. What I wanted was....

Oh... hello....

Nicky's clever, clever fingers had slicked themselves in my sex and were using the moisture to penetrate the *other* opening displayed by my propped leg.

My eyes went round, and Bracken chuckled, low and ruthless, against my ear.

"Is he playing with the forbidden, beloved?"

Oh, yes he was. "It's never been forbidden before," I panted. Bracken's cock, fully engorged and ready, thrust up between my thighs, and Bracken adjusted his position so I was eye level with his chest....

And he was fully seated inside of me.

I moaned, my mouth open against his ribs, my body shuddering at his intrusion.

"Bracken...," I whined, because Nicky was still toying with me.

Bracken arched his hips and thrust again, and Nicky's clever finger embedded itself deeper.

I groaned, beyond words, biting softly into Bracken's pale skin at the overwhelming of my synapses.

Bracken kept thrusting, but there was a fumbling at our bedstand that didn't usually need to happen. A part of me was put out that he'd be bothering with anything but me, but most of me figured out what he was doing.

Nicky didn't have a magic self-lubricating penis. And Nicky was about ready to put his penis where one should *only* go with lubrication.

Bracken made the handoff successfully, and the coolness of lubricant followed. I clung to him while Nicky positioned himself, thrust carefully, *ahhhh*....

I lost the thread of myself, used passionately and well between the two of them. Bracken controlled the speed, the fierceness, the rhythm, and Nicky clutched me to him and held on—and held himself inside.

My power slammed through me like a hurtling meteor slams through a planet. One minute I was traveling the stately orbit of sex that I knew and loved. The pressure in my backside was dark, bordering on pain but not crossing over, and Bracken's cock inside my body was huge and welcome, home and amazing in every slam into my cervix. I expected a build, a climb, a series of them to a plateau, because that was the way my body *worked* during sex, but that wasn't what happened.

What happened was orgasmic Armageddon slamming up through my pelvic floor and taking over my enlarged uterus.

It boiled up out of me, an underground explosion popping the lid off a manhole, and I was terrified of hurting either of the men with the fury of my power. I closed my eyes and let it rock me, holding my hand up to the ceiling and trusting that Green, who was on the hill as he always was, would catch the fallout.

Bracken's shout of climax was surprised, while Nicky's was stunned and indignant. We'd been riding the wave, still surfing the joy of it, and now suddenly we were cresting and exploding in tumult?

But it didn't matter. The power rippled through me, a planet twitching its skin, and I had to scramble to align my thoughts, give it a shape before it took a shape of its own.

My body contracted around their bodies, and my sunshine magic shot through my palm and fingertips, penetrating the crown of the hill and interacting with all of the elements I knew so well.

It continued to interact as my body's spasms—not content with one orgasm or two—continued to ride me as the men stayed locked inside me, milked into the same extended climax quaking through us all. I half sobbed against Bracken's chest, closing my fist and keeping the remaining power inside before I exhausted myself, and abandoned my body to the miles-long orgasm that was *not* going away.

The last of the convulsions were still pulsing along my abdomen when Green walked in and surveyed the scene. He used Bracken's body as a cushion as he leaned over to brush the hair from my face.

"You about done?" he asked, his accent thick with exasperation.

"Goddess, I hope so," I gasped. "By all that's holy…." Oh fuck, again? One more hard shudder passed through me. Bracken and Nicky each gave a reluctant moan, a final spurt, and tightened their arms around me.

And that was the end.

Oh, hell. I melted into their embrace—limp, dazed, and destroyed.

Our breathing filled my ears, filled the room, filled the world.

"That," I said hoarsely, "was really fucking unexpected."

Green nodded soberly, his oval face half-shrouded by his loosened plait of yellow hair as he leaned. "I'd say, beloved, that we should have no more unexpected fucking after that."

Bracken chuckled weakly around me, because he could never resist a good pun, and Nicky let out a chuff of laughter behind me.

I was unhappy.

"Make a… a *plan*?" I might have propped myself up to argue with him, but even if *I* could summon the energy, Bracken's and Nicky's arms lay across my body, limp with their exhaustion. "Like… like… a *schedule* to have sex?"

Green surveyed the tangle of us with beleaguered amusement. "Arturo?" he called. I made a half-hearted attempt to cover myself, even though Arturo had seen me naked and worse before and honestly didn't give a ripe shit.

Green flipped the comforter over the lot of us, and Arturo popped in as though maybe he and Green had hauled ass down the hall together but Green had been the only one allowed in.

"Yes, oh leader mine?"

"Do you have *any* idea what we just did?" He sounded seriously interested in the answer.

Arturo closed his eyes, and for a moment an aura the color of his copper-lightning eyes glowed around his body. He opened his eyes and nodded.

"We are now officially a beacon of fucking hope." He glared at me.

I squinted muzzily back over Bracken's shoulder. "Clarify the use of the expletive?"

He gave a short laugh. "Okay, yes. A beacon of hope. As in, friendly preternatural creatures will be drawn to us—will, in fact, see a sort of glow around us and find their way here."

"We sort of had that before, right?" Because otherwise we'd have people wandering the property and, say, into the pond, or into the overgrown parts of the lower hill, or… well, there was a distinct lack of morality among the lower fey. It was just as well humans had to be invited to see us.

"This is more extensive," Arturo said gravely. "And a little more deadly. Say someone like Cami or Connor or Dylan are looking for us—someone friendly. They will actually *see* us. Say Iris was looking for us before her connection to the elf queen was broken. She will *think* she sees us, but then she will wander around in a sort of no-man's-land between our borders and what you just did with our shields until someone here has pity on her and helps her out. So, on the one hand, the lost supernatural peoples will have some recourse. That's *fantastic*. On the other hand—"

"Oh hell." Because I got it. "We're something out of the… the fucking grimmest fairy tales. Rip Van Winkle, or…." I fluttered my hands weakly between the bodies blocking me. "I can't even remember. But… we can *find* them, right? And, you know…."

"Tranquilize them and drive them to the courthouse to shove them out on the lawn?" Green asked dryly.

Nicky began to snore softly into my hair. Bracken did that big shuddering yawn thing with his body that meant he was stretching *just* prior to falling asleep. I could barely focus my eyes.

"You know," I whined, "you're really harshing my afterglow!"

Green laughed soundlessly. "Understood, little Goddess. Just remember—no sex without me nearby from now on."

"I'll be sure to text," I said crankily. Instead of smiling or rolling his eyes, Green placed a sober kiss on my forehead.

"If that is an unsubtle reminder that I need to not work so much, then point taken."

Oh, this was so unfair. *Yes*, I wanted him in our bed more. *No*, it wasn't fair of us to ask him. *Yes*, I understood that he was needed to heal and bond people to our hill through his bed. *No, I couldn't do anything about that now!*

I whine-grunted. The men got to fall asleep *immediately*, didn't they?

He smiled—and no, there was no irony or regret in the smile at all. "I'm working on it," he said softly. "Now go to sleep. You're going to wake up hungry in a few, so I'll be sure there's leftovers just for you."

"Thanks, Green," I mumbled. "Sorry 'bout the wild magic."

His laugh this time was really quite kind. "It's always the best kind of magic from you, luv. No apologies."

Then he disappeared and shut off the light, and he was quite right—I slept until around ten o'clock that night, then woke up to potty and have a snack.

The angels were the only ones in the front common room, where they were playing Mario Kart. Jefischa usually won those games, but Shepherd was usually watching Jefischa.

The angels….

Puzzled me. They were friendly, yes, but Green had built them a great treehouse, which they could enclose to keep the weather off and just as quickly remake to reveal the sky. Most often they slept there—but sometimes they preferred the noise and closeness inside of the hill, and then they came in and mingled. Their wings didn't seem to take up much more room than the height and breadth of our largest sidhe, and every day they looked more and more… average. Everyday. Manlike.

But as I sat at the kitchen island and ate my cookies while quietly watching them, they suddenly stopped playing the silly, absorbing video game and stood up. As one they wandered to the great wraparound window that surrounded much of the hill and stood, shoulder to shoulder, staring out at the mist-shrouded canyon beyond.

Their wings rustled, unfurling slightly and looming over their backs. For that moment, as they stood vigil over what parts of the night I did not know, they ceased to be Shep and Jefi, new lovers and occasional blood donors. They became instead something great and mythic and dangerous, their wings casting a shadow and projecting an aura, their vigil sacred against all evil.

"Do you see it, Shep?" Jefi asked, almost bouncing in his enthusiasm.

"Yes. She made it with her sex."

"That's pretty cool. Adrian didn't tell us about that. Don't you wish *we* could do that?"

Shepherd cleared his throat and looked away, seeming supremely uncomfortable. "Enough of the world moves when we have sex as it is, Jefischa. This would frighten me."

Jefi rustled his wings so they merged and stroked as the angels stood, faces pressed against the window.

"Yes, I think you're right," Jefi said after a moment. "Right now all our world is filled with wonder."

I dropped my cookie in my milk.

All our world is filled with wonder.

I could make magic things happen with my sex, and often even without it.

My hand flattened almost instinctively on my no-longer flat abdomen.

Look what I am making in my body.

All of our world really is filled with wonder.

I managed to make it back to bed and found that Green was sitting up in one of the stuffed chairs waiting for me.

"Please tell me you ate something besides pie." He pointed to the space on the bed left by Bracken and Nicky, who had gone to have a drink with the shape-shifters as they often did when I was sleeping.

I crawled back into Bracken's space and relaxed into his warmth. Green smiled at me as he worked on his laptop, and I smiled back, truly ready for some sleep now.

"Whatcha doing?" I asked, feeling the comfort in our work to keep the hill safe.

"Just paperwork," he said, yawning. "I press Send, it ceases to matter."

"You're a good leader." I yawned in response to his yawn, dammit. "You know what, Green?"

"What, beloved?"

"All our world really *is* filled with wonder."

He paused as his fingers flickered across the keyboard and stopped to cup my cheek. "Indeed it is," he whispered. "Indeed it is."

The next week I found out he'd implemented "training" sessions with some of his most promising sidhe captains—Lambent included—in how to heal with one's body. Since the healing required subsuming all of your needs to your partner's, Green seemed to feel that the elves who could successfully do this of their own free will wouldn't want to rival Green for power. Of course Green would "collect" from his captains as well, and make sure all his people were being treated fairly.

But what it amounted to was that Green was working less. And I also realized that he hadn't been taking any business trips off the hill, although previously he'd been forced to do that.

"Andres is helping me there," he reassured me. "You bound him to us quite tightly, and I'm very comfortable with him taking over some of my business ventures. But yes, I'll be forced to leave for nearly three weeks sometime after Christmas. Some things have been put off too long."

"Well, we're still sort of fighting for our lives," I observed, because it did seem to hang over our heads. Even though it appeared we'd wounded the enemy badly and she needed time to regroup, she'd had weeks already. We knew she was planning to augment her numbers and probably plotting to add another engine to her siege since the werewolves weren't working anymore. We weren't counting her out—in fact, I was more than a little wary of her next move.

"Yes, yes we are," he said assessingly. We were having this conversation sitting kitty-corner to each other at the kitchen island while he fed me sausage and fruit for breakfast. It was Sunday morning the week after Thanksgiving, and the rest of the household was still asleep. Just this once, Green and I were at the breakfast table together and alone.

"I can deal with a business trip," I said into the silence. "I have before."

He shrugged and nodded. "This is different."

I shrugged and nodded back. "Yeah, but...."

It wasn't like either one of us would be changing jobs.

He covered my hand with his. "Beloved, you know what you can do for me while I'm gone?"

I grimaced. "Yeah, yeah. I'll have to go into the nursery sometime."

He winked, because my reluctance to go in there and admit it was a room was a Green's hill punchline by this point. "Exactly. I think it will give you comfort to go in there when you're missing me."

I couldn't argue with him. In fact, after the madness that would be Christmas and gift giving, adding the finishing touches that the sprites wouldn't have thought of would be a very legitimate project to fill my time when I was down to six units next semester.

"Do I really have to not have sex while you're gone?" I asked plaintively. Because... well... three weeks. *Sex.* "Isn't it dangerous for me to get... you know... depleted?"

He arched one butter-blond eyebrow with so much irony it practically dripped off.

"Yes, luv, you can die of sex depletion. It's a terrible risk—how could I not have seen that before?"

I stuck my tongue out. "Don't be a smartass." I wiggled a little, though, because after the big shield-refining thing with Bracken and Nicky, the four of us had rolled around and changed the wall colors again—and, much to the entire household's horror, changed the colors of every vehicle in the garage to baby pink and baby blue. Including Arturo's sky blue Cadillac, which turned pastel. Including Max's red Mustang. Including (oh horrors) Teague's precious candy-apple-red fastback. The only vehicle spared had been the one I'd "painted" over the summer in olive, purple, and gold.

The bitching had been prodigious and bitter until Bracken and I had made a conscious effort—sort of the ultimate pity fuck, from my point of view—and changed the cars back. Green had said it was a nice exercise in control, but Teague, Max, and Arturo kept checking their cars in fear now. The sex car color fiasco was not going to be forgiven soon.

"I just… I mean, we can't have a sex moratorium while you're gone!" I pointed out in exasperation. "I know scary things happen, but…."

Green let out a hmph. "See, luv," he said after a moment, resting his chin on his doubled fists, "our difficulty lies with the unpredictability of it. You can't predict what the orgasm is going to do as it ripples up your body." His fingertips danced along the side of my stomach through my T-shirt, and we both looked down at the bulge pressing against the worn gray fabric. Now, when I concentrated, I could feel the slight stretch in my uterus and the way my muscles and insides were rearranging themselves to host the parasites currently gnawing their way through sausage, eggs, and fruit.

"Well, maybe," I said archly, "if you're going to be there more at night, we can practice some more so we *know* what will happen."

He tilted his head back and laughed. "Point taken." His eyes danced. "But also—" He grimaced. "—we may want to consider that as you leave your second trimester, around February, you'll feel less and less like 'cavorting.' In fact, the larger your womb gets, the bigger your orgasm will get. It could be that, by then, the full… ménage experience, as it were, might be a bit much for you."

I had the wherewithal to blush. "So you're saying that (*a*) I'll feel too crappy to get it on, and (*b*) if I *do* feel good enough to get it on, I might want to tone it down anyway, because the full monty is going to wear me the hell out."

Green thought that one over. "Yes, beloved. Once again, you have put your elbow on the pulse of the problem."

I blushed harder. "More like my big freaking burgeoning stomach, you know?"

"That too." He touched my stomach again, palm out, and his fingertips danced along my nerve endings.

Except they were dancing on the inside, against my stomach or my diaphragm or something that most assuredly wasn't my skin.

I gasped and pressed his hand tighter against my stomach. I closed my eyes and just *felt* for a moment, the space behind my eyes blood dark until the flutters pressed against it in spreading spots of white, like handprints on a piece of black plastic.

A slow smile spread over my face, squishing my cheeks up and letting my teeth dry out.

"You felt that?" he asked, tender as always.

"Mm-hmm. You?"

"Luv, I've been feeling them for weeks. You're late to the party."

I opened one eye and saw that he was teasing me—but he was also telling the truth.

"Poor, poor, mortal-oh-me," I said, but without any real venom. I could feel our children, and Green was there, Green whom I loved before all others.

For once—just a peaceful slice of time in a quiet kitchen, with the tranquil dark sleeping around us—I was content.

TWO DAYS before the winter solstice, in the late afternoon, Nimuetia threw everything she had at us. Later we would assume it had been so we wouldn't interfere with her solstice ceremony to make more troops.

It didn't matter why.

The minute we heard the psychic shriek of the alarm, those of us who could fly ran up the stairs and into the Goddess grove so we could levitate or fly up above the trees and see what was going on.

We got there just in time to see a mass of werewolves—over two hundred people, from the looks of it—rush the borders of Green's land.

And disappear.

Everybody grimaced. We could feel the push of bodies into our defenses—sort of like eating another cheeseburger when you were constipated. (Pregnancy—so very many new experiences, so few of them as magical as that first kick.) The body of our land felt bloated and full, roiling with human gas, lost werewolves who could not see their way to the other side.

Green looked at me beseechingly. "Beloved?" he asked. Then I felt a spear of power aimed at our heart.

With a gasp of outrage, I looked out into the murky twilight of the closing gray day and saw a burn of orange on the horizon.

It wasn't the sun, which had hidden behind an iron-gray cloudbank for the past week, oblivious to the lot of us working hard at our Christmas.

It was her.

Our first glimpse of an enemy who had harried us for over a year, and unimpressive from a distance. A single woman, blazing orange— and from a guess, she was blazing with other people's power. We'd met enemies like this, ones who could steal from the preternatural creatures in their personal sway, and she was probably getting her groovy hot orange glow from the werewolves who had just disappeared into our borders.

I heard a savage oath from Bracken next to me. "She wouldn't be so fucking bright if we could break the blood bond with all her goddamned minions."

I looked at him and grinned. "Beloved, think you can make it rain in the borderlands?"

Brack looked at me, confused. "Rain? That's Green's province." Well, Green *did* control the weather in the hill.

"Not rain, my darling," I said, thinking about how I'd direct the power just *there*, and let Bracken follow my lead. I squinted through the whipping wind and held my breath. "Do you feel it?"

Everyone hovering on the hill with me, including the angels—who were flapping their wings slowly and without personal investment in the battle—stopped for a moment and held their breath.

Oh, holy Goddess, she'd mistimed it. She must have been banking on the power of twilight and the grayness of the day. That made it harder to see, and perhaps she was hoping for some of her people to slide under the defenses. Perhaps she had thought she would have won already—and it was a good thought, because two hundred werewolves was a lot of killing fury under your control.

She hadn't counted on them simply disappearing like that.

It didn't matter why, or what she had thought she could gain. Nothing mattered now, because *they* were coming.

The vampires had arisen.

Phillip and Marcus zoomed through first, followed by Grace. Then the whole kiss came boiling up from the trapdoor, covering the grove below our feet with angry bodies—souls ready for battle, born bloodletters who wanted a chance to be set free.

Oh, was she lucky we'd accidentally hidden her werewolves.

"Phillip, Marcus, Grace, need you."

Next to me, Green was having the same conversation with the other elves, the ones inside the hill. A heartbeat later, the last of the sidhe streamed outside—all of the landbound looking up at those of us who *could* fly with awe.

Lambent was one of the ones who could.

He rose up next to me and asked, just under the wind, "Can Kyle do it, Your Nibs?"

Yes, he and Kyle had been comforting each other. I didn't see it lasting—but then, I hadn't seen Max and Renny lasting either, which proved my perception in these matters was often for shit.

"Sure." I called the grieving young vampire. He rose, gaunt but focused, and listened to the mental call I gave my captains.

Very carefully he approached Lambent in the air, a march of two hummingbirds. As they hovered, bobbing with the air currents, he sank his teeth delicately into Lambent's pink-flushed skin.

The other vampires were executing the same stately dance with the lot of us, and Phillip took his turn with me. I managed a short caress of his coarse black hair before he punctured and then licked just enough to hold the blood in.

By the time he'd finished, the lot of us were holding out our hands, and the vampires' spit was pretty much the only thing keeping us from raining blood on the sacred ground of the Goddess grove. The angels had apparently been eager to donate, and Marcus was looking just a little bit drunk on angel blood.

"Bracken?"

His eyes glowed faintly in the early dark, what had been the whites pulsing instead with the dark ruby color of new blood.

"Yes, beloved?"

I didn't touch him physically, but I did join with Green and let a tendril of power twine with Green's and then Bracken's. I can't explain it any better than letting vines of our will snake together, spun like yarn.

"Do you feel that, beloved?" I asked, probing at the edge of Green's property where my shields kept the werewolves both out of the property itself and locked in limbo.

I heard Bracken's grunt. Then I felt him tugging lightly at my blood.

"Everyone ready!" Green and I called together, both mentally and out loud, and I spoke in a low undertone to Brack. "Not too much from me, beloved. The children need some."

I could feel them pulsing in my body, sending tingles to my extremities, through my fingertips, in the ends of my toes. They enjoyed the rush of power, the adrenaline running through my veins—Green had told me this, and when the lightning was crackling through my body, I could feel it too. When I touched down and let the power furl back under my ribcage, pulsing with my heart, that surety would disappear, going back to where it had been before that marvelous flutter with just Green and me in the kitchen.

But right now, I savored it. I was afraid for us, yes. But I was not alone, not even in my body, and *that* was comfort.

I felt the readiness of our people roaring in my blood, felt it ripple and swell, rise and crest—

And peak.

"Bracken, now!"

I felt his power tugging the blood from our veins, thin trickles of crimson twirling through the air like the threads of a licorice whip and joining, combining elves, sorceress, angels, all into one slightly thicker rope. Bracken wrapped it around the power Green and I sent snaking along the boundaries of the property in a steady circle like a sprinkler hose.

Almost exactly like a sprinkler hose.

I felt a wobble and gasped, handing my wrist to Green so he could heal the puncture and stop the blood flow. It took barely a brush of his hand, almost absentminded, and then both of us were twining with Bracken again, pooling the blood around the areas most populated with werewolves. In volume it wasn't much blood—we weren't exsanguinating our people, just borrowing a bit of what they had to spare—but combined with the power the vampires were giving me and that Green was taking freely from the elves, it became a small whirlpool, a blood grenade set to cleanse the tainted.

"Song!" Green called, and I remembered. The last time we'd done something like this, we'd had an entire chorus, complete with rehearsal and timing. This time all we had was a song everyone in the hill could sing.

"Rain will fall!" I shouted. And then, at the top of our lungs, with no conscious effort toward harmony or even staying in key, Green, Bracken, and I began to chant. "Rain will fall and trees will grow and rain will fall and trees will grow and…."

As the groundswell of chanting started up just like the first borrowed drops of blood, I left them to it. I sent my own voice soaring—as pure in pitch as I could manage, because when I let go of the melody line, that was when we all let go of the blood and the power and….

"You will have lovers," I sang. *"We will have lovers…."*

"Again!"

As a people we roared the word, and as the focus of our blood magic, Bracken flung the blood through our shields so hard that any body, tree, human, or werewolf would be penetrated by the fine mist and cleansed, left standing as the blood diffused through their systems, taking the mind-warping magic of our adversary with it.

For a moment, nothing happened. Quietly elves began to heal the small puncture wounds on themselves and each other—although now that Bracken wasn't pulling their blood from their bodies with magic, the vampire spit would probably keep the whole works inside their skin where it belonged.

But that was all, in that moment. And then….

Then the werewolves began to tumble into sight at the borders of our land. They were, to a one, dizzy and disoriented—and naked. But they were no longer hostile to us, and they *were* very confused to find they'd just been werewolves and now no longer knew what they were.

"Did we get them all?" I asked Green. He thought about it and shrugged.

"No," he said, not seeming perturbed. "But it's still early yet. If we try this again in a few weeks, we may be able to round up the stragglers."

I noticed his compassion for the poor lost werewolves wandering inside no-man's-land seemed to have run out, and honestly I couldn't blame him. We really were going to an awful lot of effort not to kill people, and it was starting to piss me off.

With that anger building, I looked out across the murky sky.

Our enemy was fading. Fading, in fact, and falling. A controlled fall, so not deadly, but still, we'd weakened her. Weakened her badly— and suddenly I wanted an end to it.

I don't even remember the conscious decision, but one moment I was hovering, watching with satisfaction as the newly freed werewolves began stumbling around in the frost and thinking we should probably send them some sprites to act as will-o'-the-wisps to guide them to their clothes and cars before the snow-laden air did them harm. The next moment I was streaking across the sky with a precision I hadn't possessed this summer but had honed in the attacks since.

I was barely aware of what was probably half the hill streaking after me and Green shouting my name while remaining over the grove, hovering.

I felt the power depletion the moment we left Green's land, but I had flown without that backup before. I was freezing—the hooded sweatshirt and jeans I wore weren't enough for being this far up and flying in the cold—but hot fucking vengeance was making up for a lot of heat loss.

She was *down.*

I hurtled past trees and underbrush, looking for the telltale glow of burnt orange as I passed. She'd need her power in the cold and the rough terrain, and providing she'd not been killed with the fall, she'd be hoofing it.

I was going so fast that I thought the white streaks blurring past my vision were from speed. It wasn't until my face started stinging that I realized it was snow.

I took my eyes from the horizon for a moment to register the complete dark of the sky above me and the enchantment of the falling white, and when I pulled my head out of my ass I realized I had almost missed her. It took all the control I'd learned in the past months to stop—just stop—and lower myself to the ground.

She was running, and I landed about ten feet behind her in a patch of forest that was both spare and steady, with trees about every twenty feet or so.

"*Elf bitch!*" I screamed, too furious to be a grown-up about using her name. She turned anyway, and we faced each other under moonlit snowfall and a winter-dark sky.

If, as we suspected, Nimuetia waxed and waned by the solstice, pulling her sustenance from the obscene rituals of flesh and sex that Connor and Iris had described, she was so far into the bottom of her swing she was almost subterranean with want.

Her flesh was sunken into her cheeks. Skin sagged at her neck and even flapped around the bones of her skinny forearms. Her eyes glowed from black pits like coals in a skull, and her bright, rich robes flapped around a ribcage and spine both clothed in fragile, brittle skin.

Her hair fell lank and coarse down her hips. On a good day, it was probably the color of an LA sunset. Today it was a dirty ginger—fruit-flavored bubblegum at the bottom of the subway.

Her teeth were whole and sound, though, and she pulled back skinny flaps of chapped lips to snarl.

"Is that all you've got, Cory Kirkpatrick Green?" she hissed, her voice sibilant and dry. "*Elf bitch?*"

"Nimuetia," I named her. Then I got nasty. "Mistress of putrid sex, witch-master of obscene blood rites, succubus of toxic greed. How's that?"

She flinched, and for a moment some animation returned to those desiccated features. I must have named her aright—at least in her perception of herself—because the power shield she held around herself flickered, and for a moment she was soft and sad and puzzled.

"But what *is* your name?" she whispered. "What is it? Lady Cory? We've heard that—it holds no power over you. Why can we not call your name?"

Well, for one thing, because it was too goddamned complicated for even me to remember. But for another? Well, part of elvish naming rituals involved naming what a person *was*, as well as who they were related to. I suspected she knew very little about who I was.

"I got no idea," I lied. But then, I wasn't elvish—at least not in this matter. Whatever spam filter my blood had undergone during my mother's repeated reboot of the baby thing, I had never had the stricture placed on me concerning truth-telling that the elves had. Once that had bothered me, and I'd worked hard to be just like them. Now that it turned out I *was* like them? I had no problem letting this one little similarity slip away.

"None?" she asked derisively. Oh, yes, it rankled that I could tell a bold-faced lie, I could see that.

"Okay, maybe a little, but that's not what concerns me. You know what concerns me?"

She waved a languid hand, and I swear even the skin on her fingers flapped. "I don't care what your concerns are," she said, bored.

My eyes narrowed. "Remember that I can kill you as we stand, and say that again without irony," I snapped. I *hoped* I could kill her as we stood. She was still glowing, and everything she'd done had been sneaky and defensive—what defense did she have up her sleeve?

She blinked, long and slow, and focused those burning coal pits on me as though she'd forgotten who I was for a moment and was trying to connect what I'd said with the truth.

Suddenly she started to tremble, a skeleton covered in leaves on the wind.

"Of course I care," she rasped, and the trembling ceased. "You're Green's pet human—and his best weapon. If I can get rid of you, I can have his entire kingdom, and my revenge will be complete."

A chill ran up my spine. She hadn't been *lying*—she just hadn't been paying attention. In fact, she'd had the same distracted look on her face that I probably had when I talked to the vampires.

Without warning I shot up twenty feet into the air. I barely felt the wind of their passing as two werewolves—big ones, well fed—leaped out of the shadows aimed straight at me, teeth out, snarling and slavering. And oh, holy Goddess, they'd almost gotten me. Yeah, sure, a bite from one of those werewolves might be reversed by Green and some quick transfusions, but I'd probably be really sick in the meantime, and the fight not to be taken over by the madness of holding two or three magics in one body might kill me.

It would definitely kill the children living inside me.

My stomach threatened to rebel, and I almost threw up on the snapping, slavering werewolves.

Fury flooded my veins. I threw two power balls in quick succession, almost depleting my ability to fly in one mighty surge.

The first ball hit the werewolves and cooked them fast and hard, the smell of charred dog hair and melted fat almost making me throw up again.

Before the smell even wafted up, the second power ball was in motion, aimed at that nightmare woman's glowing form. The first ball had found its mark, but I wavered, and the second ball….

Blew up the tree behind where she was standing. She disappeared so fast that I hoped she withered into dust from using that much power.

I knew *I* wasn't in such great shape after all the energy *I'd* just used.

Bracken, Grace, and Arturo pulled into the clearing and hovered near me, all of them glowering with such fierceness that I forced myself to remember what I'd done wrong.

What I came up with was that terrible moment of realizing I might have survived the werewolf attack, but the children… the children would not have.

Bracken heard my little moan first. He swooped below and caught me as my emotions sent me spinning out of control.

"I can fly," I defended, staying still in his embrace because struggling was stupid and childish, and hadn't I done enough already?

You know that way people pronounce words when they're squeezing them out through a rage-constricted throat and grinding teeth, syllable by syllable?

"I would appreciate it if you didn't."

And where the snow and the night and the flying hadn't done it, Bracken's fury did. I started to shiver so hard my vision blurred. I didn't stop until after he got me back to Green's hill, into some warm, dry sweats, and under the covers, nursing a cup of hot-chocolate-o'-shame in a stony silence.

NICKY
Fatherhood

THEIR FURY was building like an ion charge in a thunderhead.

Green and Bracken were gonna fucking lose it.

Not that I blamed them. One minute we were winning, watching the werewolves stumble out of limbo, their tie to the elf bitch broken and their own identities free to creep back at their own speeds.

And then….

Zoom.

Like a slingshot or a little dog down the street—that's how fast Cory had taken off, and that's how stunned we were when we realized where she was heading.

Arturo turned and screamed at Green—"Don't fucking move!" or something close—and Bracken was already after her. Holy hell. I flew all the time—had been flying since I was a kid—but in that entire life of flying, I didn't remember seeing anything like those humanoid forms sizzling through the air. They weren't people, they were projectiles with minds of their own, and I was just a bird. I could barely keep up.

I'd been a mile behind them when I saw the two flashes—power balls, as Cory called them—light up the ground. Then Bracken, Arturo, and Grace dropped out of sight. By the time I caught up with them, Bracken had Cory and there was nothing to do but the trailing behind on the way back to the hill.

I had time to think as we went, though, and I was one up on everybody else by the time we got downstairs.

That summer, she—there was really only one *she* as far as we were all concerned—had killed children, had almost died, and had faced the possible death of Green, whom we all loved. And in one charming, painful gesture, she had let me know I wasn't going to be a part of dealing with that. She just dropped me off at the airport so I could go visit my boyfriend, telling me that what was going to happen next was too intense, I hadn't signed on for it, and I could go heal now—Bracken and Green would take care of it all.

Yeah, they'd taken care of it, all right. They'd knocked her the hell up.

Not that I blamed them—it was unmistakably Cory's doing. Me and Cory, we were small town. I understood how wanting control over your own life and your own body could backfire that way. It had happened to a lot of people I knew. Cory hadn't been prepared for it, that was all—it was a simple human thing, and she was usually thinking far above the simple human things.

That's why they bit her on the ass.

She needed me.

That one thing had become clear to me since I'd returned to the hill and smelled that pregnant, quickening aura in our home. She *needed* me.

No, I wasn't her great love. Never would be. But when she saw me with Bracken or Green, she had the feeling her lovers were cared for when she couldn't. She needed me for that. When Green or Bracken got too intense, she needed the lover who was *not* all about sex and power, the lover who didn't eat thunder and crap lightning. She needed *me*. Yeah, sure, I was a smartass. But we had that in common. Cory and Bracken—when they argued, they could rip the hill apart. Me and Cory, we barely snapped towels on each other's ass. If we were a human couple, I could see us, hand in hand, making a baby's room and fucking shit up ten ways to Sunday—and laughing and doing our best.

Even counting Green and Bracken, there was not another person in the hill who could grab her hand and skip into the sunset with her. Even counting Teague, who was her friend but would never cross that line even when it needed to be crossed.

I'd felt that need building in her all semester when she and Bracken talked about not killing a guy when a simple protocol could put him in his place. I'd felt it when she went into the ultrasound and then needed someone to lighten shit the fuck up in the suddenly flying car. It was why I hadn't gone to see Eric that Thanksgiving and had no plans to see him at Christmas. It was, in fact, why I'd given Eric up and told him he was free to live his own life without an inexplicably tied-up boyfriend who dropped in and out like weather.

For one thing, I had Bracken in my bed now, and between him and Green I was a very happy five-on-the-Kinsey-Scale boy. (Goddess bless the Internet—apparently the Kinsey Scale was much more acceptable than the Faggot Scale my peer group had used when I was growing up.)

But mostly there was Cory. It didn't matter that I wasn't the great love of her life. Between loving her as a husband and loving her as a queen and loving her as a friend, there was no way I could love a human being—even Green or Bracken, even Eric—more than I loved her.

And suddenly, with the advent of children on the scene, it didn't matter that I was everybody's third choice.

I was going to be a father too.

And my wife was having a baby too.

I was something to her that no other man was, even if there wasn't a name for it.

And right now, that thing was exactly what she needed.

Green and Bracken were icy quiet, and I was sure they were waiting for me to go so they could have their intense, oh-my-God-everybody-could-have-died powwow with her. But you know?

I got to have my say first.

I crossed my arms and rolled my eyes as she drank her hot chocolate. Katy and Jack—gotta hand it to them. They took their roles as provisioners for the power throwers seriously.

"You couldn't have fucking waited?" I asked, making my voice as bitchy as possible.

She stuck out her tongue. "She was *falling*!"

"Yeah, I know. We all fuckin' saw. But you couldn't have, say, turned to Bracken and said, 'Bracken, sweetheart, *due'alle*, big-cocked bastard in my bed, could you go over and suck that bitch's blood out of her body for me?"

Oh yeah—she almost lost it, and she had to pull in her full lips in order to purse her mouth. Well, Bracken's penis could lighten the heaviest moment, unless it was right up your ass.

"She didn't have any blood," Cory replied soberly. "She was all skinny bitch, no blood."

I didn't even have to play. I wrinkled my nose. "Fucking eww."

"I'm saying," Cory grumbled. "Every time she moved, her skin flapped around like a Renaissance dress on a runway model. It was terrifying."

"So why didn't you take her out?" I asked, but not accusingly. That last part was very important.

"She had werewolves waiting," she grudged. Then an evil smile lit up her wide-cheekboned face. "Did you not smell the cooked dog?"

I couldn't deal. I tilted my head back, studied the newly maroon ceiling, and groaned. "Oh my fucking God. Was *that* what the stench was?"

Cory shuddered. "I almost threw up on them as they were starting to heal. That would have made it extra special."

"Fucking gross," I said, shaking my head. Then, while Green and Bracken were calming down—I could feel them lightening the fuck up, because the sense of storm was fading—I pulled up the chair and sat down next to the bed. "Cory?"

She looked at me soberly. "You gonna yell at me too?" Her voice shook a little, and I was reminded of how she hated it when we yelled.

"No." I took her hands in mine. They were icy cold, and the nail beds were still tinged blue. Yeah, we weren't overreacting—she'd been seriously cold by the time Bracken got her wrapped up and in bed. "But I am going to throw a little guilt on you, so hang on."

"There's nothing—"

"I broke up with Eric," I told her baldly.

Her jaw dropped, and instantly—*instantly*—her freckled face softened with compassion. "But... but *why*, sweetie? Why? He was *yours*—all yours!"

I nodded. "Yeah. But I would rather be Daddy Three than Eric's number one. So let Green and Bracken lay the heavy shit on you. I'm sure they'll have plenty to say. Just remember—I'm the most human person in your bed, and I love you. I love the babies. I thought you were worth giving someone up for—someone I loved—because being a part of this group was so much more important than having someone outside of it. So you find a way to make that work for all of us, okay? This thing you're doing"—and for the first time, *I* got to deliberately touch her stomach, acknowledging that there was a gift growing in there for all four of us—"it's a really tremendous thing. You don't have to go kill the elf bitch and pass all your classes and get a degree in queenship or whatever just to impress us. I mean, you didn't have to do all that before you forgot the fucking magic condom, but you really don't have to do it now. Just remember that the next time you feel like storming the castle, okay? There's a reason the queen has a knight and a bishop and a rook and shit on the board. It's so she doesn't have to fly off and die."

Cory cleared her throat, looking highly uncomfortable. But for once—and Holy Goddess, wasn't this an improvement—for once, she didn't argue with me.

"Yeah," she whispered. "Yeah, okay."

When I kissed her cheek, her skin was still chilled under my lips. "I'm going to go get you—"

"No," she said, leaning her head on my shoulder. "Don't go. If everyone's going to yell at me, I want you to be here."

"We're *not* going to yell at her," Bracken snapped.

"I don't believe you," she deadpanned.

Oh, yeah—there would be yelling. So much yelling. I should have brought a book.

CORY
Bed Rest

BRACKEN WAS trying so hard not to be angry at me, not to make me shiver, not to just let loose his frustration. It was painful to behold.

Green's face was the color of ice.

Nicky's hand in mine lent me courage the way his small-boned body lent me warmth. He'd broken up with his boyfriend for us. For all of us, including the babies. It was a sacrifice I'd never have asked him to make—but to have him here, next to me, no divided loyalties? Oh, there were not words enough for how grateful I felt.

And what was I supposed to say? That I was sorry? Well, I was and I wasn't. I was sorry I'd forgotten and gone in after her myself. But I wasn't sorry for how I felt, for the thing that had driven me.

"It's just that…," I started, feeling my throat constrict, "I'm so tired of being afraid. I just want to… to have our family, and be pregnant, and not *worry* every fucking day about this. And…." I waved the hand Nicky wasn't clenching. "I know this won't be the last time we fight, or the last enemy we have." All those damned history and politics classes, they weren't for nothing. The Roman Empire had fallen, the Aztecs had fallen, the United Republic of Consumerism wasn't doing so hot. All successful governments had weaknesses and downfalls. Ours would too. "There will always be obstacles," I said, the full weight of time and inevitability falling on my shoulders. "But for just… Goddess, just long enough to have our children, to know they're sound, to be able to put them out of danger. I just want some fucking peace."

Nicky let go of my hand and wrapped his arm around my shoulder, and some of the tension in the room changed shape, becoming an ineffable sadness.

"I can't make any guarantees, beloved," Green said, voice throbbing with a lover and child who had been dead for over a thousand years. He came to crouch in front of me, hands on my knees. "The only thing I can tell you is that if you don't show some consideration for yourself and the life inside you, you may have more peace than you can bear."

I nodded, stricken. My lower lip began to tremble, and suddenly I wasn't a queen or a weapon or a sorceress or a commander or any of those other things that I represented to the people at the hill.

Suddenly I was a young mother, and just that quickly I could see the terrible moment of sadness when that face of motherhood ceased to be.

There was no splitting hairs or being right with that one. There was only sorry.

My wail of "I'm *sorry*!" could probably be heard throughout the hill, and I couldn't be wrapped in Green's arms tight enough. There was a moment, though—I felt it—when he stiffened. Something had happened that needed his attention.

I pulled back and wiped my face with the back of my hand—'cause I'm just classy that way—and sniffled. "Go," I said thickly. "I'll be here when you get back. Promise."

He lingered for a moment, nuzzling my neck and leaning against me temple to temple, and I drank in as much of him as I could get. With a whisper of a kiss across my cheek, and a strong clasp of Bracken's shoulder, he was gone.

"I'm not gonna yell," Bracken said after a moment, looking away.

"Wouldn't blame you if you did," I offered apologetically.

He came and sat on my other side, my non-Nicky side, and wrapped his arm around me too. I leaned on him, because he was Bracken, but every now and then a shudder still rocked me when a spasm of fury fought past his mental shields.

We sat for a moment, him staring a hole through the door to our room and me staring a hole through his profile. For that long moment, he didn't look at me.

"I would have been the one to find your body," he said, voice expressionless. "Sucked dry, bleeding out, broken beyond recognition."

Oh, Goddess. "Bracken, I—"

"I would have been the one who had to bear you to Green and watch as he fell to earth and Arturo caught him."

I shook with my own sobs now, not his anger. It felt as though his anger was bleeding out with every word.

"I would have been the one facing all of our people as I held the body of their hope, their queen."

I was devastated. There was no part of me untouched by tears and sorry.

"Please," he rasped, voice breaking finally. "Please remember that. Sometime before your body starts to move would be good, but… but…." He pulled in a fractured breath. "Goddess, beloved, anytime at all before you're falling out of the sky would be a vast fucking improvement."

He was shaking, weeping, head in my lap, arms around my waist, and I could do nothing but hang on to him and be glad Nicky was there beside us, stroking his hair too and giving me strength.

I WOKE up with all four of us in my bed and Arturo sitting politely in one of the chairs on the side, leafing through one of my politics textbooks and muttering to himself as he went. Yeah, well, fucking humans. We could screw up a good thing with one deep breath.

"Wha's up?" I yawned. Arturo glanced at me, apparently unsurprised that in a bed full of immortal beings who rarely slept, I would be the only one up. I knew Brack and Green had taken turns leaving the night before, checking on the werewolves at the border and making sure they were getting the hell out of Dodge.

"Iris wishes to speak to you."

"Just me?" I wrinkled my nose.

"Actually, you and Green together." Arturo furrowed his brow and looked fierce. "I would prefer neither of you, but she will only speak if both of you are there."

"What is it about?" I sat up and yawned, showing all my teeth behind my hand. The thought of talking to her again made me snarl. "And can we borrow an orange jumpsuit for her to wear?" One of the stupid things I hated most about talking to Iris was that, even in jeans with her hair falling loosely around her shoulders, she still looked older and smarter and more glorious than I did.

Especially as the twins seemed to get bigger with every damned heartbeat.

Arturo looked at me with an arched eyebrow. "Orange would look hideous on her," he said, as though making sure that was the point.

I smiled, feeling catty but not caring. "Oh, yes it would."

He shook his head. "That's beneath you," he said quietly. I sighed and wriggled out from between Green's and Bracken's sleeping bodies.

Nicky was up against the wall on Bracken's other side, and I looked at him fondly. Ours. Completely. So be it.

When I got to the end of the bed, I made sure I was sideways, because just sitting up wasn't easy when your middle got bigger, and I propped myself up on my elbow so I could do it....

And when I was done, I glared at Arturo, because it suddenly felt like his fault. "Still beneath me?" I bitched, but he didn't smile.

"Have you seen those statues?" he asked, smiling in recollection. "The carved stone statues of fecund women quickening, growing round?"

Yup. I'd seen them. Big hips, big belly, big boobs—motherhood glorified, I guess. I pushed myself up and grunted, just grateful that, this once, I didn't feel it necessary to give myself a little jet boost with the rapidly increasing gas reserves my pregnant body produced. (So far, I'd been lucky and managed to keep my gas to myself until I got to the bathroom. Once there, though, no holds barred. I'd started locking even Bracken out but hadn't told him why. Tough. Cookies.)

"Are you saying you'd worship me?" I asked, feeling bitter. Oh, wouldn't it be awesome to be worthy?

"No, little Goddess. Those statues were carved by the women themselves. That's why the bodies are so distorted. They were time markers for the women during their gestation. They would look down at their bodies and see their breasts and bellies grow larger, and they'd know something magical was happening. Those stone dolls are a mark of celebration for new life."

I looked at him distrustfully, then looked down at my body. I was about halfway through, and my belly had begun to pooch out enough for me to see it through my T-shirt under my irritatingly heavy breasts. Everybody—and I mean *everybody*—had weighed in on my weight, including Green. He had held my hand and sort of "scanned" me with his eyes closed, monitoring my heart, my blood pressure, the way I was processing sugar and protein—*everything*. The consensus was that this was a perfectly normal pregnancy of above-normal-sized twins. My belly was large, but there weren't extra fat or water deposits where they shouldn't be.

But my belly was large.

"You saw me," I said, too tired from the night before—hell, from the past five months—to dodge the issue. "When Adrian first brought me home. All baby fat and thick thighs."

"I thought you were beautiful then," Arturo said, lowering his book. He smiled slightly, his silver-capped teeth glinting and his usually dynamic, terrifying copper-lightning eyes soft and kind.

"Well, look at me now," I said glumly, making my way to the bathroom.

"I wish Adrian could visit," Arturo said out of nowhere, making me stop halfway to the door. I looked at him searchingly. Nobody spoke of this. Once I'd realized he couldn't come, I didn't think anybody wanted to think about it—how much we missed him, how much it hurt that we couldn't talk, that there wasn't really a possibility of it, at least not until the babies were born.

"Yeah," I whispered, taking another step.

"Adrian could make you see," Arturo said. "Of your four lovers, he was the one who could make you see."

I turned toward him, realizing that he was looking at me with a terrible wistfulness. Almost the same expression my mother used to use when she wanted me to wear a dress or put on makeup or please, for the love of God, just be nice to a boy so I could go out on a date.

"See what?" I asked. I knew what he would say, because he loved me. Uncle Arturo, my friend, Green's bestie. But I needed to hear it.

"You're beautiful, Corinne Carol-Anne. And not because you're my queen, or my brothers' beloved. Not because you're a warrior or even my friend. You're just beautiful."

I started to laugh and cry at the same time and tried to wipe my face off with the back of my hand. I gave it up and used the inside of the neck of my shirt.

"Love you, Uncle Arturo," I said, my voice clotted with everything. "I'll be out in a sec."

"Of course," he said calmly.

I made it to the toilet before I really started my good cry. Made it through business as usual (thank Goddess) and into the shower and still hadn't finished my emotional catharsis.

Was still leaning, head against the wall, water beating on my back, when the shower door opened. I was almost afraid to see who it was. Who did I least want to face?

I looked down at the tiles—Christmas blue today, they were one of the many things that changed at the whim of the sex magic—and saw long, narrow feet with the faintest hint of fairy pink in the nail beds.

Bracken. He pumped some soap on his hands and lathered my shoulders, down my back, along the curve of my ass.

"I thought it would be Green," I said, voice still thick. Green was the one who usually mended my self-esteem, while Bracken often treated me like it had never been broken.

"Green was on his way." Bracken lathered my neck under my hair, then moved the showerhead so it would hit that spot. "But Arturo told him that you needed me."

Well, I'd known they had powwows over who would deal with me. His hands slid down my spine and around. He palmed the space under my breasts, sliding over my pregnant stomach, the lather making the touch sensuous and slow.

"Mm…." I closed my eyes and leaned into him. "He give a reason?"

"Something about how you wouldn't think it was pity."

I let out a little laugh. "Well, that's the truth." Bracken would never pity me. He wouldn't love anyone weak enough to pity.

Bracken rubbed his lips down the back of my ear, careful not to displace the myriad little gold hoops I wore. I used to have an eyebrow ring and a nose stud too—funny the stuff you let go of when your life changes. But the six zillion earrings, those stayed intact.

"I love your body," he whispered, his thumbs moving in lazy circles around my tender nipples.

"How much did you hear?"

"Hear?" He pinched my nipple and I gasped, arching my back just enough to thrust my breasts against his hands. "I woke up and you were in the shower. Green and Arturo were talking about Iris, and Arturo said it would be best if I joined you."

I let out a semihysterical giggle and turned sideways, the better to lean my head against his chest and give him access to my body. From my throat to my parted thighs, it was all his.

"Why?" he whispered, running his hand down my pregnant stomach, every touch slow and filled with wonder. "What would I have heard?"

"Nothing," I lied. "Pregnancy hormones making me stupid."

"Hmm." He clearly didn't believe me. He laced his hand with mine and placed them both on the apex of the stomach o' doom. "I've been waiting for this to become prominent," he said happily. "Did you know that?"

"Harder to deny when I'm taking out small buildings with my giant abdomen?"

He laughed, like that image was pleasing. "Well, that is convenient, but it's not why I was waiting for it."

The muscles in my face that had tightened and stressed when I'd been crying relaxed all at once, and I melted into his embrace.

"Why?" I whispered.

"Because." I could hear it over the shower—so much joy in that one word. "Just… because. Because it's a transition, this body. It's… it's a haven and a miracle. I know there are… painful, inconvenient things going on in there." He let out a half laugh. "You spend a *lot* of time relieving yourself, for one."

"It's like half my life," I said in honest exasperation. "How do pregnant women with five kids get anything done?"

"They don't." Bracken sounded surprised. He grabbed the shampoo and prodded me, so I turned around and let him soap my hair as we talked. "They let the older kids do things, and they let the house go, and they sit down on the toilet when they need to and nap with the younger kids, because that's what their bodies need to do. Have you not been reading?"

I leaned back to rinse, and when I'd cleared the water from my mouth, I told the truth. "What do you think I'm doing on the pot?"

There were copies of his pet pregnancy books in the magazine rack we'd *recently* placed under the toilet paper.

"Good," he purred, sounding appeased. "But that's not the only painful thing. Your breasts, your thighs, the crampiness in your back, your neck—all of it is exhausting and irritating, and I know it's easy to hate being pregnant because of it."

He started working conditioner through my hair, and I was quiet for a moment while he did that.

"I don't hate being pregnant," I said after that moment, because I thought it was important.

I actually heard him swallow, and he held the showerhead and massaged my scalp while he rinsed. "No?" Oh, Bracken Brine—so stoic. He wanted me to love this as much as he did.

I turned in his arms while he put the showerhead back, then pulled his face down for a kiss when he was done. The children were a solid, comforting weight against my cervix, and the mortifying bout of self-pity had been cleansed from my heart by Bracken's ministrations.

Our tongues tangled briefly, and I wondered if he could taste the salt from my meltdown. I pulled back and smoothed his dark hair—thick and wet, a mass—from his forehead.

"No," I whispered. "I…. It feels amazing sometimes, to have little people inside me."

He smiled then—embarrassed, proud, as earnest as any human father.

"Not parasites or aliens, right? People?"

I looked away in embarrassment. "Elves," I told him. Those little squids on the ultrasound had been very, very elf-shaped.

Oh, that smile—should be bottled as a weapon. Lethal.

"People." He nodded and pushed against my stomach gently. We both felt the little pop against his hand.

I laughed quietly and turned off the water. "So," I asked, hating to let the moment slip away but aware that the world did not grind to a halt because I was enjoying myself for once. "You and Green were keeping watch on the perimeter last night. Did you see anything?"

Bracken grunted. "Yeah. She tried to send werewolves to kill the stragglers coming out of the shield last night. We sent the vampires down to pull a Teague with the poor goobers who were just trying to find their damned clothes. It was pathetic. Anyway, a few of us oversaw it to make sure she didn't succeed. She doesn't have many wolves left. I don't know, maybe she wanted the recovering ones to get bit, and they may have a fight on their hands when they go back home, but we can't do much about that."

Yeah. Well, hopefully they could protect themselves, because we were working hard trying to do the same.

"Think she's got a site lined up for the solstice?" I asked. This had been one of our worries. If she could build up more followers, it didn't matter how many we took out.

"Yes," Bracken said definitively. "She would have stayed and fought if she didn't, because we would have had her against the ropes. But the good news is, wherever she has her next ritual, it's got to be inside, and it's going to be a much smaller number of recruits this time."

"And she's lost… how many? How many do you think we stole from her last night?"

Bracken had grabbed two towels and handed me one. We toweled ourselves down as we spoke, and then he wrapped my bath sheet securely around my burgeoning body.

"Is Arturo still out there?" I asked doubtfully. *Everyone* liked knowing I was laid and happy, but Arturo was too aware of *my* bounds of propriety to get off listening to us when we were okay.

"No," Bracken said smugly. "I just like wrapping you tight. You're a big pregnant burrito."

I cackled, honestly amused, and turned to him for another kiss. Oh, he tasted so good. "You know what I want to do the day after Christmas?"

"Please say have lots of sex and stay in bed and eat leftovers."

Oh, the decadence. "Sure," I said, nodding. "All of the above. Read my mind."

Again that gleeful, little-boy, half-shy, half-exuberant grin. Literally gave me chest palpitations.

"Good. Then let's get our work done so we can look forward to that," he said, all earnestness. "We were talking last night at dinner—which you missed, so eat when someone brings you something—and we figured she couldn't have that many wolves left. So far, she's worked in tiny pockets— the courthouse, the jail—but if she took over the whole thing, there'd be APBs out on elves, and Green and you would be most wanted. It's *deep*, but it's still *covert*. So the numbers we've been seeing and breaking away from her—they've been pretty much the same wolves."

Teague had said so, and when they'd been people, I had recognized the same ones again and again.

"You know, if she's sending werewolves to kill her ex-werewolves, I bet… I'll bet she *can't* re-recruit them. What do you think?"

Bracken nodded grimly. "So she can't recruit massive numbers and she can't get back the ones she's lost. I think… I mean, we can try to stop her for the solstice, and since none of the werewolves can remember where they're from, unless we get a flash of insight from God, I don't see how. I think we're both just going to have to build our numbers and hope the strong one wins after the solstice."

I grunted. "Yeah. She'll be building up to take us over, and we'll be finding a way to stop her. I think that's what it's going to look like."

He brushed my stomach under the bathsheet as we emerged from the bathroom. "Then we'll have to use our time better," he said soberly.

I grinned. "Any time we're having sex and not worrying about *her* makes it better!"

"May it be," he intoned, deadly serious.

I got to the bedroom and let him pull out the stretch-waist jeans and soft cotton bra. I wore a sweater—pretty, cabled, warm, and just a bit tatty. For a moment I was tempted to ask Bracken to dress me up in a power suit just to walk down to the basement, but fuck it. Wasn't going to change who I was. For the first time in forever, I was comfortable in my own stretched skin.

"HOLY GOD," Iris said as we walked in. "You're pregnant."

I smirked. I guessed it had been a month or two, really, of living in the same hill but not talking—not even coming close to each other—in the course of our day.

Quite frankly, once the screaming stopped, we'd had other shit to do.

"You're looking well," I said, meaning it. We'd sent a team to her apartment, and they'd set up an armoire down here in the vampire vault as well as bringing in another bed and giving her some room to decorate. Today she was wearing some nice camel-colored wool slacks and a cream turtleneck. She'd been doing her nails, and the reek of acetone was giving me a headache. I was just as glad she hadn't been allowed to dye her hair again. She didn't have too many grays, but what she had stopped about halfway down her head as though her roots were almost down to her chin now.

As I mentioned her appearance, she tucked her hair behind her ears and smiled shyly. "I appreciate having my stuff here," she said. "And thank you for giving my friend the chance to stay." Marshall Weller, her gay friend for all her public appearances, had actually been *more* than ready to become a werewolf. It was surprising to see someone who needed faith, a change of life, and a chance to be someone new, when he spent so much time of his life giving that faith to somebody else.

I guess even the human good guys need hope, don't they.

"It's our pleasure," I said, grabbing Green's hand just a smidge tighter. "We're sorry you're stuck here with us."

Iris shrugged. Two full moons with us—and on both moons she'd changed with the pack, becoming one of the furry, fanged, charging beasts that roamed Green's hill like his own faerie hunt. She'd been well behaved both times and hadn't tried to break free of the bonds of the hill, or out of her vampire escort's bonds.

"You treat your people very well," she whispered. "It's… as places go, it's not a bad place to end up."

"But…?" Green prodded.

Iris sighed, and a look of vulnerability crossed her face. "It's just… my dad still lives down south. I don't think he has any ties to… to your enemy, and I don't want him involved, but…." She looked away, shaking her head. "Christmas is coming," she whispered. "I would like very much to call him and say Merry Christmas so he doesn't worry."

Green grunted. Well, on the one hand, Iris might call Nimuetia to see if her ally would come rescue her, and possibly give her information. On the other hand, the odds of Nimuetia using the phone connection to break her neck and destroy her former asset were considerable as well.

I was the one who voiced this possibility.

"You know she sent werewolves in thrall to try to kill the werewolves we'd snapped out of it, don't you?"

Iris didn't look surprised, but she did look sad. "I… I'm no use to her anymore," she said at last. "I can't even *remember* her anymore. I just want… I want my dad not to worry. My career… I mean, if I ever go back, everyone else is going to have to be cured in order for me to do *my* job, so… you know. Right now I've got a place to live that's not too bad, and my best friend visits, and…." She let out a humorless laugh. "You even gave me a lover—one who doesn't mind no strings attached."

"That's most elves in general," I said dryly. "If she decides there should be strings, you're stuck with her for life." I paused, because she might not have known this. "You do know that, right? Werewolves can play around, or they can mate for life. If you start feeling too attached, you need to let her know."

Iris grimaced. "Awesome. Best relationship I've ever had, and I might blow it by getting too needy. Nothing like being stuck with someone for life."

I smiled softly, thinking of Nicky. Hell, thinking of all of them, including the two new loves in my stomach. "Nothing wrong with being stuck with people you love," I said.

"How stuck are you?" Iris asked soberly.

I winked, suddenly feeling playful. "Lady, I'm knocked up—I'm as stuck as you get." I sobered then, because I had other things to do.

"Everyone here stays from their own free will. When Nimuetia is gone, you'll be free to stay or free to go. If you stay, Green can find a job for you—or not, if you'd prefer. It's nice if everyone helps."

Iris's eyes grew red and shiny, and she wiped under them with her hand. "That's… that's stupid, you know? Offer someone a chance to stay and leech off you, and—"

"And usually they'll throw themselves in traffic for you," I said, shrugging. "I mean, they've done studies on it and everything. You know that rat in the cage who'd kill himself on cocaine?"

Iris's lip curled cynically. "Yeah, I remember."

"Well, apparently if you give him a better cage, he'd rather drink water."

She blinked. "You're bullshitting me." Her voice hitched on the last syllable of "bullshitting."

"No," I said, feeling sympathetic and wise and, quite frankly, really damned glad I hadn't made her wear the orange jumpsuit.

"I stay away from my computer for a couple of months and I miss all the good fuckin' spam," she sniffled.

I sighed and leaned forward—which was harder than it sounds because, hello, stomach. "Hon," I said quietly, "we'll be happy to let you call your father. And yeah, we're not stupid, we'll monitor the call and check the number before we dial, and even make sure you have a father since he wasn't mentioned in the jacket we've got on you. But if he's there, I promise you can talk to him. But that's not why you called us in here."

Iris nodded and sniffled some more, and I looked at Green helplessly. A tiny sprite appeared above her head and dropped a package of Kleenex in her lap, and she smiled in sort of a pathetic thank-you.

"So what was it?" I asked. Christmas was in a few days, and my shopping was only partially done. And dammit, I had to call my mother.

Iris wrapped her arms around her knees. "I… I was supposed to call you in here and kill you," she said baldly. Before the last word dropped from her mouth, Green and I were completely encircled with a shield and Iris was thrown across the room and plastered against the door. A thin trickle of crimson leaked from the corner of her mouth—I guess I had been a bit rough.

She laughed sadly. "Don't blame you," she rasped. "It wasn't a very nice thing I was supposed to do."

"Then why mention it?" I asked, standing with eyes narrowed and face hard.

"Whenever we went outside, she whispered it—*'Kill them. Just kill them. I'll give you the power. Just kill them.'* And it was… it was *relentless*." Her body shook, and I released the tiniest bit of pressure. "But you gave me Sky, and… the calling my dad."

"That was a test," I said, realizing it.

She nodded. "But… but I really want to talk to him. 'Cause I don't think this is going to end well, and now you're going to kill me, and…."

I released her, and she fell to the ground. I kept the shield around Green and me, sick to the teeth of this madness.

"We'll have Sky get you in contact with your dad," I said, standing wearily. "Iris, the next time you hear her in your brain, tell Sky, or whoever is guarding you. Most of us have some sort of telepathy—we can kick her out of your head, man. Just…." I waved my hands and scrubbed my face with them. "Just don't think you're all alone, doing this shit all alone. That's why we asked Sky if she wanted to *be* with you. Trust me, if she hadn't liked you, she would have said no."

Iris nodded, looking pathetic, and part of me wanted to go hug her. But most of me was standing with my arms crossed over my stomach, feeling very unfriendly.

Green bumped my shoulder. "Luv," he said firmly, and I glowered up at him.

"No." No, no, no, no, no.

"She needs me," he said softly, brushing my hair back from my face. It had fallen out of its ponytail because it had gotten thicker during pregnancy, and I couldn't keep it back with *anything*.

"I need you more," I said, feeling mutinous.

He nodded. "I understand that, beloved. But it's not in us to let our people suffer. I'll call her lover, but right now she needs comfort. Do we want to be people who won't comfort someone in pain?"

"Urgh!" I was feeling very protective today. Gee, I wonder why?

"Don't drop the shield around you personally," he cautioned. "And by all means stay in the room until Sky gets here."

"We have shit to do today," I hedged. He'd promised to take me shopping in Old Town Auburn. It had become tradition.

"We do, and we will. But you're being childish, and I know that's not your intention."

I nodded, completely serious. "Oh, yes. It is *totally* my intention. She was going to *kill* us!"

"She doesn't even have a weapon!" he said. Then both of us got it at the same time.

Together, we looked to Iris sobbing on the floor, and I felt the surge of implanted magic throbbing deep inside her. With a hollered "Get down!" I threw Green on the ground and covered his body with mine, feeling the thump on my stomach when it took my weight first.

For a moment there was nothing. I looked up at Iris just in time to see her glaring at me, eyes filled with tainted blood, and then I ducked my face against Green and reinforced my shields with all of my fury.

When she exploded, her bone shrapnel alone might have killed me, but it was her tainted blood—tainted with the elf queen's mind magic, apparently from a distance—that would have poisoned Green.

Both things dripped off my shield like it was a big Plexiglas bubble. I looked up in time to see her shredded sweater peel off the ceiling and hit the bubble with a "whump," where it slid down thickly.

Oh, Goddess. No shopping today.

The last of the body bomb fell to the floor, and Green said, "You okay, luv?"

"Could you get me the fuck out of here?" I begged plaintively. "I'm gonna puke."

YOU'D THINK the throwing up would get easier with time, but it didn't.

Green held me and then bathed me, and we had elves in hazmat suits clean up the vampire vault. No, it wasn't the first time someone had exploded in there, why do you ask?

"We need to start recruiting new vampires," I said weakly during the refueling process that happened after cleanup (i.e. sitting at the island in the kitchen with my nose in the trough). "Because that room is getting a bad rap."

Green was looking at me in admiration. "You were amazing," he said, sounding besotted. "You were so canny in there, luv. I'm so impressed."

I pushed my ramen noodles around moodily. I'd avoided those things for my entire childhood, but now they were the only things I could eat when my stomach was like this.

"Is it horrible to say I never saw a happy ending for Iris?" I said, feeling glum. "I wanted her to have a happy ending. I wanted her and Sky to be living in our basement forever. I just… you know. I didn't feel that ending in my bones. I mean, I know I say that about everybody—Marcus and Phillip, Renny and Max, Whim and Charlie—but I had hope for them, you know? Even when it looked bleak?"

"But not Iris?" Green asked softly, stroking the arm I wasn't using to feed myself.

"She had no hope," I reasoned. "Probably from before the elf bitch got to her. I think she saw one too many stupid kids imprisoned, lost one too many lovers because of her job, and lost hope. I think her heart was dead by the time Nimuetia got to her. But it does make me think."

"That we should call Connor in and see if he's hearing voices?" Green asked, as though he was sure I was on that page.

I stared at him in horror. "No, that's not what I was thinking, but by all means do that, because now I'm fucking terrified!" Connor, Cami, and Dylan had been attempting the ménage thing. Connor had bonded with both of them—now we had to see if that meant they were going to live happily ever after or kill each other.

Green nodded, thought for a moment, and said, "He'll come visit shortly. Now what were you thinking?"

My heart was still pounding in my throat, but I tried to hold on to my breath so I could grab Green's hand. "I was thinking that… that… I mean, it's not like everyone has to have a baby, you know? Iris might not have ever wanted a baby, and that's fine. But she didn't even have a *cat*. Hell, she didn't even have a *plant*. Her father will need to be told, but he obviously hasn't heard from her in months. It's just that… that you have to find a reason to have hope, and that sometimes, having someone to… to *give* yourself to can be your reason. She thought I was weak because I give my men my power, but it was like she didn't understand how strong you all make me. Loving the three of you isn't… it's not all getting my toes licked while someone feeds me grapes, you know? But it's worth it. It's just… sometimes the more we do for other people, the more hope we have for the world."

Green's smile was a fragile sunrise, growing bolder with every word.

"Have you started knitting for the children, luv?" he asked, and I sort of wriggled in my chair a little.

"I was, you know… gonna finish Christmas stuff first." Suddenly I glared. "Because you and Bracken *aren't* small, you understand that, right?"

That sunrise smile didn't flicker. "I understand," he said, kissing my cheek. "But when you start picking out yarn and colors and patterns, do me a favor. Let me in on that, okay?"

Usually Bracken and Nicky had to listen to my grand design plans, but, well. "Okay," I said, liking this idea very much. "After Christmas. I'll start then."

"What are you doing now?" he asked. "Since I need some time with Connor and all?"

I looked up in time to see Teague trot in, and smiled. "I'm going *running*!" I said, excited. I'd been getting two runs in a week. Between that and walking around campus, I wasn't feeling too out of shape, even though the extra weight was killing me.

Green nodded. "Do that, luv, before you get too big, okay?"

I thought about that terrible pressure when I'd fallen on top of him. I hadn't told Green about that moment of fear, because I *had* read Bracken's pregnancy books. All of them said that a fall like that wasn't necessarily a dramatic thing, and my stomach felt fine. I pushed away my half-eaten bowl of noodles and wiped my mouth. "I'll eat the rest when I get back," I told Green, kissing his cheek.

He stopped me with a real kiss. I fell into it, and for a moment both of us stopped pretending that we hadn't had a close call. Nicky and Bracken were both out shopping as we'd planned to do. While we'd shielded them both so far from the body bomb and the fallout, I knew that as soon as they got back and the gossip made its way through the hill, they'd both be as freaked out as Green and I had been when we'd emerged from the vampire vault floating in a combined shield to avoid the blood and bone shrapnel on the floor.

"Stay safe," he said. I nodded, my throat suddenly tight.

"You too."

"I'm calling Arturo, Lambent, and Whim and Charlie," he said soberly. "And we're going to have a wall of magic between us when we're talking. No," he said when I would have offered to be there too. "If this ends badly, I don't want you anywhere near it."

The unspoken understanding, of course, was that it would only end badly for Connor, and I appreciated the hell out of that.

The truth was he was shielding me from having to stand in the middle of another explosion, and I was letting him.

"Will you do it downstairs?" I asked, and Green nodded.

"Good."

"Still have hope, beloved?" he asked.

I thought about Connor and his consistent, unyielding work to do better for himself, for Cami, and for Dylan.

"I don't think he hears her," I said seriously. "I think…." I grimaced, because this would sound not nice. "I think Iris was always listening for someone to tell her she's special, that she's a hero. I think Connor has always sort of been his own hero. I think he's impervious to voices in his head."

Goddess—with all of the shielding I'd done in the past year, all of the magical safeguards, there was only one way Nimuetia could have gotten anything in here. And she had.

I really hoped Connor was his own barricade, but even if he was, he was still too spooked by women in power for me to be part of that meeting in any way.

I really would have to trust the people around me.

Which was why it was just as well I was going for a run.

TEAGUE AND I talked in shorthand as we went. We'd just hit the part of the trail with steps carved out of a hard place in the red dirt when I felt Green show me what "all clear" looked like.

It looked like Connor, very confused in the vampire vault, telling the elves on the other side of a glowing shield that he'd never heard voices in his life, and could he please go to the bathroom in peace now.

I laughed a little, then turned to tell Teague it was all good….

And twisted my ankle and fell down for the second time that day.

This time, as my stomach hit the ground, I felt a distinct pain in my abdomen.

I sank to the ground, pulling back from Teague's generous hand up and trying not to panic.

"Teague, uhm, I've got a little bit of cramping, and you know, we may want to call—"

Teague was not a big guy, but he had werewolf strength. I hadn't even gotten that far when he reached under me and picked me up, then trotted me back to the house. I clung to his neck and tried not to think of the absolutely worst thing that could happen.

GREEN
Small Celebrations

GREEN COULD feel the thinness in Cory's membranes, the temptation of her cervix to expel everything in her womb—because things were getting a wee bit tight in there, and her stomach had taken two blows in the same day, and she was exhausted in general.

He prescribed bed rest through New Year's Day, with no running until the end of her pregnancy.

"But... but... *exercise*!" Cory complained, horrified. "Green, I've been reading the rule books—they say exercise is a *good* thing!"

He nodded, sitting on the edge of the bed as she sat up under the covers looking frightened and vulnerable and trying hard not to be distraught.

"*After* your body is quite certain you're keeping everybody where they belong to cook for a bit longer, we can sign you up for water aerobics at the college," he allowed. "It will do you good to be in the water between the long car rides, especially as you get bigger, and you'll get your cardio in too. But no more running, beloved."

He regarded her soberly, hoping she'd take that as medical advice and not trying to run her life.

She nodded back, and he let out a sigh of relief. That was the hard part.

Sort of.

The *real* hard part came when Christmas rolled around, and instead of being part of the grand celebration in the front room—with the tree (still living, of course, its roots carefully nursed under a carpet of sod by every dryad on the property) to the ceiling and the swarm of sprites and pixies and lower fey lining up to give small trinkets to the queen—she was stuck in her room, literally propped up on pillows in bed, knitting.

Green had needed to take a turn out in the living room to supervise the revels—not because they got out of control, but because it was only mete their lord should be there as at any holiday feast.

Nicky had gone out to relieve him for an hour, and then Bracken, but when they weren't out in the main room, watching as groups of people wandered in to exchange gifts and eat and celebrate and then wander back out to their own quarters in the hill, they were in here.

Right now Bracken was presiding in the living room. Cory was knitting, with Renny and Katy sitting in the chairs next to the bed working on their own projects. Katy was doing needlework across a precut broadcloth that looked distinctly babyish, and Renny was making a series of tiny rainbow-colored socks.

"How many pairs is that?" Cory said, looking in disbelief at the pile of brightly colored wool booties. "I mean, I know *I* think they each have six legs, but I'm pretty sure they're regular humanoids."

Renny pulled up a lip. She was festively dressed in one of Cory's gold sweaters—from before her pregnancy—and Katy had braided her hair special and lent her some sparkly green earrings. But nothing could change the fact that she was all cat.

"Babies don't have *pairs* of socks," she said disdainfully. "Babies have *socks*. I could make you twelve or thirteen or twenty-one, and it wouldn't change the fact that every time you reached for a pair, all you'd come up with is rainbow socks. So just don't worry about how many I'm making. I'm making socks until the yarn runs out, and then I'm getting another ball and making more."

Katy finished a tiny perfect stitch in a lovely color of mauve. "And even if the ball is another color," she said, nodding as if this was law, "that's still okay. Mommies are too busy to care about perfect pairs. All that matters is that the feets are warm."

Cory grinned at her, and Green, watching from across the room, was charmed as he always was by how charmed *Cory* was by Katy. Feminine and soft, Katy was almost the antithesis of Cory and Renny, but it was that difference that seemed to bring the girls together. He appreciated that. It wasn't as though he needed his beloved to appear traditionally feminine—and he'd never in a million years imagined her doing something as domestic as sitting in a knitting circle—but seeing her talking with her friends, being creative and productive and so uniquely female, that made him feel as though his home was a better place. Of course, if she'd been into building cribs instead of knitting blankets, he would have felt the same way—but then somebody would have had to teach her to knit anyway, because you couldn't build a crib when you needed to stay flat on your bottom.

In fact, he remembered, bemused by his train of thought, she had learned to knit in the first place because she'd been laid up and recovering from another crisis. Life had a funny way of turning circles, didn't it?

He fingered the fine work of his own sweater, cream colored with tiny cables. She'd given herself a break, and it wasn't as elaborate as some of the others she'd done, but he liked the simplicity.

He could feel the magic of her love for him in the fibers.

She was doing that, right now, for their children.

Her first day on bed rest, Cory had asked for her laptop and spent the day poring over city plans and reports, trying to find out where the solstice rite would take place.

Well, she had company. Pretty much every elf, werecreature, and vampire was doing the same thing on their own time, and had been since the equinox.

But the next morning they'd had to concede that solstice was over. Whatever recruiting the elf queen had been able to do, she'd done. They gathered their people to the hill for safety, but also for celebration, because yes, the war was still on, but so many of them had lived through so much.

There was truly much to celebrate.

That didn't mean all work stopped, though. Green had moved his computer desk to the group bedroom—they all slept with her now every night—for the holidays, partly to get it out of the main room for the Christmas revels and partly to keep her company. He hated working during the holidays, hated it, but the bid to buy the hill that had started in August had gotten serious. The American government was sticking its nose into Green's property rights, and he was at least a little worried.

He was also too obsessed with their immediate physical enemy to pay as much attention as he should. Of course, now that the solstice was over, he thought he'd accidentally located the property where the ritual had taken place. Finding it had been pure serendipity—he'd been researching other places where the government was making claims where it shouldn't, and this property had met all of their criteria. As frustrating as it was to be Johnny-come-lately, although they couldn't go back in time and stop Nimuetia's last recruitment, they *could* violate the building and break any power circles she'd set up there. She might still have her werewolves, but the hill folk could interfere with her ability to draw power from them, and definitely force her to go look somewhere else for her spring ritual.

And *that* could be when they'd get her.

But Green was putting that aside for the moment. Part of his beloved's celebration was the actual planning for the baby blankets, and she had spent the day before ordering Nicky and Bracken to drag her yarn out from under the bed, spread it out, then put it back in the boxes and put it back under the bed, then drag it back out, then put it back in, and bring her this pattern book here, and this one there, and then....

Grace had walked in with two complementary colorways of yarn and a simple basket weave pattern that *Green* could probably do in his sleep, and told her briskly to just fucking start already.

"You'll never find the perfect pattern," she'd said with a wistful smile. "There will always be a pattern you'll wish you'd had time for, another one that would have been more practical. I've brought you wool that is beautiful and can be washed. I've brought you a pattern you can knock out in about a week, if you're stuck here. So by the time you go back to school, you'll have two blankets. You may make six more by the time you're done, and a layette for each kid. But the fact is, all you're *really* going to need is two blankets, some diapers, and a package of onesies for each kid. Then you can go back to school and say you're ready."

With that, Grace had turned around and walked out, leaving them all bemused—and plenty ready to give up Cory's quest for the perfect blanket.

Now Green eyed Cory, fingers busy with her knitting while she listened to Renny and Katy gossip about their particular husbands, and thought about Grace's timeline for blankets and children. He wondered if she'd realized that she would be out of the battle for the spring equinox.

He was pretty sure she hadn't.

When she figured it out, keeping her in bed would be both their primary worry and the last thing on their minds.

He was startled from his reverie by a knock at the door. Then Bracken peeked in, looking pained.

"Beloved," he all but whined, "your mother's here."

The charming little domestic vibe that had permeated the room not five seconds before melted away like sugar in the rain.

"Yeah, fine," Cory sighed. Although everybody in the room heard her reluctance, Green was pretty sure that was because they all had superlative hearing.

Her mother didn't seem abashed in the least.

"Cory?" she asked, coming into the room with her father in tow. "We didn't realize you'd be laid up for Christmas."

Cory gave a shiny patent-leather smile that was obviously a lot of work.

"Yup. Just a little spotting. Green says I need to rest and give the young a chance to get resettled, and I can be up and about by the time school starts in January."

She looked at Green for reassurance, and he nodded. Yes—she wanted those children to live with all her soul. For this, she would be compliant and eager to please. Anything, anything, just let their children be all right.

It was both gratifying and terrifying at once.

When she was in denial about there even *being* children, then she could be strong. But when she admitted her weakness? He wondered if she could find her strength without her bravado.

He wondered if she would have the strength to stand down when they needed her to stay on the hill.

But she wasn't thinking of that now. She was thinking of how to keep her parents from worrying, because she didn't want them to acknowledge anything had changed.

Her mother, at the very least, wasn't willing to let that happen.

She looked at Cory and then at Green, and by the way she squinted, widened her eyes, and squinted again, he could tell she was making a conscious effort to see him as he really was and not through the glamour that her memory had left behind. Then she touched her husband's shoulder, and he looked up and smiled.

"Yeah, Ellen, I know. I thought you saw the same thing."

Cory smirked. "Way to go, Dad," she said, holding her fist up. Her father didn't leave her hanging, bumping knuckles with her and flaming out his fingers.

"So the two little ones, they're going to look like them?" he said a little wistfully.

"Well, they *are* prettier than I am," she quipped, and Green's heart stopped.

Cory's father had always struck Green as a little absent. Well-meaning, but not necessarily tuned in to his daughter.

But that one bit of self-deprecation, meant to charm, seemed to devastate the little weathered man. He grimaced and wiped under his eyes.

"I always thought you were beautiful," he said in earnestness. "I was hoping they'd look like you."

She bit her lip and looked shyly at him. "Don't worry, Daddy. I'm sure there will be freckles somewhere."

He grinned. "That there is a load off my mind. I like freckled little kids."

Cory laughed self-consciously, but Green could tell she was pleased. Her parents sat down on the bed to chat for a bit, while Katy and Renny set their projects down and excused themselves to go round up some food.

"Just not too much sugar," Cory cautioned.

Renny shook her head. "Martyr," she accused.

"I'm not doing anything to burn it off!"

Renny made an inhuman sound and slid out the door, all fur and liquid in spite of the girl shape.

"Mommy, you're making babies in your stomach," Katy admonished. "That gets Christmas cookies on Christmas Day."

Cory looked around her mom, making eye contact with Green. "Can I?"

"You're eating plenty of protein and greens," he said mildly. "I don't see why not."

She was actually a much stricter monitor of her diet than anybody else—it would be good to see her enjoy something.

Bracken had remained in the doorway, auditing the conversation cautiously, and Green didn't blame him. The last time he'd been there, it had gone terribly, terribly wrong.

"I'll make sure they get you some meat," he said after an uncertain moment. And then, reluctantly, "Mr. and Mrs. Kirkpatrick, can I get you anything to eat, or will you be dining downstairs in the formal room this afternoon?"

"Well done, Bracken. Your mother would be proud."

"Shut up."

Green kept his laughter to himself.

"Oh, we'd love it if we could eat in the downstairs room," Cory's mom said anxiously. "Is that okay, sweetheart? I just—"

"She dressed up," Tom Kirkpatrick said dryly. "She likes the people downstairs, even if she just figured out that they're different people than she originally thought, and she dressed up."

She had indeed. Was, in fact, wearing a cream-colored sweater and Christmas earrings, and even some Christmas sparkle in her hair.

Cory grinned at them—relieved, yes, but also appearing to be genuinely happy that they would find a place.

"By all means, then, go downstairs and play. There should be live music and spontaneous dancing, just like last year."

Her mother's smile was delectably shy. "I mostly just want to listen," she said. Green imagined she did. The music often started out as traditionally Celtic, because that was where many of his people originated, but given how many other influences they were exposed to now, what came out was lively and modern, with just enough of the beat for Green to know from whence it sprang.

They talked about music for a moment, and Cory's mom asked if Cory was going to sing to the babies. Cory blushed. "Well, I'm pretty sure we'll all sing to them," she said, catching Green's eye for the umpteenth time. He might have been sitting across the room, but he was definitely a part of the conversation.

"Of course, beloved," he said softly, and she smiled, rubbing her hand over her belly protectively.

Katy and Renny came back with two plates piled high—one with healthy choices and one with enough sugar to rocket her into diabetes if she chose to eat it all. Her parents stood up to take their leave, but before they went, her mother dropped one last troubling bit of information in her lap.

"Cory, I know you're not going back to him, but if you could give Dr. Nieman a call and tell him you're under care...." Ellen Kirkpatrick shook her head. "I don't understand why he's so obsessed. Janine doesn't remember that you folks even came in, but Dr. Nieman's been calling me, sometimes two or three times a day. It's really unprofessional, but I can't seem to get rid of him."

Cory nodded. "Mom, do you have a card or something? Give it to Green and he'll take care of it."

Her dad looked at Green and grinned, showing a missing incisor but a rather puckish sense of humor that Green hadn't seen until this moment.

"Bet you've got some good moves up your sleeve, don't you, sir?"

Green grinned back, delighted. "Indeed I do. And if I can't get him to go away, the vampires will most certainly be able to."

Cory's father made a little O with his lean lips. "Vampires. Think they'd be up now?"

Green shrugged. "I don't see why not. You've met a few of them, actually—Grace, Marcus, Phillip—"

Both Ellen and Tom gasped, and Cory erupted into a happy cackle.

"Go on, both of you. Play guess the superpower—best Christmas game ever!"

Cory's mom paused in the act of bending down to kiss Cory's cheek. "Do *you* ever have to play it?" she asked, as though seeing something important.

Cory shook her head. "No, Mom. From the minute I first saw Arturo, I pretty much saw everyone."

"Oh," Ellen said softly. "You really *are* special, then."

Then with a kiss from each, they were gone, and Cory was left to plow through the massive quantities of food Renny and Katy had brought.

After that she was visited quietly by one or two people at a time— and Bracken was very efficient at limiting the queue to the people she was most comfortable with. She was in the middle of eating a sugar cookie and talking to Teague about what to do with the shields, because the sleep spell was still present and they weren't sure it was still a great idea, when suddenly she set the sugar cookie down and fell asleep.

Just that quickly, exhausted by the visitors and what was happening inside her own body.

Teague eyed her with laconic surprise, then picked up the sugar cookie and finished it off. "You about done with that row, Katy, darlin'?" he asked softly.

Katy nodded and finished what she was doing, then carefully tucked the needle in her work and tucked the work in a quilted bag at Cory's feet. Renny muttered to herself, obviously in the throes of turning a sock heel, and Teague waited for a hushed moment until she'd packed her bag as well.

He stood up and took Katy's hand, placing a gentle kiss on her forehead. "You ready to go save Jacky? He's downstairs in the were common room having a drinking contest with Max."

"What are they drinking for?" Katy asked, surprised. "No one gets drunk here! How do you know anybody wins?"

"They throw up," Renny said in disgust. "Max is, like, king of this game."

Katy's eyes got big. "I say we don't go," she said, pursing her lips and shaking her head. "I say, if Jacky is stupid enough to do that, he deserves to come home and find us in bed."

Then Teague's eyes got big, and he started to laugh—obviously pleased and appalled at the same time. Renny shushed him, and together they moved quietly out of the room. Teague stopped, letting the women go first, then turned to Green.

"She needed this—the quiet Christmas. Thanks for letting me visit."

Green smiled benevolently. Teague was continually a surprise—rough-hewn, angry, hurt, and Galahad to the gentle heart of him.

"You're on her short list, mate. Even Bracken let you in!"

"That boy didn't let his own mother in," Katy said, sounding both admiring and appalled.

"That woman is *busy*," Teague grumbled, and Green took "busy" to mean *too* busy for the recovering queen of the realm.

With that, Teague turned to close the door, but Green stopped him.

"Teague, I'll be out in a moment. Could you send Nicky or Bracken in? I think there's something that needs to be dealt with quite soon."

Teague shrugged. "Sure, boss. Anything else?"

Oh, this was unfortunate. "Yes—if you could perhaps postpone your liaison with your wife, Teague, I think you need to be in on this."

Teague rolled his eyes. "She wasn't serious, you know. She's going to be there with a cold cloth and glass of water, making sure he's aw bedda, wight?"

Green laughed. "Right. Thank you. I'll be out in a moment."

He closed his laptop, having finished the few business matters necessary to have a pleasant holiday, and sat down on the bed, shifting Cory from her back to her side and tucking the pillow under her head.

He was pulling the blanket up to her chin when she shifted around, making herself more comfy. "Mmm...." She grabbed his hand as he fussed. "Sorry. Didn't mean to crash on everybody."

"No worries, beloved. It's been a busy day."

"Remember last year?"

He remembered, all right. "You made yourself sick. You were exhausted, and you ran out barefoot in the frost to give Teague and Jack and Katy their house."

"I was thinking about when we made love the night before that," she said, but her voice was still murky with sleep.

"Yes, well, I was thinking I'm just as glad you're resting today."

She breathed deeply, and for a moment he thought she was back under. Then—"You heard. You're worried."

Yes. Yes, indeed. "I did, and I am. You're good at the mind-wipe, luv. It was your first talent. I'm not sure if it's because you were in a hurry, or if he just has such a connection to the babies—"

"He was a prick," she mumbled. "No imagination, all scientific curiosity...."

He laughed silently. "Shh. We'll talk about him later. Sleep now." He probed gently with his mind and found she was completely out, no help from him necessary. He'd just stood up when Bracken came in, looking ready for rest and carrying a full plate of honey tarts—his personal favorite, probably made by his mother.

"You look done in," Green said gently. Bracken smiled, handing him a tart.

Green nibbled gratefully, using the opportunity to move closer. Ah, Bracken always smelled so good. Between Green, Brack, and Nicky, they were a sunny meadow, a bedrock mountain, a bird surfing the wind. No wonder Cory was so comfortable between the lot of them—together they were the day and the wild, the earth and the ether of the hills in which they lived.

Bracken chuckled in a sleepy, sated way and moved a little closer, rubbing his nose down Green's jaw line and blowing playfully in his ear.

"I need peace," he whispered. "My lovers in my bed."

Ah... yes. Cory had been abed for five days, and they'd been so busy. Sex was necessary to all of them, even if Cory simply lay and watched and stroked their brows.

"Yes, Bracken Brine," Green whispered, tilting his head back and appreciating Bracken's lips along the side of his throat. "I need."

"Good," Bracken took Green's chin between his long fingers and turned Green toward him for a potent, feeding kiss. Green groaned softly, enjoying the taste of honey tarts and Bracken's strength. Bracken pulled back and smiled, looking evil as only he could manage when talking about sex. "How long has it been since someone took care of you, leader?" he asked softly.

Ah, yes. Bracken wasn't talking about penetrating or being penetrated—no, elves thought beyond that when they thought of sex. He was talking about *taking care* of Green. Being the dominant one, being in charge of Green's pleasure from beginning to end.

Usually, Bracken was the one pleasured. He was the youngest sidhe, the darling of the hill—it was how he was made.

Apparently he'd grown up, these years without Adrian—or these years with Cory.

"Tonight?" Green suggested, feeling the low hum of anticipation fill him as it hadn't in nearly a week. Oh, he loved his calling, loved how his body could make others feel, loved that he healed with a touch.

But sometimes, as a vessel, he needed to be filled.

"Yes, leader," Bracken taunted. "Tonight. Now go do big important things, and leave us to our peace."

Green slid his hand down the side of Bracken's fine, handsome sidhe face. "Of course, *due'alle* of my *ou'e'eir*."

"Is there a word for us?" Bracken asked, those unique, shadowed eyes crinkling at the corners.

"No," Green said, smiling back. He reached behind Bracken's head and held him in place as he plundered Brack's mouth mercilessly. That low thrum of anticipation filled him, pitched, until Bracken groaned and pulled away.

"There's about to be a word for me fucking you senseless," he gasped crossly. "Now go do your thing, leader. She needs her sleep."

Green chuckled and adjusted his slacks. Then, since one of Brack's hands was still carrying the plate full of tarts, he reached down and adjusted Brack's equipment in his jeans.

Bracken growled irritably until he was done. Green gave Brack's impressive package a nice little pat before he sauntered out.

"Enjoy your *rest*!" Green taunted. Then he left, still chuckling.

Oh, that was a Christmas present if there ever was one. There could be no bad spirits when you were flirting with a lover like Bracken. Or like Cory or Nicky, for that matter.

And speaking of Nicky….

"Are we gonna?" he asked, practically skipping up to Green before the door was closed. "I mean, Brack and I were talking about it, and you know, she loves to watch, and…."

Green turned a look of pure disbelief on the little shape-shifter, charmed as he always was by Nicky's excitement regarding anything sexual.

"Dear Penthouse Forum…," Green intoned, invoking the name of the human porn icon. Porn always seemed a little superfluous to the elves—sexual experience, whether voyeuristic or actual, was for the having. But Nicky, being born and raised in the human world, had acquired most of his sexual knowledge from porn.

Teasing him about that never lost its joy.

Nicky nodded. "Well, duh! C'mon, Green, it's been a *week*!"

Green laughed, wrapping an arm around his shoulders and kissing his temple. "Yes, it has, my lovely boy, and to go another night would be a shame. Now come on, we need to plan an op *without* Cory before we retire to our bed of debauchery and lust."

Nicky stopped so short that Green's arm around his shoulder almost knocked him over. "Uhm…."

Green cast him some playful censure under lowered brows. "Oh, come on, Dominic—you're one of the bravest warriors in the hill. Don't tell me you're afraid of a pregnant woman taking a nap."

Nicky narrowed his eyes and shook his head, causing his rust-colored hair to ruffle around his face like feathers. "You look nice and all, Green, but you are an evil, evil man."

Green chuckled, low and dirty, then pulled Nicky into his arms and made a positively filthy suggestion about what "evil" might possibly entail.

Nicky moaned and melted against him. "Yeah," he rasped. "That. That right there might make it worth my while."

Green laughed throatily and pulled Nicky down the corridor. He had not yet spoken at his own feast, and it was time to put some matters to rest.

"NICE SPEECH," Arturo said as Green sat down—finally—to his own food. "Did you rehearse that?"

Green arched an eyebrow. "Did it sound rehearsed?" he asked sweetly.

"It sounded half-assed. But that's fine. They really just wanted to hear that their lady will be well."

Green didn't try to hide the trouble in his smile. He hadn't confessed half his worries, but he didn't need to. Arturo had the same worries.

"This semester is going to be very hard on her," he said quietly. "I think we need to start asking our sidhe women how early our children can be delivered and still maintain their health."

Arturo nodded soberly. "Green, we will need to keep her safe. Her power is fine—she might have taken Nimuetia out if she'd been ready for the werewolves—but her physical body...."

Grace sat down on Arturo's other side. "It's rough on her," she acknowledged. "But whatever you and the boys have planned tonight might give her more strength, you know. Sex and sunshine, Green—it's what she runs on. We've taken away the sex, and we're in the middle of winter."

Green inclined his head, not bothering to blush or protest about having his personal life so rudely butted into. Grace had been butting into his personal life pretty much since Cory's arrival on the hill.

"Are her parents still here?" Green asked, looking around.

"They're asleep in one of the guest rooms," Arturo answered quietly. "Do you want us to have someone drive them home?"

Green shook his head. "No, but if you could perhaps spell them asleep tonight, that might make everybody a tad bit more comfortable, yeah?"

"Absolutely."

At that moment Green caught Teague's eyes from across the room and gave a nod with his chin. Max too, with Renny at his heels. And then, simply because he'd been so valuable in July for a similar mission, Professor Hallow.

"You planning anything else?" Arturo asked, truly surprised. Green ignored him and turned to Grace.

"Grace, lovey, what can you tell me about human doctors? The ones who deliver children?"

Grace snorted. "Ob-gyns? Well, some of them are okay, I guess. Most of the real work is done by the nurses." She seemed to ponder for a moment. "Except catching. Apparently there's extra paperwork if the nurses catch, so that's pretty much all the doctors do. The nurses deal with the patient, know what's happening, make the recommendations, understand when to push. And the doctor catches."

Green, Hallow, and Arturo looked at each other in horror, then looked out at the people who had once been human.

"It's a wonder you survived," Green said, shell-shocked. "It's a bloody miracle. I'm giving extra thanks to the God, Goddess, and other tonight that you all made it through your first breath." He turned to Grace again. "That's bloody barbaric. I can't believe this man even touched her!"

Grace looked surprised. "What man?"

Well, they had been pretty preoccupied. Apparently this story hadn't made it through the general sense of warfare permeating the hill.

"Oh my God," Renny burst out. "Did *you* miss out on that one. It was like… I mean, parental manipulation at its most extreme. Jesus, no wonder Cory was so excited about escaping home!"

Green stared at her. "You were just lovely to that woman to her face!"

Renny nodded. "It's the social lie, Green. It's what keeps us from killing each other. I know you've heard of it. Anyway, Grace, there was this whole ambush thing at the doctors' back in October, are you sure you didn't…."

Renny launched into the story, backed up by Nicky and, after a moment, by Katy, who wandered up to see what the confab was about. (Apparently Jack really *was* throwing up, which considering his metabolism was impressive.)

By the time they were done, Grace had gone from outrage to horror, and finally to thoughtful regard.

"Children," she said, cutting them all off in the middle of their excited chatter, "I think this is important. Green, why are we talking about this now?"

Green looked at all of them. "Because apparently this doctor has *not* forgotten about us—about *Cory*—as we'd hoped. And I think it's dangerous for her to go back there."

"Indeed," Arturo agreed, appalled. "Did they manage to clear all the records?"

"Yes," Nicky said, "but only at the one computer terminal. We found out that a copy of the records was sent to the terminal in the exam room." He grimaced, obviously unhappy with the mistake. "You've got to understand— Mrs. Kirkpatrick was freaking out a little, and Cory was trying with the brain-wipe, and there was some…."

"Confusion," Green allowed. "Yes, I do understand. Well, there's no confusion about him continuing to ask about her." He looked at all of them. "I seem to remember we had a human problem like this in the summer."

Hallow, Max, Renny, and Arturo all regarded him evenly.

"I think Lambent was here for that as well," Renny said quietly.

Green looked up to the far table, where Lambent was busy teaching Kyle a drinking song. He had two puncture wounds in his neck that were dripping just a tad, probably because he'd let Kyle feed until Lambent was light-headed from blood loss and Kyle was light-headed from elf blood, and neither had remembered to be neat.

Lambent was drinking mead fermented with wildflowers, available in limited quantity. It was one of the few things that could get an elf drunk. While Green looked up, Lambent smiled sloppily and raised his mug.

Green inclined his head and smiled sadly, urging the elf to grieve in the way that suited him best.

"I think we can leave Lambent out of this one," he said, and the others nodded in agreement.

"Right, then. We need to make sure the records are wiped, and we need to make sure this doctor can't remember Cory's name, or our appearance."

"Green?" Max said cautiously.

"Yes?"

"I think we should wear masks, whoever does this. If magic hasn't wiped his mind yet, it might not. We might need to come back with some sodium pentothal and a rubber mallet. You'll need someone who knows what cops look for at a crime scene. And I think we should do this when the nurses aren't there, because we don't want them in any danger of seeing. And perhaps we should wipe his mind at home—a two-front operation, where someone breaks into the clinic at night and—"

Green held up his hand. "Arturo, would you have any objections to taking orders from Max in this matter?"

"None at all," Arturo said, inclining his head.

"Good. Then we're going to put Max and Teague in charge here. You have any vampire you need at your disposal—"

"I'll do it," Grace said. "Or I'll grab Marcus and Phillip. We're good."

"Thanks, lovey." Green nodded. "Then I'm going to leave the logistics to you, Max. Pick your team and run it by Arturo and me tomorrow night."

"Can we have Arturo and Hallow?" Max asked before Green could add anything else.

Green looked at Hallow. "Are you up for another round of this?" His old friend—his *oldest* friend, truth be known—had related the grim details of his last attempt to excise the memory of elves from a stubborn human. Hallow had done… unforgivable things to that cockroach of a man, and his heart had been troubled.

Hallow looked at Max, whom he had worked with during that venture too. He blinked his wide-set azure eyes and shook out his silver-spangled hair, not preening exactly, but more… settling things inside himself. Hallow was thoughtful that way.

"Of course," he said soberly. "Only…." He grimaced. "I would rather not kill again."

"No worries," Max said, sounding completely at ease with the thought. "That's why we're bringing Arturo. He's got no problems with that at all."

Green stared at him. "And neither do you?" he asked to make sure.

Max didn't even think about it. "Since August, Green. Those fuckers have been attacking *my home* since August. And you guys are great—it's all 'Protect the were-animals! Bad blood! Bad blood! Alert alert alert!'" The once *very* human Officer Max pulled back his upper lip and exposed growing incisors. "I have a body that's made to protect people, and I haven't been able to protect my queen. Let me protect my queen!"

Renny snarled in agreement, her own incisors permanently pointy.

Teague and Katy followed suit, and Grace exposed her own feeding face to hiss intimidatingly. (Green could smell Arturo's arousal from across the table. She was formidable, his vampire warrior.)

Green nodded. "So may it be," he said simply.

He let them chatter for a few moments as they got into the planning, but at the first lull in the conversation, he spoke.

"It's Christmas, children," he said gently. His voice carried, though—it quieted all of them, including Arturo and Hallow, who were very much older than he was. "It's Christmas, and for tonight I think we should revel. Teague, Katy, by all means see if Jack feels better. Everyone else, I wish you a warm bed and a full heart this night. I wish you peace and joy and kindness. Tomorrow we can fight to protect our own, but tonight let us enjoy what we have."

He stood then, full of noise and party chatter, full of the excitement. He had not realized how much he appreciated the excuse that afternoon to simply sit in a quiet room and watch women execute a time-honored craft as well as share the common moment of being young women of a certain time.

It had been peaceful. He needed more peace.

He bowed slightly and looked across the table to where Nicky had just stopped an animated discussion with Teague as to whether or not it would be simpler just to go in through the skylight of the clinic building. Nicky caught his eye, grinned, and stood. As they left, Nicky slightly behind Green, they both heard Arturo say—for their ears alone—"Now *that* was a speech!"

NICKY TORTURED him on the way up the hall. Tantalizing touches down the line of his back, in his hair, along his backside. As they neared the top of the stairs, Green whirled, lifting the smaller man by the waist and pinning him against the wall.

"Growing impatient, darling Nicky?" he purred, and Nicky opened his mouth in a smile.

Green kissed him hard, plundering and taking, tasting sugar and surprising steel and an incredible joy.

Cory had been in awe of Nicky's sacrifice—giving up his boyfriend for his family unit. Green was grateful, but unsurprised. Green, Bracken, Cory, they could be enough for their darling Nicky, and now was the time to prove it.

Nicky groaned, lifting his legs to lock around Green's hips and grinding his erection against Green's stomach.

"I'm never patient," he whispered against Green's tongue. "You took me to your bed, and I can only want more and more and more…."

Green laughed, feeling wicked and… *young*. Goddess, Adrian had been gone from the grove for months, and he'd felt that loss keenly. He and Adrian had been *young* in this hill, and they'd fucked like gods, like the touch of skin and the joining of bodies had been invented for them. War, worry, impending parenthood—it had pulled the youth from their bones, from him and the lovers in his bed.

He wanted to claim it back.

"Want more? Anything you want more of, Nicky?"

"Nungh…." Nicky arched his body into Green's, but Green knew what he loved the most. Oh, how he loved to be possessed, taken by a man, pounded hard and used well. Green and Nicky had used each other many times thusly, and it had never gotten old. Sidhe were famous for using and abandoning lovers, and Green had enjoyed his share of bodies who were, quite simply, not Cory, not Adrian, not Bracken or even Mist.

But Nicky was not one of those. He was a lover to savor, to enjoy, to be grateful for, and Green showed his gratitude in this darkened hallway by shoving his hands under the boy's jeans and reaching back to spread his bottom, using his longer arms and fingers to tease Nicky's crease suggestively and taunt him with what was to come.

Nicky's love bite on his neck stung deliciously, and Green probed harder, grinding against Nicky, occasionally even putting pressure on his own prick as they rubbed.

"I want it all," Nicky begged. "Oh Goddess, Green, fucking use me…."

"Is that what you want?" he whispered. "A quick one in the hall? Or do you want to be truly used, boyo, on hands and knees—me reaming your arse, Bracken rammed down your throat, groaning between us while our queen watches and pleasures herself?"

"I heard that!" Bracken demanded in his head. *"Get a move on!"*

Green chuckled, egged on by his own filthy words, by his lover's hands shoved between his sweater and skin, by a need they'd all denied too long.

"What?" Nicky begged. "What's funny?"

Green opened his mouth above the boy's jugular and sucked hard. He released the sweet flesh with a pop and licked a line up Nicky's ear. "Bracken is listening in on our thoughts," he taunted. "He's watching us… *wanting* us…."

Nicky moaned, bucking against him. "Green, I'm gonna cream my fuckin'…."

Green *blurred*—ran so fast even other sidhe couldn't see him, but could only feel the wind of his passing. Six stairsteps, three around the corner, and Bracken was holding the door.

Green slowed down enough to move to the front of the bed, Nicky still held to his chest. "Did our beloved make your sweater?" he asked, pretty sure it was so, because the wool was fine, rust-colored cashmere with bronze highlights and fit tight against the young man's chest.

"Yes," Nicky hissed. He held his hands above his head, tightening his stomach muscles while Green supported his lower back with one hand and helped him strip off the sweater with the other. Bracken took the sweater from his hands and then, Green noticed, crouched by a now awake Cory, whispering in her ear, murmuring against her temple, probably arousing her with his words as Green had aroused Nicky.

"And the jeans?" he asked, licking a line down Nicky's hairless chest, teasing a cinnamon-colored nipple with his tongue. "Do you—"

"Fuck the jeans!" Nicky begged, so Green threw him on the bed and ripped the jeans off his hips.

They fell to the floor in two pieces—no underwear to speak of, no shoes or socks either. Green bent his head and swallowed Nicky's erect, dripping cock to the back of his throat.

"*Yes!*" Nicky arched off the bed, grabbing Green's hair in both fists and thrusting his hips hard as Green sucked him down.

Green had plans. He'd made promises to Nicky—to use him, to fuck him fast and brutally. He let some saliva slide down Nicky's cock and spread it around his opening. Nicky loved to be penetrated, and even as he was gibbering for Green to suck harder, he reached down and spread his bottom, readying himself.

Green teased Nicky's rim as he sucked, thrusting one long finger in, then two, and he was relaxing into the rhythm, getting ready to ask Bracken to do the honors at Nicky's mouth, when Bracken moved without Green's plan.

He moved behind Green.

"Mmff…!"

"Keep doing what you're doing," Bracken whispered. He tugged on Green's hips a little so Green was bent inelegantly at the waist as he pleasured Nicky. He opened his mouth to explain his plan—he was the leader, yes, and between Green and Cory, they *always* had the plan—just as Bracken stripped Green's slacks off, leaving him bare from the waist down.

In sheer surprise, Green pulled harder at what was in his mouth.

Nicky cried out, spurting just a trace into the back of his throat.

And soft hands, smaller than a man's, worked insistently at his sweater until he was forced to wriggle out of it. It hadn't even been whisked away before Nicky grabbed his hair and jutted his manhood up again, begging without words. Green had just enough time to go back to work, fingers penetrating, mouth and tongue moving in concert, when….

Bracken's tongue, bold and obscene, began to pleasure his backside without mercy.

Oh! Oh, dear Goddess!

Green couldn't remember the last time he'd been taken like this— surprised, surrounded by….

"*Ammmmfffff….*"

The vibrations in his throat made Nicky scream again, and Green looked up to see the boy pinching his own nipples hard as Green used him. His head was thrown back and his eyes glazed, which was good, great, wonderful, because Green was in no position... because Cory was in exact position... because.... While Bracken was lubricating his entrance, probing, stretching, filling him with dark pleasure and utter abandon, their beloved was crouched at his knees, eyes luminous with joy as she pleasured her husband's prick with her mouth.

Briefly releasing Nicky to his own fist, Green took a moment to wink at her as she sat there, her giant T-shirt still shrouding her growing body and her mouth stretched wide with only the hint of a smile at the corners of her lips.

Oh, she did love taking her lovers into her mouth. She loved to taste them, to give them sweet pleasure and great release.

She craved them filling her mouth and her throat. She'd told him so. As she lowered her head and swallowed, a wave of black crashed behind Green's eyes. He concentrated on his fingers in Nicky's backside and his mouth on Nicky's prick for a moment, pulling himself back from the brink of climax, enjoying being taken just a moment... just an instant... just an....

He shuddered, losing his mind, his balance, his place in things completely. Bracken had positioned his mighty behemoth of a cock at Green's entrance and begun to push slowly, inexorably in. Green's palms grew damp, a sheen of sweat tracking down his back, and only Nicky, holding him in place, using Green's mouth as Green had planned to use Nicky's arse, kept him from just lying face down on the bed and groaning in preclimax repletion, the sound rising like an alarm or a siren or the tide.

Nicky cried out, filling Green's mouth with the sour-bitter taste of shape-shifter's seed. Green kept milking him, kept thrusting his fingers inside until Nicky gave one last, almost pitiful whimper of orgasm and rolled to his side with his knees to his chest, clearly in recovery.

Green had nothing left to ground him, keep him sane, and he abandoned himself, head buried against the comforter that still smelled of Nicky's sex and musk. That dreaded, out of control sound emitted from his mouth so often that he lost himself in the sound, feeling his pleasure and climax surging and receding, building and pulling back and building, and again, like his helpless cries into the mattress.

Bracken picked up the pace, slamming harder, using Green roughly, taking all the control that had so wearied Green and using it to give Green all of the pleasure, all of the body joy he could handle.

Nicky's hands, sticky with sweat, stroked his hair from his face, and Nicky's breath puffed gently against his ear.

"We've got you," he whispered. "Look at him, Green. You should see him pounding you, possessing you. She's sucking you, and it's glorious. Let it go. Let it all go. Climax, Green—she'll drink you down, and he'll fill you up. We're here, beloved. We're yours. We'll take it all. All of it… ours…."

Oh! That was no fair! Green closed his eyes against the prickle of tears and the kind reassurance from a lover who was only to have been casual, only an inconvenience, until he found his place.

His place was with them.

Green pushed up on his hands, wanting to open his mouth and tell Nicky that he was beloved too, but Nicky took his mouth in a kiss, the same kiss he'd given Cory during their first combined tumble into joy.

The kiss that set them both free to love the people in their bed in any way their hearts saw fit.

Green's cry of orgasm was lost into that kiss, but it didn't matter. The ocean wind of climax washed over him, cleansing his body of worry, his mind of fear, and his heart of shadows. Nicky swallowed Green's shriek of completion as Cory swallowed his spend. Green shuddered, convulsing in their embrace, taken over by their ministrations as he hadn't been in a hundred years, since the lover three of them missed so keenly, since Adrian.

He couldn't bring that name here, not tonight.

Cory's mouth moved gently on him, cleaning him off, and then Bracken pulled out, leaving the mark of his spend inside Green's body. Green would have fallen then, languorous, debauched, into the great bed, but Cory crawled out from between his legs and Bracken lifted him into his arms. Nicky pulled the covers back so Green could fall into it, naked, for once not on the outside edge but against the wall, Cory in his arms.

Bracken took the outside, Nicky mashed up against his chest, and by the time everyone was settled, Brack was already growly.

"You are ruining the mood," he threatened. "If you keep grabbing at my prick, it's going to get hard."

Nicky purred. "Then you'll let me clean it up," he said playfully, although Green seemed to recall a washcloth somewhere in all they'd done to get him to bed.

"It's quite clean," Bracken reassured him.

"Well, I could get it dirty," Nicky teased, inexorable.

"And I could fuck *you* until you screamed too," Bracken said, sounding so matter-of-fact he almost made Green hard again.

Cory let out a whimper against Green's chest.

"You don't approve?" he asked in surprise.

"I want to see it so bad," she confessed, kissing his sternum between his nipples. She liked doing that to both Green *and* Bracken. Product of being so tiny in a household full of giants. "But I'm falling asleep," she yawned. "I'll miss it."

Bracken reached over Nicky and stroked her hair. "Sleep, beloved," he ordered. "Nicky and I will wake up and play when you get up to pee."

For some reason that made her giggle against Green's chest, but Green was too replete to ask why.

TEAGUE
Second Bananas

THE FIRST time Teague had met Maxwell Johnson, Jacky had been dying in the back of Teague's car as he'd sped toward Green's hill and a new life.

Max had been cordial, matter-of-fact, and no-bullshit then, and he hadn't changed. They'd worked ops together as humans and run together as animals, and the cat/dog thing that could bother some people in the hill (or the cat/cat thing that Max and Charlie did on occasion) did not seem to bother Teague or Max.

When Max was a cat, he was cocoa-colored, with crossed blue eyes and a rather placid disposition. If he'd been a house cat, he would probably have been the type who didn't disturb the houseplants and groomed meticulously.

When Teague was a wolf, he was just as tough, scarred, and no-bullshit as he was as a human.

Teague didn't let ego get in the way. He'd had no problems taking orders from Cory, and he had no problems taking orders from Max.

This irritated Max for some reason. It was probably a cop thing, with all the vying for promotion and hoping to make detective. When Teague had been having problems with Jacky—and brother, there had been some fucking problems—the entire hill had gotten some use out of rebuilding the small house across the driveway that Teague had been given to keep his family in. But the house had been finished while Teague was recovering, so working shit out that way was not an option.

Still, Teague was not surprised when Max greeted him with a shoulder bump as he came inside the kitchen of the hill proper.

Teague grunted. "Milk and cookies." Because he'd just run, goddammit, and now that he wasn't eating with Cory, he could eat whatever his werewolf metabolism and deep-seated childhood issues demanded.

Max grunted. "I'm tuning up my 'Stang. Come help me." He grabbed a gallon of milk from the huge stainless-steel refrigerator that Grace and the pixies kept stocked to the brim, and Teague grabbed a package of Oreos—fresh, unopened, the double-stuffed chocolate kind—with green icing in deference to the holiday season.

Grace kept an entire cupboard stocked with just cookies, because that woman was more than any man deserved.

Teague stuffed three in his mouth while he followed Max at a trot down the stairs. The middle level housed most of the shape-shifters and some of the elves as well as the shape-shifter bar. Teague looked in and waved at Jacky, who was doing something on his computer with Nicky. They both waved, and he picked up his speed to keep up with Max.

A breath of heat at his back told him he'd acquired a visitor.

"I did not see you in there," he grunted.

"I was hiding in the corners," Lambent said snidely. "Where I heard the most interesting thing from your mate."

Teague groaned. Jacky did *not* have a bone of empathy in his body. He would not have guessed why they hadn't included Lambent in this op, and he would not have thought to keep silent.

"You were fucking drunk last night," Teague said through another mouthful of cookies. "We thought we'd let you recover."

Lambent's hand on his shoulder was not surprising, but the hurt on his fine-boned, ruddy face was.

"Recover? I've about full up on recovery, you manky prat. Full up on being holed up like a badger in the first home I haven't hated, full up on being treated with kid gloves by a bunch of gestating daddies and a pregnant woman who could stomp out our enemy like a cockroach if she was ever let off the fucking leash—just fucking full. I want some bloody action, yeah?"

Lambent was shaking Teague, his hand gripping hard enough to burn. But Teague saw the hurt, the desperation in his eyes, and didn't snap at the hand on his shoulder in spite of the blisters forming under his new running shirt. He took a deep breath and held up the box of cookies.

"Want one?"

Lambent's jaw dropped, and he flailed his hands. "Want one? Do I want a bloody—Oh. Fuck."

The charred black handprint at Teague's shoulder flaked away to reveal the burned, blistered skin. The faint odor of cooking dog assailed them both.

"Fucking sorry." Lambent's voice cracked. "Hold still."

Teague did as ordered, not feeling anything but the sympathy of a pack mate as Lambent bent over and breathed softly on his shoulder. The pain—and it had been considerable—faded instantly, and when Teague looked again, his skin was whole and healed.

"Thank you," he said soberly. "Please take a cookie."

Lambent did, closing his shiny blue eyes as he crunched down. "Tha's good," he mumbled. Teague threw a friendly arm around his waist, because Lambent was an obscene size, even for an elf.

"It is, and Max is downstairs with a gallon of milk to share. He's going to work on his car and talk about why I shouldn't feel bad about not leading the op, and then we're gonna fuckin' plan. Want some goddamned cookies?"

Lambent nodded and finished off the one in his hand, then leaned his temple against Teague's in a way that Teague took to be companionable and not sexual. Well, his libido had pretty much locked itself against anyone not Jack or Katy over the summer, which was fine with him.

"Sounds amazing," Lambent said thickly. "Why *don't* you feel bad about not leading the goddamned op?"

"Because being the top dog doesn't mean shit to me," Teague told him. "The pack's all that matters. Besides, Max can make sure we don't get caught with this one, and that's what's important."

They had continued down the stairs and through the grand banquet room. If they'd taken an abrupt turn to their right as they got to the bottom, they would have gone into the heart of the vampire darkling, with their common room—mostly oxblood leather couches and blood-colored rugs, ick—and the vault where people kept exploding. Again, ick.

They didn't. Instead they turned to the staircase on their left, going down one more level into the garage, where Max was already bitching at the top of his lungs.

"Goddammit, Teague, you *looked* into the common room—*tell* me you did not suddenly decide to get la—" Max stopped midrant as he saw Lambent and jerked so hard he hit his head on the trunk of his '69 cherry-red Mustang.

"Hi, Lambent," he muttered, rubbing his head with one hand. In the other he had a box of tools, a drop cloth, and—God help him—a mechanic's jumpsuit that some sort of creature probably kept pristine for him.

Teague usually just wore his old T-shirts and jeans. Yeah, the creatures or sprites or pixies or whatever raided *his* laundry too, but since he didn't ask them to, and since he *tried* to do his own laundry, when his shirts shredded from the umpteen-zillionth washing, he wasn't responsible for cleaning up the carnage or a burial ceremony.

But Teague was wearing neither T-shirt *nor* jeans today. Instead, he was wearing a new long-sleeved microfiber shirt and lycra running tights—the mortification was acute—given to him by Lady Cory for Christmas. Shit. A *once*-new long-sleeved microfiber T-shirt. Lambent had burned a hole in the shoulder, and now his Christmas gift was no more. He looked around the garage and grimaced.

And then had a horrifying thought.

"Hey, you're not going to make me wear—"

He caught the jumpsuit in the face and swore. Then realized that Max was already wearing one of his own, and Teague had gotten a spare one.

"You're terrifying," he said on a note of pure loathing. "I can't even begin to fucking tell you."

"Shut up and get dressed," Max muttered. "You can't work on the car wearing that shit—even if it's melted. Lambent, do *you* want a jumpsuit?"

"You do realize that cars make us sick unless we bless them with the equivalent of elvish holy water, don't you?" Lambent asked acidly.

Teague could scent Max's embarrassment. "Yeah. Forgot about that. Was just trying to be—"

"Don't be considerate of my bloody feelings," Lambent snapped. "I lost someone. Haven't we fucking all?" Then he snorted. "No, of course not. You, Officer Max, have lost nobody. I'll grant Teague grace because we've almost lost *him*, almost since he was born. But stop trying to tell me I should be so goddamned careful with myself. *I want to kill something!*" he snarled.

Teague grunted. "Join the fuckin' club. But not on this run. This run is about deleting shit off a computer and keeping the damned doctor from tracking Cory down."

That brought Lambent up short. "Wait—this the git her mother took her to? And why haven't we wiped that bloody woman's mind, by the way? Just a little woop-blip and she forgets she even had a Cory, right?"

Teague and Max stared at him in horror. "That's fucking heinous!" Teague snapped.

Lambent held up both hands in mock surrender. "Yeah, whatever, at least we wouldn't have to worry about her practically throwing up whenever she realizes she's looking at someone not human."

Teague laughed a little, suddenly sympathetic with Lambent. He'd spent most his childhood wishing his own father had forgotten his name and regretting when he didn't. "Yeah, well, I admit to flashing a little fang just to freak her out, but we're still not divorcing her from the family. Cory's gonna pop those kids out—"

"Like tomorrow, if her belly's got anything to say about it," Lambent said in disgust. "And it can't be too fucking soon."

"She's got until late April or early May," Max muttered, pulling out a socket wrench. Oh, okay—tune-up. Easy. Well, on an older car, it was. Teague had needed to take some classes on the diagnostic equipment for Green's fleet of SUVs. It was what he did when he wasn't being an enforcer, and it was actually even more fun than the models of muscle cars he made during his "family" time with Jack and Katy. (They had discovered much more enjoyable and creative uses for family time. Teague approved.)

"May," Lambent said, his horror completely unforced this time. "Gents, that little thing isn't going to make it."

Teague and Max looked at each other and swallowed. Nobody had wanted to say it. She obsessed over every bite of food, ate like an angel, had thinner ankles now than before she got knocked up—but it wasn't going to change the fact that she was carrying two babies too big for her, and threatening to get bigger with every breath.

"We're going to have to trust in Green for that," Teague said after a moment of hush. "We're going to have to trust Green and Brack, and Hallow, even, to keep her healthy. And the rest of us are going to need to pull our weight."

Max grunted. "Amen."

"What do you mean?" Lambent asked, as alert as they'd ever seen him.

"Don't you get it?" Max asked, bitterness sounding right at home in his crisp, no-bullshit voice. "All those battles, you guys soaring over the fucking hill, why do you think we haven't been sending shape-shifters on the ground?"

Lambent let out a grunt. "Because we don't want them to bite you. We don't know what'll happen. I thought even you two would have picked that up."

"Yeah, well, if they had risked a few of us, we might have been able to figure out where she's holing up," Teague supplied. "Because it can't be too fucking far. It's got to be a big house, probably about ten miles from us, which would make it one of those cabin-in-the-woods places, like here, but hella smaller. Big enough to house her lieutenants, but not her whole military, because she seems to draft whoever wants to get laid. It's not something someone can find from the air—but I know it's fucking there."

"Makes sense," Max said slowly. "She's setting herself up to be Green—she's going to want a base of operations nearby."

"Right?" Teague slid into the jumpsuit just because he thought better when he was tinkering with a car. "Give me the gap measure, Max. I'll gap 'em, you get 'em out of the fucking block."

Max did, and Teague measured the gaps in the clean plugs and set aside the ones that needed replacing, all while they talked.

"It's just… you know. The elves and the vampires are all flying, and we could sense her on the ground, but everyone's afraid they're gonna have to—"

"Pull a Teague?" Lambent supplied and then laughed uproariously at his own joke.

Teague regarded him with flat, unfriendly eyes. "That's actually a great idea, smartass. We do it at night. She never attacks at night anymore—I think the vampires freak her out."

"They would," Max said thoughtfully, pausing in the middle of wrenching on a stripped plug. "I was there, remember? I met the elves from the old country who were trying to take over. They really loathed the vampires or shape-shifters—in fact, they considered them less important than cattle, really. They…." He suddenly looked really sad. "I mean, it's how *I* felt about them, actually, and then I just saw… it was just so fucking ugly, you know? And I didn't want to be like that."

Teague grunted. "You think I wasn't one of the bad guys too? No worries, Max."

Max shrugged, and they worked in silence for a moment. "It's just that Mist and Morgana's people, they would have thrown werewolves to die against our shields the way the elf queen has. They would have kept the elf lieutenants close by and protected. They would have avoided the vampires, *especially* after they turned the tide of a battle, because they want to pretend they don't exist."

"Wait," Lambent said, curling his lip at the obvious. "If this woman thinks she's going to run Green's hill, what does she think is going to happen to the vampires and shape-shifters who live here?"

They all contemplated for a moment and then had one of those collective orgasmic shivers that people do when they all run into the same dreadful conclusion.

"Over my dead fucking corpse," Lambent snarled. Then he brightened. "Or my live body while I'm fucking my corpse—that would be fun too."

"Jesus!" and "God in Heaven!" Teague and Max groaned, but Teague recovered enough to gap the next plug Max handed him.

Oh, it was good to have someone who got swearing, too.

"So we need to stop her," Teague said. "That's… I mean, we need to fucking stop her. And we need to change tactics. And maybe do the same thing we're doing tonight."

"Sneak out of the house without telling Mom?" Max asked, throwing some bright yellow sarcasm into it.

"Dad can know," Teague replied evenly. "Two of the dads can maybe go with us. I'm just saying that after we take out the doctor tonight—"

"Wait—you're going to kill him?" Lambent asked, horrified. "I thought that was the whole reason you didn't invite *me*!"

"We're gonna brain-fuck him," Max said in disgust. "And that *is* the whole reason we didn't invite you."

"But I'm great at the mind-fuck!" Lambent said delightedly. "Finesse work—you all know I can do it!"

Teague grunted meaningfully and looked at his shoulder. The charred handprint in his new shirt was right under the brown fabric of the jump suit.

Lambent grimaced. "Well, not my finest hour, but you're bringing *Hallow* and not *me*?"

"You could always ask Hallow if he wants to change places," Teague suggested, looking at Max.

Max pursed his lips. "Yeah, but…."

They looked at him.

"Last time…. Lambent, you were there, right? Hallow did that… that *thing* where the guy looked inside himself and it melted his brain?"

Teague swallowed. "Ew."

Lambent's and Max's eyes met.

"Blood ran out his ears and mouth," Max said flatly. "You have no idea how much ew. Could have lived my whole life without seeing that, and I've seen some heinous shit. But…."

"You're thinking, set that power on nonlethal?" Lambent asked, uncertain.

Max shook his head and leaned on the car, and Teague took advantage of the break to reach inside the front passenger seat for the gallon of milk while it was still cold.

He tilted it up and started drinking as Max spoke.

"Not so much nonlethal as… *karmically* nonlethal," Max said. Teague stopped gulping and looked at him, sticking his tongue out to capture the milk running down his chin.

"I'm fuzzy on this karma shit," Teague said into the considering silence. "Maybe clarify?" He tilted the jug back again and gulped some more, expecting Max to talk into the pause. Max did not. When he was done, he wiped off his mouth with his arm and looked up to see Max and Lambent staring at him. "What?" He held out the remaining quarter of a gallon. "You all wanted some?"

Lambent shook himself all over. "Not the milk, wolfman. Glory, how you make that look sexy…."

Max's mouth hung open. He closed it with a snap. "God, this cat thing is fucking with my head. I'm straight, and I *still* want to lick milk from his chin."

Lambent nodded, and both of them exchanged horrified glances.

"I am not that attractive," Teague told them. "Get over it."

Lambent sniffed the air for a moment, then grinned. "Oh no, gents. That's not our werewolf here, although having him bond was a loss to us all. That was the smell of happy leader sex. It's permeating the hill—can you smell it?"

In spite of the fact that they'd been down in the garage for half an hour, Teague looked instinctively to his own Mustang, terror pounding in his heart.

Oh, good. Red, as it was meant to be.

Lambent grunted. "No, idiot, nothing changed color, because *she* didn't come." He looked honestly glum for their little sorceress. "She probably can't—not on bedrest. But everyone else did, and they all did it together, and we should be bloody well happy about it."

Teague nodded. "Yeah. We're stronger when they're happy. We know that. That's why we've got to do that…. Wait, Max, what *did* you mean by karmically… whatever?"

Max was still looking at him funny. "Maybe it's the milk," he pondered. Then he shook himself. "Okay, the thing is, you know how Cory put that thing in the air that had people who meant us harm falling asleep?"

They both nodded. Genius, that. Teague was the first to admit it blew him away that she could do that with sex. He always thought he was lucky if he just got the other two people with him to come.

"Well," Max continued, "what if we could do that brain melting thing, but only if he deserved it?"

Lambent sucked Oreo off his teeth and reached for another one. Teague had put the package on the roof of the car, and he helped out by pushing it across the hood a little closer.

"Sure you don't want milk?"

Lambent's eyes narrowed. "Sure you don't want to watch me yank my sausage in the middle of a car park?"

Teague actually felt his throat close in horror. "Oh dear Lord…."

"Well, then stop yanking around my libido, wolfman. Just because your interest has closed up shop doesn't mean the rest of us haven't had our fantasies."

"Weird," Teague pronounced. "So can you do it?"

Lambent munched, still thinking. "Yes, yes I can, but I don't think I should," he said carefully.

"Why not?" Max had apparently given up on the car, because he carefully wiped off his hands and moved around to Lambent's side to take a cookie out of the carton. "I mean, it's… you know, poetic and shit. The guy's a shitball, his brains explode and he dies. He's not a shitball, and he just forgets he ever saw Cory, game over."

Lambent shook his head. "You don't get it, mate. There's shitballs, and then there's *fanatics*."

Teague squinted. "He's a survivalist?" he asked dubiously. "Like, one of those hosers in the hills with a semiautomatic shooting the fuck out of deer?"

Lambent rolled his eyes. "So cute and yet so bloody dumb. *No*, asshole, like *you* and *Max* before you got all hairy and nocturnal. Are you feeling me?"

All of a sudden, Teague did. "Oh. Oh. Oh shit, yeah, Max, bad idea."

Max's blue eyes were *truly* crossing with the effort of thinking about it. "But I don't see—"

"'Cause you weren't a bad *guy*!" Teague said, wishing Max was Jacky so he could smack him upside the head. From the corner of his eye he saw a shadow flit down the stairs and then around some of the SUVs. Awesome.

"Well, no. I was… you know. Misguided. Ignorant—"

"Yeah, but you weren't *bad*." Teague actually got this—oh dear Goddess, it was something Green had been trying to tell him since he'd arrived at the hill. "This guy, he looks inside his head, he's not gonna see greed or sloth or… you know. Any of those other vices. He's gonna see… I don't know. Scientific curiosity, or even a desire to help pregnant women. He's gonna see… whatever is driving him, he's gonna see it without the twist. I mean that's what makes people like… you know, Trump, or Hitler, or Republicans, so fucking terrifying. They look in the mirror and they don't see evil. They don't see the twist in themselves. They see that…." He grabbed two cookies and flailed crumbs all over the vast garage. "They see the *purity* of their vision, or whatever. They *don't* see what it's doing to decent people."

Max stared at him, openmouthed. There was a glob of green Oreo frosting on the front of his teeth.

"So," he said after a moment, sucking his teeth as he spoke, "that wouldn't work at all."

"No, boyo. In fact, that might make him even more fanatical than he already is."

Teague felt the thrill of discovery leave him, and he deflated slightly. "It was a good idea, Max. Just… you know. We can try the mind-fuck this one time. Maybe split off, have two teams. One goes with the mind-fuckers to the guy's house at o-dark-thirty, and the other goes to the hospital with a mind-fucker of his own and takes out the computer system."

Max nodded his head enthusiastically. "That's a great idea! Yeah— okay, let's do that, and I'll take the…."

"You should take the clinic," Teague said decidedly. "You'd know how to deal with a break-in as a cop, so you'd be the best guy to cover the tracks. I'll take dealing with the guy at his house. That way I can take Lambent and Kyle, and you can take Hallow, Marcus, and Phillip—"

"Grace and Arturo want to come too," Max said. Teague rolled his eyes.

"No. Just no. All this 'But the shape-shifters are gonna be infected and shit!' blah blah blah—no. Those two go, the hill stops running. I *would* like Mario with me—"

"And I wouldn't mind Nicky or Bracken—"

"You're gonna get your wife and be happy about it," Teague said grimly. "She's been listening to most of the discussion anyway."

Max gaped, another glob of green cookie on his teeth. "She's been—"

Lambent cackled. "Oh, glory—like you'd have a chance of getting the daddies out on the field right now anyway. No, gents, it's time for the kings and the queen to retire, and the bishops with them. Up to the rooks and the knights, yeah?"

Renny appeared and rubbed herself along Max's legs. He hmphed and scratched the ruff behind her ears. "You don't strike me as a rook or a knight, darlin'. What are *you* in this little game?"

She shifted—slight, willowy, feral—and licked his ear. "Wild card," she purred, then slid right back into her cat form and slipped beyond the cars to the spring-loaded shape-shifter's entrance toward the side of the hill. One shove and she was out scaring whatever was flying in the gardens. Teague would have supposed it was for mice, but he'd seen niskies, now that he knew what they were, running in flower-colored droves taunting her, and he assumed it was an old game.

"I adore her," he said, quite sincerely. "She's funny."

Max snorted. "You know what's funny?"

"That you drive this thing when you can't even finish gapping the fucking spark plugs?" Because they'd only gotten through about four of them. Teague was going to have to go back and redo the whole thing so Max's beloved car could run the way he needed it to.

"No, genius. What's funny is that Green told me I was in charge of the op, and you just planned the whole damned thing."

Teague stared at him blankly. "No, I didn't."

"Yes, you did."

"No, I swear I didn't."

Lambent smacked him upside the head. "You so did. Doesn't matter. I'll follow either of you. We've all been learning from Her Nibs—you'll do fine."

Teague grunted and sagged against the Mustang. "So, we do fine with this one, you know what that means, right?"

They were all quiet for a moment.

"Means we need to go do that other thing," Max said.

Teague met his eyes square on. "And we've got to enlist help."

"So, does this mean we can't ask Green? Don't you think he'd let us—?"

"He'd tell her first," Teague said, then stopped. Green had become more and more protective, the further along Cory had gotten. Must be like a spider on a web in a hurricane, trying not to put her in a glass jar on general principle but keeping her safe from herself and half the supernatural world. "Well, maybe he wouldn't. But he could also tell us no."

Max whistled low from between his slightly gapped teeth. "Yeah. That would be bad."

"Yes, it would be," Teague said, nodding.

They both looked at Lambent, all of them in accord. No, they could *not* go against Green's orders. All of them owed their lives—their *souls*, when it came to that—to their leader, who had proved again and again that they were all valuable and loved.

But they could, maybe, make plans of their own. Green tended to want his people independent, right?

And under no circumstances, none at all, would they breathe a word to Lady Cory.

LATER THAT night Teague, Kyle, Lambent, and Mario sat in one of the SUVs in the dark of a frost-lit suburb in Grass Valley. The trees provided the shadows, and their extra senses gave them an advantage in the silver light of the moon. About two feet of snow had fallen since solstice, and Teague had been grateful for the SUV's extra-deep snow tires as Mario had given them directions via Google Maps.

"That's it, huh?" Teague asked, looking at the nice house with the brick edging and manicured lawn.

"What it says—Dr. Roger Nieman." Mario wrinkled his nose. "He lives with a wife, both kids in college. She's with her parents in Aspen for the holidays with the kids. Sounds like a warm family."

"He got any hookers in there?" Teague asked with curiosity. "Any side pieces? Poker games? Half a key of blow he's gonna shove up his nose while he's got the house to himself?"

They all stared at the house, trying to impart a glamour to it that the plain, well-heeled residence simply did not possess. White house, brick trim, no topiaries, no prize-winning flower beds, no dog.

"You are giving this man credit for sexiness that he quite simply does not possess," Mario told him bluntly. "Some people, they're all work. This one, he's all work. No play, no sex, just a bottle of bourbon and his medical records is all he needs."

Teague turned his head away from the house to regard Mario thoughtfully. The bird shifter's eyes glowed faintly gold in the dark, but otherwise he was the same plainspoken, stocky, quite frankly *beautiful* Latino man who accompanied Cory and the others to school.

And the past summer he had harried an actual vampire bear from the air while Teague had run for his life to get away from the damned thing.

Teague would trust Mario in any matter, but—"How do you know about the bourbon?"

Mario's teeth glinted. "Anyone want action on that?" he asked wickedly.

"I'll take it," Lambent said. "Five dollars says birdman here is right. Kyle?"

For a moment Teague was afraid he wouldn't respond. Lambent held himself apart, body quivering slightly, as though expecting his lover to reject human companionship altogether.

But Kyle surprised them all. He turned his attention to the people inside the car, rather than what was going on across the street or in the shadows beyond, and flashed a smile. "Twenty dollars says there's at least two bottles in the trash," he challenged, and even though Teague thought all of them were right, he was heartened to see the young vampire taking any sort of interest in his surroundings.

"Deal. You go check, and while you're at it, let us know if this neighborhood is as dog free as it sounds."

He was not necessarily talking about the regular loud yappy Chihuahua, and they all knew it.

"Will do. Can I have Mario to spot me from above?"

"Done. Good hunting."

"Roger that."

Kyle had begged nicely and managed to get a sip from Green before feeding from Teague's wrist before they left. Green hadn't seemed suspicious, and the double feeding not only made their bond tighter, it gave them limited telepathy, same as feeding from Cory the night of the flaming RVs. If something went wrong, Teague would at least know that and have Kyle's back.

Mario stepped outside and flapped away almost instantly, but Kyle settled for walking across the road with no stealth at all.

"Smart," Teague approved. "If he'd looked around, it would have seemed like he was hiding something."

"Yeah, the boy did good. He came up with the old vampire kiss in Folsom, before Her Nibs killed them all off."

Teague wasn't surprised often. "Really? I had no idea."

"Yeah." Lambent sighed and looked out into the night. "And then his girlfriend—human—got to know Her Nibs through school. Didn't turn out so well for the girl. Not Cory's fault, though. Poor boy. He's… he's got a good heart."

"You don't have to defend him to me," Teague said. As far as he knew, it was the first time Lambent had actually spoken of the relationship with the young vampire. "Have you *met* Jacky?"

Lambent let loose a breath and tilted his head back. "I am… I am unused to being attached," he said, almost to himself. "Started out as fun, right?"

"Hurts," Teague said, remembering moments when he'd thought Jack had been dead. "No fun then."

"No fun," Lambent sighed. "But necessary. He is becoming very, very necessary."

"One of you having babies?" Teague asked, just to lighten the load.

Lambent cackled—score one for Teague. "Nope. How 'bout you, mate? You and Cop-Fuck gonna be our next couple of daddies?"

All the gears in Teague's brain fused together as though they'd been dipped in water and frozen solid. "Hrk…."

Lambent cackled some more and was still cackling when Kyle returned, with Mario landing just as he opened the door. They hopped in together, bringing a blast of arctic wind with them, which allowed Teague to shake the vision of Katy, baby in her belly, doing something fancy with the embroidery floss and tiny needles.

"What's up, gents?" Lambent asked, voice still ringing with the knowledge that he'd completely fucked Teague up.

"We all win. Somebody owes us money," Kyle said. "He's got two empty bourbon bottles in the trash—top-shelf stuff, but that's his one vice. I say we wait until about two minutes after the light goes out and knock on his door."

Teague grunted. "Genius. What're we gonna say, 'Pardon me, sir, we're just poor lost circus performers'?"

Lambent's cackle could really get on a guy's nerves. "No, ducks," Lambent said with confidence. "Leave that to me and Kyle, here. We'll go deal with him. You and Mario get in the house through the back and look for files, right?"

Well, that had mostly been Teague's plan, outlined as they'd driven in.

"Right," Teague agreed. "Break."

They hopped out of the car the way Kyle had crossed the street—as though they had all the time and right in the world to be there.

Teague sort of regretted being the guy going behind the house, because he didn't get a chance to see how the brain-fuck went. He and Mario slid open the guy's back lock as soon as they heard him answer the door, and thank God the alarm was disabled as soon as he did.

They slid silently and more than silently into the back of what looked like a *very* nice house decorated by someone who lived at *Better Homes and Gardens*. Cherry hardwood floors and carpet runners made with high-quality wool greeted the two of them as they ghosted through the house, their heightened senses making the break-in as easy as blinking and breathing.

The hallways were marked by silver photo frames like milestones—here is the happy family twenty years ago, eighteen years ago, fifteen years ago. Teague watched Nieman's hairline go from thick and full to widow's peak to nonexistent, and he watched Mrs. Nieman's physical distance from him widen as their kids got bigger and her teeth got pointier.

The house was ranch style, one story, and all the furniture was that same incriminatingly pricey cherry wood—so damned expensive. And the place was big enough for Teague and Mario to take turns walking down the hallway checking the rooms.

Young woman's room, yes, complete with Stanford banner on the wall. Young man's room, check, complete with USC banner on the wall.

Parents' room, check, complete with two queen beds like a hotel room. Ouch. How do they explain *that* to the kids?

Teague was going to turn around and go check out the living room, which would have been dangerous—but he could hear Lambent and Kyle having an animated discussion in the front room. Something about how the two men were lost and looking for their friend, young woman, pregnant, had a gigantic husband, what was her name?

From what Teague could gather, the problem was exactly what Teague had said it would be. The guy wasn't *evil*, just misguided.

Teague looked over his shoulder toward the living room, then back into that sterile bedroom with the white hotel comforters. And that's when he realized that there was a large bathroom to the left, and two doors to the right. If one of them was a walk-in closet, and he had no doubt it was, then the other one would be....

"C'mon," he whispered. "I think there's a study next to the bedroom."

Together they ghosted through the darkened room, noting that one of the beds had been barely slept in before Kyle and Lambent had started their lost tourist routine. Around the beds, past the dresser, and hey, hello, here you go, a tiny study that....

"Holy God," Teague said just as Mario whispered, "Merciful Goddess."

Oh hell, no.

"Where did he get those pictures?" Mario demanded. Teague looked at them and shuddered.

"Got no idea, but this shit goes *now*!"

The room looked like a stalker's wet dream, and the man had... how had he done that? There were pictures of Cory from first grade up, school pictures showing her progression from a plain, sturdy, freckled five-year-old with a big smile to a surly, black-haired goth chick with a terrifying snarl.

He had pictures from what must have been junior college, the DMV, and even her application for a gun permit, all of which were blown up and thumbtacked to a big corkboard behind the desk.

Post-its littered the little shrine, with big red writing on them. "Goes Armed," "Was so confident in my office," and, most alarmingly, "Corinne Carol-Anne Kirkpatrick... what? There's another name there besides Green, but I can't read it."

"Oh, Jesus," Teague breathed. "Whatever happened in this guy's office, he's fucking obsessed."

The crown jewel of Dr. Nieman's little shrine to the patient who got away sat dead center in the middle of all the pictures of Cory: in black and white, three stills of young fetuses—with oversized heads, elongated bodies, and very pronounced tails. In one picture they were just hanging out, doing what babies do, swimming in peace. One of them was sucking a tiny thumb. In another one, both little faces seemed to be pointed toward the camera, and the inhuman placement of the eyes and ears and cheekbones was unmistakable.

And then that third picture, where the very forms of the babies were blurred and their features distorted, the only thing clear—and clear to Teague, who knew babies for shit—was the oddly large, misshapen heart in each tiny chest.

Teague and Mario looked at each other. "This shit has to go," Teague said decisively. He and Mario started ripping out thumbtacks and collecting incriminating, invasive pictures as quickly as they could.

"He doesn't have any from the campus now, at least," Mario noted.

"Hard to stalk someone when you have a day job," Teague muttered back. He found a big manila envelope on the doctor's desk and started stuffing it full of evidence.

Mario grabbed another one, and between the two of them, they cleared the board and were left with nothing but the doctor's small laptop on the desk.

They looked at each other.

"He's probably got the info somewhere else," Mario said.

Their dilemma was obvious—the man was a doctor, and that was information on other patients. Destroying that computer….

Corinne Carol-Anne Kirkpatrick... Green. He was a Bracken and a Nicky away from figuring it out.

Teague shook his head at his moment of indecision, closed the laptop screen, and cracked the whole thing in two over his knee. He gave Mario a half, and they both cracked their smaller halves in two, then put the remains on the floor and started stomping on them. Yeah, he might have had backups online, but they'd have to hack the system later. For now, if they were going to brain-wipe him, the less visual evidence, the better.

"What was that? You two gentlemen need to leave. I don't disclose patient information about *anybody,* do you hear me?"

The doctor's voice, raised in irritation, was punctuated by the slamming of a door.

"Fuck!" Teague could hear Kyle in his head, and he sent a firm thought of *"Got it all nailed down"* to calm the young vampire.

"What do you need?" Lambent said in his head.

"When you hear the ruckus, open the back door."

Teague reached into his back pockets, pulled out his wallet and cell phone, and gave them both to Mario. "You can get them to the car, right?" he asked, pretty sure the Avian's ability to hold things as he shifted went that far. Mario shoved them in his jacket pocket. "No promises. I lose the jacket in trans, and they're molecules," he whispered. They could both hear the doctor stalking back through the house.

And they could hear his side trip to the kitchen for what they assumed was a shot of bourbon. Well, that helped.

Teague stripped off his denim jacket with a sigh, and the shirt as well, and then slipped his key lanyard over his head. There was no way for them to get down the hall without being seen—not if Nieman had gone into the kitchen.

Well, let's make sure he has nothing to see.

Teague continued to strip all the way down, stowing his clothes and boots behind the desk.

"Won't the cops find that?" Mario whispered urgently, tugging on his shoulder.

"What's he going to report? Someone stole his murder board and got naked?"

Teague stacked the two envelopes neatly and then shoved them in his mouth.

Mario opened the door, and they both changed.

Mario almost flew straight into Nieman, and Teague let out a growl as the intrepid doctor raised his hands over his head and gave a shout. With a leap Teague jumped on top of the man, knocking him to the floor and thumping him solidly on the chest. Mario continued to flap, a giant bird in a slightly smaller house, and Teague yipped three times.

The back door banged open hard enough to crack the plaster with the doorknob, and Mario flew out with Teague hugging his wingspan. Lambent reached back and grabbed the knob, hauling it shut and cracking the doorframe. As a unit, the three of them blurred back to the car. Lambent opened the car using the keys hanging from Teague's neck, and Teague jumped in, turned human, and slammed the door.

Lambent didn't even smile as he slid out of his jacket and threw it over Teague's shoulders. "Here, brother."

Teague turned the ignition and looked urgently around for Kyle. "What the fuck is he do—Oh."

He felt the feeding link snap into place and heard Kyle, loud and clear, telling the doctor to forget Connie Lynn Fitzpatrick and her husband, Bart.

The good doctor fought him—hard—and Teague could feel that too, but that wasn't what was important.

As Kyle flew toward the SUV, barely a foot off the ground, and through the door that Lambent held open, Teague gave thanks for smart vampires and smarter elves.

"Good what you did with the name there," he said, so fucking grateful.

"What'd he do?" Mario asked.

"Fed him the wrong one. It's close—damned close. But the doc won't be able to get a handle on it. You know, you get someone's name wrong once, and—"

"You can never get it right," Mario agreed.

Teague put the car in gear, thinking that his ass and his tackle were both freezing on the seat. He drove silently down the street without lights for a good mile, the Christmas lights on the more active houses plenty of luminescence to guide the way.

They turned on 49 and headed for home.

"Augh!" Lambent let out, when they were sure they weren't followed. "That was a clusterfuck. We're fucking doomed!"

"Oh my God," Teague added. "You assholes don't even *know*!"

Mario turned around with the saved envelopes, and Lambent and Kyle both took a look at what was inside.

"Teague?" Lambent said weakly as Teague took the left down Bell Road.

"Yeah?"

"Don't take this the wrong way, but I think you should have torn the guy's throat out. Good intentions or not, I've got a bad feeling about this."

Teague grunted. "Next time," he promised. "Maybe when I go back to get my clothes."

Max actually went back later to get Teague's clothes, as a cop, under the pretense of checking out the crime scene. The guy had reported it after all—but he left out the part about stalking his patient because of his obsession with her children. But before Max grabbed Teague's clothes—Teague liked those boots and jeans, so he was grateful—they had a little confab where they reported to Arturo.

The results shook them all up, more than a little.

"He had the same thing set up in the clinic," Max said. "It was fucking freaky."

"Did you take it down?" Arturo asked. Oh, how they'd wanted his input, since the news was so very bad.

"I already told you, we burned the whole place down," Max told him. He looked at Teague and grimaced. "No casualties, but Hallow asks if next time maybe Lambent couldn't get pyromania duty."

Teague grunted. "I'll try to arrange it."

They both looked at Arturo, who nodded.

"The clinic will put him off his stride for a bit," Arturo said. "But yes—if the good doctor asks Cory's mother again, there *will* be a next time."

He got up to leave the living room then, presumably to report to Green, but he turned back to Max and Teague before he left.

"By the way, you two, well done. Green couldn't have left this in more capable hands."

Teague smiled tiredly at the praise, aware that it never got old. "Thank you," he said.

"But next time, assholes, don't leave me home like an irritating old relative. Do you think you're the only ones who get bored?"

With that he stalked away, the folders held tightly in his hand, and Max and Teague caught each other's eyes.

"Yeah, fine," Max conceded. "When we do the other thing, we'll let him in on it."

"Good," Teague said, grateful. "I was afraid you were gonna bail on that."

Max smiled, the bloodthirsty smile of a feline, and Teague remembered his story of Renny running—naked—from room to room spraying gasoline all over the clinic in psychotic glee.

"Are you kidding?" Max asked, keeping his voice down under most creatures' hearing. "This pregnant-queen shit is just getting fun!"

CORY
Sidelined Goddammit

KARMA'S A bitch when she bites you in the ass.

Especially because she's a *sneaky* bitch. There you are, thinking you're having a decent moment, and then you realize that somehow you have lost complete control—not only of your own wayward body, but also of your entire fucking life, household, and kingdom.

And you can't get it back. Maybe not for a couple of months. Or years.

Or ever.

To start with, I didn't hear the vampires' need of me until two nights after Christmas. Bracken had me lying on my side after a snack, the better to feel the tap-dancing babies.

He had Flogging Molly playing from the computer, and in the middle of "Float," the sugar from the milk and apple kicked in and the kids started really going at it. Brack had pulled my T-shirt up just under my breasts and rolled my pants down under my belly, and I watched in fascination as the skin of my stomach jumped in time to the music. (Yes. In time. I assume it had something to do with being elvish, because those people love their music.)

Bracken had rubbed cocoa butter on me, because the stretching itched something awful, and there was something hypnotic about watching the taut, shiny skin of my stomach undulate as though it was animated.

And maybe because my mind was engaged in nothing more than music, the muted purple light of our darkened room, and what was going on inside my head, I heard them.

The vampires. They needed me.

It was a quiet hum of neglect, a sadness none of them wanted to voice. I used to spend a night a week in the darkling, sharing blood with whomever was needy. Nobody had taken advantage, and if they did, Bracken dealt with them quietly and effectively. (Maybe it was his blood power, but he scared the fuck out of most of them. Go figure.)

I hadn't been down in the darkling since Iris had detonated.

I made a sound of discomfort, sorrowful beyond belief, and linked my mind with Grace, Phillip, and Marcus.

"You three. Five more. Choose carefully."

"Cory?" Bracken looked at me curiously, and I reached out and brushed his hair back from his eyes. He forgot to cut it—most of his life he hadn't needed to, because it had swirled past the back of his knees. In the past months it had grown shaggy and wild, and some days he just grabbed one of my elastics to pull it off his high forehead.

"There are vampires coming," I said softly. "A small number. Don't turn them away. They need me."

Bracken grunted. "They haven't said anything," he said sullenly, but I could tell by his tone that he'd guessed.

"It's perfectly safe—I asked Grace. She said if I were going in for tests every week, they'd take between one and five vials of blood a week. A small bite tonight, one tomorrow, a few days of rest. Repeat. They're pining, beloved. They haven't been able to fight since October, their friends are in danger, and their queen is… just fucking absent. They need attention, or they'll start to go rogue."

I was overstating the rogue thing. But they were lonely and lost— that much I could feel.

Bracken grunted. "I'll go round up some shape-shifters to fill in the real hunger," he protested, pushing himself up from the floor.

"Bracken…." I grabbed his hand and looked up, biting my lip. He sighed and bent down, kissing me softly and sliding his tongue between my lips to taste.

"You're right," he conceded. "Was just… nice, this past week. Only sharing with Green and Nicky. We…."

"Were a family," I said, feeling the loss of that privacy too. This was why people had their own rooms or, like Teague or the Avians in the Eyrie in Sheraton, their own homes. Because the hill was lovely, yes it was, but spending every day at the pool party was exhausting. Sometimes you just wanted your own room and your own people.

We didn't always get what we wanted.

"We're still a family," Bracken said, rolling his eyes. "Just, you know, we've got a fuck ton of cousins and they're all *next door*."

A subtle knock sounded, and he dropped my hand and let out a breath.

"Or *at* the door," he amended, then strode to the door.

Grace came first, bearing food, of course.

"I just ate," I protested sleepily, pushing myself up on my elbow.

"It's a protein smoothie," she said, "and stay down." She set the smoothie on the table—all thirty-two ounces of it—where it chilled in a little container of ice.

"Well, at least let me fix my shirt," I grumbled, and Bracken yanked it down from under my armpits as I wriggled up from the bed.

"*Now* stay down." Grace smiled and pulled up a chair. "Thank you for this," she said softly, brushing my hair back from my brow. "I've already fed today—I just need a drop. And I'll share with as many people as I can."

"I know," I said, catching her hand. "Sorry I didn't think of this sooner. I could have been doing this for a month—"

"We've *all* been preoccupied," she said firmly, squeezing my hand. "But this was… kind. And timely." She smiled slightly. "Now that Christmas is over, they realized how much they missed you on movie nights."

"I miss them too," I said with a lump in my throat. They were my last link to Adrian. I blinked back tears. "We can't forget this—not even after the babies are born, okay?"

She kissed the back of my knuckles softly. "Of course not, my queen."

I swallowed against an irrational yearning, a terrible fear. "You'll help me, right?" I asked. "After they're born? I mean…." My mother would come visit—I had no doubt—but she wouldn't understand. The things I knew in my bones because I'd lived in Green's hill for so long would need to be taught to my mother, and she still wouldn't always see.

Grace laughed. "My darling, you will have so much help. You will never be alone if you don't want to be." She bit her lip, one canine popping out as she did so. "But you will want to. Silly songs, nonsense games, plans, worries—you'll want to tell your children everything while they're tiny. You'll want to hold them forever, just so they know they're yours." Her eyes watered with crimson tears. "There is not enough time in the world. There is *never* enough time in the world. But when you need it, there will be help." Her grin was starlight bright. "If nothing else, Bracken's mother is *dying* for a shot as a daytime nanny."

I laughed. My one mother-in-law had spent an hour the day before flitting from one corner of the room to another, talking about the things we *could* put there, if I *wanted* them there, and the things I'd *want* to put somewhere else, and maybe, just maybe, could I go look in the nursery and see what we could do there?

I promised that I would. I really wanted to. But at the moment, if I so much as veered a little to the left on my way to the bathroom, the guys would lose their fucking minds. If I didn't want to be carried in to pee, I would have to put the nursery off until later.

"Yeah," I said fondly. "She's exhausting. I hope *she* can keep up with two elvish children, because I'm a little scared now."

"You know, I think pixies are the reason the human race survived," Grace said. She'd wiped the blood from her eyes with the back of her hand, and the sudden melancholy lifted from the room.

"Really?" I was charmed. "Why?"

"Because! If they liked a human family, they'd keep their eye on the babies—keep them entertained, keep them out of trouble when Mom got too busy, that sort of thing. And those babies, they'd grow up to be poets and artists and musicians, because their childhoods were full of wonder."

Oh, it was beautiful, this bit of whimsy—or maybe history. This was, after all, Green's hill.

"These children will grow up full of wonder," I said, feeling complete peace about the life in my womb for the first time since I'd conceived.

"And our vampires are growing hungry," Grace said briskly. That was it, our moment of quiet bonding. That was okay—I was pretty sure we'd have more.

I offered my wrist, and she punctured so smoothly that I didn't feel it until she'd pulled her mouth away and swallowed. Her first grimace told me the taste of flowers and patchouli hadn't gone away, but the look on her face after she swallowed....

Oh, Goddess.

She let out a groan, her face tilted upward toward an invisible sun. For a few moments, she just sat there and shuddered, until the door opened and Arturo ventured in. Quietly he wrapped an arm around her shoulders and led her, still inarticulate, out of our room.

Marcus and Phillip came next. Marcus pulled out the extra chair and gestured for Phillip to sit, then sat himself. Bracken had been hovering at the foot of the bed the entire time, but now that the boys were making themselves comfy for a visit, he tapped my feet. I curled up just a little tighter to make room at the foot of the bed, where he sat with one hand cupping my calf comfortingly through my sweats.

"You guys look great," I said, resting my head on my hand. "I'm sorry I didn't see you on Christmas, but—"

Marcus held up a hand. "No worries, Lady Cory. We stayed away on purpose." His cool hand touched my brow, much as Grace's had, and I realized it was unconscious. They needed me—and if they could not have my blood, they would settle for my touch. "They're our babies too," he said, tapping my cheek with his knuckle.

I raised my hand up to seize his and Phillip's too. "Don't stay away if I'm well," I told them. Phillip's hair was clean and pulled back into a half queue. He was wearing black jeans and a turtleneck with a black leather jacket over it—new, and probably from Marcus. Marcus's curly hair was a riot, as always, but he was dressed neatly and casually in jeans and a ski sweater.

"How did you do it?" I asked them quietly. "In August…." I bit my lip. We'd put them through battle after battle, when Phillip had needed to recover, and he had just kept rising to our need and beyond. "We thought we'd lose you."

Phillip smiled his thin-lipped smile. No one would consider it kind—but there was kindness there, nevertheless.

"You gave me something to fight for, my lady. You trusted me to fight." He smiled and used his free hand to ruffle Marcus's hair. "I had to stay sharp to keep *his* dumb ass out of the heat, you know?"

Yeah. By all reports, Marcus had been a sturdy second to Grace. But Phillip really *was* back to full speed, and apparently love really *was* the answer.

Well, and kicking a little werewolf ass as well.

I offered my wrist to both of them, relieved and joyful. They were very considerate and scalpel swift, and both of them screwed up their faces like a human drinking pure lemon when they took their one swallow.

But the slow roll of ecstasy that passed over their faces almost had a sound.

This time, since they were men and we hadn't spoken as Grace and I had, I closed my eyes and allowed myself to link with the two of them.

I saw darkness and two SUVs taking off—one with Teague, Lambent, Mario, and Kyle, and the other with my two vampires, Max, and Renny.

I saw a covert break-in, a frantic search, and—

They both snapped their minds shut just as my eyes popped open.

I felt my mad hurtling through my chest.

"Bracken?" I asked, my teeth gritted. "Could you possibly fetch Green and a few other folks for me? We're going to need to have a little powwow when I'm finished with the other vampires." I remembered a face from the images I'd seen, a vampire who might give me more information. "And make sure Kyle is among them."

I glared at my lieutenants, who looked back blandly.

"Somebody has been *very, very* bad."

I TRIED not to hurry through the next five blood exchanges—and some of them had to be true blood exchanges, as I was getting a little dizzy by the end. The effect of tasting a vampire's blood was always disconcerting—I usually got a rush of the best moments of their lives, and my recitations of who they'd been when their hearts were beating and they'd had loved ones and living families was usually something people looked forward to during the exchange.

But this time the vampires who could manage to sit still for that first bitter/sour painful swallow were mostly too blissed out to appreciate the recital, which was a relief for me. Their images were so crystal clear they cut my soul, as though their experiences were somehow amplified by the children in my womb.

The thought of them experiencing my vampires' lives was both reassuring, as though I were passing a blessing on to my young, and disturbing.

Very often our vampires' lives had not been pretty before they'd become ours.

But then, my own parents had done so much damage trying to shield me from the world I'd inherited. How much damage would I do to *all* of us if I refused to take my vampires' blood in return?

So I did what so many mothers have had to do as they made their way in an uncertain world—I hoped for the best.

And when I was done hoping for the best, I watched as the last two vampires were led away, slack and dazed and stoned to the gills, then turned to the crowd that had been gathering in my room as I'd finished up with the vampires.

For a moment I was embarrassed. The bed was rumpled, and as of an hour ago I'd been lying in my pregnancy sweats watching my stomach move. Everything about this situation spoke of casual and intimate, right down to my hair, which was only partially pulled back in an elastic.

But then I remembered what *Kyle's* blood had revealed—how Teague and Mario had burst out of the good doctor's house where they'd been *trapped*, and how Kyle and Lambent had clenched hands so tightly as Teague had driven them home, half-naked, that Lambent's fingers had turned blue.

My mad hit me all over again, and I surveyed my group of primary offenders. As I was glaring, trying to project a presence, Phillip, who was sitting sideways with his back against the closet, belched softly and fell into Marcus, who giggled into his hair.

Then Kyle gave a replete groan, toppled forward onto the carpet in front of the bed, and just lay there twitching, apparently as baked on pregnant sorceress's blood as any stoner on the finest Colombian Gold.

Everybody in the room looked at the tripping vampires and burst into giggles.

Including me.

Dammit. When we subsided, I looked at them all again and shook my head.

"You assholes."

"I told them to do it, beloved," Green said patiently.

"You're included," I snapped.

"We weren't!" Bracken and Nicky protested almost in tandem.

"That's a real fuckin' shame," Teague said frankly. "We could have used your help. Lambent and Kyle were having no luck at all wiping that guy's mind."

Augh!

I was suddenly tired.

"Okay, that's frightening," I admitted, wishing I could stand up and pace. The dull ache in my lower back—the one that had been there persistently since I'd been laid up in the first place—told me I couldn't.

"But so is you guys going out on a run without me! Couldn't you have waited?"

"Until you had the babies?" Teague asked, apparently the only one who wasn't afraid of me. Renny had been a cat since she first walked in, and she just sat there in front of the bed, hind leg extended, licking her own asshole directly in my line of sight.

Bitch.

"I'm not going to be on bed rest forever!" I protested. "Green said I should be up and about just fine by the end of the break. I'll be able to go to school, so I should be able to help plan runs—"

"Their plan was excellent," Green spoke up, apparently taking one for his team.

"Did you see the same op I did?" I asked suspiciously. "Max and Renny burned down a clinic."

Renny looked me right in the eyes and licked her whiskers.

Did I say "bitch"?

Green nodded. "And yet there were no casualties." He said that. My beloved said that with a straight face. "And we have valuable information, and young Kyle there—" Kyle twitched, still facedown on the carpet. "—managed to throw Nieman off the trail, hopefully for long enough to figure out how to break the hold his obsession with you has on his mind."

"We were sort of hoping to kill him," Max said apologetically.

Green grimaced but then reconsidered. "Yes," he said, absolutely okay with that. "It might come down to killing—which is fine."

"Fine?" I squawked.

"Yes, beloved," he said, his patience fraying. "If he's obsessing about you, killing is fine. This is not just you and not just him finding his way to the hill. This is *our children* he is thinking about hurting."

That drew me up short. I looked at Teague and Max for backup. "Was he really thinking about hurting us?" I asked, feeling the shock of it already starting to penetrate.

Teague looked uncomfortable. "Not… hurt," he said, looking at Max for confirmation. "That's not how he's thinking about it. He's thinking he's *rescuing* you. You have imperfect babies, and he wants to be your savior—the guy who delivers those babies and makes you see they weren't supposed to live."

I wrapped my arms around my middle—which was jumping madly, by the way—and snarled. "Okay, fine," I conceded. "If he doesn't back off, kill him. But you couldn't have *asked* me?"

"Dad knew," Teague drawled. "And you know what? That's all who needed to know."

My mouth dropped. Then I closed it and tried to swallow, and then it opened, and then Bracken handed me a glass of water and I gulped frantically trying to get my thoughts together.

"You will explain that," I said, eyes narrowed.

"Yeah, sure."

Oh, I should have known giving someone like Teague some self-worth would be a mistake. The cocky bastard plopped down next to me and clasped his hands between his knees.

"See, the thing is—in a good relationship, Mom and Dad only get half the info in a day as it is. I figure Mom talks when she's taxi service, and Dad worries about the kitchen and finances and whatever. And then they meet in the middle and tell each other their halves of it. That's what you guys do, anyway, right?"

I gaped at him, completely at a loss. "Teague," I said, knowing this was going to sound bitchy as fuck. "You, uh… you never *had* a mom and dad." I didn't count his progenitor. Mother*fucker*.

Oh Goddess. The look he gave me—for a bantam-tough, cynical, cocky asshole, it was the purest look of faith I had ever received. People had put me on some scary-assed fucking pedestals, the kinds surrounded by soft lights and perfect chords, the kinds it was impossible to live up to, but this look put the look we gave the angels in the trees to shame.

"No," he said, that look never fading. "But I imagined. You think people with shitty childhoods don't imagine?" He looked away, past the people in the room, past the walls surrounding us to the walls of his own heart, maybe. "Ever since I first saw Jacky, I tried to imagine what parents would do—real parents, a real family. When I saw Katy again, I tried to fix her into it. When we got together, all that fighting, all that fear, it was all because I didn't have a clear picture—what does a mom do, what does a dad do, how do they talk without fists and screaming."

His attention suddenly fixed exactly on me. Really me, not the me-on-a-pedestal that I found so frightening. "You and Green, you and Bracken, you and Nicky—you're our mom and our dad, and we learn from you. It's okay if you let the dads take some stuff. You're busy *being the mom*. Being the mom doesn't always mean kicking ass."

I must have looked stricken, because he did something remarkably un-Teague-like and tapped my nose. "Not that you have to retire for good," he said soberly. "And not that we don't miss you. But you got more important things to do."

I nodded, feeling forlorn and left behind. "You couldn't have even *told* me?"

"Yeah," Bracken grumbled. "You couldn't have even *told* us?"

"So you could have gone with them and she could have worried?" Green asked acidly. "Because that worked so well a year ago."

Nicky cackled, the sound incongruous with the waiting hush of the room. "Didn't Bracken call that a domestic dispute of epic proportions?"

"Yeah," Lambent reminded us. "Right before we killed all the wolves!"

"*Almost* all the wolves," Teague and Mario said with extreme satisfaction. Well, *they* got to kill some people in mortal combat.

"Lambent got to set shit on fire," Max said brightly. "I mean, seriously. It was sort of a win."

And part of me wanted to cry, because it *hadn't* been a win, it had been a *prelude* and a *bloodbath*, but that wasn't what my guys needed to hear just then. They needed to hear "Good job!" and "All win!" and I didn't blame them.

"Yeah," I agreed, sacrificing my own temper tantrum for what they needed. "It was a win. Good job, guys. Maybe next time, some warning before the vampires share blood and I get it close up." I turned to Teague, shaking my head. "You drove home naked, you dumbass. Didn't you remember to pack the sweats in the SUV?"

Teague grunted. "By the time we felt like we could quit running, we were halfway home. My assprint was already on the seat."

There was a collective groan, and Teague turned to the room. "Yeah, think on *that* the next time one of you wants to drive, assholes."

I smiled because I had to. I'd committed. I wasn't going to tell them I was hurt and left out, or that I worried they'd never let me back into the little club that I'd worked so hard to build. I wasn't going to tell them that I felt cheated because I'd finally gotten used to leadership and now I had to give up the reins when my body—which I had always known was frail and human— had assumed a different purpose than I'd envisioned six months ago.

But some of the sadness must have permeated my smile, because Green cleared his throat. "Now that this has been addressed, people…," he said delicately. One by one they all filed out, sort of. Lambent was carrying Kyle like a groom carried his bride, and Teague and Max had Phillip and Marcus between them the same way.

"It's a shame these guys don't show up on film," Max chuckled. "I'd want this pic."

"I would so totally post that in the front room," Mario agreed. "With captions and…."

They disappeared outside and down the hallway, presumably going toward the darkling. Renny drew up the rear, her tail twitching as if to say "That was fun, let's go kill rabbits now," and I watched her leave with dark purpose in my eyes. If that bitch thought I was going to knit her another pair of socks….

I welcomed the shift in the bed as Green sat on one side of me and Bracken sat on the other. I was still a little miffed at Green and sympathetic with Bracken, so I leaned on him and wound my hands through Nicky's hair as he crouched on the floor next to us.

"They left us behind," Nicky said, the sulky hurt in his voice a perfect counterpoint to what I felt.

"Yeah," I whined, unable to comfort him.

"You ordered them to do it!" Bracken stated, glowering at Green over my head.

"I did," Green said blandly. "But please note: I didn't go with them. And did you notice who *wasn't* in the room?"

"Grace," I said promptly. I'd taken her blood—she hadn't even known about the run.

"And Arturo," Nicky said. "I knew he was pissed about *something* today."

"Indeed." I looked up at Green and saw a slight smile on his lips. "They were sidelined too, children, like Mom and Dad, while the kids went out and took care of the young-people thing."

I thought about the dynamic in my room just a few minutes past and let out a small laugh. "Yeah. That there was… yeah." I sighed. "God, I feel old."

"What are we, luv? Twenty-one?"

I grunted, that "little bit tired" moving over into exhausted. "Twenty-two."

"In your dotage," Green said, rubbing the salt in.

"Good, boys. Grandma needs her nap."

Was anything resolved? Sort of. Apparently I wasn't going on runs anymore, and someone had to. Apparently Green got to call some of those shots, and we'd all been reminded a couple of times that he was good at it. And apparently if I was getting sidelined, the entire A-team was getting stuck with me.

Green moved to scoop me up into his arms, and Bracken stripped the covers off the bed. It was two in the morning, which was about two hours later than I'd stayed up all Christmas break. The men climbed in with me naked, even though I knew Green and Bracken would probably get up after I fell asleep. It didn't matter.

Yeah. We really were in this together.

A MONTH later, we were in the home stretch.

Green had let me off bedrest and okayed me to go back to school, which was a relief, and Hallow did his mind/administrative mojo thing and got me into a water aerobics class during my rather lengthy break.

I was officially in my third trimester, and getting out of bed to go to the bathroom felt like an Olympic event. The thought of walking the campus this way scared the hell out of me. The idea of swimming was heavenly. The idea of pulling a swimsuit on over the *thing* my stomach had become, not so much.

The day before school started, Bracken—who had done this drill with me before—approached me cautiously, a two-piece lycra object in his hands.

"It's green," I said suspiciously.

"You look good in green." The caution was well-founded, given the pile of *other* lycra objects already discarded at my feet.

"I look like shit in everything, Bracken. Stop the bullshit and tell me why I should try on this *particular* thing."

Bracken straightened his massive shoulders, threw the top over his arm and held out the bottom. "Note," he said, "the gusset that pulls out for the stomach, the lycra shorts meant to hide your—in your words— massive tree-trunk thighs. Also note the top is completely serviceable, with a fully functioning foam bra to house your girls, which even *I* know are in screaming pain, and an expando-apron to cover—again, your words—the entire other planet rising up from your body without your permission. Note the flattering color, a nice emerald green with little butterflies on the hem of the apron, and the way the apron buttons to the lycra shorts so that it does not—your words!—float up like a circus tent that will haul you down to the briny deep."

I tried. Goddess, I tried. But I couldn't hold a straight angry-cat face—not after all that meticulous attention to detail.

"Do they have it in burgundy?" I asked.

He nodded, a flicker of hope in his pond-shadow eyes.

"Then get both colors."

"You're not even going to try it on?"

I looked down at the dead soldiers at my feet, all of them presented with such hope, only to be thrown away in a hormonal burst of self-loathing.

"No, beloved," I said wearily. "I'm going to trust your judgment, sit down and knit, and try not to panic about getting through the next few weeks without Green."

Bracken sighed and ventured closer with the swimsuit. (He'd caught a bikini in the face early on in this endeavor—I didn't blame him for not wanting to come near.)

"Try it on," he said, palming the small of my back. I was standing in a bra and underwear, my ginormous stomach exposed and drooping. "You will look beautiful, your body will be supported, and you'll feel like you can do something for yourself that will make you feel better."

I smiled gamely at him. "You and Green gonna make out while I do?" The guys had made love almost nightly during the past month, all combinations of the three. The charge it gave the hill—and me—wasn't nearly as big as when I was involved, and I was getting *seriously* backed up. Green and Bracken had become experts at… well, Nicky called it a "lick-me-up," but that felt a little crude for their tongues between my thighs, and that hopeful way they looked at me as I arched in a gentle climax that *didn't* overtake my entire expanding uterus.

I missed being small enough to get thrown around between the lot of them like a fuck muffin. I just *really* did, and I was wondering if I would ever get back enough of my body to do that again.

And Bracken was being so patient with the bathing-suit thing when normally he would have given as good as he got, and I couldn't decide if it made me feel better or worse. On the one hand, I didn't mind a good shouting match. On the other, it felt like if he really did yell at me, I'd fall apart. I think he was unsure as well—hence his serious work for the position of husband of the year.

I leaned on him and sighed, letting him help me with the bottom and taking my bra off so he could slide the top over my head and do the catch behind my neck.

I stared at it in the mirror behind the bathroom door, feeling cumbersome and obvious and stupid. Then I felt his palm at my back again and his breath feathering my temple. I looked at him in the mirror and saw his eyes, overlarge as they were, shiny and besotted and luminous.

He's not just blowing sunshine. He really thinks I'm beautiful.

My heart stuttered and my own eyes got shiny, and at that moment Green walked in. He looked at us in the mirror first, his eyes taking in my body at almost seven months along and the acceptance on my face, that rare moment when I felt unapologetically beautiful, and his mobile, full mouth softened into a sweet smile.

He ventured closer and flanked me, putting his hand between my shoulder blades and leaning down so I could look at the three of us.

"You look lovely carrying our future," he said.

I nodded, biting my lip. "Yeah?" So uncertain. I'd finally gotten a handle on how much they loved me, and then everything changed with the growing life in my body.

"Yeah," he confirmed. He put his hand on my taut belly and smiled. "They're awake, but quiet. What do you think they're thinking when they're like that?"

I thought darkly about everything I didn't know about babies, elvish or otherwise. "Mischief," I said succinctly. "How to drive me bugshit when they come out."

Bracken smirked, and Green smiled delightedly. "I suspect so," he agreed. "Bracken was a lovely baby, though. Curious, and his mother was terrified once we realized he was vulnerable to bleeding out. He could barely walk, and you know the first place he went, don't you?"

I smiled and couldn't stop the stupid tears, because it had been seven months of pregnancy and seven months of not even seeing his eyes watching us, remembering us, yearning for the time when we could touch. A part of me wished he would just stay gone, because... because peace, right? He would be at peace. But a part of me was holding on to the moment when he would come back, and when the child I'd been before I'd conceived children of my own could live again.

"Adrian's," I whispered, heartbroken.

Their arms wrapped around me, and for a quiet, communal moment, we missed him together. But I didn't have any more time to dwell on his absence than I'd had since he'd last been seen in the garden. I had newer, more immediate griefs to tend.

"So you leave tomorrow?" I asked, trying to keep my voice brisk. We'd been facing this ever since we'd first come back from San Francisco flush with victory, expanding Green's holdings and his measure of safety.

"Yes," he said, voice aching. Of course he ached. He'd had to leave a pregnant wife before—and it hadn't turned out well, had it?

"I'm not helpless," I said, making my voice as sturdy as I could, considering I was talking against his chest. "I've spent a couple hours in the common room for the last two weeks, and I can keep doing that." We'd discussed this before. "Bracken's like… like the maiden aunt I never wanted, so he'll make sure I don't get too tired, and Nicky can pick me up and take me to bed if Bracken gets busy." We'd actually had a trial run of this, because even though I understood magic shape-shifter strength, I still didn't believe a falcon could lift a Volkswagen. Apparently, one could.

"I know," Green said patiently. He understood that I needed to reassure us all, so he let me keep talking.

"And Hallow is at school too. LaMark and Mario are… are they really doing *nothing* but following Bracken and me around all day?"

They didn't even have *classes*. LaMark had apparently taken enough to graduate, the lucky fucker, and Mario had decided he didn't *want* to graduate—he was happy enough being on the new A-team with Teague and Max and Lambent. I was trying very hard not to hate them all.

Speaking of which—"Renny's coming too," I remembered. "She and Nicky have the same classes this semester, so they're together." Jack was taking the Monday-Wednesday-Friday track this semester along with Cami, Dylan, and Connor. I realized that I was going to miss Jack— not least because he was finally proving of use to us and no longer being one big passive-aggressive ball of hatred-o'-Cory. But I would also miss the chance to see Teague when he dropped Jacky off, and the fact that our little A-team was being all secretive and doing something that none of the parents were supposed to know about had *not* escaped my notice, not with the blooding of a couple of vampires every other night. (I found if I had them bleed on a saltine and then ate *that*, I wouldn't get nauseous. Fucking saltines, they were the superpower of food.) It had just been nice to know that I'd have an excuse to see Teague and maybe get him to confess what the kids were up to, since Mom and Dads had all agreed to let them play.

"You will be well taken care of," Green said, pulling back and kissing me on the forehead. I looked into his beautiful green eyes and felt the same magnetic pull I'd felt almost three years ago, when I'd thought Adrian would be my first and my one and my only. Funny, I didn't *feel* older and all grown up when I saw Green like that. I was just as young and just as starstruck as I'd been when I'd realized Green and Adrian were lovers, and I wanted them to remain so, and I wanted to be with them too.

Bracken pulled me against his back, and I closed my eyes, stupid in love with him too.

"We'll be fine," I said, still melancholy but also feeling better. I *was* older. I *had* dealt with his absences before. We had a routine now, and I had survived all sorts of shit I hadn't known about then. I wasn't sure if I was going to handle being a parent, but I had *this*.

It would all be good.

BRACKEN
Pop Goes the Weasel

It was *so* not good that Green was gone.

For one thing, he had apparently been unconsciously fixing her acne since she'd first developed it with pregnancy. The day he left, she started to develop blotches. By the next day, they were spots. She was too proud to ask anyone to fix them, so I talked to Lambent and Hallow, and they started taking her arm as they walked by just so they could cure her of spots before she realized she was getting them. Such a small thing, such a human-vanity thing, but it was one more thing she didn't need.

Her ankles started to swell by the time she walked across campus the first time. She complained because her shoes were too tight, and when I realized how swollen she was, I scooped her up and took her to Hallow, ignoring her protests that we had a class and Hallow had his own office hours.

Hallow was as invested as the rest of the hill in making sure she survived this pregnancy. He didn't even wait for us to knock, already very sweetly asking the undergrad in his office to leave as I drew near.

He actually took Cory from my arms in the hallway, then brought us both into the office and sat with her on his lap, monitoring her breathing and heart rate.

"Elevated," he said after a moment. "Cory, your blood pressure is elevated."

"Should exercise help that?" she said hopefully. "I mean, the walking, the swimming—"

"Yes, and I recommend both things. But no running through campus to get to your next class. Let Bracken help you."

She half laughed. "But aren't people going to notice when he's carrying…." She gestured to herself. "You know, *me*?"

"They already think he's freakishly strong," Hallow dismissed, and I tried not to take offense at the word "freakish." "The thing is, Lady Cory, you can't get winded, not with high blood pressure after such a long time off your feet. Walk until you can't, then let Bracken help you. Swim and exercise that way, and make sure you walk, just up to the garden or around the house, on your off days. But don't push it too hard. Your muscles are stretched to the limit right now, and your heart is laboring with the extra people. Please listen to me and take it easy."

I was almost alarmed when she nodded meekly and sighed. It wasn't until later that I realized that, for once, she really *did* plan to follow all of Hallow's instructions without fighting him.

When I broached this with her, knowing my eyebrows were doing that "suspicious Bracken" thing she complained about so much, she looked at me with a little bit of fear chasing across her features.

"Green's gone, Bracken. I'm not going to tempt fate *now*, when he's not in my bed every night to cure me!"

Nevertheless, I told Green at his phone call that night, and watched in relief as he ticked two days off the electronic calendar he'd had installed on all our phones.

The one *good* thing I could tell him was that swimming seemed to be a success. I had not been allowed into the all-women aerobics class, but I *was* allowed to sit in the bleachers on the side. I'd spent much of the time watching her perform the water calisthenics, deciding that the exercises really *were* good for her, and part of the time smelling… sensing… the air.

There was a strange werewolf in that class.

At the end of class, I stayed at my seat and pretended to read while the women grabbed their towels and walked toward the locker room.

The chlorine confused me—strong human chemicals really did interfere with a sidhe's sense of smell—but by the time the women were done filing by, I'd narrowed it down to three or four of them. I wished I could say more, but they'd all been eyeing me with suspicion and irritation, and their hostility *definitely* threw off my sense of smell. Apparently Cory wasn't the only woman who didn't like being seen in her swimsuit.

LaMark and Mario had agreed to break for lunch while she was in the pool, and Renny had the same class. I almost welcomed the time alone, something we didn't get too much of at the hill. I used it to do homework—we had a class in warfare that employed a war game model. For that first day of class, I sat and plotted three ways to defeat Napoleon. Cory said I was awesome, and I told her that if humans had been meant to wage war, they wouldn't have been mortal. The fey could regenerate limbs and come back swinging—they got *serious* about their war games. It was easily my favorite class after the engineering courses that had taught me how to help break into the jail. Not that I missed hurtling through the air and busting a hole through a concrete prison, but it had been nice to use those skills.

Cory's second day of school, I sat quietly on the bleachers near the towels, watching from under my brows as the women pulled out of the pool and migrated to their little spot of property in the pool house.

I liked the women in aqua class. Some of them were *very* large and were exercising in the water to stay healthy because losing weight on land was so very difficult. Some of them had joint problems or chronic pain, and some of them just enjoyed the freedom of the water coupled with the hard workout of water resistance. These women were funny and fit—and the minute Cory arrived, they fussed over her in a way that would have done my mother proud.

Cory, usually exhausted, swollen, disheartened, and in pain, brightened as soon as she put a bloated foot in the water. She didn't work out with any less heart than I'd seen her run, but in the water, her pregnancy weight was supported and her blood pressure stayed steady, and she was much healthier for it.

And I could tell from across the pool that it felt so very good to use her body.

This second day of her workout, I was already planning to ask Green if we could make arrangements with the kelpie to build a pool nearby. If we left his pond alone, the pool could be fed by the springs Green had first called to the hill when he was building. The water could be recycled through a filter, and it could be kept fresh through a combination of baking soda and fey magic if only we could convince the niskies to....

My mind wandered off into the land of invention that had been my gift from Cory's education, and for a moment I neglected my duties as watcher.

Then I took a deep breath, having figured out how to sanitize the water without hurting either human or fey, and broke into excited coughs.

She was *right there*—I could *smell* her—oh my God! I automatically looked up to check on Cory and instead met the surprised brown eyes of a woman with dusky skin and riotously curly hair.

She gasped, taking two steps backward, and I stood up.

"Wait," I said, looking frantically for Cory. "Wait, we don't want to—"

The frightened werewolf turned and darted for the exit, and I kicked off my shoes and darted after her.

We were fortunate that during my woolgathering everybody had left besides myself, Renny, and Cory—and our werewolf. I do not "dart" gracefully, and there was so much equipment around the edge of the pool that every time I tried to use hyperspeed, I tripped over lane lines or buoys or, Goddess help me, the big bucket of foam-rubber belts that bore people up in the water.

As the belts scattered across the pool's surface, Cory came to the edge with the stairs, calling "Bracken! Brack, what's wrong? Dammit, Bracken, stop chasing her, you're freaking her out!"

Renny, seeing what was happening, made a feral growl, and for a moment the strange werewolf and I stared at her in shock as she changed right there in the pool and began to swim toward the stairs herself, a pissed-off cat in a one-piece bathing suit, spitting mad.

"Goddess," I breathed. I looked with panicked eyes at our poor werewolf. "She's gonna be *pissed* when she gets—"

Renny emerged from the water spitting and half-drowned—the brown one-piece hanging from her feline body in twisted, uncomfortable ways—and bounded toward me and our werewolf, lips pulled back from her teeth and claws exposed. I saw her pull a paw back to bat the werewolf, and in the next moment, the poor woman had changed into a big, handsome wolf with dark cocoa fur and a slightly darker ruff. She growled, snarled, and launched herself at Renny in a preemptive move, her bright red bathing suit binding her body like a rope.

A true cat/dog brawl is fearsome to behold, lightning quick, and full of sharp claws and wicked teeth. I did what any sane man would do and vaulted to the top of the lifeguard platform, looking down at the frothing mass of teeth and claws in horror.

Cory had pulled herself up to the second stair, right where the water started to drop from her hips, and was looking at the mess with the same helplessness I was.

"Is she friendly?" Cory called over the noise.

"I think so—she's not tainted."

"Fucking awesome. Get down from there and push them in the pool."

I stayed exactly where I was. "A power bubble would do the same thing," I said, liking my skin where it was better than scattered throughout the pool house.

Cory let out a shocked laugh. "Yeah. Yeah, it would. Sorry!" And with that, she held out her hands and surrounded the two fighting animals with a shield. They were too locked in trying to kill each other to notice when the floor under their feet became power and then shifted. Cory kept them in a levitating cage-match over the deep end of the pool while she pulled herself out. Then, as soon as she got to the top step, I put my bare feet in, scooped her up, and walked to the far corner of the pool room. It would be best to have an escape plan in case this whole thing backfired and those two pissed-off wild animals decided to eat us both.

"Ready?" I asked her.

She nodded and let go of the bubble.

Renny and the werewolf crashed into the water from about ten feet up. They surfaced in their human forms, sputtering and trying desperately to fix their suits over exposed patches of flesh.

Cory and I burst into laughter, and I settled us down on the bleachers where we could listen to them swear.

At that moment, the instructor—a nice woman in her forties who believed in what she was doing—came striding out of the locker room.

"What in the holy hell—"

"They were racing," Cory said, throwing some power into her voice. "We were cheering them on. Sorry we were so loud!"

The woman nodded and simply ceased to see the two women struggling to stand up and fix their clothes and not kill each other while she was there.

"That's okay. Glad to see your friends having some fun. Who won?"

"It was a total tie," Cory said blandly, looking out at both of them. "Wasn't it, Renny? Cerise?"

Renny glowered at Cory, then smiled and nodded at the instructor. Cerise, as her name apparently was, looked at me distrustfully but nodded too.

"Excellent! You ladies should get into the locker room quickly, though, because I'm going to have to lock up in twenty minutes."

Oh, hells. Cory *had* to get changed. It was cold outside, and it was bad enough that she wasn't going to have time to dry her hair.

"We'll lock up," I said, and the poor woman blinked and gave me the keys. I made a mental note to have them returned to her before the end of the hour. I looked to the pool where Renny and Cerise were pulling themselves out, the glares between them icy enough to freeze the pool over. "Right, ladies? We will all leave together."

Some of the fight drained out of Cerise's spine. "I was going to have to talk to you all anyway," she conceded.

"I'm going into the changing room," I said quietly to Cory. "I don't care what you have to do to make me invisible, but I'm not leaving you in there with her until we have this out."

"Yeah, I hear you," Cory agreed, sagging on my lap in what was probably exhaustion. She would get home tonight and sleep for a good ten hours, only getting up to pee and snack on saltines, and I didn't know how to make it better. Every discussion we'd ever had about this semester had boiled down to "Yes, I know it will be difficult, but I will overcome."

She would not overcome without our help.

Without asking, I stood up, taking her with me. I told the obliging professor that she could go now and we'd get her keys back to her later. She nodded, eyes unfocused, and turned toward the exit. In my head I told the sprites that followed us invisibly to make sure the woman didn't get hurt, and then I led the way to the locker room.

Forty minutes later I bore Cory out of the locker room, wishing I'd had a chance to call Teague.

"What do you mean, protect me?" Cerise asked plaintively, and I didn't blame her. "Look, like I told you, I went to a party with a guy and…."

"Things got out of hand," Cory said from my arms. "You drank drugged water and participated in an orgy, but then, during the *real* climax, where you were expected to do something totally heinous, you woke up and didn't do the big heinous thing. But you *did* get bitten by a fucking wolf, and that's still your problem. Have I covered everything?"

She sounded sharp—but then, we all had places to go.

"Yeah," Cerise said, disheartened. "I… it was right before Christmas, and… I mean, I lost my job because I couldn't control it a couple of weeks ago—"

"The week of the full moon," Renny said patiently. Apparently beating the hell out of each other in their alternative forms qualified them for sisterhood now. "I know, it's horrible. It's so hard to control it—it's like trying not to take a poop when you've got the runs. Been there."

Cerise whimpered as we walked out of the pool house, and I turned behind me and locked the outer door. With a thought the sprites appeared before me, tiny humanoids lit from within and sporting all sorts of animal and insect variations between them. The three who had been following me since birth were all female, all combinations of human and field mouse, and all very obliging. They landed in my hand, chattered briefly, and then took the keys and disappeared.

I looked up to see Cerise holding her hand to her mouth.

"They're beautiful," she said, her big velvet eyes meeting mine without a trace of suspicion or anger.

"They are," I said, smiling a bit, then adjusted Cory so I had a better grip on her. She *was* heavier, it was true, but I could still carry her easily if I could balance her first.

"If I let you help me out," she said after a couple of footsteps, during which the extent of her despair seeped in, "what will you make me do?"

Cerise had gone to a party with her boyfriend and woken up to a nightmare. She'd managed to take off, but her boyfriend had disappeared. She'd been stuck alone for the holidays, enduring the change alone, with nobody to explain it, and she'd lost her job as a result.

She'd come to school because it was paid for, and because when nothing else made sense, she understood how school worked, until she looked up from her PE class and saw me.

"Nothing," Cory said. "We would like some information—that shit you saw the night you were changed has to be stopped. But other than that? Help out when you can. Teague's your pack leader. He'll be happy to show you the ropes. But right now…. Here, Brack, put me down."

"No," I said, not sorry even a little. "Continue on."

Cory sighed and didn't fight. That was the biggest reason I didn't think I should set her down. "Okay, fine. You need protection, Cerise. If she finds out about you, she'll come after you—and she doesn't care if she has to convert you or kill you. She's easy that way."

As we walked across the campus, Mario, Nicky, and LaMark came trotting up to meet us. LaMark had a travel mug of hot chocolate for Cory, and Nicky and Mario had sandwiches for the rest of us. Renny took hers—mostly roast beef and pickles—and gave half to Cerise.

Who ate it no questions asked, as though she hadn't had a full stomach for a week or so.

"Mario?" I asked, knowing I had to take Cory to the library to nap soon. "We need you and LaMark to brief her. And someone needs to call Teague. He can come down and talk to her and, I don't know, escort her up the hill, or—"

"On it, chief," Mario said smartly. LaMark nodded a little too, mostly in Cerise's direction.

"We'll take care of you," he said quietly. "We probably don't need Teague down here right now. Can you follow us home?"

Cerise nodded through her sandwich. "I've sorta been living in my car," she said. "No job, no rent, no nothing."

"Goddess," Cory swore. "So vulnerable. Look, we'll take care of you. Place to stay, way to get your shit together, whole nine yards. But you need to stay with these guys until we get you home, okay?"

Cerise nodded, shoving the last of the sandwich in her mouth. "I… I kept driving," she said softly. "Do you guys live up near Auburn?"

We all grunted an affirmative, and she went on.

"I *felt* something up there. The other night, right before I ran out of gas, I saw this glow, but I ran out of gas and had to coast back down the hill." She wiped her eyes. "Thanks for not killing me when you could have."

"Not a problem," Cory said genially.

As Nicky and Renny followed us to the library, I heard them talking.

"Did you see?" Nicky asked quietly.

"I'm not saying anything," Renny said stubbornly.

"But… but they're planning on…."

I turned around and pinned them with a glare. "They're planning on what?" I asked, suddenly very wary.

Nicky shook his head. "Nothing. You know, just the standard recruiting thing. Nothing wrong. Just, you know, let's get Cory to the library, okay?"

I should have known better.

But Cory was so weak, so tired, and the excitement with the fight and the shield had only made it worse.

But I should have known—Nicky was lying to me, and Renny was hiding, and Teague had gotten a taste of what it was like to have the power to protect what he loved. However it all fell out, I had some blame because I turned away from that feeling in my gut that they were holding out on me and turned my attention inward to my wife and children. I have thought since that this is how the world has fallen to hell when it is mostly populated by good men.

Good men are forced to make their worlds small in order to protect their families.

Bad men and women have no qualms about reaping destruction from the inattention of good men.

GREEN
Afar

NICKY'S EX-LOVER looked sad and distraught, and Green could find no way to make that better.

Green and Eric both owned properties in a coalition of small oil companies that employed earth-friendly practices. They had to attend a board meeting at the beginning of every year to check in on the state of their holdings, and in the past, meeting up like this had proved both profitable and pleasurable for both of them.

Two years ago, when Nicky had been at his lowest and most depressed from having his life so rudely rearranged by magic mating practices and having his sexuality thrown into some harsh light as well, Green had brought Eric home—and Nicky had discovered that, apart from Green and Cory, he had a sex life and an appeal all his own.

Green and Cory had encouraged the relationship, but long-distance lovers are difficult at best. And when one of the lovers is involved in a ménage on the other end of the jetway, well, that made things even more difficult.

As the rest of the businessmen filed out of a conference room with a stellar view of the Austin, Texas skyline, Green touched Eric's elbow and pulled him aside.

"I'm so sorry," he said without preamble. "We had no idea Nicky was going to call it quits until…."

Eric shook his head, waving away Green's apologies with grace. "No. No, I… I mean, we had a great couple of weeks in the summer, but I guess when he got home, everything had fallen apart, and suddenly… suddenly I realized, you know?"

"What?" Green asked, knowing the answer but hoping it would do Eric good to say it.

"He's yours," Eric said, twitching his mouth into a sad little smile. "He's always been yours and Cory's, but… but he's Bracken's too, and… just, I thought he could be mine, but he couldn't."

Eric looked so dejected.

Green had been training journeyman elves to take some of his duties in healing and solace. Being away from his family had seemed especially hard during Cory's gestation—he'd wanted to be the one close to her, but more often than not, Bracken or even Nicky had needed to bear the weight.

But here, with an old friend looking heartbroken, Green felt his sexual vocation pulling at him again—not as an onerous duty, but as a calling and a joy.

"Eric?" Green said, looping an arm around the young werecoyote's shoulders.

"Green?" Eric asked hopefully, his narrow, boyish face appealingly alight.

"Would you like some comfort tonight?"

A couple of years ago, that was how one of the most remarkable nights of Green's life had started. This night wouldn't even come close, not in sexuality or wonder, but Green was fine with that.

This would be the night he'd apologize for stealing Nicky from the world, and the night his body would reward him with joy in his calling once again.

LATER—AFTER DINNER and conversation, flirting and innuendo, and finally, at Eric's lovely condo, consummation—Green lay with Eric's head pillowed on his chest and called home.

Bracken answered, and because he was Bracken and spoke with more passion than linearity, the entire werewolf debacle fell into Green's lap without a "Hi" or "how are you."

By the time he was done, Green didn't need a "Hi" or "how are you."

He sat up in bed, pulling Eric's lean and wiry body with him because he enjoyed the touch of those tight male muscles under his hand. Eric lay still, taking in Green's terse replies with wide gray eyes, and Green was grateful. He would talk to Arturo after Bracken, but having Eric there— someone who was naturally submissive but enjoyed establishing a safe territory—gave him a way to ground his panicked thoughts.

Cory was the last voice on the phone, and she sounded drifty and close to sleep.

"So how's the new recruit doing?" he asked, hoping she could reassure him.

"Fine, I guess," Cory said softly. "Teague's been talking to her most of the afternoon, along with the younger shape-shifters and Marcus and Phillip. I mean, I told them not to inundate her—she's pretty shaken up—but Grace found her a room and stuff, and…." Cory yawned. "She had most of her clothes with her. She's moved in, right?"

Oh, of all the things his beloved usually was, sleepy and incurious were not among them.

"How are you doing?" he asked. "Any bleeding?"

"Bracken carried me around most of the day," she protested, laughing. "I'm all fine, Green." Her voice dropped. "Missing you. Remember the last time you and Eric were in bed and me and Bracken were—"

Green laughed. "Yes, my love. Give my regards to Twilight, yes?"

She chuckled lowly. Twilight, the dark-purple-skinned elf that Green had brought home after that adventure, had actually been cured as a result of Cory's newfound power. It had been one of the first times she'd ever changed the shape of the world with sex, and for a moment he wondered how they could have ever taken that for granted.

"I will," she promised and then yawned. "Look," she mumbled, "I have this feeling… you know, how Teague said he'd tell half of us about stuff?"

Green grunted. "Oh yeah, I remember."

"I don't think he's telling half of us even half of what he's doing."

Green's eyes popped open. "Who *is* he telling?"

"Mm…." For a moment he feared she'd fallen asleep. "Nicky. And Max. Jacky, of course. Lambent. Maybe Kyle."

"I need to talk to Arturo again," Green said, feeling a little panicked. "I need—"

"She's asleep," Arturo said darkly. "And I've had about enough of this school bullshit."

"You ask her," Green said wretchedly. "*You* ask her if she's willing to give up the one dream she had before Adrian—before *any* of us."

"But it's not giving up, it's postponing—"

"Until when? Until she's done breastfeeding? Until the babies are old enough to walk? They don't go to human school—when does she leave them during the day? What if they're freakishly powerful, Arturo, and she's the only being on the hill who can calm a tantrum? What if we need her to actually leave the hill, because she *knows* things about business and law and history that even *I'm* fuzzy on at this point? The one thing she's *ever* asked of us, ever, is that she finish her education. And she's one lousy semester away."

The silence hung heavy between the two of them, and Arturo sighed first.

"I hate to see her this miserable," he confessed stonily.

"Join the fuckin' club," Green snarled, prompting Eric to sit up and look at him curiously.

"Yes, brother, but you're not seeing her this way," Arturo countered. "You're off doing other things, and I get it, I do, but there is still a war on. We were damned lucky it was one escaped werewolf instead of twenty tainted ones."

Green took a deep breath and let spill the one business matter that had frightened him the most this trip.

"Someone is trying to buy our land," he said, hating himself for letting his voice fracture. It had been a low, persistent hum of annoyance for the past year, one he had let no one in on, one he'd only truly come to recognize recently himself.

"Well, say *no!*" Arturo burst out, causing Green to roll his eyes.

"Yes, Arturo, that idea completely escaped me. I shall just tell the United States Government that their attempts to procure my land to add to the national forest acreage are ill-advised."

"But the government can't force you—"

"They can if I don't dot my fuckin' i's, now can't they? And that's not the worst part."

"Please. By all means, hit me with it," Arturo said. Green could hear how stunned he was from two thousand miles away.

"The worst part is it's a cover. The senator writing me isn't part of any committee related to buying land. Someone has the man in his pocket, and I suspect the land would be purchased and then sold at auction to our prince with the deep pockets, don't you?"

"Has this been happening around us?" Arturo asked, proving once again that he was both smart and canny.

"No," Green said with satisfaction. "No, because while everybody was playing up in Redding this summer, I was going personally to all of our neighbors and making them a better offer. Now Deep Pockets has to deal with *me*, and *only* me, and our land has expanded enough to take in all of the werewolves when this war is over."

"It's like you knew this was coming," Arturo said with admiration.

"If I knew it was bloody coming, don't you think I would have sent an assassin into this bitch's bed a year and a fucking half ago?" Green snarled.

There was silence on the other end of the line. Then, to his shock, Arturo laughed.

"What?" Green pushed hair back from his face, feeling sullen.

"Nothing, leader. Just… I forget. We've been so domestic and happy for the last couple of years. You forget that it's always a fight, you know?"

Green grunted. "I'm sort of with Cory. It would be lovely if we could at least bear our children in peace."

"Yeah," Arturo sighed. "Was there anything else?"

"Teague."

"He's planning something." Arturo sounded pleased, as though he'd been expecting this.

"So…." Green flailed with is free hand. "Stop him!"

The silence on the other end of the line sounded definitely puzzled. "I would do that why?" Arturo asked.

Green met Eric's eyes and shook his head. Holding his hand over the phone, he muttered, "You got off so easy. You could have been part of this madhouse, and you left just in time."

Eric stood up and stretched, tight and lithe as only a coyote could be. While Green still had the phone to his ear, Eric leaned over and stroked his cheek.

"I'll go get us a bottle of wine," he whispered in Green's free ear. "You and I can drink it while we plan to get you home early."

Green nodded at him with naked gratitude and talked into the phone. "Because he needs *backup*," Green ground out. "Because launching an offensive is a major ordeal, and he's going to need the vampires and the elves—"

"He pretty much has everyone but me and Grace," Arturo said, sounding disgruntled. "Apparently we've just aged out of the cool kids' group."

Green grunted. "Remember last year—"

"When he couldn't grab his own damned box of Oreos? Yeah, Green, I remember. But he's grown into his potential, and right now his potential is to go out and save our asses while we gather around our queen."

"I've played chess for over a thousand years," Green snapped. "The knight's gambit doesn't always turn out so great for the knight—do you remember that, Arturo?"

"Yeah, but it turns out absolutely *awesome* for the fucking queen, and right now she's the one with the swollen ankles and the high blood pressure that she's trying not to let anyone tell you about."

Bracken had already told him—and if Cory didn't know that, she really was slipping. Green's head hurt.

"Don't let him do anything until I get back," he ordered, hoping he was being absolutely clear. He used to be able to handle autocracy better than this, he *knew* it.

"I will *ask* him," Arturo said, proving that Green was even worse than he thought. "But Green, if he's got a way to end this war, I don't want to stand in his way."

"End the war, wonderful," Green snarled. "But we *don't* sacrifice people unnecessarily, and we *don't* leave our queen unguarded. She almost *died* keeping that stubborn Irish motherfucker alive this summer. We had better make sure he survives the next few months."

"Yes, leader," Arturo said formally. Green was tempted to feel like shit for pushing the leadership thing, but then Arturo threw one more wrench into his night.

"And Hallow says three."

Green crossed his eyes. "But the gestational period—"

"Ten and a half months, yes. But they can survive early. Hallow says she can't make it past nine and a half."

Green tried to keep his heart beating evenly in his chest. "When I get home, I'll talk to her about school," he said, feeling defeated. "But no promises."

"But the children—"

"Will come in their own time," Green said. "If they need to come early, her body will make that happen. But we can't force her to have them—I know they can in the human world, but those medicines will make her sick. You know what happens if she takes so much as a Tylenol, Arturo. And if it hurt the fetuses, she would never forgive herself."

He heard a gentle, repeated thunk.

"Are you beating your head against the table?" Green asked, alarmed.

"The wall."

Green pinched the bridge of his nose, then reached for the glass of wine Eric was offering. No, he didn't enjoy the alcoholic effects the way humans did, but as Eric did, apparently, he found the taste soothing and… civilized.

"Let me rework my schedule one more time," he said, wondering how in heaven's name he was going to appear in—where was it?—Colorado on one day and back in California the next. "I don't like being away from home any more than you like having me gone."

The thunking noise stopped, and Nicky picked up.

"Green?"

"Yes, Nicky?"

"You know, Renny and I are going to school too. Jacky too. You'll have help—we just have to get through this first."

Green glanced at Eric, who was looking away. Yes, Eric could hear Nicky's voice over the phone. Yes, it hurt.

"So, you're over there with Eric and he's listening, right?" Nicky's voice trembled for a moment, and for the first time Green got an inkling of what it might have cost him to give up a lover of his own.

"Yes, Dominic," Green said gently. "Yes, he is."

"How's he look?"

Green reached out and lifted Eric's chin up with his forefinger. "He's beautiful, as always," he said. "But he's still hurt."

Eric's gray eyes shifted away. "Always, with you guys," he said softly. "It's always the truth."

"Well, you know. Me too," Nicky said, his voice showing how much. Then he snapped right into the Nicky who had kept them all functioning for the past few months. "Tell him I miss him. And don't worry too much about what Teague's got planned. It's just recon right now, no assault."

"Tell him not to move until I get back," Green urged, but Nicky had already passed the phone to Bracken.

"This was reassuring," Green said acidly into the phone.

"If you meant for us to blow sunshine up your ass, well, you took the funnel with you," Bracken snapped. "Do your business, we know it's important. Know we miss you, keep yourself safe."

"Talk to you tomorrow," Green finished, and Bracken grunted good-bye before ending the call.

Green downed the glass of wine in his hand as though he really *could* get drunk.

Eric's hand between his shoulder blades soothed him in ways he didn't think possible. "Feel better?" he asked sweetly. "I've got more superexpensive wine, if that will help."

Green grinned at him and tapped his freckled nose. "I'll just bet you do," he said, trying to keep his humor. "But now for the hard part."

"How to get home early?" Eric asked. He reached behind him for the bottle and refilled both their glasses. "That's easy. You let me attend those meetings in your stead. No voting power, but I can be your eyes and ears—your representation. We've done it before."

Green grunted. "Yes, before you had your own oil empire, Eric. Why would you want—"

Eric sighed and rested his cheek against his knees. "My father died last year," he said, out of the blue.

Green regarded him, completely neutral. Eric's father had been an oil magnate who'd disowned his only son for being gay. Green had found Eric, starved and half-dead of disease, and had linked him with the werecoyotes and given him an education and the backing to execute his revenge.

Three years ago, he'd been able to buy his father out—and go visit his mother and his little sisters again.

Green was not exactly sure how his father's death would have affected the young man, not after so much bad blood.

Eric laughed bitterly. "Look—I *could* be a bastard because my lover, who was yours to begin with and pretty much out on loan, decided that his real loyalty began and ended with family. Or I could remember that you're my family too. You were my father more than my real father, Green. You were my mentor and my supporter and my cheerleader. Yeah, I miss Nicky, but he's not dead." Eric leaned his head against Green's bare shoulder and swallowed. "You're trying to be a dad, Green. Don't you see? If anyone deserves children—flesh and blood children—it's you and Cory and Bracken. Give us a day to prep for those meetings. Two. We'll drink wine and order in, and I can have my very own healing elf to myself, as well as a damned fine business mind to learn from, and in two days you can go back to your loved ones and let me go to the meetings in your stead. Is that a deal?"

Green leaned his temple against Eric's.

"That's a deal," he said, his eyes burning. He hadn't wanted to admit it, hadn't wanted anyone at home to see, but he'd been panicked too. So overwhelming—how was anyone to have the answers when the world had gone bloody mad? "You know that day I saw you in the square? Bought you a cup of coffee?"

"Offered me a life?" Eric finished, smiling slightly.

"So much bloody reward for one act of kindness, mate. I'm not sure I deserve it."

Eric pressed his mouth against Green's, swept in his tongue, tasted the wine and the frustration, the fear and the relief.

"I am," Eric whispered. "Nicky is. It's why he left. So he could be part of something bigger. This is *my* chance."

"It's all yours," Green whispered back.

Eric deepened the kiss, and Green gave to him because Nicky couldn't. For a moment he didn't hear the clock ticking the seconds that would send him home.

TEAGUE
Tactical Error

TEAGUE LOOKED at Cerise again and tried to determine what was off about her.

He'd had the vampires blood her, more than one, and the consensus was that her blood really was untainted. He'd fed her angel blood and Lambent blood, and the results had been… well, she said her hair had grown three inches overnight, but he was going to take that at face value.

He'd had Jacky and Nicky check into her story, and they'd found eviction notices and unpaid bills and even the record of her hiring and firing from the local chain restaurant.

Teague even knew that she'd failed her English 120 B class once and had needed to take it again.

But there was something… something not….

"You smell funny," he said, the third night he'd gone in to interview her. Unlike Iris, they hadn't put her in the vampire vault—but Teague had asked Lambent to set fey guards on her, the tiny ones that Teague never knew were there.

Cerise looked at him blankly. "Funny? Like… birthday cake or a clown party funny? Eau de chocolate ice cream?"

Teague grimaced. The problem was, he *liked* Cerise. Maybe it was because she was Dominican, and her accent reminded him a little of Katy's. Maybe it was because she seemed so much like Cory, so much like him and Katy—working hard for a better life, not assuming it would be given. She'd gotten a tough break and had lived in her car and kept going to school. He recognized that drive, not just in Cory but in his own husband.

But just because he empathized with her didn't mean he *trusted* her, or the information she seemed to have delivered right to their doorstep.

Too neat, too pretty, too wrapped up in a bow.

Too important to resist.

"No," Teague muttered, wishing Cory was there to help him deal with her. But the whole point of this moment was to leave Cory alone to gestate—to fucking sleep and rest her exhausted body.

He'd seen her ankles after a few days of walking around at school; they were really freaking him out.

"Look," he said after a moment of pacing Cerise's room. She'd been driven to school for the last two days—she had four days of classes instead of just two—and Teague and Jacky had been her guard dogs for the off days. Connor, Cami, and Dylan also helped since they had M-W-F classes as well. He was getting damned good at drawing complicated schedules, when what he wanted to be was damned good at killing elf bitches who were fucking with his home.

"Look, what?" she asked—not even trying to be a smartass, just honestly confused.

"Look, I've got an idea!" he said, not sure where it had come from. "You're Catholic, right?"

"Yeah, sure."

"You ever prayed to a guardian angel?"

She had naturally skeptical eyebrows. He liked that—if he hadn't been bonded, she would have been just his type. As it was, he had hopes that one of the very few straight or bi guys who ended up at Green's might actually have some mate potential here, because she was resourceful, funny, and tough.

But first he had to make sure she wasn't full of shit.

She raised one of those naturally skeptical eyebrows, and Teague looked at Max, who was slouched in the far corner of the room.

Max still hadn't admitted there were *actual angels* living in the Goddess's grove, so he looked blandly back. Teague didn't see why that should be any different than pansy-shaped people who opened the trapdoor for him, so he nodded maniacally.

"Yeah," Cerise said slowly, crossing her arms in front of her. "I prayed to a guardian angel, why?"

"How'd you like to meet one?"

It was February, so even though there was still snow on the ground in the Sierra Foothills, there was also a slightly warmer promise of spring.

Teague stood in the climate-controlled Goddess grove, perfectly warm in a hooded sweatshirt and jeans, and called to the angels in the treetops.

"Shep? Jefi? You guys up there?"

Those guys were *always* up there. Apparently they had waited *four millennia* to fall down to earth, live in Green's treetops, and fuck like rabbits.

Yeah, sure, nobody wanted to *say* "fuck like rabbits" when you were talking about angels of the Lord who had sort of deserted their posts, but Teague knew what those guys were doing up there in their open-sky tree house most days, and he knew it wasn't planting daisies.

Which was fine—Teague was getting laid plenty himself—but he wasn't going to pretend that what Shep and Jefi had going on with their musical angel moans and poetic angel sighs was not the exact same deal Teague had going on when he banged Jacky from behind as Jacky had his face buried between Katy's thighs.

Good shit, yeah, and there were times when it was even holy, but unless those angels were coming silver and gold tinsel, Teague was pretty sure the whole reason they'd crashed into Green's party was to party like the people did.

So they got to be interrupted just as often as Teague and Jack and Katy did, and that was pretty damned often if you included Jack and Katy going to work and Teague doing everything from auto maintenance to listening for when Cory went for a walk so he could be on designated-friend walking duty to make sure that all went well. Right now it was designated-friend waddling duty, and often she needed to lean on Renny's feline shoulders to finish her short loop around the hill. It hurt him to see her so slow, but it didn't surprise him. She'd been fond of throwing her little body around as though it weren't no big thing, but Teague had been old enough when he'd been bitten to know that eventually your body got you back for shit like that.

In the garden, Teague waited for a moment until he heard… oh yeah. Shep had a sort of sonorous groan when he was coming, like a french horn climaxing in a symphony.

And there, right there… Jefi's sigh, like bells.

Okay, wait to make sure they're done… yes. The low laughter. Mmhm. Well, Teague really was bonded to his mates, but trying to match *his* postcoital sounds to Shep and Jefi's was making him *really want* his mates. In the hard-cocked way that left him even more impatient than usual. Next to him, Max made an uncomfortable sound that told Teague he wasn't the only one—and unlike Teague, Max wasn't bonded for shit. Apparently angel sex didn't subscribe to heteronormative values any more than it obeyed Goddess-get-mating strictures.

"Are they doing what I think they're doing?" Cerise asked, her voice as earthy as it was curious.

"Oh, Shep—do you hear? There's humans in the garden again." Jefischa sounded very excited, although people must come to the garden all the time.

"No," Shep corrected, because he *was* an officious fucker. "One of them is a werecat, one is a werewolf, and the other one is… well, she's a werewolf, but…."

Teague heard some rustling, followed by that powerful, near-silent whoosh-whoosh-whoosh as the angels swept downward. Teague was grateful they'd both put on jeans, but their bare torsos testified that yes, they really *had* been sent down from heaven to fuck like lemmings.

Well, Teague had always guessed sex was sublime with the right person. Now he had his proof.

"So, yeah, guys," Teague said, nodding to both of them. "Max and me want to know exactly what she is."

"She's a werewolf," Shep said, squinting at her.

Cerise stared back, her mouth parted a little. "Holy God."

"No, my friend," Shep said patiently. "We were once agents of our Lord, and then we fell."

Jefischa's laughter had a positively dirty ring to it. "Falling was the best part."

Cerise's big, black-fringed brown eyes were almost Looney-Tunes big.

"They're totally freaking her out," Max pronounced. "Great idea, Teague, now she'll be a basket case."

"No," Teague admonished. "Look, they already know there's something going on with her—"

"I told you the truth!" Cerise protested. Teague patted her shoulder almost unconsciously.

"That you know," he said. "This woman has set traps with people before. Guys? You remember how awful it was when Iris exploded?"

The angels had been nearly inconsolable. Green had needed to send people—elves, shape-shifters, vampires, only the purest of heart would do—to hold them and stroke their hands until the psychic imprint of Iris Masterson's death had faded.

"Yes," Jefi said soberly, nodding. "You'd like very much for this one not to explode."

Teague smiled. "That's pretty much why I'm here."

Shepherd was all business. "Come here, child," he commanded. Cerise ventured forward tentatively, her arm outstretched.

"Can I touch…."

"No," Shepherd apologized, and just as her hand would have made contact, the feathers seemed to part and jump away from her touch. "The only one who comes close is your little Goddess, and we're not sure why. But I would like to simply hold your hand, if that is acceptable?"

"Yeah," Cerise said, humbled. "Sure. Why not. Vampires in the basement, angels in the garden, fuckin' elves and were-*everything* in between." She looked over her shoulder at Teague, almost accusing him. "Do you know a vampire cooked me dinner last night? She told me to tell her if it needed more garlic." Cerise's laugh was semihysterical. *"Garlic!"*

Oh, no. Teague had dealt with enough tough, self-sufficient women to know when a breakdown was imminent.

"Max, uh, you wouldn't want to get my wife, would you?"

Behind them the trapdoor opened, and for a moment Teague thought maybe some sort of mate telepathy had kicked in and it really *was* Katy.

Then Cory called down the steps, her voice shrill and irritated, "See? I got to the top, Bracken. On my own power. It's a fucking miracle. Should I take my underwear off now and show them to you? I'd better be fucking careful or they'll catch wind and I'll parachute away!"

Then she looked up and met the horrified eyes of her audience.

"Oh. Fucking awesome." Her freckled face flushed. "None of you get to see my underwear."

"Thank God," Teague said, honestly and sincerely grateful. He walked forward and offered his arm. "Now sit down before you pass out."

She glared at him. "Shut up. What are you—" She looked around and did a mental head count. "—five conspiring about today?"

Teague put his hand on the small of her back and escorted her to the bench in spite of her reluctance. God. Goddess. Whatever. Her face was pale under her flush, and she had bags under her eyes he could ship to Tahiti.

"There is no conspiracy here, my lady," he said primly. She rolled her eyes.

"Don't bullshit me. Please. I am in no mood for bullshit."

"Then you should stay out of the fields to the south," Jefischa said, nodding. "They have a *lot* of cows."

Cory smiled at him, obviously charmed in spite of her irritation. "Thank you, Jefi. I'll be sure to avoid cows at all costs." Her eyes narrowed at Teague. "And perfidious best friends—"

"Enforcers," Teague said evenly. "In this matter, I'm an enforcer."

She rolled her eyes, and even *he* felt how wrong that was. "Whatever. What is it we're doing here?"

Well, that was actually easy to answer. "We're having the angels look for any, uhm, time bombs. You know, like—"

Cory's mouth thinned. The memory was probably as unpleasant for her as it was for the angels. "Iris," she muttered. Yeah—only Cory and Green had been in the room, but the legend of the cleanup had permeated the hill. Bad. Just... bad. "So, any luck?"

Shepherd hmmed in his throat. "There's... uhm, a tick under her skin."

They all stared at Cerise as her eyes widened. She opened her mouth and gasped a few times, then scared the hell out of everybody by screaming, waving her arms, and crawling up Shepherd's back squealing, "Get it off get it off get it off!"

Teague, Cory, and Max looked at each other in surprise and then burst into horrified laughter as they watched Shepherd try—with dignity—to divest himself of a screaming, spazzing girl, so human in that moment she didn't even think to turn into a wolf.

"Little Goddess," Shepherd asked, the restraint never leaving his voice, "a little help, please...."

"Of course," Cory gasped between whoops of laughter. "Not a problem." Without even standing up, she held out her hand and engulfed Cerise in a blue power bubble, which detached itself from Shepherd. Then Cory held the girl about twelve feet off the ground and waited for her to notice that she was, once again, locked in a force field.

It took about five minutes, and she only stopped spazzing because she exhausted herself.

In the meantime, everybody on the ground looked at her in fascination as she ran around in circles, her hands grasping at skin and ripping through hair as she screamed "Get it off, get it off, get it off!"

"Oh, hey," Cory said after a moment. "Look. Through the shield. Do you see it? In her bicep?"

Teague looked and knew his eyes widened. "Oh, wow. Max?"

"Yeah—it's purple. Like, the shield shows it… is that under her skin?"

"Yes," Shepherd said mournfully. He was sitting on the ground between Jefi's knees as Jefi groomed his hair and feathers gently, soothing the scratches on his face and neck with gentle fingers. "That is the tick."

It was, in fact, a bite mark. "So that's how elf-bitch did it," Teague murmured. "The wolf who bit her must have just fed from elf-bitch. Not like Connor, who got a werewolf bite and got away. I'd hazard that this wolf had just freshly re-upped. Just enough to leave a little bit of whatserface lodged in her flesh."

Cory squinted at the wound through the bubble. At this point, Cerise had collapsed into a whimpering tick-phobic heap on the bottom of the shield.

"Okay, so we know it's there, but it doesn't seem to have any destructive properties—it's not a hook or a bomb like Iris had. It's not driving her insane. What is it doing?"

As Cory started to lower the shield bubble slowly, so as not to frighten its inhabitant, Max began to growl. When Teague looked at him, his upper lip was pulled back, and he was panting with his tongue out like a cat.

Teague allowed some of his wolf out and growled back.

Max shot up into the air, spitting, then landed at a crouch. It wasn't until his knees hit the ground that he remembered who he was and what he was trying to do. He stood up fluidly and didn't even brush at his clothes, just casually pretended it had never happened.

"It's a bug," he said shortly. "A supernatural bug. Whether she means to or not, that thing is spying on us."

Teague pondered. "That would be a shitty bug," he said after a moment. "It would be like the vampire bite for beginners, don't you think? Before telepathy kicks in. You know—all emotions, no clear picture of what's going on in her head or around her?"

Max studied his cuticles. "I don't know. It's not really just a *dog* bite, you know? It's more of an… an *elf* bite. I say it's a bug."

Teague took a few paces forward, rubbed the base of his skull, then turned around and paced back. He ignored Cory, who was still sitting on the bench and apparently laughing at him and Max through her hand, because fuck that, this was important.

"I say it's something else," he pondered. "'Cause it's blood. And this bitch has been using blood magic on us almost from the beginning. It's like, I don't know. It's how the elf bitch finally broke into the hill—that thing on her arm."

"But why so elaborate?" Cory mused. "Why not just attack us at school?"

Teague looked at her and smiled. She was so unassuming, but she'd gotten very used to being the center of the world. "Because you're not the point, Miss Universe. Green's the point. This whole thing has been about taking over his hill. She sees you and Brack as tools. She knew you'd take Cerise in—she'd seen you do it before with the happiness triplets and the jailbreak—so she sent something in this way. I say Cerise is maybe her way of getting through the shields."

When Cory glared at the poor woman through the power bubble, Cerise was frightened enough to back into the bubble, hackles rising like a newly born beta pup.

"I didn't mean to!" she protested, her voice not muffled in the least, proving she'd heard the entire conversation. "Please don't chop my arm off or anything. I swear I didn't mean to!"

Cory took a deep breath and looked down, rubbing the back of her neck. Very, very carefully she lowered the shield bubble.

"I'm not going to hurt you," she said, sounding oh-so-weary. "I just need to fix the shields. Right now they're based on tainted blood, but if we let you in, and you've got that blood mark under your skin, I don't know how to… to tweak that." She looked down at her burgeoning body and then looked up at Teague apologetically. "My, uh, usual way of charging to rework our defenses is right out."

Teague shook his head. "This shouldn't all be on your shoulders—"

"That's my job!" she laughed, and the part of him that was a friend cracked wide open.

"*Bullshit*," he snapped. "Bull. Shit. No. Just… *no!*" He paused, scrubbing at his face through his stubble, hoping for better words as she regarded him kindly.

"Teague, it's just the way it is. I'm the weapon. I've been the weapon since I came here—it's how you and I got to be friends. I can't afford to be weak now that we're under attack, and you know it!"

Max let out a sound between a "Hell no!" and a "Mreowl!" and Teague whirled to face her. "Your weaponry is *not* the sum total of your value to this hill, my lady," he growled.

Cory waved him off, but he was so angry that his vision went red and he felt his snout elongate. It took a conscious effort—and a heavy-duty one at that—to force himself not to go hauling off into the wild blue decimating the rabbit population.

"Cerise, honey," she said, her voice soothing, "I'm going to drop the shield. *You* are not in trouble in any way, do you understand? We just need to figure out what to do about the broken blood seal, okay? Not your fault. You found us. You needed to. Nobody's ever gotten in trouble for coming to us when they didn't mean any harm."

Cerise nodded at her, her lower lip trembling. Cory looked at Teague and Max as though expecting something, then shook her head. "I so miss Green," she muttered. With that she dropped the shields and held out her arms.

"C'mere, bunny," she said kindly. "C'mere."

Cerise threw herself at Cory, crying softly. "Get it off," she whimpered. "He said it was a tick… get it off…."

"Shh…." Cory stroked her hair. "He just meant it's under your skin, precious. Don't worry. We're going to talk to the vampires and feed you some more angel and elf blood and see if we can't just sort of bleed it away, okay? You know, your blood replaces itself every six weeks. What's it been, three?"

Cerise nodded, full lower lip quivering. "I don't want bad things here, Lady. You've been so nice to me, and I'm so scared."

To Teague's horror, Cory's eyes grew bright. "It's okay, really. We're all scared. But we're stronger together, right? You stay here and huddle under Shepherd's wings—he's very protective, you know. If anything bad goes down, he'll keep you safe."

Shepherd nodded as though he hadn't thought of any other duty. Well, from what Teague had seen, he really hadn't.

With murmuring little noises, maybe learned, maybe instinctive, Shepherd moved in, his naked torso pale and beautiful and sexual in a way that would probably have horrified him. He gathered Cerise into his arms and then nodded Jefi over. Without a word exchanged, Jefischa took over the cuddle duty, and Shepherd turned to Cory and Teague.

"My lady?"

Cory smiled—but even though she obviously put her whole heart into her smile, Teague could tell she was getting tired. When he threw a look over his shoulder, Max nodded and disappeared down the stairs. Yeah, it was time to pull in the big guns.

"My lord angel," she said playfully—but also with greatest sincerity, "what can I do for you?"

"I've given my blood freely to help you fight this terrible battle, and I would give even more to preserve this place."

Cory's lips parted softly—oh, yes. She was taking this *very* seriously. "We're very grateful. Please let us know if you are giving too much. Jefischa as well."

Shepherd nodded. "It's just that, until this moment, I had never… *touched* what we were fighting. And now that I have?"

"Yes?" Cory said eagerly, leaning forward in a way that *had* to be cramping her stomach.

"I recognize it, but… it's masked somehow. There is something very old and very evil and very powerful masking that blood from our gaze. But now that I know what I'm… tasting, I think I can tell you where it is."

"And I can tell you why it's hidden," Teague said, dancing in his excitement. "*That's* why I brought her out here, my lady. She had something *very* interesting to report, and I needed to make sure the intel was good."

Cory leaned back and shifted, a look of pain crossing her face. She put one hand behind her to brace herself and then pushed up from the bench, standing and stretching when she reached her feet. Teague realized with a pang that the granite bench—the one with Adrian's likeness on it that she and the elves loved so much—was probably hell on her back. She must have been coming out here for some peace, and he'd thrown work at her instead.

"So," she urged, leaning forward on one foot and rounding her shoulders, pushing out. "Spill! What would hide that power from us? What did she see?"

Teague reached out and touched the small of her back, fixing her form. "You'll throw it out otherwise," he cautioned. Then—"Okay, so the thing is, Cerise there said she and her boyfriend went out to a party up in Colfax. It was a big deal, right? Getting out of Sacramento, whatever. So to *her* it's a bunch of driving out to nowhere, every road is acres of turns, she doesn't remember any names. *But* they get to the place, and it's like we thought—sort of a big mansion, one of those places bought before the crash that people couldn't keep up on the payments for. Makes sense, right? Except there had been *previous* squatters there—she said she could tell, because there were a couple of buildings that looked like munitions storage. Concrete, lots of steel—no place you'd put a cow in, right?"

Cory shifted her feet, this time stretching out her chest. "Right," she grunted.

"Anyway, she said that one of the outbuildings there was a little chapel—or that's what it looked like from a couple hundred yards out. Anyway, before everyone drank the magic wine and shit, these guys— what'd you call 'em, Cerise?"

"Matched set," Cerise mumbled from Jefi's chest. "They were like… like Bracken, you know? But two of them—twins."

Cory raised her eyebrows. "Awesome. Twin elves."

"We saw them," Teague said soberly, remembering the garnet-glowing eyes and the hip-length ruby hair. "At the courthouse. We *thought* they took out the judge."

Cory nodded. "Yes, I remember. I'm sure there's some sort of power squared going on. They were…." She frowned. "The werewolves. That night I flew out and almost got her. The werewolves that I cooked— they were twitching when Bracken came and got me. So, twin redheaded bad guys. What did their glamour look like?" she asked, trying to peer around Jefischa's wings.

Jefischa maneuvered himself and Cerise so they were *both* facing Cory, but he still had his arms around her chest. Okay, well, everybody in the house had somebody bigger and stronger to protect them—that's just how it worked out. Teague had had Cory and Max; from what he could tell, Connor, Dylan, and Cami had Arturo and Lambent; and Cerise had landed herself two guardian angels.

Teague had certainly lucked out, and that so *rarely* happened that he gave a little prayer of thanks. Shep and Jefi would have driven him bugshit in short order.

"Their glamour?" Cerise frowned, and for once Teague felt like he knew something important.

"It's their public face—the magic they use to look human."

Cerise's eyes widened. "Oh! Okay, I guess… yeah. Your man, he looks different here than at school—that?"

Cory nodded. "Yeah, hon. *That.*"

"Oh. Uhm… I dunno…. Oh! Redheads. They were both redheads, but the kind with that real pure skin. No freckles. Just this fire-red hair down their backs."

Cory grunted. "If they'd been human, there'd be freckles. Always fuckin' is."

Teague looked at her as she rubbed on the tight skin of her belly. "Will your kids have freckles?" he said, thinking of his own. Freckles were supposed to be a sign of innocence, but he'd lost his innocence a long time before he'd lost his freckles. The thought of two little kids playing in and out of Green's hill, freckled noses scrunched up in their mother's no-bullshit squint—well, it just made Teague happy in an inexplicable way. It just fixed something inside him, that's all.

"I hope so," Bracken said, swinging out of the trapdoor in time to hear their last comments. "But we won't know for a few months, so it's time to come inside now."

His tone brooked no argument, and Teague could tell by the furrows in his forehead that Green's absence had left Bracken vulnerable and on edge. It must be terrifying to be on his own with Cory—Teague would just fuckin' bet.

"Hold on," Cory said, holding up a hand. "I'm almost done with my neck stretches, and Teague and Cerise were going to tell us why the elf queen has been in Colfax this entire time and we haven't seen her."

Bracken glowered at her—but he didn't scoop her up in his arms and blur down the stairs, which he could have done. Renny came up behind him and rubbed against his calves, making Teague think they'd been calming each other down while Cory came up to the garden to stretch.

Teague brought his attention back to the task at hand. "They had a chapel," he said. "But it wasn't… I mean, I don't think I've ever heard of one of these that's really holy. I mean—"

"It was filled with bones. Practically made of them," Cerise said, breaking through Teague's ramblings. Well, she probably should have, because Teague didn't know shit about the sort of magic that Cory and Green had been wielding. Yeah, it all sort of stemmed from touch, blood, and song, and Teague got *that*—but the rest of it? Such a tremendous stretch of thought from those three cornerstones to what Teague had seen happening with the werewolves.

Cory stood up straight and sucked in a breath. "An ossuary?"

Everybody but the angels blinked. "Is that a chapel with bones?" Teague hazarded.

"Yeah—an ossuary."

Renny blurred into a naked human girl and said, "Why do you need an officer fairy? Max is straight." Then she blurred back into a cat again, sat on her backside, stuck both legs out, and started licking her crotch.

Cory put her hands on her hips and stared at her girlfriend in shock.

"You came up here just to say that?" she asked.

Renny looked up, tongue half-hanging out, and nodded. Her legs still pointed obscenely, and Teague wondered exactly what had been going on to make Cory come out alone and Bracken and Renny team up and be pissed off.

"Don't be a bitch," Cory grumbled. "You want your fucking degree too."

Renny growled and pulled all four legs underneath her. She hissed and spat and then just took off down the side of the hill. Teague wondered if there were any jackrabbits left around at *all*.

He turned to Max. "You going after her?"

Max shook his head and looked at Cory. "She's got a point," he said quietly. "They both have a point. There's no law that says you have to—"

"When?" Cory asked, her voice wobbling. "I mean, when can I go back? And look—Teague just said 'bone chapel,' and I know it's an ossuary. And I know they're usually made by the most holy of the congregation in anonymity, and I know from the sidhe that they're really fucking powerful, and I know from *school*, where I'd like to *keep going*, that they're scattered through Europe. If we ask the elves, there's probably some who remember those—the ones in Great Britain and the Czech Republic and shit—and they can tell us what they *do*. So the school has already done us a favor—I just need to…." Cory closed her eyes and wiped the moisture away with her fingers. "I just need to finish."

She turned back to Teague, as though he'd be an ally in this fight.

"Just let me finish here," she whispered. He found himself nodding, even though he was pretty sure he agreed with Bracken and Renny. "The thing is, any place made with as many bones as she's saying is a big deal. I think the others were made with the bones of the believers. That would increase power, right? That would make *you* more powerful…." She started to pace just as he had—but she had her hands on her stomach, and instead of striding, she sort of waddled from one end of the garden to the other.

She looked around. "But what if your ossuary was made with the bones and blood of your enemies?"

"It would… wouldn't it weaken you?" Bracken asked. She turned toward him, something like gratitude on her face.

"Yes. You *could* get power from it, but it would be fighting you. Remember? I saw her before solstice, and she was desiccated—down to flapping skin and hollow bone. So maybe it's not just because she's fighting Green's mark and giving her power to her followers. Maybe she's also fighting her power… focuser—the thing that's focusing that power and directing it toward them. So it gives her power, but she needs more of it at every Goddess sabbat."

"But why would you do that?" Max asked. "That's like… I mean, why not build a temple out of her believers? She's got no problem throwing lives away—"

"Yeah," Teague said, disgusted, "but they're not really *her* followers, anyway. As soon as the ritual wears off or we counter with blood, these people don't know her fuckin' name."

"*That's* why an ossuary," Cory said, voice grim. "And that's why she spent the summer going after the Dylans and Camis of the world. We thought it was just a side effect—and maybe it was—but I would bet she started importing the bodies for her fucking temple."

"So those shape-shifters that went missing at the beginning of the summer?" Teague said sickly, and Cory nodded.

"Yeah—that's probably exactly where they went. And… and any of the people that didn't drink the elf blood, as it were. You know, the folks at the courthouse who didn't fall in line, or any werewolf that balked at her bidding—enemies, enemies all."

"So she built a tiny chapel with bones and used it to focus her power. Do you think that's what she used for the winter ritual?"

Cory nodded and looked at Bracken.

"She must have been building it since we killed the fall equinox," Bracken said grimly. "But she must have been *planning* for it since the summer."

"So it's got to be taken out," Cory said decisively. "And then we can take out her lieutenants—and if it's not just one of us alone, we can take her out as well."

"Any capture?" Teague asked, as though it was purely theoretical.

"Fuck to the no," Cory snapped out. "No. No, this… this bullshit has gone on long enough. I'm done. We offered her amnesty once, and she does *this*? Every werewolf who threw themselves at us until they were dead deserves justice. Every fucking one."

Her voice was breaking again, and she paused to knead at the muscles of her lower back.

And that, apparently, was when Bracken decided enough was enough. With a grunt and a heave, he lifted her up into his arms and blurred down the stairs—the way, Teague would hazard, he'd wanted to do from the very start.

But he hadn't. Because they needed her. Not the weapon, but the way she thought, the way she led.

And now Teague had what he needed to protect her.

He looked over to where Shep and Jefi were standing, chest to chest, with Cerise sheltered under their shoulders.

"Guys?" he said, getting their attention. They turned their heads only. "Guys, thanks. And thanks for taking care of her. Make sure she gets downstairs in time for dinner—I think Grace made her favorite."

"Fuckin' garlic," Cerise mumbled. Teague laughed, feeling sad. That was actually Cory's favorite, but she hadn't been eating much, and what she *had* been eating was vampire blood on saltines.

CORY
Home Fires

GODDESS, I was tired. Not just from school, or from missing Green or worrying about the war.

I was tired of being at odds with everyone in my life.

Bracken strode into the bedroom, where I was lying on my side doing my reading. I looked up at him and cringed. What was it now? I was hungry, but I didn't feel like going into the front room—not tonight. I was tired, but I was resting, dammit. Couldn't he leave me alone? I was *not* going to quit school, and I was *not* going to stop trying to exercise, and I was *not* going to stop blooding with the vampires, and—

"Hey," he murmured, crouching in front of me and moving my textbook out of the way. "What's the matter? I haven't even said anything yet."

I was crying.

"Don't be mad at me," I wailed. "I'm so tired…."

"Shh…," he whispered. Then he did this amazing thing. He sat on the bed, took me in his arms, and just held me. I didn't come apart, really—I was done with it. Besides, sobbing was sort of fighting your body, and this was just… silent tears.

I finished, soothed by his big hand rubbing between my shoulder blades and the patient way he breathed in time with me.

"Have you eaten?" he asked when it was clear I was done.

"No," I said, almost afraid I'd get another round of lecturing.

"Good. I'll go get us some food. Stay right here."

I looked up at him, naked gratitude written clearly on my face. "That's it? No lecturing, no 'the people need you,' no 'you're too tired'—"

"No," he said with a weary sigh. "I'm tired too." A slight smile flickered over his drawn features. "I want to touch you, and say hi to the guys, and maybe make love to you—as much as we can do. I don't want to worry about fighting anymore. You know why I think you shouldn't go, and I know why you think you can't quit, and you know what?"

"What?" I asked cautiously.

"We're both right. And we're both wrong. And I'm fucking done."

I half sobbed and nodded my head, not wanting to leave his lap. He still made me feel small, when not much else could.

A subtle knock sounded at the door. Then Nicky came in, a tray of food in his hands.

"Oooh…," I said, suddenly ravenous. That had been one of our bones of contention as well. Between school and the third trimester, the nausea had returned, but now nausea had a new friend—heartburn. Eating had been both necessary and horrible. I was always hungry—but after about three bites, the nausea would kick in, and about an hour after that, the heartburn would rear its ugly head. Grace had started giving me papaya juice with my saltines, because the little roll of papaya-enzyme tabs had apparently been too humanly processed for my delicate elf-infected system. In fact, *everything* was too humanly processed. I couldn't just have *bread*, I had to have bread made from organic flour and baked here at Green's hill. Apparently Grace and Katy had made a spreadsheet to see what I could and couldn't eat, and even the *yeast* had to be homegrown.

Grace had started ordering things like organic rice, and she'd even planted a garden on the hill *for my vegetables alone*. I was starting to realize that all of those "fairy fruit" stories were not just analogous to fairy sex, as Green had first supposed. If you were carrying fairy offspring, your body was more the Goddess's than God's. I knew mine was becoming increasingly fragile, in spite of my efforts to convince Bracken otherwise.

Maybe that was why he was so angry with me when I told him it was all okay. He knew I was lying, and he couldn't even lie to me and tell me it would be all right when he didn't know that himself.

Nicky set the tray on the end table, and I moved to get off Bracken's lap.

"No," he said quietly. "Just… just stay."

I nodded, and Nicky handed me a bowl of chicken with rice and veggies. I dug in gamely. Something about being in Bracken's arms, not feeling the telltale chill that still lingered between us when he was angry, made my stomach not quite so tetchy. Go figure.

Nicky stood uncertainly while I ate, apparently taking in the intimacy of the two of us. "Do you, uh… you know. Want some privacy?"

I closed my eyes and leaned against Bracken. On the one hand, I *longed* for the two of us in bed together, me screaming out his name. I longed for the same thing from Green. But that wasn't happening. Penetration was not going to happen, not for a while—and as much as I longed for it, that was how much I needed to put away the thought of it.

"No," I said, holding out my free hand. "Just stay."

Nicky sat down in the free chair and we spoke quietly about school, about the water class, which I loved, about how I missed working in the yarn store, and how I swore I wasn't dodging my mother's calls.

"We tried to explain that you were resting," Nicky apologized. "But then she told me that whatshisname had asked about you, and I hung up."

I laughed in surprise. "You hung *up*?"

"Well, *yeah*!" He threw his hands in the air. "I didn't even want to *tell* her what we were thinking about doing to get him to leave you alone."

I sighed, hating this discussion. "But… you know, he's a *doctor*!"

"Yeah, so was Josef Mengele!" Nicky snapped back. "But everybody says he didn't die soon enough."

I thought about my WWII history. "He really didn't," I said, considering. "I mean… the guy *really* needed to die much sooner, and much worse."

Nicky nodded. "I'm *sayin'*!"

"Well, this guy hasn't performed any experiments on me yet," I told him, disgruntled. I couldn't even believe we were *having* this discussion.

"So we wait until he does?" Bracken said, horrified.

I took a dogged bite of organic protein and seasoned carbohydrates, hoping they would soothe my stomach. "How 'bout we just hope he doesn't?" I said, chewing. "Who wants to change the subject? All in favor say—"

"I think me and Bracken," Nicky said, out of the blue. Goddess help me, I was so used to putting sex in the little box labeled *Not For You* that I didn't know what he meant.

"You and Bracken what?"

"You know—me and Bracken. Do the thing."

"Kill the doctor?"

Nicky growled and pulled out his phone. Tap-tap-tap, and *boom*! He flashed us a picture of two very nicely built, clean-cut young men, naked, sucking on each other's cocks.

My giant maternity panties soaked through, like *bam*! And I knew they could both smell it too. Under my bottom, Bracken's member got hard so fast he had to adjust himself.

"Give me the phone," he ordered, and Nicky handed it over with a grin.

"Don't look," Bracken told me, a faint smile on his lean mouth. I closed my eyes and took an automatic bite of dinner. "Swallow," Bracken commanded—and yes, there went a big pulsing throb to parts unmentioned—"and then look."

I swallowed and looked.

There was a smaller man riding a much larger man's cock. The big guy was fisting the little guy's member, and the little guy was… given over. Utterly abandoned. Being serviced and enjoying himself.

I made a strangled, longing sound.

"You like?" Bracken asked, pleased with the picture.

"Very much," I whispered. My only regret was that there wasn't a girl in the picture about ready to be taken by both of them—because it would be nice to think that *some* girl was getting laid, even if it wasn't me at the moment.

Bracken showed Nicky the phone. "Look at that and touch yourself," he said, as though he wasn't just autocratically talking about sex.

"You want me to—"

"Look at that picture," Bracken said patiently. "And take off your clothes while she finishes dinner. Please be hard by the time she's done."

Nicky whimpered. I watched, fascinated and dripping as he remembered to lock the door and then stripped off his clothes while we looked on. Nicky loved his clothes—he was always meticulous. He folded his pants and put his underwear in the hamper, then hung up the shirt, which was good for another wear. Then he sat in the stuffed chair he'd just vacated, cock bobbing, and spread his legs so they hung over either side of the chair.

"Like this?" he asked huskily, the first words spoken since Bracken had given his order.

"Yes," Brack said, seemingly unmoved. He checked my bowl—which was, shockingly enough, empty—and then set it on the end table, taking the damp cloth that had come with the dinner and wiping my mouth, chin, and hands as I stared at Nicky.

Boys really *did* know how to work their own equipment.

His hand slid up, around the head, then down. He wasn't circumcised, so he played with his foreskin—up and over, up and over, up and—

"Slower," Bracken told him. "You don't get to come until I'm ready."

Nicky whined. "But you're still *dressed*!"

"Yes, yes I am."

Gently he stood and helped me find my feet. I was wearing a loose, flowy skirt and a long-sleeved peasant blouse, because they were comfortable and cotton and didn't feel too condescending to my humongous body. Bracken crouched at my feet and reached up, palming my thighs and spreading my legs gently, sliding his fingers into all the teasing places in my body before he slid my pregnancy panties down to my bare feet.

"You don't want me naked?" I teased, threading my fingers through his hair.

His smile—so wicked. "I know this does it for you," he told me. And yeah, I liked being naked under a skirt. So sue me. Then he reached up and unhooked my bra in one movement, deftly pulling it out of one sleeve and then the other.

I let out a slow breath, my body aroused by something as simple as taking off my underclothes—and watching Nicky stroking himself for our pleasure.

Bracken stood up, being sure to palm my thighs, spread my bottom and knead, and then drop my skirt and move his hands to my midriff and my still-tender breasts. I kissed him ravenously, greedily, and he pushed me to the bed, pulling down the covers and sitting me down, then shoving me gently until I was propped up on my elbows.

"Watch him," he ordered. Then he pushed my knees apart and put his head under my skirt.

Oh, it felt so wanton, so *good*, to be a sexual being again. I wasn't going to get fucked sideways or banged like a screen door in a hurricane—but Bracken's tongue, the flat of it, was dragging slowly from my backside to my oh-so-sensitive bundle of nerves, and I was heading for a short, sharp, glorious climax.

I caught Nicky's eyes, his hand on his midsized cock, his own legs splayed out like mine were, and we both groaned in tandem. I watched the reddened end of his member grow shiny and slick as he rubbed his thumb across the head and then sucked the liquid off.

I screamed.

The orgasm rocked me from core to tingling breasts, and I gushed my own come on Bracken's tongue. He kept licking until I grabbed his head and pulled him out, still shaking with orgasm. Another climax and I might lose control of my magic—and control of what it could do to my body.

Bracken grinned at me wolfishly, his face slick and dripping. I parted my lips, expecting a kiss, but he shook his head. "Nope," he said playfully, and oh, it had been so long—so *very* long—since anybody in this room had played like that in bed.

Nicky was panting slightly, his eyes closed, wanton, and Bracken turned from servicing me and kneewalked to service Nicky.

I moaned, the sound soft and unnoticed in the sex-saturated room. Bracken started by parting Nicky farther and performing the same service for Nicky's exposed parts that he'd just performed for me.

My sex—swollen, dripping, still sensitized—shivered, and then again when Bracken very carefully took one of Nick's balls in his mouth.

"Brack, I'm gonna…."

"Am I fucking you, little man?" Bracken asked. Again, it was spooky how unmoved he sounded.

"No…." Nicky's voice shook.

"Then you won't. Now stay right there."

Bracken stood and stripped. Jeans, sweatshirt, all of it thrown in a pile near the hamper, because clothes had never been as important to him as sex, thank you Goddess.

When he returned to Nicky, still splayed on the chair, he went to his knees again but didn't squat.

And I got a good look at his manhood for the first time in forever—huge, stiff, long, and demanding.

"Bracken?" I asked throatily, both shy and needy. "Can I… can I taste that?"

He looked at me over his shoulder, then stood and scooped Nicky up with his hands under Nicky's ass, legs straddling his waist.

Nicky let go of himself long enough to hold on until Bracken dropped him in the middle of the bed without ceremony.

"Same position," he said. Nicky let out a groan.

"God, you're killing me—"

"Legs spread, little man. I *do* need to fuck you."

"Weak," Nicky whimpered. "Just making me fucking weak."

I smiled at him, lewd, open, ready. Then Bracken approached me, staff level with my mouth, and I opened my mouth to devour him. Oh… oh, his taste, his girth stretching my lips, his length.…

He didn't use me, which was a shame, but he thrust gently in and out, my spit and his precome making him slick and ready. He pulled away reluctantly and kissed me openmouthed, carnal and needy as hell, and I returned it. Ah… oh, the taste of sex, of juices and musk on a lover's lips. I *needed* these things. I could actually feel my body growing stronger, more accepting of the twins, more powerful, from the repletion of orgasm and the joy of being touched and given pleasure.

He moved away too soon and positioned himself to invade Nicky. His precome was so thick, so slick and lovely, I knew Nicky felt no pain at all. Slowly, gently, Bracken thrust his way into Nicky's resisting body. When he was completely seated, they both groaned.

I wanted to be part of it.

I leaned over and kissed Nicky, openmouthed, giving him the same taste of carnality Bracken had given me. Nicky knotted his hands in my hair and let me, while I reached down and grasped him in a slickened, firm stroke designed to bring him off at the same pace Bracken was setting.

I hadn't counted on the fact that he was overstimulated as hell. That's all it took—a few thrusts from Bracken, a few pumps from me, and he was shouting into my mouth and spilling over my hand, hot and sticky and male.

"You're not done yet," Bracken threatened. Then I *had* to move my hand, because Bracken was a man on one single mission.

He fucked Nicky blind. Fucked him hard, fucked him fast, fucked him unmercifully. Nicky grunted, shouted, *begged*, all of it for more— more of Bracken in his body, more of his spend sliding down my hand.

I stroked him until my shoulder got tired, and then I rested my head on his chest and contented myself with licking his nipple until he whined through one more giant come. This was the big one, I guess, the big kahuna, because it rocked him up off the bed, still impaled by Bracken, and he squeezed so hard that Bracken shouted, convulsed, and collapsed on top of Nicky and me while he was still pumping into Nick's smaller body like a man possessed.

I pulled away slightly, resting my head on my upper arm and shivering in repletion, clenching my thighs together to stave off the aftershocks.

For a moment the only thing in the room was our heavy breathing. Then Nicky gasped, "I feel cheated."

"Cheated?" Bracken asked, clearly outraged. "How was that cheating?"

"I really *did* want to sit on your cock."

Bracken chuckled and rolled off him, leaving Nicky in the middle with the two of us linking hands over Nicky's limp body.

"Next time," he mumbled. "Next time. I promise."

I shivered again—because, yeah, no underwear created a draft— and Bracken got us both out of bed and cleaned up and into sleep shirts. Then we all settled in for a cuddle, even though it was still early out in the front room. I was exhausted, and for once I was *happy* tired, and so was Bracken. Neither of us was going to break the new good thing by trying to milk one more hour out of our night. Before I fell asleep, I realized that the sprites had come to clean up our dinner, but I was beyond complaining. *Thank you tiny winged people/creatures for cleaning up after us. I may have to expect you to do a lot more than that, but not right now. Not when I'm happy and replete and two of my lovers are close to my heart and the third one is working on getting home soon.*

Right now, I've got peace.

SOMEONE WAS calling my name.

I woke up suddenly, kicking at the covers on the bed, restless as fuck. Bracken was sitting up next to me, e-reader lit up but eyes focused on something else entirely.

"Do you hear that?" I whispered.

He looked at me, chewing on his lower lip. His elongated ears were practically twitching.

"Cory. Corinne. Corinne Carol-Anne. Lady Cory. Corinne Carol-Anne Kirkpatrick."

"Stop that!" I muttered, and he jerked his attention to me like a laser.

"Stop what?"

"Someone's calling my name," I said, swatting at my ears. "But they're doing it wrong."

Bracken let out a long, slow breath.

"Where's Nicky?" I asked, somewhat suspiciously. We'd gone to sleep all sexed out and happy. Why wouldn't Nicky be in bed with us?

With a frown I looked into the closet where he'd been keeping his clothes. The shirt he'd hung there when he'd undressed for Bracken—that shirt was gone.

So were his carefully folded jeans.

"I don't know," Bracken said, clearly as alarmed as I was. "But that's not the real question. The real question is, why is it so quiet?"

I closed my eyes for a moment and listened past the annoying buzzing in my ears. The hill was never completely quiet. Thousands of people lived there—it was an apartment complex with inhabitants who had a lot of sex. There were usually voices in the common rooms, and there were two on our level, or people in their own rooms watching television or getting off or arguing or....

"It's not empty," I said, pondering. "Just... half-capacity? A third?" Okay, folks, someone had to have answers. *"Grace?"* No answer. I sat up in bed abruptly. Fuck. Grace wasn't answering. How could she not answer? I was her *fucking queen*!

"Corinne Carol-Anne Kirkpatrick, Queen of the Vampires—"

"Stop that!" I snarled it this time.

"Marcus? Phillip?"

"Not so loud! We're almost there!"

I opened my eyes and looked at Bracken, tugging on his sleeve. "I'm gonna fuckin' kill them," I said. His look of outrage told me all I needed to know about having secrets kept from you.

"They went without me?" he gasped, sounding hurt and outraged at once.

"Yes, Daddy Bracken, they went without you. And...." I looked at the closet where Nicky's clothes were. "And Nicky sexed us both up so we'd sleep through it!"

Bracken blinked. "That little fucker...."

"Corinne Carol-Anne Kirkpatrick, Vampire Queen, lover...."

Oh no. Oh, no. "Shh!" I hissed in annoyance, even though I didn't think it was going to stop.

"I didn't say any—"

I held a hand up to his mouth.

"I'm being quiet. No words." Marcus and Phillip both turned part of their attention to me. I put a picture of Grace in their minds. What I

got back was an image of Grace and Arturo watching quietly as shape-shifters and vampires filed quietly out of the shape-shifter common room, all of them heading down to the garage.

Grace was in the hill, but she *wasn't* answering.

"Bracken," I said quietly, "you and Arturo link a lot. See if you can find him."

Bracken closed his eyes, then opened them and shook his head.

"Corinne Carol-Anne Kirkpatrick, Vampire Queen, lover of two men, wanton slut, student…."

I didn't shush the voice this time. It was getting shit wrong. I didn't correct it in my head either—that shit was important. The elves believed that names held power over us, and I believed it too. This voice thought it knew all my names, but the more it got wrong, the clearer-minded I could be.

"You and me," I said, voice so low Bracken had to lower his head to hear. "We're going to try really hard to connect with Green in a minute. Then I'm going to connect with the vamps and see where we are."

"What's—"

I held up a finger, this time just mouthing my words. *"She is in the hill."*

Bracken's look of fear and revulsion was reassuring. I was literally scared pissless, and that hadn't happened in seven goddamned months.

NICKY
Not a Moon

LEAVING THEM was hard.

I can't lie—I almost backed out. Teague gave me the option—called me Daddy, told me seriously that I was part of the expectant family and should stay home. And seeing them sleeping—*truly* sleeping—for the first time since Green had left for his business trip, I almost did. Teague was right. I *was* an expectant daddy.

Two nights before, I had gone down on my knees in front of Bracken while she watched and approved. After Bracken spent in my mouth, he'd pulled me up and kissed me, then left us both doing homework while he made his nightly rounds and touched bases with everyone Green and Cory usually spoke to on a normal night. He'd been so tense, so worried—giving him my sex, my mouth, my attention, felt as natural, as necessary, as it felt with Green or Cory or even with Eric during our intense whirlwind weekends together. Seeing Bracken's face relax, even for that moment after climax, was all the reward I needed, all the proof I ever *would* need that I was family.

After he'd left, I spent an hour sitting next to Cory and reading my history homework, my hand resting gently on her stomach. The twins were dancing up a storm.

At one point, after what probably felt like a barrel roll to her, I looked up and saw her eyes, sober and bright, resting on my face.

"They like you," she said, her voice whisky rough. "They only do that for Bracken and Green."

My smile—I felt it to my gut, to my groin, even to the place where my shape-shifting rested.

When we'd first bonded, I'd told her she would need to have my baby. With my hand on her stomach, Bracken's seed still on my tongue, I knew she already had. These babies were mine. She wouldn't need to have a baby with my DNA to answer the call in my blood. Maybe that was just a myth, a legend, a boogeyman that all Avians believed. I'd tell Green that later, but right now?

Right now I knew these babies were mine. They had answered that thirst in my blood, and there would not need to be another child.

I thought Cory might want one anyway. She'd reached out and touched my cheek with her fingertips, as gentle and tender as any man might want from a lover.

When I'd first met her, I thought she would be the only lover I'd want or need—but now, now I knew I wouldn't have been happy with only a woman in my bed for "as long as we both shall live." But she loved me for who I was, for what I desired, and I wouldn't trade being her husband for all the cocks in Green's hill.

But then, thanks to Bracken and Green, I wouldn't have to.

So when Teague gave me the way out, the daddy escape, I could have taken it.

But why?

Why would I not go fight, when I was *aching* to fight back? When Cory was suffering and Green and Bracken were worried, and all the people I loved were in danger from this woman and her frightening tainted werewolves?

No. If the shape-shifters and vampires were going to bring the fight to the bad guy, my family had to be represented. I was there to represent.

They didn't stir as I slid out of bed and got dressed, and I thought that was pretty telling. Cory had been sleeping in hard little spurts, probably because she had to get up so often, but she'd been restless too. Without our little adventure—and I never got tired of those—she might have caught me.

And Bracken—whom, it seemed, almost *never* slept, especially when Green wasn't there—*definitely* would have.

But I'd done my job and tuckered them out, and I was free to join the stream of people walking quietly down the hallway from the first-level bedrooms to the staircase. There was also a back stair from the darkling, and I'm sure there was a river there too.

"Not everybody," Teague had warned, looking Arturo and Grace in the eye. He'd been planning this for a week—had sent out vampire scouts at night, telling them what to look for this time—and yes, we'd discovered the grim little chapel. The outside had been Tuff Shed, of all things, but vampires are pretty sensitive about blood and bone. They'd definitely been sensitive about *this*.

"It smells… like the *opposite* of Lady Cory," Marcus had said, shuddering when he'd returned. "Cory… she smells like flowers, and she tastes like lilies and lavender, which is gross, but…." He and Phillip locked eyes. We got it already. Whatever feelings Cory's blood evoked, they were powerful and personal. She'd blooded a couple of vampires each night, and the experience had consistently knocked them into euphoria until their next rising.

It had also made them stronger, faster, more powerful, but not even Grace had told Cory that.

"She'd feed us more, or hell, probably get knocked up more, if it meant she could keep us strong." Grace had been mumbling it to Arturo one night, but I'd heard her and agreed. We didn't need Cory pregnant again, or weaker in this pregnancy than she already was.

What we needed was our enemy gone. What we needed was some breathing room.

Teague's plan to give us that was simple.

"The way I figure it, Cory's shields send the enemy to sleep, right? Well, that's great. The shields are up, so—"

"The shields aren't up," Arturo said grimly.

We'd been talking in the shape-shifter common room, which Green had outfitted like a dive bar with hardwood floors and pedestal seats around shiny wooden tables. They even served alcohol for the people who still enjoyed the taste, and dinner. Cory usually ate dinner in the front room of the hill and held court there—this meeting was later and almost subversive.

She *knew* we were planning something, but she didn't have details and was too exhausted to track them down. Our logic in defying her was simple—if she'd been well enough to come with us, she would have already had us pinned to the wall and confessing. She wasn't well enough, so we needed to protect her.

It was logic I could live with. Apparently so could everybody else, because the only one not here was Green, and Arturo had told us he approved.

But we still wanted this done before he got home.

"What do you mean, the shields aren't up?" Teague asked. I knew he wasn't the only one who felt a shiver of fear right to his bowels.

"They're up, but that… that bug the girl brought in changed them. Someone with definite evil intent *will* get caught in the shields. They'll get lost, they'll fall asleep, they'll wake up at the edge of the territory and maybe find their way home or maybe stay there forever. It's a crapshoot because the shields have been fucked with so many times. I like it that way. The randomness makes me *very* happy—I've found some of those werewolves who were lost in the borders, and they were shitting their pants. The more random we keep it, the less manpower she'll throw at us that way. *But.*"

"I knew it would be coming," Lambent muttered. Of the all of us, he seemed the most afraid to do this without Cory. Well, he had another vampire to lose, didn't he?

"What's the 'but,' Arturo?" Teague asked seriously. "I've got my teams all set up to go. This could be a pretty big 'but.'"

"But with so many people *out* of the hill, and that thing *inside* it, the shields are going to be trying to shield all of *you*. I can't guarantee we'll be insulated and safe in here."

All of us sat, paralyzed with indecision.

Teague was a wise man—he must have been—because what he said next was damned smart.

"Ask Green what he thinks."

The next night when we met in the common room, Arturo had news. "He says go on the night of the full moon."

We all gasped.

"But the shields!" Lambent said for all of us.

"Lambent—you, me, Hallow, Whim, Twilight, some of the others—we're going to try to fix them in the morning."

"Do you think you can?" Teague asked. We all held our breath. He was one answer away from calling the op off, and we knew it.

"Cory is powerful," Arturo said, nodding at Lambent. "But even without her, we've got one of the strongest groups of sidhe I've seen gathered in one place in my entire long life. Talk to us tomorrow night, and we'll tell you if it's a go."

The next night I'd passed Cerise, and her arm had been bandaged. Apparently she'd woken up with a searing pain where her old bite had been—a burn had just appeared out of nowhere. None of us told her it was a side effect of Arturo's amping up the warning system around the hill. Lambent had healed it, and that had been that.

But that night Teague had told us that if Arturo said we were good to go, he'd take it on faith. We'd made plans to move out the next night, vampires by air, shape-shifters on the ground. The vampires would hover nearby, the better to rescue the shape-shifters if they got caught in the shit, and the Avians would fly recon.

Besides elf queens and their entourages, we also had some new crazy people in the hills with shotguns trying to declare racial purity for Planet Earth. I sort of wished they'd get caught in the crossfire myself, but I knew that was probably not charitable of me.

It didn't matter. If they hurt me or my people, they were fucking going down.

The night of the attack, as we streamed quietly down the stairs and out the garage, I felt a moment of remorse. We weren't flying out of the hill proper. That would alert the angels, and so far they hadn't even been able to tell a social lie, similar to the elves but without the puking. That could cripple our covert operation, and nobody had wanted to put them in that position. We'd sent Cerise up there under the pretext of delivering some dinner and asking them how they were doing. (They were doing great! Fucking like minks and enjoying the company of anyone who came to visit. If word got out that falling from heaven could bring all the angels a sweet gig like this, pretty soon we'd be ass deep in angels who only wanted each *other's* asses.) Cerise didn't know that two-thirds of the hill was leaving, and hopefully we'd be done by the time she figured it out.

So we ghosted out from the base of the hill, going northish to Colfax. Mario, the other Avians, and I turned bird pretty much as soon as we got to the invisible border that separated Green's lands from all the rest of Placer County. As we darted under the full moon, I could see the other shape-shifters leaving their clothes at that border and turning furry before trotting into the mist.

The mist was actually perfect—just thick enough to muffle our movements, not too thick to steer through. We thought "Gee! What a stroke of luck!" as we trotted, flitted, and flew through the shadows under the moon.

We would figure out later that the enemy had been waiting for us to cross that border in the mist so they could cross in the opposite direction. Too much movement, too many people, too many *different* people—not even magic could account for it all.

But we didn't know that until later.

All we knew right then was that we had fifteen miles to travel cross-country, and we needed to be quick about it. The vampires needed to be back at the hill an hour before dawn, and it was ten o'clock already.

Just like we knew when our feet touched Green's earth—we could feel the vibrations in our bones—we could feel the desolation, the earth-sucking destruction, the corrosive purpose and villainous intent when our feet touched the enemy's land.

The wolves, cats, coyotes, wolverines, badgers, deer, pumas, Labrador retrievers, mountain lions, and Goddess-knew-what-else down there let out a collective whine as soon as they crossed from Green's land to the enemy's.

Arrows came out of nowhere, and at first dodging them was no big thing. They got thicker, though, a hail of them, and when one nicked me, I could feel some sort of astringent coursing through me.

Not silver, thank fuck, but something—a toxin to vampires, perhaps, but not to shape-shifters.

Then I saw Marcus get hit by an arrow and rip it out of his shoulder without a problem, and I realized who the arrows were for.

"Guard the elves!" I shouted—and bless our people, we did. The vampires formed a midair phalanx, taking the arrows grimly because the arrows could hurt but not injure them. After I shifted and flew behind them with the other Avians, I got a good look at the three big stables Cerise had described. All of them had ports for firing weapons.

I was pretty proud of us as we flew through that hail of arrows, heading with the vampires to rip apart the outbuildings beam by beam. Then I got a look at what the arrows were guarding. Oh, Goddess. We'd known. We'd known they were out there, but hells—not how many. Phalanx upon phalanx of werewolves, stacked out on the lawn, ready to charge into the brush and take out the shape-shifters—and possibly any elves who were left untouched by the arrows.

A trap. Jesus, this was a fucking trap. We'd walked right in—and as far as I could tell, not a one of Green's people were ready to turn around and run with their tails between their legs.

The arrows were getting thicker, and my attention turned to dodging them. Left, right, up, down, almost like a drill, except... *ouch*! One of those fuckers got through! My attention narrowed. I lost the global sense of what we were doing and settled into the rhythm of every soldier, probably since ever—keep going, stay alive, keep going, kill. Keep going, stay alive, keep going… *kill*…. Mindless, just sentient enough to keep from getting skewered, I didn't even wonder what we were going to do with the fury at the end of the tunnel.

It wasn't until the vampires started to glow that I realized that we could take the fight away from the girl, but there was no way in hell the girl was going to let us take her out of the fight.

CORY
The Joys of Raising a
Family in a Two Front War

"THEY'RE UNDER attack!" I snarled, and the voice—the one calling my name—suddenly ceased to fucking matter.

"Call Green first!" he snapped.

Bracken grabbed my hand, and together we sent out a big psychic distress call to the elf we loved most.

At first, it was like screaming at a wall.

We both opened our eyes and looked at each other, trying not to panic. Then Bracken, of all people, started to laugh wolfishly.

"What?" I asked, taking deep breaths and shoving a pillow under my lower back.

"They've obviously never seen you break through a wall," he said.

The panic, the pounding in my ears, the fear for my physical person and for the children I bore, all of it faded away.

I was remembering me, Bracken, and Arturo tucked inside a magic bubble while we crashed through a brick wall.

I knew that feeling—whether it was made of psychic energy or concrete, I did know how to break a wall.

First I needed help.

"Arturo!" I called out loud. "Grace! Get your asses in here!"

I could hear their feet pounding from outside so quickly I knew they must have been there all along.

"Why couldn't we feel them?" Bracken asked. I slid my reply into his mind because I was afraid to say it out loud.

"She put psychic blinders on them—rendered them insensible to power. That doesn't mean they weren't right there!"

He smiled at me, nodding. At that moment I heard the call again.

"Cory. Corinne Carol-Anne. Beloved. Due'ane."

Bracken jerked and looked startled, and I was swept with an overwhelming sense of relief. It wasn't just me. Finally, he could hear it too.

"No more with the psychic thing," I said, and he nodded.

As Arturo and Grace broke into the room, I held a finger to my lips. My phone was charging next to the bed, and I grabbed it and opened a text box to Green.

They're in the house.

Psychic thing bad.

She's calling my name.

The vampires are under attack YOU ASSHOLES and I need us to hold hands so I can do shit.

I looked at the text box for a moment, hoping Green would reply, but we were so good at the mind-link thing now, so adept, that phone texting seemed superfluous.

Well, teach me to depend on magic when I had tech, right?

"Kk," I said, swinging my legs over the bed. "Grace, you stand watch. I can draw from you anytime. Arturo, think sexy thoughts about me. Bracken, hold on tight, we're gonna pull a jailbreak with our minds."

I wouldn't say it was effortless, but it did feel familiar.

Bracken's hand was comfortable in mine, and a corner of my mind realized I should never take that thrumming, the joy in me that drove my power, for granted. Arturo's hand was sturdy and capable, and while I'd joked about him finding me sexy—as if!—the fact was that it just needed to be the potential for sexual attraction. Arturo had been attracted to my person from the very beginning—that enjoyment of me, that personal love, *that* turned my key as well.

I closed my eyes and let myself fill up with that power. It was heady, whirling, and tremendous, and we were only three.

I spooled power like copper wire around a magnet and visualized us as a glowing steel ball. Bracken and I kept coming up against that force, the hard blanket that stood like an insulating shell around the hill, making us psychically dead to each other and separate when we were used to communicating effortlessly.

I charged… charged….

And I punched us up through that wall, exploding our consciousness beyond the crown of the hill and into the night.

"GREEN!"

My mind found his driving down Foresthill Road, the silhouette of the double-lane bridge in his rearview.

Oh, sweet Goddess—he was ten miles from home.

GREEN
Terrible Choices

He had only told them he was coming home early. He hadn't told them when.

Green and Eric had prepped hard for the meetings Green was supposed to make in Colorado—both in the lovemaking that helped Eric heal and in the actual business dealings that Green was leaving Eric to proxy.

With every other thing going on in their world, the *last* worry they needed was losing the hill to the government.

It was their home. It was home to nearly an entire city of full-sized humanoid people, and hundreds of tiny cousins who filled in the corners.

The government could never know that.

As far as the government was concerned, Green's hill was the residence of Green, his wife, Corinne, and their two friends Brack and Dominic. Explaining why those four people couldn't just up and relocate had, in recent months, become one of the many banes of Green's existence.

Putting the future of his hill in the hands of the young man who had once been his protégé was one of the hardest things he'd ever done.

Part of it was that Green had managed to do his people proud in sheer honest duplicity. He couldn't just fund his household expenses from his business profits—that would be a tremendous amount of cash to pay for four people, no matter how rich. No, he'd labeled the entire hill "Green's Hill Enterprises," and everything from food to electronics to Cory's special organic flour was funded as an expense in product development, which was paid for by Green's *legitimate* businesses.

It was a tricky dance between what was true, what was legal, and what Green could get away with to keep his people in their home.

It was a good thing Eric was damned good at what he did.

The night before all hell broke loose at Green's hill, Eric bought Green the plane ticket himself.

"You're driving me batshit," he said frankly. "Green, you can't even settle down to make love!"

Green—shirtless and sitting at Eric's glass table, a bowl of ice cream in front of him and his laptop open and more than warm—managed to pull himself out of his distraction long enough to groan.

He'd left Eric *in bed* on the pretext of getting a glass of water, and here he was again, making sure he could leave his life in the hands of a friend—and that nothing they did would be irrevocable.

"I'm sorry," he said, feeling as lost and vulnerable in that moment as he had the day… oh Goddess… the day Adrian died. "I'm not there for them," he said, looking up at Eric and swallowing hard. "I left them at *war*, do you understand that?"

"No," Eric said, cupping his cheek. "But then, that is why you're the leader. You make the hard decisions. I…." He looked away. "Someday, Green, when not being with Nicky doesn't hurt so much, I *will* come back to you."

Green stared at him, surprised. "Why would you do that, mate? I thought you were perfectly happy—"

"My mother, my sisters, they're glad to have me back. That's fine. But…." He bent and dropped a kiss near Green's ear. "I've only ever had family in one place, Green, and it's not Texas. So, yeah. Someday, after my family has drifted apart, when I'm feeling the sting of living so very much longer, I'll find my way to your hill again. I'd *really* love for it to be where I left it, yeah?"

Green smiled, his eyes closed, and allowed himself to be comforted by Eric's animal warmth.

"Absolutely," he agreed.

And that was when Eric had bumped him aside and made his travel arrangements, brooking no argument. "If you can, meet me in Colorado in a week. If you can't, I think I'm prepped."

That had been the end of it.

Green had already made his phone call for the night—he knew everybody would be in bed, and if they weren't, they should be. And by the time he could tell them about his arrangements, he was already on the plane. He'd figured that just about the time Cory was thinking he should be calling the next evening, he would be arriving home.

And then she, Bracken, and Arturo all screamed in his head and he almost wrecked his specially prepared rental car.

He got it back on the road—after rubbing fenders with the guardrail over the canyon, not that he'd ever tell them that—and did what he did best.

"I'm here."

"Green, Teague made the raid tonight. It's an ambush. They've got poisoned arrows aimed at the elves, and they're going to need help."

He tried to remember to breathe.

Chest, diaphragm, there was a whole working-in-conjunction thing, and then....

Then he touched his beloved's mind and did some thinking.

"Why the three of you?"

"The enemy is here."

Oh, Goddess. He actually thought his vision was going to go dim. He kept his eyes furiously focused on the road ahead, on driving at a reasonable pace, at *not flooring the gas and driving into the canyon* and on being safe. They needed him.

"And you want me to go help the battle?"

"We've got this locked—"

"Shite!"

Oh Goddess, he'd couldn't do this, not again. He'd left her—he'd left her once, and she'd been broken, violated, stripped, and bleeding, their dead child on the floorboards between her knees. He'd left her again and invading forces had taken over… *were inside his home*, threatening his lovers and their young, and she was telling him not to go help?

"Calm down." She sounded irritated. But Hannah was never angry. It was *Cory* who sounded irritated. And pissed off. And capable. *"Look—they need you on the field. I almost took this bitch out by myself...."*

He heard it in the back of her mind, because they were so closely linked.

"Cory. Corinne Carol-Anne. Corinne Carol-Anne Kirkpatrick. Slut, tool, weapon, ou'e'eir, due'ane—"

Oh, sweet Goddess. His own call to her was desperate and pitched. *"Cory!"*

"Cool your jets. I just wanted to see how much she'd gotten."

"She doesn't have it—"

"Yeah, I know. Let her fucking guess. She'll never unlock the whole of it, Green. She doesn't understand. Just get your ass to go help Teague, because—oh shit!*"*

For a moment his heart failed him, and he found the car hurtling dangerously fast as he contemplated whether there would be enough of him to scrape off the canyon floor if she'd just been killed.

"I'm linking with the vampires now—all three of us. They need you, leader—"

"I can't leave you!" Oh Goddess! The whole reason he was here at all was that he couldn't leave her alone—he couldn't *bear* to have her hurt, violated, broken because he wasn't there to keep her safe.

"You're here. Have some faith in me, Green. I'm not helpless. The whole reason you fell in love with me was that I could hold my own."

Oh, he wanted to call her names, to get her to listen. It was so automatic for them—the endearments had become part of their souls. But he couldn't, because there were other ears, and he didn't even want to think the words.

"Beloved...."

"I won't leave you, Green. Now have some faith. Have some faith in us. We'll do you proud."

All those times of sending her away from him into the field and believing she would come back whole and sound, and the hardest thing he'd ever do was going to be leaving her home.

He came to the fork in the road, the almost invisible left turn that would take him to Colfax, to the place Nicky had told him they thought the current compound was located. Turn left, and help his people. Go straight, and ride to Cory's rescue, being the knight in shining armor he'd always wanted to be.

Turn left, and do what he'd promised.

Turn left, and risk losing everything he'd worked for, yearned after, loved.

Go straight, and lose friends, lovers, and his beloved's faith.

You had better be fucking right.

The car—a Lexus—didn't skid when he made the abrupt left, but he did come close to the trees on the side of the road.

"Thanks, beloved," she said clearly in his head. *"Now go ahead and let me work."*

TEAGUE
Disasters and Mercies

TEAGUE GOT hit in the heart with the first arrow.

Good thing it was steel tipped and not silver, or he would have been dead. As it was, he turned human, ripped it out of his chest, turned wolf, and led the charge into the compound. It wasn't until Nicky's shout that he realized—the arrows weren't really aimed at the shape-shifters, were they?

He turned human again, naked and pale in the mist, feet sinking into the bed of pine needles and rotted leaves that made up the floor of the forest they'd hidden in, and shouted, "Shape-shifters, pick an elf and guard him!"

Or her. Elves of all flavors were drifting into the night with the shifters and vamps, many of them with lethal silver-tipped spears. As he stood and watched, he saw scores of arrows blocked and destroyed by those spears, and he was grateful the elves were good enough to leave some space for his guys to work. His guys—and girls—weren't doing bad in the working area either. The ones who were more comfortable furry were batting arrows out of the air. Many of them had strapped weapons to their bodies—Teague had a machete in an elastic harness around his back should he need it—and they were using those to defend the elves. Arrows—seriously? Gunfire, yes. They'd been prepared for gunfire, and Teague had spent the last week prepping plastic bottles of the herb water they used to counteract silver in wolves and iron in elves. But arrows *stuck*. Unlike bullets, which would cause damage that a shape-shifter could heal with just a little magicked herb water, an arrow shoved the poison *deep* inside the body—and it needed to be ripped out, which caused more damage too.

Yeah, humans were more vulnerable to guns, there was no doubt about it, but in the supernatural world, arrows were a stroke of genius.

Well, fuck. Arrows from people hidden in the outbuildings— what next?

He gazed across the lawn toward the compound and saw enemy werewolves massing on the lawn.

"Marcus!" he called. "See that?"

"We got it!" Marcus called back. The vampires pulled together vertically, stacked on top of each other, taking most of the arrows and not caring. Jesus, that was scary. Teague watched one of them rip an arrow *out of his eyeball*, eat the fucking eyeball off the arrow like a shish kebab, and then chuck the arrow like a circus knife thrower—*thunk* into the heart of one of the wolves on the ground. The wolf yelped and ran away, but didn't die.

But neither did the vampire. In fact, his eyeball would probably regrow before the battle was over, but… hell. That was fuckin' gross.

And he didn't have time to dwell on it.

The enemy wolves had seemed disoriented and confused as they'd arrived on the field. Teague had a distinct vision of one of them shaking his head, uncertain as to what he was supposed to be doing on the moonlit field of milling bodies. But all that changed when the two glowing giants strode from the farmhouse in the background onto the field.

The arrows stopped when the giant elves appeared, and Teague had to squint his wolfy eyes to figure out what he was seeing.

Suddenly he yearned to have Cory next to him.

He wanted someone in his head—someone to say the funny, frightened thing, someone to make it all better.

Holy fuck, he thought to himself, *those are the sidhe, clothed in naked power*.

No wonder Cory got amped fucking those guys.

They weren't six feet plus—they were eight, nine, ten feet tall, their size swelling and contracting with what seemed to be their heartbeats. Their skin was beyond pale, beyond white or glowing or marble—it was so bright it seared Teague's eyeballs, every movement of the naked giants imprinted on his brain like a photo negative.

They wielded whips above their heads, the whips glowing like blood or rubies or heartblood fire, and the hair they shook out past their hips was the same color.

The enemy werewolves went insane.

Snarling, snapping, yowling, they charged, and Teague flashed grimly on the quiet good-bye he'd bidden Jacky and Katy before he'd begun the march. They always knew—*always* knew—there was a chance he might not come back. This might be that—

The vampires started to glow.

Dammit. Just fucking once….

Well, too bad. If she wasn't watching over them, she wasn't breathing, and apparently she was watching over them.

Teague looked up in time to see Phillip, acting as the focus as he always did, laughing maniacally and holding his hands out as he channeled power into the werewolf pack, scattering the mass of them and cooking those in the center where they stood.

Then the glow from the vampires increased and a shield formed, keeping the hill's shape-shifters safe from arrows, werewolves, and apparently a stray breeze—but it couldn't last.

The younger vampires, the weaker ones, were moaning in pain—Cory's power was *not* meant for vampire consumption—and even as Teague blinked, the glow around some of the outliers faded. Those vampires fell from the sky, taxed beyond endurance, even beyond the ability to fly.

But not Phillip—man, that brother could fuckin' *kill*—and he was doing it with glee, until Marcus started yelling, "The elves, asshole! Get the fucking elves!"

Phillip turned the power on the giants with the whips. At their first howl of pain, a cheer went up.

Then Phillip screamed—power, pain, it didn't matter. Marcus flew behind him and grabbed him around the waist, screaming, "Enough, my lady, enough! We can fight!"

There was a flicker in the shields, in the vampire ranks, and Teague wondered at the titanic struggle inside Cory as well.

Hurt her friends, or leave them open for the enemy?

Or have faith that they could defend themselves.

The shields shut off abruptly. Then Phillip and Marcus dropped out of the sky, landing about three feet from Teague.

Teague could hear Phillip's giggles and sobs as they landed, and he thought Green's people could either break or rally.

He changed to human again and decided to help them rally.

"*For Lady Cory!*" he screamed and then ran—naked and joyful, bounding over the fallen vampires with his machete in his fist.

The roar at his back nearly knocked him forward—loud, savage, fierce, and pissed the fuck *off.* These were *his* people and they'd been attacked in their own home, made to fear leaving it, afraid to drink the water outside their walls, afraid to get so much as a traffic ticket in case the invaders took them out.

They'd been made helpless while the elves protected them, while their queen even at her most vulnerable fought for them, while the vampires lifted them out of the fray like house pets even though they were dangerous predators all.

This was the cry of a warrior army, furious and angry, ready to fucking *kill*.

"For our lady!" Teague cried again. "Ignore the werewolves—go for the fucking *elves*!"

The two redheaded giants with whips paused for a moment and shrunk in a few throbs of fear, allowing Teague to get another good look at them.

Not giants. Not gods. Elves. Powerful still, terrifyingly powerful, but dammit, Teague wanted some fucking elf blood!

Elves flooded from the outbuildings. They were probably the ones who'd been shooting the poisoned arrows at the hill's people—all of them armed with silver-and-wood weapons, their movements fluid and graceful as they made to stand by the twin giants.

The werewolves, no longer driven mad by the elves, took one look at the screaming, writhing, furry mass of shape-shifters, yelped, and ran away.

"You *cowards*!" screamed the giant elf on Teague's left. "Get back to your ranks!"

He cracked the whip again. Even though it didn't fall on any werewolf backs, they must have been conditioned by the sound. Some of them yelped, others growled, and Teague could sense a general return of purpose, of *hatred*, to the rank soldiers of this lot.

"Oh, *fuck* no! *Fuck* the werewolves—kill the fucking *elves*!"

He was laying about with the machete, and he knew how to use it. Hack, chop, slash—yes, most of the werewolves would be getting up again, but not anytime soon. Even for a werewolf, it took *time* to reattach a severed limb, and time was something the enemy didn't have.

Teague wasn't the only warrior making his way to the front. Max had strapped six clips of steel shot to his back, and when they got close enough for Max to aim, Teague heard the reports, sharp and wicked, rip across the clearing in front of the ranch-style house.

Five elves went down before the redheads started calling for a shield. With a few cracks of the whips, the werewolves were driven to a frenzy again, tearing and ripping at the Green's hill shifters.

Teague found himself surrounded by werewolves—being one of six or seven lone naked humans in a werewolf fight *did* make you sort of fucking conspicuous—and he was one snap away from getting his leg shredded by a werewolf who was probably tainted beyond redemption when Teague felt that now familiar sensation at his middle.

"No! No, no, no, no, no, no, goddammit, *no!*"

"Too bad!" Marcus singsonged in his ear. "Besides—you and Max can do a lot more damage close up. As soon as we take these assholes out, the werewolves will curl up and sleep."

"Goddammit!" Teague groused. "Can we at least call it 'Pulling a Max' from now on?"

"Not on your life, wolfman!" Marcus crowed, then dropped him just out of reach of the redhead's whip.

Teague jumped backward barely in time, and as he dodged out of the way of the whip's crack, he realized the damn thing wasn't made of leather as he'd first assumed. It was made of vertebrae, no doubt from the elf queen's enemies. Those jagged bones crackled with power around Teague's head as the elf wound up, but Teague pulled out his machete—sharpened steel, all the better to kill elves with—and slashed the air as the whip fell down.

And then whirled sideways as the severed piece of whip flew from the rest and what looked to be elf blood spattered from the pulsing end. Teague screamed as it splatted his face, burning, and he thought he was going to have to use his handy-dandy herb gel to clean that shit off.

Just as soon as he was done killing this guy and doing his part for the cause.

But the battle wasn't going as well for the other warriors as it was for Teague.

The giant elves weren't the only ones stoked with power.

As the werewolves whimpered and fainted at the enemy elves' feet, those elves swelled and grew. They were enormous—aliens, giants, gods—and if Teague hadn't had the boiling blood of one of them eating at his flesh, he would have thought the fuckers were invincible, because none of his guys seemed to be getting in a decent blow.

Max aimed his Glock point-blank at the other redhead, but the bullets skidded off and up—something impossible with a normal target, but then, these were elves. The freaky fuckers defied gravity, and Teague was done thinking about it. He had enough problems just *staying out of the fucking way*.

Max was playing happy-dancing too—except his elf had a silver blade, and Max didn't have anything to parry with. Teague saw a stave on the ground and jumped over the whip stump, rolling to come up with it in his hand.

"Max, catch!" he shouted, tossing the stave over a couple of werewolf/werekitty skirmishes between them.

"Got it, thanks!" Max shouted. "But do you got any other bright ideas?"

"Kill them?" Not Teague's smartest moment, no. But killing them *had* been the idea before he'd led this little shindig—it was just proving damned harder than he'd planned.

"That'd be fucking *brilliant*, wouldn't it?" Lambent snarled. He was hand-to-hand battling another elf, and for the moment it looked like he was winning. Lambent had cast off his own glamour and was standing seven feet tall with flames for clothes, his ruddy features lit up in blue fire. Hellific, furious, he could have been the Christian devil, and the elf blood spattering his mouth and hair didn't make that any less likely.

"Got any idea *how*?" Teague swung his machete again. This time it clanged off the shield covering his opponent's body—preternatural body armor powered by demented werewolves. Where in the fuck was *this* in Teague's battlefield strategy, huh?

"Yeah!" Lambent shouted, face suddenly lit with unholy glee. "Get the fuck out of *his way*!"

Was Lambent fiery? Were the enemy elves glowing? Were *they* giants among men?

Green appeared—a brilliant flickering conflagration, an emerald holocaust of furious movement, a giant among giants—clothed only in the glory of his people.

Teague saw him striding with nothing in his hands but a pure bolt of energy fueled by love, by sex, by loyalty—none of it constrained, and bright enough to hurt the eyes and feed the soul.

Not sunshine, but *life*—love, lust, sex, touch, kindness, growth, spring, oak roots, lime acid, wooden thorns—crawled over Green in the flames of power given to him freely by the people fighting for him in that moment.

With an energy bolt shaped like a sword—a light saber, Teague wanted to say, but it wasn't, it was a *power* saber, but that sounded dumb—he cut a swath through the werewolves before him. Then he strode through the bodies—not healing, these bodies, not reconstituting or recouping—and came face-to-face with the twin Teague had been fighting.

That twin lost some of his stature, and Teague saw a distinctly human swallow.

"You ready, Green?" Teague asked, tossing his machete from hand to hand.

"More than ready, sir knight," Green snarled. He raised his voice. "You fight proudly, my people! Now *fuck them all!*"

LADY CORY
Vacant Chambers

I PULLED my power from the battle—partly because Marcus and Phillip had had enough, and partly because I was growing weaker with every heartbeat.

But mostly because I had seen Green's car about two miles away from the viewpoint of the vampires.

We weren't losing, and help was coming.

And I had shit I needed to focus on a little closer to home.

"Cory. Corinne Carol-Anne. Lady Cory. My Lady. Wife, slut, tool, student, menial crafter—"

I grunted and looked at Bracken, Grace, and Arturo. "That last one was just rude."

Arturo shook his head. "Where is she—I mean, *how* did she get past us all?"

"She just walked in, Arturo," I told him. "When she's not all skinny and shit, I'm sure she looks like every other elf. There's thousands of people here—especially while people are filtering out, you're not going to notice one figure, probably coming up the stairs, and…."

I closed my eyes and listened.

"Ou'e'eir, due'alle, slut, wife, tool, student, kid, menial worker, white trash—"

"She's close," I said. "Is she in Nicky's room?"

A look of revulsion crossed Bracken's face. "No, that's not Nicky's room," he snarled.

For a moment I was going to be sick. Then my mad charged into me like a rampaging rhinoceros.

"She is getting the fuck out of that room," I threatened. "C'mon, Bracken, help me up. This is you and me—"

"And me," Arturo said, matter-of-fact. Well, he was like my uncle, sort of. Grace cleared her throat grimly, and there you had it. Mommy, daddy, extended family—

Everyone was going to visit the babies' room.

Bracken helped me up, my knees creaking grimly, and I waddled to the connecting door that I hadn't opened since I'd created it, not even when Green had asked me to visit it in his absence.

I'd thought I had another week.

There was never enough time to prepare. I should have known that—I should have learned that lesson with Adrian. With Green. With Bracken and Nicky.

I should have learned that lesson when I'd found out I was pregnant and couldn't even say the word. But time was up—it was time to face facts, and time to see who was waiting for me in the nursery.

She wore robes the color of blood, and her hair was just as red spilling down her back.

She faced the opposite wall, sitting in a rocking chair—one of those laminate ones that glides back and forth that you see in all the maternity stores.

All of the furniture was wood laminate, and I frowned as I looked at it.

"I didn't pick any of this shit," I snapped. Bracken glared at me as the elf queen whirled around. "Well, I didn't!" I protested. "This isn't my furniture! Who picked it?"

Oh, Jesus.

I glowered at Nimuetia. "*You?* You sneak into *my* house, you call me all the wrong fucking names, and you try to decorate my fucking nursery? Who in the fuck do you think you are?"

She must have fed well enough. Her face was pure alabaster, and her eyes glowed ruby red. Gone was the desiccation, the flapping skin, the ruin. In their place was whole, healthy elf, with one exception.

Green's mark—*our* mark, the wreath of oak leaves, lime leaves, and rose trailers—twisted along her skin, on her face, up her arms. Her robes weren't just the color of blood, they dripped with it as well, as the mark crawled along her body, doing its job.

It was supposed to constrain her not to act against Green or his people.

The blood, the sparkler burst of madness in her eyes, the defiance, the fucking war—all of it ripped its vengeance out of her skin and demented her even more.

But even that dementia couldn't contain her surprise.

She took me in—swollen ankles, swollen face, swollen belly, bloated anger—and her mouth dropped open.

"You're *quickening*?" she hissed. "*You're* the one who's pregnant? How—I thought it was an *elf* concubine! They *impregnated* you? You're trash, that little human sorceress—" She snarled. "—the *singer* we saw that night!"

Oh, Jesus. We all knew she'd been there the night we defeated Green's old lover. We'd known she must have been one of the overthrown elves.

We just hadn't counted on how much she still didn't know us. Well, hell—*that* was something we should have exploited while we'd had the chance. No chance now, though, just pregnant me and the backup squad.

And the monologuing villain.

"Bitch, I may be white trash to you, but here I'm the fucking queen, so maybe stop trying to know me." Bracken grabbed my hand like maybe he could hold me back.

"I *do* know you!" Her face twisted—and you know what? She wasn't all that attractive when she looked like she wanted to rip my throat out. I mean, *I* was bloated and swollen, and I had bags under my eyes and bad skin and greasy hair, but *she* was fucking scary.

"Yeah?" I snapped. I realized that I wasn't afraid. Maybe I should have been, but mostly I was just mad. She was in *my* nursery, with cheap furniture, as though she was taking over *my* house? "What do you know about me?"

She snorted dismissively and gestured to the tacky furniture in the darkened room. "I know I picked better than I knew. I could feel the life building here—*elf* life. I didn't know it was some half-breed abomination!"

"So you teleported shitty furniture for a real elf baby?"

Yes, yes I was stuck on the furniture. *It was my fucking nursery!*

"I was trying to make a statement!" she snapped.

"Make a statement? Terrorizing hundreds of innocent people to kill for you isn't a statement? Tainting the water supply of the entire county wasn't a statement? Big fucking orgies where you *forcibly* created werewolves—that *wasn't a fucking statement*? Lady, you need to take an English class, because I don't think you know what a statement is."

"No!" the woman snarled. "You don't get to tell me what or what not to do! I watched you and your lover destroy my entire *world*. You're upset because a few humans were marked? *A hundred elves* were marked against their will. You destroyed our leadership and just… just *took over*, forcing *us* to work with… with the… *kymutxha* of the universe."

"My mother wouldn't even let me hear that word," Bracken said in wonder. "So *that's* what it sounds like. Talk about *kymutxha*!"

As she'd spoken, Nimuetia had been throwing power spikes at me—subtle, invisible, but unmistakable. So the situation was grave—very grave—but that didn't stop me from smiling at my beloved.

"You were very sheltered," I said cheekily.

"I was," he agreed with a modest nod. A power surge hit us—hard enough that Nimuetia glowed blue for a moment—and our hands tightened around each other.

I turned to our adversary without a trace of levity in my expression. "We gave you an out, O lady of misplaced vengeance. Did you petition us at Imbolc? Did your brethren?" I had sat through those meetings at Green's side, the very picture of the leader's consort. We'd received five petitions, all of which we granted, provided the petitioners moved overseas or to Vancouver or hell the fuck away from us. This bitch had not been among those five.

"Why should we petition?" she asked. "We *lived there first*!"

"Well, we were doing just fine with that until your people sent some sort of mad fey hybrid to kill our lover!" I snapped. Adrian's ghostly absence was a seven-month throb in my heart. "Did you think that shitstorm blew through your life because you were *innocent*?"

"I had nothing to do with that!" Nimuetia's cry bespoke honest anger. "My liege lords did as they saw fit, and I followed! Don't your people follow *you*?"

I couldn't help it—I smiled. I'd been getting flashes of the battle with every power surge, and I'd seen Teague and Max, Renny and Lambent, and Green—my gloriously alight, gentle lover—wielding teeth, claws, blades, guns, and blinding power on the battlefield.

They were covered in blood, in viscera, and in battle fury, and if I'd had my way, they'd still be in Green's hill where we could have kept them safe.

"Sometimes," I said, my smile grim. "But not always."

"Then you're weak," she said with deep satisfaction, "and deserve to be destroyed."

Then she started to glow magnesium bright, emanating power like a charging phaser. I drew from Bracken, from Arturo and Grace, and kept my power shielded from Green and Nicky on the field. If I hadn't been practicing power control in our marriage bed, particularly in the last month, I couldn't have done it—I would have sucked them dry. They would have fallen in battle, and all would have been lost.

But I managed. My knees may have wobbled a little, but my specialty, the power shield, clamped itself over her magical glow, forcing her to back off or self-immolate.

"So, you're a follower," I said, panting a little. Well, I was out of shape. "That's something to add to the résumé. You sat passive while people did bad things. You refused to take appropriate peaceful options when you found your situation was not to your satisfaction. You're like a pathetic stalker, really. You want what you can't have, so you try to terrorize the people who have it. Have I missed anything?"

"You *cunt*!" screamed Nimuetia, her push against the shield frenzied and hard. "You—you're a *child*! You know nothing of the world—nothing about love, about what you would do for your children. This room was *vacant. Empty.* And you—a woman with sidhe twins should be treated like a *queen*. Pampered, petted, *worshipped*. You were on a battlefield, a common soldier—I didn't even suspect you were pregnant. You can't even acknowledge you're having these children. How would you know what a *true* sidhe mother will do to further her children's cause?"

In my head I saw them—as Cerise had described, as Green was seeing in battle. Two boys with hair like blood and rubies, white as alabaster, beautiful and cruel.

"You sent your children into *battle*?" I asked, horrified. "You… how could you?" *My* power spiked, and Nimuetia cried out and hunched over, moaning. "How could you? Do you know what I've done, what my *people* have done, to make sure I can raise my children in peace? Do you think I let them put themselves in danger *willingly*? They left to protect me, because some rabid fucking… cum-pshaw or whatever kept trying to kill me and mine. My friends left to put their lives on the line for *me*. I fought in all those stupid battles to make my home safe for *all* my children, the ones in my home and the ones in my womb! My *ou'e'hm* is trying to *kill your children* right now because he wants to keep us all safe! You want to be a good mother? Stop trying to give your children territory and start trying to save their lives!"

"My boys will win," she said, very human tears trickling down her nose. "My boys will win, and your lover will die, and I will suck in all that released power like a sponge!"

"How do you figure?" Arturo asked, surprising me. And thank Goddess—I was a breath away from bursting into tears myself. I was pretty sure I could have held the shield steady, but I might have constricted it until I squished her like a bug too.

Nimuetia looked at him as if he'd sprung from the ground fully realized. She hadn't even *seen* the people I'd come in with, and that was important too.

"It will be free for the taking!" she sneered. "This one will simply melt into grief. Not even her children will keep her whole. Look at her— she's human, weak. Her leader is all that's keeping her alive, because her body can't bear our kind!"

"None of that is true," Arturo said conversationally, and my heart tried to accept his words as real. She'd hit me there in the places I was most tender. Would I keep going to save our children? Would my body give out on me? We'd achieved such a crucial balance—what would these two lives inside me do to disrupt that? "She's so much stronger than even she knows. But you're funneling all of this power through a bone chapel—even *if* Green goes down, and our people become yours for the killing, how will that work? You could use our leader's thighbone as a straw, and the ossuary would *still* scatter that power to your enemies before you had a chance to channel it. It was a terrible risk."

It was, wasn't it? I thought about that battle and how it was all focused on the elves.

"Marcus, Phillip, get some helpers to destroy the chapel. Dismantle it bone by bone if you have to."

They were startled—I'd caught them in the middle of… well, of eating an enemy werewolf, both of them ripping strips of flesh away from his throat to his heart. The taint in the blood was doing strange, rabid things to my vampires, goddammit, and I needed to split myself again.

"My guys! Stop eating the poisoned werewolves, for sweet fuck's sake, and destroy that fucking chapel stat!*"*

I got to most of them. They responded sluggishly, dazedly—but still, they responded.

"My children will protect it!" Nimuetia's shout pulled me back from the battle just in time for her to try to burst out of the shield.

For a moment she succeeded.

Bracken and I were thrown backward, and only Arturo and Grace—anchored, grounded both physically and mentally—managed to keep us from being thrown back against the wall. Arturo caught Brack, and Grace, bless her vampire strength, caught me, levitating us both up and letting our upward momentum take care of some of the thrust without an impact.

Before we were even stable, I threw that shield back over her, screaming with the effort.

She started to chant my names.

"Cory, Corinne Carol-Anne, Corinne Carol-Anne Kirkpatrick, Corinne Carol-Anne Kirkpatrick Op Bracken Green, Corinne Carol-Anne Kirkpatrick op Bracken (Get it right, bitch!) *Green, student, weapon, tool, breeder,* kymutxha—"

"Oh, that is it!" I howled. "I'm so fucking done with this bullshit. You are Nimuetia, the mother who kills her children, the bloodthirsty bitch who would rather be right than protect her beloved ones, destroyer of the innocent, vengeance before mercy, blind follower, man hater—"

"I am *not*!" she gasped. Oh, she wasn't the only one who could hit tender spots, was she?

"Oh, yes, you are. Look at Iris. You picked Iris and other strong women because you thought they were just like you. You hated men so much, you only picked weak ones—the uneducated, the frightened and hurt."

"The women were strong enough to do what I needed!"

Had she looked beautiful when we'd come in? No more. Her hair tangled over her face, and every etched line of the tattoo was dripping blood. Her struggles against my shield made those lines bleed faster, and it occurred to me that she must be hemorrhaging power with every drop.

I didn't want to admit that I was too.

My magic—yes, that was as strong as ever, but my body was… failing. My knees and legs could hardly support me, and my pulse was beating too fast, too strong—in my throat, in my eyelids, throbbing in my fingertips. The children were being unusually still given all this activity, and I wondered if my body was releasing stress toxins or something to put them to sleep while I worked.

Well, good. I wanted them to sleep through this. I wished *I* could sleep through it as well.

But I had no other course of action but to carry on. I let Grace hold me, support me, and sent her a little mental plea to set my feet on the ground but stay right where she was so I didn't collapse.

"But you couldn't count on your men, could you?" I asked, feeling pity, actually. Green and Nicky were on the battlefield together. No matter what happened, I knew that they loved me, and they'd do their best to see it through.

"What men? *My* men died at your little dinner party."

Oh, hell.

"So you decided to wage war on my entire people using werewolves?" A year and a half. This woman had been trying to build an army for a year and a half. "How could you even think you were a leader?" I burst out, because my head hurt and my vision was getting spotty. "How could you even think this would work? You couldn't confront us in person *once*? Let's go back to the name thing, shall we? *Coward.* You're a bloody *coward*, and you're manipulative, and you *hate* your men for leaving you all alone with only this shitty, half-planned vengeance within your grasp!"

"You're weak," she growled back, her face now a mask of blood. "You're weak, and you depend so much on your men that your body is failing without them. You mourn *everything*, even people who should be beneath you—or *would* be, if you weren't beneath *everybody*. White trash, fat, ugly little human bitch, so worried about her own worth she'd put her body and her children on the line to prove that she belonged in a faerie hill where she had no business—"

"*This is my home!*"

Oh, it was fucking *on*. Bracken replaced Grace to support me, but Arturo and Grace stayed on either side, and the rest was light show. Nimuetia threw her power out while I tried to keep her from blowing our entire fucking hill apart, and us with it.

The nuclear ball, in the center of what would now *never* be the nursery, grew brighter and brighter and brighter. Even as Nimuetia screamed, I could feel the heat scorch my skin and my pulse throb from my feet to my throat. My vision grew darker and my knees grew weak, and I knew I would keep my grip on that shield until my heart exploded in my chest.

It was coming.

C'mon, Green, save my life.

BONES AND BATTLE

Teague

TEAGUE WAS getting winded, and he hadn't thought that was possible. That damned elf giant—fucking fast, fucking merciless, and fucking *armed*. Teague had managed to cut off two more sections of that bone whip, each one accompanied by more blood, but the pain only seemed to spear both twins on. They both screamed when each cut was made, so Teague guessed they really *were* that close, but their shared pain wasn't helping him now.

In fact, the only thing helping him now was Green.

They'd developed a rhythm, with Teague dodging in low and swinging madly while Green engaged both twins at once. Max was beating the hell out of the other twin at the same time, and they were winning, cut by cut by blow.

But it was a war of attrition—and *that*, Teague wasn't so sure they could win.

The vampires were helping, but every werewolf they killed became a bloody temptation, and Teague had the feeling that vampires were falling out of commission with every corpse.

And there weren't nearly enough corpses on the ground for the shape-shifters *not* fighting the elves to be able to win.

As far as Teague could see, between the enemy elves sucking the werewolves' power as fast as they could and the vampires falling from the sky drunk and sick on werewolf blood, it was going to be a toss-up to see whose resources were exhausted first.

That damned bone whip scourged another bloody strip from Teague's sorry fucking ass. He howled, stumbling to one knee and holding the machete up to catch the blow he knew was coming.

The bone whip curled around his throat instead, and Green turned his attention from the other elf (who was bleeding and bruised but still fighting like a fucking *beast*) to cut the hemorrhaging weapon right out of the redhead's hand.

Teague expected to be dead first. The whip was hauling him in. He couldn't breathe, couldn't fucking gasp, and the bone spines were cutting into his flesh. His feet kicked, and he *dropped* his machete, grabbing futilely at the whip. Just as his vision started to go dim, he heard Max shouting, "Change, you dumb motherfucker, *change*!"

And then two things happened at once—Green's blade fell just in time to part the elf's hand from his wrist, and Teague went werewolf, healed his wounds, and ripped a big wolf-sized hole in the twin's stomach.

That screaming moan of pain just urged Teague on, because *damn*, didn't it feel good to taste the blood of his enemy! *Damn*, wasn't vengeance a fucking fine wine! He ripped, tore, and shredded that elf's belly while the elf screamed and beat his bloody stump against Teague's head.

Gruesome and horrible, but the rage driving Teague had been a year and a half in building and had only grown stronger, more acidic, as he'd watched the only home he'd ever loved fall further and further into danger. He was gonna disembowel this fucker, eat this chump's liver, put his heart in a blender and drink it while the guy screamed! He was gonna—

A rending sound stopped everything. Everybody. Every sound on the battlefield ceased as the vampires, gibbering in glee, tore apart the tiny outbuilding that had been ignored in the general melee. Teague never got a look at the ossuary, but the vampires would describe it later, and it curdled his blood. Underneath the vinyl poly of the Tuff Shed sat an altar made of skulls and walls made of crossed arm and leg bones, a ceiling lattice of broken ribcages, a floor tile made of laced fingers and toes. The bones hadn't been cured, Marcus reported, and gobbets of rotting flesh hung from them and from sinews that had been woven in and under the bones to tie the whole thing together.

A monstrosity, an abomination, meant to pull power given by the unwilling from the constrained receptacles. Its presence should have made a hole in the universe.

Its absence certainly caused a fucking commotion.

Green

GREEN FELT the wrongness of the ossuary's power-funnel in his *soul.* The elves, supernaturally charged and lethal, were functioning on stolen power, bent to their use by an obscene instrument of magic and will.

But he'd set his course when he saw Nicky, Max, Renny, Teague, and the other shape-shifters engaged in mortal combat with the power-mad elves.

They were his. They were Cory's. They needed to live.

He threw himself into the battle with all of the fluid grace of the sidhe, and with all of the power and experience of nearly two thousand years on the planet. The love of his people fed him—many of the snarling, spitting warriors on the field had been the sweetest, neediest of lovers in his bed, and he had fed deeply from them. What looked to Teague like a fight between a sword and a whip was really a whirling dance of magics—the magic of anger, the magic of love, the magic of destruction, the magic of entropy—love and lust grown so great it could ravage all in its path.

Green had no flaming sword in his hands—not to his own eyes. To Green, their battle was a liquid dance of raw boiling power.

The destruction of the ossuary sounded like the shriek of a thousand tortured souls freed to afterlives of their own choosing.

For a heartbeat Green was distracted, pulled in the direction of healing that torment, dying at the thought of those lost souls trapped into service.

He didn't see the flick of the bone whip that wrapped around his throat.

If he hadn't been sidhe, the ripping strength might have decapitated him. As it was, he had just enough time to fill his cells with full sidhe power before his air was cut off.

He grasped at the whip, shoring up the tender flesh of his neck with all the energy he possessed, and locked eyes with the mad glare of the redheaded warrior who was going to kill him.

And saw only grief.

He expanded his perception and saw more of the battlefield than just the enemy in front of him. Teague was only a few feet away, snarling over the entrails of the other twin. Even as Green watched, that sidhe's eyes lost focus and filmed over, and his body shrank to normal size, releasing his soul and magic into the universe for another Cory to find.

"I'm sorry, my brother. We didn't ask for this fight."

Green's antagonist heard him. For a moment the pressure of the whip relented, and Green was consumed by sorrow for a soulmate, for the other half of a lost heart.

"I know this feeling."

Ah, the wrong thing to say. The bereft elf let out a howl of rage and jerked back on the bone whip. Green was falling into dispassion, into void, his oxygen failing, his heart sore and aching. *"Cory… love them well…."*

"Fuck that, mate!"

Green smiled even as his lungs stalled and his heartbeat bulged in his ears. *"Adrian—we've missed you."*

"Well, backatcha—now get your ass up and fight!"

Green beat feebly at the whip around his neck, but even he knew the movements were drunken and desperate. *"Kinda stuck here. So much to do…."*

Adrian stood right in front of him, blue eyes blazing, white-blond hair a frenetic halo around his head. *"I will come visit again, you wank, but now is not your time!"*

With that he pressed transparent lips against Green's, and Green felt it—the bubblegum taste of him, the tongue, and then….

Air. Or not-air? Ghost air? *Something* filled his lungs, pushed the darkness back, gave Green the strength to grab the whip and yank with all his might.

The enemy elf faltered long enough for Green to pull real air into his lungs but then jerked the whip tight again.

A streak of feathers and talons screamed from the sky, aiming a razor beak at the whip-wielder's naked eyes. Just then, Teague turned from the dead elf at his feet to hamstring Green's antagonist. The sidhe stumbled to one knee, covering his bleeding eyes with one hand and wildly flailing the bone whip with the other. Green fell to all fours, hauling air into his lungs as the whip curled around Nicky's wing and yanked it out of its socket in an explosion of quills, blood, and bone.

Nicky stalled and started his fall out of the sky as a man while Max leaped at the struggling sidhe's throat, claws fully extended, teeth bared with rage. Green didn't see the rest. He ran—lungs laboring, heart pounding, because Nicky….

Oh, his darling Nicky….

All that power floating through the air for the taking, so much of it meant for hatred, for vengeance, for anger and pride. Green threw open his arms for a moment—a single moment—of stopped time and pulled it all into his body.

And blurred, faster than light, up into the air so he could clasp Nicky to him as he plummeted to the ground.

"Nicky!"

Cory's scream in his head told him more than he wanted to know about her struggling heart and Bracken's valiant efforts to keep her failing body together. In that moment of supreme fear, the link that bound them all snapped into effect.

Nicky wailed in pain as Green's feet touched the earth, and Green had no choice but to pour all that power into his maimed and savaged form.

"Green... I can't live if I can't fly."

Blood poured out of Nicky's body at the severed shoulder socket. Green turned his face to the heavens and roared, pleading for the strength to heal his most inconsequential, most accidental, so very much beloved lover.

Bracken

I CAN'T heal—I can't heal! My body is made for blood, calls to blood, *thirsts* for blood—and as I wrapped my arms under her arms, it was that very element that was killing her. It pounded through constricted vessels, forced her heart to labor too hard for such a fragile human organ, throbbed in the delicate network of veins in her fragile brain.

In desperation, we turn to what we know.

Her body was failing her. I knew nothing of healing, but I knew blood.

"Heed my call!" I screamed to her blood, her platelets, her cells, her iron. It knew me. Some of my own blood—a trace, a memory, however small—still ran through her veins from the last time I'd given her my life.

"Slower, my lovely, slower!" I followed the rushing river of blood and sang to it. I flowed through her heart and soothed it, calmed it, eased its suffering. I threaded through the network of veins in her gray matter and whispered gently to move with ease, to—oh please, beloved—just once, just this once, don't fight all the things, don't fight the enemy, don't fight your lovers, don't fight your body, not all the things, oh please, Cory... please....

"Hello there...."

I found myself flowing through the umbilical into the tiny bodies of our children.

"Father... Father... Father...."

In this place I had only one name.

"Rest, my children... sleep and be at ease. Your mother is keeping you safe."

Perfect touches, filled with wonder, like chubby fingers patting my cheek. That was the touch of their growing minds upon my own. *"I can't wait to tell Nicky and Green...,"* I thought at them.

"Father and Father and Father... Father and Father and Father... we shall love them too...."

I emerged, chasing the next heartbeat through her arteries to her fingertips. How tightly her hands were clenched in mine. *"Relax, beloved, be at ease.... I have your heart, your body, your blood. You do what you need to. I will care for you."*

The grip remained, but the sweating and desperation softened. I kept a part of myself, my magic, within her, giving her the strength of my blood when her own human frailty would have betrayed her, giving her the rest so she might protect us both.

The magic she channeled so effortlessly still flowed through us both, but her body, the precious receptacle for her vast and mighty soul, could survive the force now.

I was weeping with the effort, with fear. I'd seen the transparent walls of her blood vessels, knew the ones in her brain and heart were growing thin. They were scarred from bulging and had so very nearly burst.

And in one blowback of magic that was rotten to the core, all of that was forgotten.

The elf queen screamed, both psychically and out loud, her cry filling our heads until I held my hands to Cory's ears and blocked her eardrums with power, because I could see the blood running into her hair and felt my own doing the same.

"Garnet! Oh Ruby, your brother! Ruby!"

As she was screaming, Cory screamed, but only in her mind—and in the collective of the entire hill.

"Green! Green! Nicky!"

Oh, Goddess! I saw them, Green blurring across the battlefield, cloaked in a chaperon of magic to catch Nicky as he fell from the sky. His body was wrong... was wrong... was....

"I don't want to live if I can't fly...."

Cory, Green, and I—all of us, all of the hill, as a booming heartbeat, sang *"Don't you fucking dare!"*

Cory and I, a joined consciousness, could see the power floating like dust motes in the black of the battlefield. Together we watched them stream, a river of stars coming to Green's call.

Our lover, our leader, the father of our children, the father of us all, lay hands on our beloved and fed power into his maimed and bleeding body as I had fed blood into Cory's—was it only seven months ago?

Cory moaned in my arms, and I tightened my hold, but our hearts were on that field, over trees and brush, over a canyon, up a mountain, far away.

And then Cory spoke, her voice echoing in the defiled nursery and startling all of us.

"Holy fuck, Brack—what time is it?"

I was sidhe. My blood surged with the tides, and I had loved a vampire for my entire life.

"It's nearly four," I said, my voice far away. "Order them home."

I wanted to join her, mind to mind, on that battlefield, but I couldn't. I had to attend to our home.

I looked around the room first, only a little sad that Cory hadn't taken this first moment of belief in who we were to become and made it beautiful. But we all knew that first joys, first loves, first pictures of what life should be, they were so rarely the truth of things.

Nimuetia sobbed, a crumpled heap of grief on the floor, so broken that Green's mark no longer twisted through her flesh. I hefted Cory into my arms, aware that she was struggling with the vampires in some way. She would win—but that was not my task, not right now.

"Elf queen," I said harshly. She looked up at me, her eyes as red as her hair, as her cloak, as the blood that dripped from the ends of her fingers and pooled at her feet. "Tell me now—do you want forgiveness or oblivion? You have this moment in which to speak."

She bared her teeth, the grieving mother gone. "I will murder you as you sleep."

"Oblivion it is."

I backed out of the room toward the hallway, nodding at Arturo and Grace to go first. When they were out, I looked at Arturo to see if he knew and could help me.

"Arturo, how many rooms does Green's hill have?"

"One less," he said, putting his hand on my shoulder. Together we looked into the testament to motherhood gone awry and watched as the walls closed in.

Smaller and smaller, the integrity of the hill maintaining its shape just as the hill had remained the same when Cory built the room. The doorway shrunk before us—eight feet tall, seven feet tall, six feet....

Nimuetia began to scream. She pulled her power to her, suddenly conscious of what was happening, but it did nothing. This was our home, mine and Arturo's, Grace's and Cory's—hell, the new ones, Connor, Dylan, and Cami, could have done this, if only we'd told them how.

But we would not.

Because Nimuetia's scream echoed in my ears long after the doorway shrank to nothing and the room ceased to be.

And the elf queen, the tainted bitch, the bane of our existence for so very long, blinked out of creation with it.

She got off easy. I had endured grief and fear and pain. Oblivion is a trip down a river of blood compared to what her heart would have done if she'd lived.

Cory moaned in my arms. I took a step toward our bedroom door, realizing only then that the hall was full of people, terrified and needing guidance.

This was usually not my job, but I thought I would do for the moment.

"The battle is over," I said. It was a testament to our people that they waited for me to finish speaking before they cheered. "Nicky has been gravely injured, and the vampires are... drunk on tainted blood. She's trying to convince them to come home."

"Is that all?" Grace asked, irritated.

"Brack, they're not listening to me. They... they just roll around and belch."

Grace leaned over and kissed Cory's brow. "Don't worry, my darling. We'll take care of it."

"We need drivers for every car in the fucking garage, and all those damned fire safety blankets I stocked up on last year," she called. "Pixies, drop them in the cars. Drivers, meet me downstairs at the pegboard. Move out, people—we need to go pick them up!"

And then the cheer—strained and tired, but happy. Everyone in the hill had someone out on that battlefield. They wanted to know how their loved ones were doing.

Katy and Jacky pushed through the crowd, which was thinning enough for me to get to the door.

"How is he?" Jacky asked, looking nervous.

"Teague's fine," I reassured. I'd seen him, when Cory and I had been joined. He'd looked beat the hell up, but fine.

Jack's mouth twisted. "I meant Nicky," he said softly. "She would have told us, Brack. I have faith."

I swallowed and felt tears start. I'd heard Green's desperation, his plea. *Darling Nicky.* It had been his pet name for Nicky from the very beginning, when I'd hated Nicky and feared that he'd distract Cory from me. I'd finally been ready to bare my heart. How dare he lay claim to my beloved when I'd waited—had been ready to wait lifetimes—but needed her so badly once Adrian was gone.

"We don't know," I said, my voice rough. "It's all so tangled, everybody's minds, and the vampires…." Their minds were a dark and twisted disaster. I shook Cory gently. "Beloved. Beloved, leave them be."

"The sun, Brack," she complained, like a child wanting more sleep. "The sun will—"

"Grace and the others are riding out to get them. We'll get them home, okay?"

"Okay," she whispered. She was sopping wet in my arms, her body taxed and sweating from the battle. "Okay. But Nicky…."

"What about him?"

"My brain hurts," she whimpered. "Oh, Bracken, it feels like my head's gonna pop off…."

I kissed her temple. "Shower," I said, knowing it was something to do while we waited. "Jacky, did Hallow go into the battle? Did Whim?"

"Whim did not," Jack said, sounding relieved. "And neither did Charlie."

"Could you make sure they're not driving to pick up the vampires? We need a healer here. She's… her blood pressure. It's bad."

Jack nodded grimly, and I staggered into the bedroom and started to undress us both without even closing the door.

We were in the shower. She was weeping with exhaustion, with weakness, with worry, when Green's faint voice sounded in our head.

"I swore he'd fly again."

Oh, Goddess.

"Will he?" I asked. Avians—so many perks and so many fucking drawbacks. They didn't regenerate limbs. They had healing, but only to a point. Almost as fragile as humans. And his wing had been ripped out from the socket.

"It's growing," Green said with some satisfaction. *"But I can't do it alone."*

Cory began to laugh against my chest, and I laughed with her.

"What's so funny?" Green asked, sounding offended.

"Oh, beloved!" she said. *"We're never alone."*

It was truth—all the truth I needed to give me enough strength to get her to bed and see her in Whim's care.

The vampires began to arrive by caravan scarcely half an hour before dawn. Grace and the lower fey put them in their darkling beds, cleaned them of the tainted blood, and threw their clothes into the incinerator as well. Arturo found Grace in the laundry room, fighting day death like no young vampire should have been able to and dodging into the shadows of the room. He swept her into his arms and blurred her to her room in the darkling before the sun could touch her.

The shape-shifters and elves came straggling in through the trapdoor from the garden about half an hour after that. The pixies had met them in the Goddess grove with buckets of water, towels, and homemade glycerin soap.

Teague, Renny, and Max were some of the last ones down, smelling faintly of lemon and hyacinth even in their furry forms. Jack and Katy met Teague and took him to the front room, where they fell asleep in a love seat with Teague across their human laps like the family dog. Max and Renny, for all I knew, fell asleep on the floor of their room, curled together like the cats they were.

At the very end, with Arturo at his elbow and Lambent two steps behind, Green arrived with Nicky cradled in his arms.

Green was naked and clean, and so exhausted the dark circles under his eyes were practically translucent. I took Nicky from him before he could protest, closing my eyes and nuzzling our boy's temple in gratitude. He was asleep and breathing evenly. The hole where his arm had been was healed over, filled in smoothly with skin.

From the center, where the joint of the shoulder would be, a tiny embryonic wing had begun to grow.

I closed my eyes and felt the tears start.

"Thank you," I whispered to both of them. Ah, Nicky. Every silly joke, every game sally into the grim and terrible affairs of sorceresses and elves. "Oh, our darling Nicky—we'd be so lost without you."

Green wrapped his arm around my shoulder and kissed my temple.

"Shall we go see our girl?" he asked, voice shaky.

"Yes," I said, holding Nicky tighter for a moment. "She needs us. She needs us all."

CORY
Little Acorns, Tall Trees,
Inconvenient Motherfucking Squirrels

I KNEW that healing quiet in the hill. Was it awful that it comforted me?

Green, Bracken, Whim, and Hallow all ganged up on me and put me on bed rest for the week after the battle. Hallow gathered up all of my schoolwork and the lectures on YouTube with every intention of letting me do my own homework, but Bracken sat stoically and silently and did it all for me.

He did Nicky's too, but Nicky didn't object to not doing his own work the way I did.

Nicky was too busy trying to wheedle hand jobs from Bracken as he nursed his own healing body.

"C'mon, Bracken," Nicky cajoled on our fifth day in bed. "Look at it!" He flapped his withered, half-formed arm and hand as they tried hard to grow from his body using what the military calls PFM. "I need one hand to pinch my nipples and the other hand to grab my peter—how am I going to get anything done?"

But no amount of Pure Fucking Magic could take away Bracken's terror of something bad happening to the two of us.

"I'll go get you some water," Brack said abruptly, standing up to rush out of the room.

Nicky watched him go unhappily. "Is he repelled by it?" he asked, flopping it around for effect.

I glared at him over my second baby blanket. "You are so stupid," I snapped. "I can't believe you could jack off when you *had* both hands."

"What's wrong, then?" he asked, serious for once.

"He was *worried* about you, asshole! You spend the last seven months changing your relationship, making yourself vital to *everybody*, dedicating yourself to the fucking family, for sweet Goddess's sake, and you don't think that's going to deepen how much he cares about you? Jesus, Nicky. Grow the fuck up!"

His wide, smiling mouth made a juicy, cherry-ripe little O as he got it. I leaned in and kissed him, because we were confined to bed and I could.

"Don't worry about it," I murmured when the kiss was done. "Bracken's growing up too."

He'd been... well, practically catatonic with worry when we'd woken up after the battle. Green had been pretty silent too. Neither of them said anything, but Nicky had come damned close to death on the field, and I hadn't been doing so hot myself when Bracken had gotten all heroic as a caller of blood.

"Yeah? What's got him all nutted up?"

I turned and stroked his shoulder and the skin of his regrowing limb. "Besides almost losing both of us? We all lost friends, Nick. And... and an enemy was *here*. In our home. He... he had to unmake the nursery. How do you think they're going to replace that?"

Nicky shrugged and winked. "I thought they were just going to use my room, since I'm mostly sleeping here or in Green's room."

"I'm all for that," I said, so glad he belonged. "But honestly, I think once the babies are born, nobody in this room is going to get much sleep."

"Well, why don't we put them in bassinets in here and then move them to cribs when they start sleeping through the night?"

I stared at him.

"What?"

"It's... I don't know. Sort of fucking brilliant."

Nicky grinned. "Thanks! And my room is damned big. And right next door. How about I keep a part of it with a bed and some drawers, and we put the squids in the rest of it. I mean jeez, all I have to do is tweak your nipples and we've got ourselves a partition with a door, right?"

I laughed tiredly. "Someday I *will* have sex again."

He leaned his head on my shoulder in honest consolation. "Yeah. I know. So will I."

"Well, so will Brack."

Green didn't have to wait. Green was up to his eyeballs in comfort sex, and so were Lambent and Sweet and Twilight.

We had lost two elves, five vampires, and over two dozen shape-shifters on the battlefield that night.

I had blooded with the vampires, had eaten with the shape-shifters, had learned poetry from the elves. Bracken and Green had expected me to put up a fight when they'd sentenced me to more bed rest, but I couldn't. I was too heartsore to fight them, too sad to want to do anything but let my body heal, feel the children in my womb, and grieve.

When Bracken returned to the room with the glass of water, I saw his own grief etched on his face. He thrust the glass at Nicky with a mumbled "Here," but I took it and set it on the end table instead.

"Here," I whispered, cupping his cheeks.

He stared at me—too surprised, I think, to cloak his sadness, his fear, his worry for the both of us anymore. He sank down on the edge of the bed, and I took his hand and rested it on my stomach. "Here," I said. I looked at Nicky and took his hand too. "Here."

I held their hands over our children for a moment, and we closed our eyes and simply *were*. "A boy and a girl," I said, and they hmmed in assent. "The boy, we'll name Drian," I said with decision, "until he decides on his own name. The girl will be…." I was going to say "Adria," but that wasn't what came from my mouth. "Silver," I said, surprised by the simplicity, the perfection of it as the name issued forth. "Silver and Drian. Did you feel them, Brack? That night you talked to my blood?"

"They're sweet," he said, voice filled with wonder. "So sweet. They know us. All three of us. We're their fathers."

"Yes," I said. "Their fathers. Who all kept their mother and their home safe when it was under attack. Their fathers are wonderful. Their fathers are heroes. Did you tell them that when you were in there?"

Bracken turned and used the generous portion of bed I'd left him so he could slump against me, his head on my shoulder. "I told them they were loved," he said hoarsely.

"They are," I told him. "They're so loved that all of their people ventured out to fight a battle to keep them safe. They destroyed a temple of bone and set free bound werewolves to make sure they grew up free and happy. Some of them gave their lives for a free and happy home. That's the story we'll tell them."

"It's a beautiful story," Green said, standing in the doorway.

I met his eyes, mine shiny and bright with unshed tears. "My children have beautiful fathers," I said as the tears spilled over.

"And their mother is mighty." Green moved forward so he could crouch next to us. He leaned his forehead against mine, and his tears plopped down to brush my cheeks.

I didn't argue with him. I didn't complain that I wasn't up to the job. I protected my people and comforted my lovers. I would protect and comfort my children. I'd seen a blueprint for what not to do—I was pretty sure we would be okay.

The next day, Bracken, Nicky, and I went up to the Goddess grove alone with Green. We watched him hold his hands over one of the twisted boles of a fused oak, lime, and rose tree. He passed his hands in a dance—like a bird floating on air currents, or a raft feeling the veins of a river beneath it—and sang softly. Our song. Rain will fall and trees will grow and we will have lovers… again.

Underneath his hands, a shape began to form.

It emerged slowly, the wood electing to peel back from his gentle persuasion. When I realized what he was doing, what it would be, I wept. Two feet by three feet, all of one piece, a cradle on two rockers, too sturdy to tilt unless it was flipped over on purpose. He gently separated it from the living wood and set it by my feet.

Then he turned to another likely bole and began to pass his hands again.

It took him hours, and we stayed with him, silent and reverent, the whole time. After the first one, Bracken lifted me up and sat me on his lap as he rested on Adrian's bench, and we watched as Green sang softly to the wood, smoothed it, cured it, made it silky under his hands. A sprite appeared with linseed oil, and he used that to finish the two cradles, then cleaned his hands off on a handy-dandy sprite-prepared cloth and left them to dry in the emerging late February sun.

When I went back to school the next day, Nicky's room had been cut in half as he'd suggested. While we were waiting on cribs that would be gifts from the lower fey, in Bracken's and my room, standing waist-high and carved out of living wood, there stood two cradles—beds of safety and love carved for my children by one of their fathers.

On each cradle, I'd placed one brightly striped, loosely knitted cotton blanket in a basket weave pattern with a lace edging.

Grace had said they'd like to play with the lace on the edge.

She'd made two cradle pads the night before, of simple white flannel, and two quilts, one in turquoise and purple and one in yellow and green.

We would need other things, of course. Clothes, I was sure, and a dresser to put them in, as well as a changing table and a rocking chair.

But when I went back to school after the battle for our home and our souls, I went knowing that if those babies were born the next day, my home and my heart would be ready.

A MONTH later, I was more than ready.

I could barely walk, and nothing stayed down. Bracken carried me more often than not, and even I had to admit that I was losing weight under the burden of the not-so-tiny bodies inside mine.

But when your mother asks you—politely and as a peace offering— if she can take you shopping for little cotton onesies and T-shirts with bears on the front, it's not nice to whine. Bracken and Nicky agreed to chaperone me, and Renny had just slid into the car without asking. Even though Nicky was just showing off his whole, hale, and *very pale* left arm, I was so grateful that I didn't mind the way he posed and flexed with every garment he picked up.

It felt good to laugh again.

The night before, the boys had pretty much banged each other comatose—oh yeah. Every tab in every slot, and I lay on my side in the corner of the bed and said things that felt silly in the cold light of day but felt pretty damned good at the moment. ("Oh yeah, fuck him harder!" just sounded so porny in real life. In the bed, fine. In the baby department at Target? Oh dear Goddess no.) And when they were done, they had turned their attention on me.

No, penetration wasn't happening, and even orgasm was looking pretty risky, given how tired Green said my body was getting. But they weren't touching me to stimulate me—they were touching me to *sate* me. From my toes to my thighs, over my flanks, over my stomach, gliding up my arms and over my neck, even massaging my scalp through my hair, every touch had been infused with love, with their own pleasure, with the sex that had pleased us all.

I still waddled—and sat down a *lot*—and my hair was still greasy, and I was pretty sure elves were bumping me in the hallway on purpose to cure my acne, which would have just been all over the fucking place without them.

But I had been well loved the night before, and even though my body was a giant gestating oven right now, I felt a *promise* of sexuality from that touch, a promise of selfdom, of being a fully contained person after I gave birth and had these two little people to care for.

Yes, I wanted it to be done because I was exhausted and miserable, but more than that.

I'd felt them dance against my palms, and against my liver. I'd sung to them, read them poetry, and told them to dammit, stop that!

I had imagined braiding my daughter's hair—and my son's. I imagined them playing outside on the banks of the pond, terrorizing the kelpie and being tossed in the air by the vampires as Adrian used to toss Bracken.

I imagined Nicky rocking them to sleep at night, and Bracken holding them in the morning, and Green remembering what it was to be young again and playing with them in the day.

I imagined taking them to the garden and watching to see if they could visit the ghost who would, I just knew, return upon their birth.

All of that imagining—dammit! I wanted to meet them now! They'd had a hell of a buildup, right?

But according to Hallow, Whim, Lambent, and Green—who all consulted now, after touching my stomach and letting their eyes roll back in their heads—it looked as though I had a couple weeks to wait, if my body was holding up, and I wasn't really known for my patience as it was.

So shopping with my mom on a sunny Saturday in April was fine. The lower fey had carved two big cribs and then used cotton to tick hand-sewn mattresses for them. I might have said something about, hey, hello, plastic mattresses for leaky all-cotton diapers, but at this point, I figured what the hell. I hadn't done my own laundry in nearly three years. If they wanted to wash the mattress pads, that was their business, and I'd leave them to it.

But the all-cotton onesies—those, Mom and I could buy.

She held them out for me—pink for girls, blue for boys—and even though I was supposed to be more evolved than that, I was still conditioned by Western culture. Sue me. Pink for girls and blue for boys was cute as hell.

"Knock yourself out, Mom!" I said from the hard plastic bench that had become my throne. "They're adorable."

Mom preened. I guess I wasn't the only one who could flower under a little praise—it was nice to see that I had the power of dishing it out too.

"I'll just go get these," she chimed, pushing a laden cart toward the register.

Bracken bent down and kissed my cheek. "I'll just go pull the car around," he said. "Nicky?"

"I wanted to go look at iPods," Nicky said. I could see the electronics aisle from where I sat. "Will you be okay here for ten? I'll come get you after Bracken has the car." Bracken had needed to park in the farthest reaches of the parking lot—and traffic was fierce.

"Where's Renny?" I asked. I'd gone to the bathroom for the five hundredth time, and she'd followed me there and back but had wandered off as soon as I could see Bracken again.

"On the other side of the partition—see?" Nicky waved his pale arm at the formal baby clothes my mom *hadn't* bought, and I saw Renny absorbed in a teeny-tiny tuxedo.

So I knew where everyone was. What the hell, right? I was still a sorceress, and we were no longer at war.

"Yeah," I said, tucking my hand behind the small of my back and leaning my head against the hard wall behind me. "I'll be fine. Brack, buzz us when you're waiting."

Nicky would be mostly in my line of sight—I wasn't worried.

"I want ice cream when we're done here," Nicky said pertly. God, he was so milking this arm thing.

"Of course, my liege," Bracken said, rolling his eyes. I grinned at him and pushed his dark hair from his face.

"Don't you forget it!" I murmured.

He kissed the end of my nose, and he and Nicky lit out on their separate quests.

We figured it out later—much later. Doc Nieman must have been stalking me for months. But the broken shields had been reinstated before I went back to school. How many times had he followed one of Green's vehicles back to the driveway entrance and then driven away, baffled because he couldn't remember losing the car in front of him? How many times had he seen me at school—demented to the point of alienating his family, distracted by the loss of his clinic, heartbroken by the loss of his chance to practice medicine, and disturbed by the things he'd seen the night of Teague's abortive break-in?

How long had he plotted to see, just see, just get to the bottom of what had started the whole chain of events? How long had he waited for me to be alone?

This time he must have sensed victory, because he had Nurse Janine with him, and I wasn't afraid of her at all.

"Cory! Hon, how you doing?" she asked, coming around the corner natural as could be.

"Janine? Hey. I heard your clinic burned down—sorry to hear that." I glanced around for Renny and saw her flyaway hair peeking out over the partition.

Janine's once open face closed, and later I would remember that she was wearing scrubs and that her clothes didn't match what came out of her mouth next. "Yes, well, it's been rough. Had to go back into the rotation, you know, and injured my back all over again. I'm out on leave now—we're hurting."

Dammit. "Well, I understand the clinic is close to being rebuilt."

"Yeah. It will be nice to get back to work." Without asking, she sat down next to me. I had to crane my neck to look at her, her hazel eyes guileless in her lean, tanned face.

"That's—ouch!" I turned, and there he was. Dr. Nieman, the man I'd set on the road to obsession and then blown off. As I watched, rubbing my arm, he palmed a small hypodermic needle and I felt the sudden urge to blow chunks.

Oh, Jesus. I couldn't even drink coffee out of a plastic cup these days.

My body was taking the sedative hard, and my eyes were at half-mast as I told him the honest-to-Goddess truth. "Man, you've got one chance to save your own lives. My men will fucking kill you."

"Shh, Cory," Dr. Nieman soothed. "We'll get those babies out of you and to a nursery just as fast as we can. You're at your due date already, and I'm sure your blood pressure is through the roof."

I tried to summon power even as I slumped over. "Well, it is now!" I mumbled. And then I was lost in a queasy, pukey, hallucinogenic darkness, dreaming about frying Doc Nieman's testicles and serving them to him on a platter.

THE CHILD-RAISING VILLAGE

Nicky

So I just turn around and she's gone? That's it? What in the hell?

I went hauling ass through the fucking store, my panic so great that Green popped into my head right before I grand jetéd over a toddler in the toy aisle.

"What the fuck—"

"She's gone*! We left her sitting in Baby Essentials, and I can't see her!"*

That pause… was worse than the fall from the sky, the paralyzing knowledge that part of what made me *me* had been ripped off my body forever.

"She's… she's under. She's been drugged. Meet Bracken and Renny in front. Now!*"*

Goddess help me, I forgot about Cory's mother until I almost plowed into her standing at the curb.

"Nicky, where'd Cory go?"

I swung open the front door to the SUV before it even came to a stop. "I'm going bird. Green will relay directions."

"I saw them load her into the car. Brown Toyota Sienna, heading up 49, probably toward Grass Valley. I'll ask Green to get directions from Teague."

"God*dammit*!" I snarled, because if anyone would know the self-loathing that came with letting someone down like this, it would be Bracken. His hand on mine stalled that, though, and put it into perspective.

"Not your fault. We underestimated him, and he underestimates her. Be careful, birdman. Stay over the roads, because her shit's gonna come exploding out the fucking roof."

Ooh… good point. I squeezed his hand back. "Drive safe."

Cory's mom had been throwing bags of baby clothes and baby wipes and plain cotton diapers—which she claimed you could never have too many of—into the back of the SUV. She swung into the backseat and leaned forward, forcing Bracken to turn toward her and release my hand. Renny ghosted in after her.

"Where'd Cory go again?" she asked, puzzled. I winked at Bracken in spite of the grimness of the situation.

"Good luck, brother. Don't kill her before we get there."

With that, I shifted into a bird right before her eyes and launched.

I scanned the horizon desperately, going in the direction Brack had suggested. Fucking cars. Fucking hyper-clear bird vision. Brown Toyota Sienna my feathered *ass*. I was all movement, all prey to my predator, all....

Hello.

"I see her, Green. Glowing power burp, north on 49, past Bell Road, continuing on toward Grass Valley."

"Keep following her, Nicky. We're all on our way."

Bracken

"She was abducted by who?"

I was going to kill my mother-in-law. Would that be matricide? If I wore her blood like skin, would she be a blood relative then? These were questions I might just answer if the wretched woman didn't *shut up and let me fucking drive*!

"She was abducted by the doctor you took her to against her will," I said not so patiently. I tried very hard to forget that I had been the one to suggest the ultrasound, the one who was guided by his curiosity and heedless of the consequences. "He's been obsessing about her, do you understand?"

"But... but don't you people have mojo or something?"

I ground my teeth. "Mojo? Yes, we have mojo—but not every human is susceptible to 'mojo.' Some of them are curious or practical or *fucking obsessed*. We used our mojo, and we ended up burning down the clinic and breaking into the guy's house to *erase her from his memories*."

"You're the ones who burned down the clinic!" she crowed. "I *knew* it!"

I breathed heavily through my nose. "He had a *stalker's board*, Mrs. Kirkpatrick. He had her pictures, from birth through high school. He even had her driver's license picture, and he didn't get that legally. He had her schedules, her whereabouts on what day, and a fuckton of long-range shots highlighting the baby bump and estimating how far along she was compared to how far along she claimed to be. He estimated her weight gain, her baby-weight gain, her actual physical weight loss… it was a nightmare! He even tried to estimate what minerals she was getting through her diet by her skin tone—"

"Stop!" Cory's mother sounded close to tears. "Why would he do that?"

"Because she's *not human*!" I shouted. "Our *children* aren't human! And he *is*, and he's *curious* and dedicated, and he's going to fucking *die*!"

"Die?" she said blankly. "Die?"

I thought I'd recovered from the night of the battle. I thought I'd regained my equilibrium. Nearly three years—wasn't that what it had been? Three years in June? I'd lost my brother, my lover, my friend, and for three years I'd been trying to recover from that loss.

But I'd held Cory's failing body in my arms, had seen Nicky fall from the sky, heard the stories from Teague of Green—*Green*—struggling for breath and dying by the heartbeat.

I was not okay. My beloved was in danger, our *children* were in danger, and whatever polite fiction Cory had told her mother for the last three years was done.

"*Nobody* puts my beloveds in danger," I ground out through clenched teeth. "And nobody puts *her* beloveds in danger. If she doesn't kill him, I will. And if I'm late, Nicky will—and so help me, if the three of us fail, *Green* will. And I don't care if he's misguided or well-intentioned or fucking insane. We're *not* human, and we *don't* live by human rules, and if you're not ready to be a part of that, then you need to get out of the car when we stop and run like hell."

Tense silence roared in my ears like the ocean. I couldn't even hear Renny breathe.

"Would she really?" Ellen Kirkpatrick asked. "Would she really kill?"

In my mind I saw a hundred vampires vaporized by a thought. I saw piles of werewolf bodies heaped in front of her lethal shields. I stood back to back with her as we fought with guns and blood, surrounded by shape-changers and vampires who wanted us annihilated. I watched her flying through the snow fearlessly, determined to destroy a threat to all she loved.

I sat, a quiet passenger in Green's mind, as she held a little girl in the sunlight and comforted her before she conflagrated into ashes.

"Can she kill?" I asked, my voice breaking. "She's *glorious* at it."

"Teague's given me directions," Green said in my head. *"Are you ready?"*

"Hit me," I ordered—and just before Green could start giving me pictures, I flashed a glower at Cory's mother. "Don't you dare."

But Ellen Kirkpatrick was busy staring out the window, her face bleak. "What am I supposed to do with that?" she asked, half out loud.

"Be proud," I told her, concentrating on Green's pictures, grateful the route was simple. "She's a warrior."

"Left, straight for two miles, left, and there... got it?"

"Got it, Green. How are you getting here?"

"GTO."

"Call Max to meet us there."

Because if it was Teague's Mustang, that was Teague driving like a bat out of hell—and Teague was great if we needed a part-time criminal, but Max was *awesome* if we needed a part-time cop.

I didn't even want to guess who was in the backseat, because... oolf! We were there.

We rounded the final corner in the little rural suburb, and I looked around with dazed eyes. It appeared quiet, unassuming. It was Saturday, right? Shouldn't there be kids in that neighborhood? Something?

The For Sale signs on half the lawns barely registered before Nicky flapped down across the street and landed in the tree in the yard across from us. His wings looked... singed—and when he turned human while still seated on the branch, his bare feet dangled, and about the only clothes he had left were the now holey jeans that barely covered his ass.

"Oh, thank God," I said, getting out of the SUV. "We're here."

A car, a tiny Ford Fiesta, tore away from the front of the house so quickly I had to leap back as it roared past me. Cory's mother said, "Hey, was that Janine?"

The nurse. Great. I looked at Cory's mother and said, "If she talks about this, we'll kill her. You make sure she knows that."

"I'm pretty sure she knows," Nicky said, dropping out of the tree, and that was our signal. Together we started jogging across the lawn.

Cory

BY THE time I came to, they'd put the IV in with the Pitocin. I could tell because I was puking all over myself, and because the pain that slammed up my body, from my thighs to my ribcage through my cervix, was huge and all encompassing.

I was surprised the foundation of the earth didn't crack.

Janine offered me water, and I swished out my mouth gratefully while she tried to clean me up. Oh, great—my wardrobe was reduced to giant empire-waist muumuus, and this green one had been a favorite. Now the neckline stank of vomit, and I'd never wear it again without remembering what it felt like to be restrained on a gurney in what looked to be a converted garage.

I looked around, saw the scrubbed walls, the vinyl flooring over the concrete, the newly tiled sink and what looked to be a fully equipped delivery room surrounding me, and I realized I was right. It a *was* converted garage, and I was stuck in a bed staring at the connecting door to what was probably the kitchen, with my knees propped open and my weehoo facing whoever walked in through that room.

Somebody had cut off my giant pregnancy underwear.

I turned to Janine in a black fury as another contraction slammed up through my thighs.

I could deal with pain.

I breathed long and deep while that fucker moved through me, and let my consciousness ride the wave. When I looked at Janine again, she was about to inject something in the IV. I managed to shout "*Stop!*" loud enough for her to startle before the needle punctured the injection port.

"It's just a painkiller," she said soothingly. "It won't hurt you—"

"It *all* hurts me," I panted. "Don't you understand? That's why no doctors. Your shit—it's not good for me!"

She looked at the needle in her hand, confused. "But… but Cory, your chart didn't say anything about allergies—"

A wave of black nausea chased through my body, but this time I managed to keep it down. "I'm allergic to mankind right now!" I snapped—and oh, Goddess, that condescending smile.

"Oh, honey, I know it feels that way, because inducing labor isn't a joke, and—"

"*Holy mother of fuck!*" Oh, *Goddess*, those contractions felt like muscular train wrecks, giant steel balls transferring energy up from the thighs, straight through the weehoo, cracking my cervix open like a walnut and ending at the grand finale of uterus, diaphragm, taint, asshole, and lower intestine.

And this woman was *not* listening.

As the contraction receded, she went to inject the painkiller again. I reached out with the motherfucking force and slammed the hypodermic across the garage, where it lodged in the wall and stuck like a dart.

"*Listen to me!*" I snarled as she turned startled eyes toward me.

I let the glow of power coat me as a shield, and her eyes got even bigger.

"Is he paying you?" I asked, feeling guilty about the people we'd put out of work, in spite of my anger.

"What?"

"*Money*, Janine. Are you doing this for money? Because you could lose your license, and I know it."

"Yes," she whispered, voice broken. "I need the job, Cory, and the insurance. I've got two daughters, and one of them is in college. I'm—"

"Desperate. I got it. Well, listen…." Oh, fuck. Another one. They were coming fast and they were coming hard, and my hold on myself, on the power that seemed to up in amperage with every roll of muscles, grew looser and looser. On the hill, I'd have Green and Bracken, I'd have Nicky, and Grace and Arturo and Katy and Renny—so many people to calm me down, to help me hold my power, to catch it when it exploded. But not here. Not in this converted garage with this terrified nurse who didn't know what she was in for.

I almost let power slip through this time. Almost. My hands were bound to the fucking gurney, and it had nowhere to go but up and out— right up until my body turned into a giant electric fence with nowhere to ground.

"Janine," I gasped, making eye contact again. She was holding her hand in front of her face, so I tried to tamp down on the glow and maybe partially succeeded. "Janine, I am going to *kill* whoever is in this room with me that I don't love. Do you understand? *Kill.* Dr. Nieman is a fucking dead man—if I don't do it, my husbands will."

"Husbands—"

Oh… fuck… not yet. "*Focus, bitch!* We will *kill him.* If you're here, so help me, I won't be able to stop…."

Mother of fuck*!*

I opened my mouth and silently screamed, sunshine pouring from me up through the garage roof, turning it black and charred and unstable—and from there, I had no idea. I was spending all my energy trying to save the goddamned nurse and none of it trying not to kill the whole neighborhood.

At that moment Dr. Nieman burst into the garage, partially gowned and looking as cool as any country-club doctor in his own examining room.

"Janine, can't you sedate her? I'm trying to get the incubators warmed up and prepped."

"I… I…." Janine held her hand to her mouth and flicked her eyes from the charred ceiling to my glowing body and back. "I… I can't do this…," she announced finally. Then she bolted. I heard the garage door slam as she took off for parts unknown, leaving me with the obsessed doctor and twins on the way.

"Miss Fitzpatrick—"

My eyes bulged. "Stay the *fuck* away from my babies!"

"Now calm down—"

"You have until my next contraction to get out of here before I fry you like bacon," I snarled. Oh, I felt it. *Fucking* Pitocin. It would have happened slower than this—and fast was bad, fast was *so* bad with twins, and nobody there with a hand in my hoo-ha to make sure they were coming out okay, and nobody ready to open a seam in my belly and lift them out gently.

Oh, Goddess… they were early. They were early by elf standards, and they would need Green—they would need the whole collective of us to care for them, to make sure they could breathe, could think, could eat.

I didn't let this one come. I couldn't. "You've got to go," I sobbed, fighting for all I was worth. The force of the contraction grew bigger even as I tried to stave it off. "If you touch my body to deliver them, somebody is going to die. I'm not human. They're not human. Why do you think you're so obsessed? What do you think is going to happen when I give birth without my family around me?"

Oh… Oh hell…. He had me on my back. On my *fucking* back. I felt the contraction recede as I squashed all the oxygen along my spine, another wave of black fucking nausea chasing up my body. I turned my head, tilted my shoulders, and threw up, so miserably queasy, so dizzy with cut-off blood and fear and the horrible fucking allergy to whatever was in that IV that all I could do was whimper.

It hit me for the first time that if I *didn't* kill this man, I was vulnerable to him, as vulnerable as a woman could be, and that he could let me die in childbirth and cut the babies out of my belly without remorse, if that's the way his obsession ran. With a heave, I cocked my hips, letting the humongous pregnancy belly flop to the side and screaming with pain as my sinews snapped and pinged and muscles tore.

The oxygen rushing my spine made me dizzy—and I couldn't control it, couldn't anticipate it as the next contraction roared through me like a nuclear freight train carrying a coal car of death.

I screamed in pain, in fear, in panic, power pouring from my mouth. And deluded or not, the doctor was caught in the power wash, thrown against the door to the garage, and cooked—the way I'd once cooked a computer in a library, the way I'd always feared to cook the men in my bed if I did not learn control.

His body shook, the fat ran down, and his skin shriveled, went black, and flaked off, all before the next contraction passed—but he did not scream.

His neck had snapped at the first impact, and even as my vision blackened with panic and pain, I knew true fear. I was secured spread-eagle, contractions roaring through me, and I had no way to get loose.

"Shh, beloved. Nicky and Bracken are here."

"Green," I sobbed, my fury transforming to tearful relief in less than a heartbeat. "Green, where are you?"

"On my way. On my way."

"Cory!" Bracken shouted, crashing through the side door. "Cory!"

"Oh, thank Goddess. Bracken… Bracken, let me out of here. Get rid of the Pitocin. Please, Bracken, please…."

I was dimly aware of Bracken and Nicky working on my restraints, and my mother too, but mostly I was aware that Bracken was *there*, touching my face, whispering soothing things in my ear, and that Nicky was holding my hand and they were *there*, my men were *there*, and I wasn't going to have to have my babies in this terrible place after all.

Green

THERE WERE bats in hell eating Teague Sullivan's dust and wondering what had happened to their lives and reputations by the time the Mustang pulled up to the little suburb in Grass Valley.

Green had been inside her mind for the past five minutes, since Bracken and Nicky had crashed into the converted garage, and after talking to Bracken and Nicky, he was certain of one thing.

His children were coming, they were coming *right now*, and there was nothing they could do to stop it.

Green slid out of the front seat of the car, not even registering the cramps in his legs from the small space, and Katy slithered out right after him. Before Teague could kill the motor, Green slammed the door and stuck his head back in the window.

"Car carriers," he said crisply. "Two of them. We're going to need them on the way back."

Teague's jaw dropped. "Holy mother of *fuck!*"

"Yes, that's what Cory said—but you'd better get a move on, because the minute they're stable, we're getting the hell out of here. Now call for Lambent to finish the cleanup, yeah?"

"Yeah," Teague conceded, reaching for his cell phone even as he peeled away.

Green didn't bother looking over his shoulder. He was too busy finding the side door of the garage to the rather well-heeled home that the doctor was foreclosed on.

He walked in just in time to hear Nicky say, "So seriously, Cory, who's the giant pot roast?"

Bracken groaned. "Little man—"

Nicky sounded honestly contrite. "Sorry. So sorry, Cory."

"Don't be," she panted, moaning with each breath. "I sure as hell am not. Oh… oh… Bracken… can't you make them stop?"

"Nobody can," Green crooned at his most soothing, coming into the room with Katy on his heels, and ever so glad to see Renny. "Ladies, I need a big pot of boiling hot water and some alcohol to sterilize things. If the good doctor had any of those gloves, I think I'll take a pair too, right?"

"On it, Green," Renny said, sounding surprisingly put together for someone who often needed to put on sweats in the back of the car because she'd been a cat for most of the day.

Green trusted they'd do that for him and concentrated on the sweating, crying woman on the gurney in front of him. He moved Nicky a little to the side so he could pull her ravaged hair back from her face, and he was immeasurably cheered by how much she stopped trembling at his touch.

"Hey, luv. Not quite the in-home birth we had planned."

"Can't we make it stop?" she begged. "Green, I don't want to have my babies here. Not in this place, with the...."

He followed the direction of her gaze. "Burnt pot roast indeed," he said, laughing gently. Then he kissed her brow. "Lovey, do you think these children don't know their mother is a warrior?"

She swallowed, and he could feel the pressure rushing up her body. He held his hand over her stomach and sucked in a breath. Nicky and Bracken did likewise, because, Goddess knew, they were getting that same pressure on their hands as she squeezed.

"Sh, sh, sh," Bracken breathed, calming her more. "Corinne Carol-Anne, don't panic. Don't cry. We know what you are, and we love you. They'll love you too."

"Kestrels would have eaten that guy already," Nicky said cheekily. When she laughed, Green rejoiced.

"We can do this," he promised, kissing her brow one more time. "Now, I'm going to go look at ground zero, yes?"

She nodded, miserable and embarrassed. Bracken spoke more surprising poetry in her ear about how she was doing something awesome and amazing, while Green used the boiling water and plain Ivory soap that Renny had brought him and the gloves that Katy held out while he waited for Cory's next contraction to pass.

Her thighs were spread and parted for him, and he smoothed his hands down personally. Not proper for a doctor, no, but perfectly acceptable for a husband who was going to do something intimate for his wife.

He pushed the skirt of her once-pretty dress up under her bottom and over her stomach, not surprised that she didn't argue with him about propriety. The inside of her body was slick and powerful, and it clenched and rippled around him as he felt for her cervix to try to measure its effacement and dilation.

Oh, dear.

"Beloved," he said, stroking her flank with the hand that *hadn't* made the journey, "you are ready to go—but the children not so much." Her body couldn't take much more. He would need to take them out if she was going to survive.

"Oh, Goddess," she panted. "He's probably got scalpels here somewhere, and…." Her lower lip trembled. "I know I don't get anesthetic, and—"

"No anesthetic!" her mother exclaimed, and Green looked at her for the first time. She was standing by what appeared to be a baby-care station, which she had apparently organized to her liking as Green had been checking on Cory's progress.

"Don't worry about pain," Green soothed, looking meaningfully at Ellen. "Love, it's me and Bracken. Bracken will make the incision, I'll dull the pain. Between the two of us, there will be no more pain than the tree felt when yielding the cradle. You remember?"

She nodded, tears of relief flowing freely. "That was beautiful, Green," she whispered, sounding young and lost and so very determined to not lose control again. A contraction rippled through her, this one more powerful than the last, and he felt the knots in her body as all of its effort went for nothing because the creatures it was meant to expel were lying sideways in Cory's womb.

"You're beautiful, lovey. Now hold on to Nicky tightly, okay?"

"Got her, Green," Nicky said staunchly.

"Renny, Katy, you get a baby each. Mrs. Kirkpatrick seems to have a cleaning station over there—make sure she's got water and cloths."

"The pot roast had a fuckton," Renny said, carrying the bundle to the table. "I've got warm water too."

They were good to go.

"Bracken," Green said gently, calling his husband, his lover and partner in this endeavor to his side. "I'll need you to part her flesh—gently. Just the skin, really, and the membrane, and—"

"I've been studying diagrams for nine and a half months," Bracken muttered. "Got it, healer. Just hold her and keep her from freaking out."

It sounded brusque, but Green saw one hand shake as Bracken rested it on Cory's bare and glistening belly.

Then—very, very carefully—he ran his finger down Cory's bikini line, asking the skin and flesh to part, asking the blood to flow around the incision and not through the parted skin. Oh! Oh, there... the tiny body, impossibly folded and unutterably cramped, slid into Bracken's hands like the missing piece to a puzzle. Bracken pulled the child out and smiled gently.

"Look, Green. She's all sidhe."

And she was—elongated features, great oval eyes, long limbs, fifteen ribs, and all. Bracken gazed sweetly into their child's eyes, and she gazed back, not crying at all, just blinking slowly, apparently puzzled by all the goings-on. Green looked with him, keeping his hand cupped around Cory's calf while he peered over Bracken's shoulder, and together they marveled at the miracle of their child. Cory moaned, and Green absorbed the pressure of the next contraction, which reminded them all that they had to hurry. Bracken smiled at their child again and said, "Okay, Miss Silver, time for your first bath," before he handed the babe to Renny.

"Hold her while I cut the cord."

With a pass of his finger, no clamp was necessary.

Renny brought the baby to Cory's mother to wash first and then swaddle, and Bracken and Green moved on to their sturdy boy.

Oh, he was sturdy too. Wider than his sister, his shoulders had more breadth even though they were both sidhe long. He met Bracken's gaze fiercely, like a man, and Green looked over Bracken's shoulder for his first look as well.

"He's a fighter," Green said proudly. "Like his fathers."

"Or a healer," Cory interjected breathlessly, "or an engineer, or...."

"Or a sidhe," Bracken said with smug satisfaction. "He can be all of us, beloved. No worries."

This one too was severed from his mother, and while Bracken was doing that, Green very carefully lifted the two placentas out of Cory's uterus, marveling at how perfectly intact they were—and making sure Bracken stayed far away from Cory as he was doing so.

"I don't want to see what your touch would do to her wide-open body," Green said softly. Bracken nodded, sober and attentive, before going to help the women with the children.

Green was delicate and detailed as he reconnected his beloved's flesh. There would be no scar, no chance of reopening, no parts of her body left savaged by surgery. When he was done, he passed his hand over her much flatter belly and pushed as much of the bleeding she would need to do down her birth canal as possible. It poured out in a gush, and Green took great care cleaning her up from that as well.

When he looked up, Cory was looking longingly at the clean, eerily quiet children.

"Bracken won't let me hold them yet," she said, yearning throbbing in her voice.

"One of them has my talent," Brack said, his voice matter-of-fact. "I can feel it in our little boy."

"Drian," Cory said without hesitation. "Baby Drian."

Green ran his hands over her again, wishing they had some clean clothes for her, anything but the pile of blankets in the corner. "She'll be fine," he said, feeling weary and happy at once. "She'll be fine. We'll all be…."

Oh Goddess. They would, wouldn't they?

They would all be. He'd been so focused, so determined to make do in this terrible place, to take away her pain, to make sure their young were safe and well…. He hadn't realized there would be this moment, this heartbeat, this terrifying, deliriously happy truth.

He closed his eyes and swallowed. When he looked out again, there they were. Cory, holding their boy child. Nicky, smiling happily at their little girl. Cory's mother, giving brisk orders to the two girls, and Bracken….

Bracken was coming around to the end of the table and embracing him, hard and without compromise.

"Fine," he whispered as Green felt the panic sobs take him over. "We're all going to be fine."

Oh, Goddess. Goddess, they really were. They were going to be fine.

CORY
Not a One-Woman Show

THANK GODDESS I don't remember much about the next two days after the twins were born. We made it back to the hill, and I got to spend *lots* of time in the shower sitting on the bench Green had moved in for me.

Then I got to spend *lots* of time in bed, propped on pillows, having my nipples chewed on by the two little aliens that Green had produced out of my womb like rabbits. "Hey, Rocky, watch me pull a rabbit out of my cooter!"

Or at least that's what it felt like for the first two days. I remember the men feeding me, holding the children, touching me absently. But really, at this point I was a postgestational cow and too exhausted to even bitch about it.

My life was a blur of visiting Mom and Dad, of hill folk coming in to pay their respects, of breastfeeding and me-feeding and tiny alien things who seemed to need me all the time.

So strange, so disconnected. It was as though that strange interlude in the doctor's garage hadn't ever happened. I'd gone shopping with my mother and had come home with two completely new beings who were now the center of my life.

I wasn't sure what to do with that. Even when Hallow told me that my professors had given me two weeks for maternity leave, I still wasn't really sure what I'd done to deserve that. It had been a battle, right? After most battles we just came down from the high, but now I got to be a mommy?

But then, one night—probably around nine o'clock, because the vampires were up but everyone had been kicked out of the bedroom for a bit—I heard that baby noise. Not crying, because creepily enough, they *didn't cry*. This freaked the fuck out of my mother, who said it was worse than Dr. Pot Roast (oh, the shame), and I had nothing much to say to that. She'd seen a guy I'd fried like meat, and still wanted to hold my children. I couldn't complain about my parents anymore. It was official, they'd passed parenthood. They'd had to take some remedial courses in personal acceptance and taking your child on faith, but some parents never pass that shit at all, so they were doing okay.

So this night, when my children were two days old, my room was suddenly… empty. And quiet. Lambent had just left, after telling me that the strange fire in the almost empty suburb in Grass Valley had been declared a result of natural causes. I had no idea how Lambent did that, but he didn't want me to thank him for it, so I left it alone. And without that to think about, I was suddenly awake with my cooing children.

It felt like the first time we'd been alone together.

They were both in bed with me—which was sort of funny after all that fuss about the cradles—but honestly, with the breastfeeding, it was just as easy to roll over, open the neck of my nightgown, and flop a boob into someone's mouth so I could allow myself to be milked like a cow. (Bracken told me that the next time I said moo when I did this, he was going to buy me a black-and-white spotted sweat suit. I only said it *very* softly after that.)

But right now they didn't need the milk bar, and they didn't want Bracken or Green or Nicky. They were just lying there, flailing their little limbs around with great enjoyment and making vowels into the quiet room.

I propped my head on my hand and stroked their little cheeks. Both of them made those little happy cooing noises and leaned into my touch.

"Hiya," I said quietly. "I don't know if you caught this, in all of the excitement of the last couple of days, but I'm sort of your mom."

Drian caught my finger then—oh, so strong! I had no idea if human babies could do this yet, but I was understanding the delight of that strong little grip.

"Oaooaaaaoooooo…." Could have meant anything, really, but I took it as a sign of disbelief. *Me?* I was on board for parenthood? Jesus, what was the world thinking?

"Yes." I nodded at him. "Your mother. I will make mistakes, you know? I mean, I cooked the first ob-gyn who tried to deliver you. Nobody has said anything about it, but even I know that wasn't cool. But I'll try—I promise I'll try. I'll be the best mom I can, okay?"

He blinked sober green eyes at me, and I took that for acceptance.

The other baby, Silver, let out this… it wasn't even a coo. It was this… this sweet little vowel that probably didn't exist in English. And when I caught her flailing little fist, she didn't just catch my finger—I could swear she brought it to her cheek.

Then she smiled.

"Hello, Silver," I said quietly. She regarded me with wide eyes that were a suspiciously familiar color of silver-spangled blue. "You and me, we're going to have to work hard to be friends, aren't we? I'm sort of in-your-face, and you're a real little lady."

She rubbed my finger against her cheek again, and then Drian let out *the* most tremendous belch. He smiled too. And there. Boom. It happened.

Both of my children. I had officially fallen in love.

I THINK any new parent will tell you, those first couple of weeks happen so fast.

I mean, the sleep deprivation didn't help. Even with a thousand people who wanted to hold the babies and smile and coo and sing songs to them, the milk bar got priority seating. There *was* no pumping the milk to put in a bottle, and there *was* no "daddies feed too." What we had instead was a mom who didn't cook, clean, organize, or shop. My one job—*one job*—when I wasn't at school was to nurse the children.

Given how badly *I* had reacted to anything chemical or human when I'd been in labor, I certainly wasn't going to try to change that.

They were a wonder, really. I would find myself singing—anything from rock and roll to show tunes—and catch their eyes on me as though I'd done something amazing, marvelous, something that no other human being or sidhe on earth could ever do.

Green told me that he would never let me stop singing again, and I was so high on breastfeeding endorphins that I sang "Rain Will Fall" for him with no prompting whatsoever. I was holding Drian as I sang it, and Green teared up, so deliriously happy with fatherhood that I resolved to sing to him *every* week if I could manage.

Of course, those are the sorts of promises that we break to ourselves when our lives get busy—that's the nature of living in a bustling household. The ability to remember those promises sometimes marks our ability to hold our lovers to our hearts.

My lovers, all three of them, were doing a pretty good job of keeping their own grip on the lot of us.

There *was* no "primary parent" thing going on here. I may have been the milk bar—but at the hill, when a baby needed to be fed, the first person near the baby brought said baby to me. Everybody changed diapers. Everybody gave baths. Everybody, at one time or another, fell asleep propped in a corner with a sleeping baby on his or her chest.

Of all the times that I missed having Bracken and Green on film, *those* were the times I ached with that the most. There was a pureness to that moment, a terrifying vulnerability. In Green's hill, those daddies with the sleeping babies on their chests were the most carefully guarded beings in the world.

After two weeks I had to go back to school. We had to take separate cars. Bracken, Nicky, the babies, the baby gear, and me—we filled up an SUV. It was amazing.

It was also frustrating—and a good way to get back in shape—because I insisted on pushing that damned stroller all over the place. We kept it covered at all times—and, of course, darling little hats over their ears. If anyone who caught a glimpse of them thought they were too deformed to be human, nobody was rude enough to say so.

And after a week or two of pushing that stroller around, I started to feel a little better about my thighs, my stomach, my back, and my grades.

Again I was blessed with circumstance. I could not have brought my children to school to breastfeed if they had been human babies.

Human babies cry.

"There's got to be a horrible penalty involved here," I told Bracken during our first school day with quiet children. "Something terrifying and real that will make us say, 'Jeez, I would have traded a thousand sleepless nights with a colicky baby if only to avoid this!'"

Bracken smiled at me, his perfect oval of a face so gentle and so noble that I was forced to remember the way he'd sung to my blood and the way he'd cut so gently into my body that he hadn't even left a scar.

"They get to be sexually active at sixteen," he said soberly. "And they *will* tell you *everything*."

I blinked, and the full horror descended. I looked into Silver's eyes, and she regarded me back with equanimity. Her hair was starting to grow, so blonde it was colorless. I was pretty sure that within the year it would be butter yellow.

"That's a horrible thing to do to your mother," I told her, truly rocked.

She actually smiled around my nipple and laughed, apparently all done.

I traded her for Drian and gazed into his green eyes. "And *you*, you shouldn't consider doing that at all."

The look he gave me was pure Bracken.

For a moment I thought smugly that I knew whose baby was whose, and then he smiled beatifically and I realized I'd never know.

Nor did I care to.

Nicky came around the corner with a giant mug of juice and ice for me, which he'd snuck into the library like the miscreant he'd love to be.

"How's our guys?" he asked, waiting until Drian was sucking away to hand me my much needed drink. "They going to make it doing this for another two weeks?"

"Our guys are fine," I said. Yes, there were breastfeeding endorphins that *did* make me mellow, but there was also a sense of relief. There would be other battles, but for today, sitting in our sunny spot in the back of the library, I could smell books and smile at my handsome husbands and know that when we returned to Green's hill, he'd be there with open arms.

"In fact," I said, closing my eyes against the sun coming through the window, "I'm going to pretend that it's all gonna be fine. For just a moment. I think it's some peace well-earned."

SAC STATE held graduation at the end of May. The twins were six weeks old, and as big as six-month-old human children, but still I was almost horrified when Green insisted we take them off the hill for the graduation ceremony I'd never planned to attend.

"But Green, I don't even need the ceremony…," I whined. In truth I was a little embarrassed. Yes, I'd taken my finals, and I'd even written my final papers—a feat only manageable because my babies had about seven nannies in addition to their three fathers.

It just didn't feel fair to be making such a big deal out of a degree—okay, two bachelor's and a master's, so *degrees*—that I hadn't really been there at the end to earn. And I was pretty sure Hallow had manipulated my damned professors to accept the papers and not give me shitty grades on them. Either that, or the fact that I had to breastfeed newborns before, during, and after classes had just sort of pushed the pity button on all of them.

It didn't matter. Green got stubborn, much as he had before the jailbreak in August. I *would* have a damned graduation ceremony, and I *would* have robes and a little hat, and I *would* walk across that stage when someone I didn't know called my name.

I sat there on the hot, crowded floor of Sleep Train Arena and fanned myself with my program, scanning over the sea of bodies until I found my family.

Like all thirty of them. Hell, it would have been more if the ceremony wasn't at one in the afternoon.

Green had one baby and Bracken the other—from the floor, I couldn't tell which, although I did see a spark of daddy-generated glamour around them both. Nicky had the baby bag. My parents both had armloads of flowers, and everybody else had some sort of card or gift in their hands too.

Silly, pure vanity on *their* part, because they could always give me gifts back in the hill, and why did I need cards or flowers or any of that other shit anyway?

Except… except they were my family and my friends, and they'd followed me through hell and back, and who was I to tell them that we couldn't celebrate this moment, this one moment, when for once I got the thing I'd been working for my entire life.

Even if it turned out to not be the thing I wanted most anyway.

The announcer called out my name—shortened, of course. "Corinne Carol-Anne Green."

I took my two steps across the stage, expecting a big ruckus, but that wasn't what happened.

The entire auditorium went still, and I turned toward my family, who took up almost an entire section in the second row. To a one they all stood up—my husbands, my friends, my subjects, my joy—

And they all, hands to their hearts, bowed low at the waist in the breathless hush of the arena.

I stared at them openmouthed, then held my hand to my heart and bowed back. And then I walked across the stage, wiping tears and makeup from my face as I picked up my diploma and shook hands with the president of the university.

It was official. "Student" was no longer my name.

But "Mother" was.

THAT NIGHT, after the inevitable banquet and celebration, and the joyful recap for the vampires of absolutely everything that had gone on during the day, Bracken, Green, and I did a thing we'd almost feared to do for the past six weeks.

We sat out in the Goddess grove, allowing the balmy air of May to wash over us and dandling the babies on our knees, talking softly about every burp, fart, coo, and smile, because they were *all* magical.

Green had pronounced my body "good" that morning. All of the postpartum bleeding had cleared up, the incision was completely healed, and although still recovering from being stretched like a rubber band, my stomach was… well, not ginormous and swollen. It was human—that was it. Human and soft. Even my ankles were thinner, which was some sort of miracle in itself.

In short, once the children were asleep in their cradles—and the cradles put in *Grace's* room for a blissful night of babysitting—my husbands and I were going to do something intimate and pleasurable and almost forgotten. We were going to fuck like hamsters on Viagra, and I was *so* excited.

But first, this.

We all took a breath as the breeze washed through the garden and let ourselves yearn. Then we let ourselves hope.

"Please, beloved. You promised Green… you promised him…."

"Hello, luv," Adrian said, his voice as transparent as his gently smiling face. "Aren't you going to introduce us?"

Next to me I heard Green exhale softly, and Bracken make a broken little sob.

I smiled at him, tears burning my eyes, so joyful in that moment I almost couldn't speak.

Almost.

"Hi, beloved," I said softly. "Would you like to meet our children?"

I felt his hand pass through my hair, slightly more solid than a breeze, and I didn't imagine the kiss on my brow.

"Look," he said in quiet delight. "They can see me."

Oh, they could, both infants staring at Adrian's ghost in the ambient light of the garden.

"Of course they can," I said, my throat tight. "You're going to be part of their lives. Ready to get acquainted?"

He beamed at me, then sat himself cross-legged in front of us and met the boy we'd named after him and the girl with the silver-spangled blue eyes.

AMY LANE is a mother of two grown kids, two half-grown kids, two small dogs, and half-a-clowder of cats. A compulsive knitter who writes because she can't silence the voices in her head, she adores fur-babies, knitting socks, and hawt menz, and she dislikes moths, cat boxes, and knuckleheaded macspazzmatrons. She is rarely found cooking, cleaning, or doing domestic chores, but she has been known to knit up an emergency hat/blanket/pair of socks for any occasion whatsoever or sometimes for no reason at all. Her award-winning writing has three flavors: twisty-purple alternative universe, angsty-orange contemporary, and sunshine-yellow happy. By necessity, she has learned to type like the wind. She's been married for twenty-five-plus years to her beloved Mate and still believes in Twu Wuv, with a capital Twu and a capital Wuv, and she doesn't see any reason at all for that to change.

Website: www.greenshill.com
Blog: www.writerslane.blogspot.com
E-mail: amylane@greenshill.com
Facebook: www.facebook.com/amy.lane.167
Twitter: @amymaclane

Choose your Lane to love!

Purple

Amy's Alternative Universe Romance

Vulnerable

The First Book of the Little Goddess series

AMY LANE

Little Goddess: Book One

Working graveyards in a gas station seems a small price for Cory to pay to get her degree and get the hell out of her tiny town. She's terrified of disappearing into the aimless masses of the lost and the young who haunt her neck of the woods. Until the night she actually stops looking at her books and looks up. What awaits her is a world she has only read about—one filled with fantastical creatures that she's sure she could never be.

And then Adrian walks in, bearing a wealth of pain, an agonizing secret, and a hundred and fifty years with a lover he's afraid she won't understand. In one breathless kiss, her entire understanding of her own worth and destiny is turned completely upside down. When her newfound world explodes into violence and Adrian's lover—and prince—walks into the picture, she's forced to explore feelings and abilities she's never dreamed of. The first thing she discovers is that love doesn't fit into nice neat little boxes. The second thing is that risking your life is nothing compared to facing who you really are—and who you'll kill to protect.

www.dsppublications.com

Wounded
Volume One
The Second Book of the Little Goddess series
AMY LANE

Little Goddess: Book Two
Volume One

Cory fled the foothills to deal with the pain of losing Adrian, and Green watched her go. Separately, they could easily grieve themselves to death, but when an old enemy of Green's brings them back together, they an no longer hide from their grief—or their love for each other.

But Cory's grieving has cut her off from the emotional stability that's the source of her power, and Green's worry for her has left them both weak. Cory's strength comes from love, and she finds that when she's in the presence of Adrian's best friend, Bracken, she feels stronger still.

But defeating their enemy is by no means a sure thing. As the attacks against Cory and her lovers keep coming, it becomes clear that their love might not be enough if they can't heal each other—and themselves—from the wounds that almost killed them all.

www.dsppublications.com

Wounded

Volume Two

The Second Book of the Little Goddess series

AMY LANE

Little Goddess: Book Two
Volume Two

Green and Bracken's beloved survived their enemy's worst—with help from unexpected vampiric help.

But survival is a long way from recovery, and even further from safety. Green's people want badly to return to the Sierra Foothills, but they're not going with their tails between their legs. Before they go home, they have to make sure they're free from attack—and that they administer a healthy dose of revenge as well.

As Cory negotiates a fragile peace between her new and unexpected lovers, Green negotiates the unexpected power that comes from being a beloved leader of the paranormal population. Together, they might heal their own wounds and lead their people to an unprecedented place at the top of the supernatural food chain—a place that will allow them to return home a better, stronger whole.

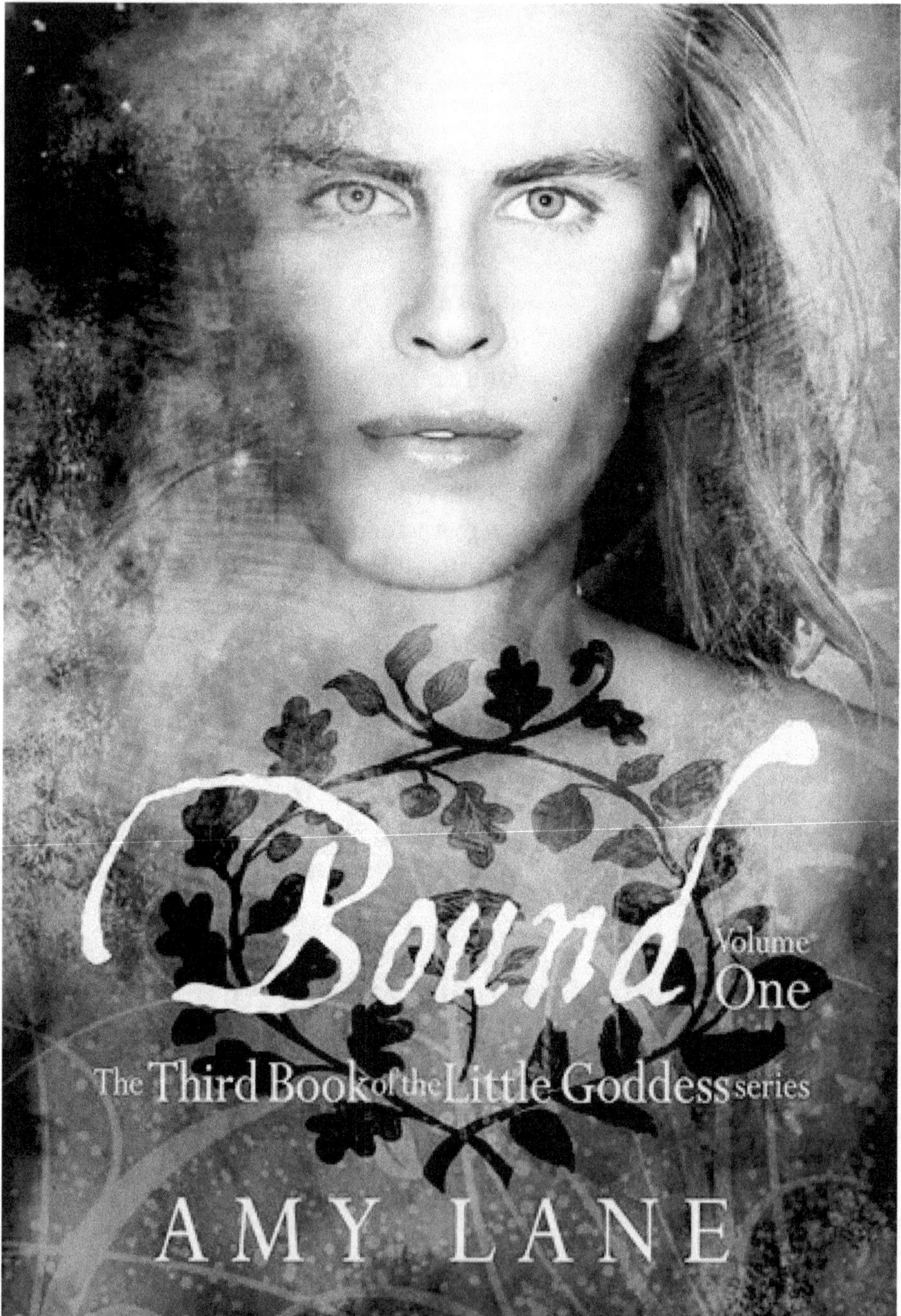

Bound
Volume One
The Third Book of the Little Goddess series
AMY LANE

Little Goddess: Book Three
Volume One

Humans have the option of separation, divorce, and heartbreak. For Corinne Carol-Anne Kirkpatrick, sorceress and queen of the vampires, the choices are limited to love or death. Now that she is back at Green's Hill and assuming her duties as leader, her life is, at best, complicated. Bracken and Nicky are competing for her affections, Green is away taking care of his people, and a new supernatural enemy is threatening the sanctity of all she has come to love. Throw in a family reunion gone bad, a supernatural psychiatrist, and a killer physics class, and Cory's life isn't just complex, it's psychotic.

Cory needs to get her act and her identity together, and soon, because the enemy she and her lovers are facing is a nightmare that doesn't just kill people, it unmakes them. If she doesn't figure out who she is and what her place is on Green's Hill, it's not just her life on the line. She knows from hard experience that the only thing worse than facing death is facing the death of someone she loves.

Loving people is easy—living with them is what takes the real work, and it's even harder if you're bound.

www.dsppublications.com

Bound
Volume Two
The Third Book of the Little Goddess series
AMY LANE

Little Goddess: Book Three
Volume Two

Cory's newly bound family is starting to find its footing, which is a good thing because danger after danger threatens, and Green can't be there nearly as often as he's needed. As Cory learns to face the challenges of ruling the hill alone, she's also juggling a ménage relationship with three lovers—with mixed results.

But with each new challenge, one lesson becomes crystal clear: she can't be queen without each of the men who look to her, and the people she loves aren't safe unless she takes on that queendom with all of the intelligence and courage in her formidable heart.

But sometimes even intelligence, courage, and steadily increasing magic aren't enough to do the job, and suddenly the role of Cory's lovers becomes more crucial than ever. Nobody is strong enough to succeed in every task, and Cory finds that the most painful lesson she and her lovers can learn is not just how to deal with failure. Cory needs to learn that one woman is only so powerful, and she needs to choose wisely who sits outside her circle of family, and who is bound eternally in her heart.

www.dsppublications.com

Rampant

Volume One

The Fourth Book of the Little Goddess series

AMY LANE

www.ingramcontent.com/pod-product-compliance
Lightning Source LLC
Chambersburg PA
CBHW070430120726
47910CB00003B/729